Madame Royale

A NOVEL
Being the sequel of *Trianon*

By Elena Maria Vidal

The Second Edition
MAYAPPLE BOOKS
UNIVERSITY PARK, PENNSYLVANIA

Cover art from a miniature of the Duchesse d'Angoulême by Jean Baptiste Augustin

Cover design by The Russell Organization

Author's photo by Virginia Crum

ISBN 978-0-557-56092-9

"Ah! In my prison every day I prayed.

How long, O God, before some help will come?

Oh, can this be a dream? I feel afraid –

Can I have died, and be at last at home?" – Victor Hugo,

"Louis XVII: Capet, éveille-toi?"

"The present generation is instructed by the misfortunes of the past; be then the future instructed by the history of ours." –A. Barruel, *Memoirs illustrating the History of Jacobinism.*

Other Books by Elena Maria Vidal

Trianon: A Novel of Royal France

The Night's Dark Shade: A Novel of the Cathars

Please visit www.emvidal.com and the Tea at Trianon Blog,
http://teaattrianon.blogspot.com.

TABLE OF CONTENTS

Part III: THE DEBACLE

Part IV: THE BUNDLE OF MYRRH

PREFACE

"But what happened to the daughter?" everyone asks.

Madame Royale was written as a response to readers of *Trianon*, who wanted to know more about the surviving personages of the story, as well as some additional historical background of the Revolutionary Age. The present work deals in particular with the daughter of Louis XVI and Marie Antoinette, and the search for her little, lost brother. All of the major characters were real people, and the situations are based upon fact. (Chateaubriand did not begin frequenting Madame Récamier's salon until 1819, rather than 1815, but this is the only great liberty taken with actual chronology.) The heart of the novel is the mystery of suffering; not the dramatic agony of martyrdom and death, but the long travail of years amid duties and disappointments, the suffering of living. It is patient endurance for the love of God which gains blessings for the multitudes; such an existence is rich with unforeseen joys and an overflowing of grace.

The period which follows the fall of Napoleon Bonaparte, called by historians "the Bourbon Restoration" (1814 1830), was outwardly one of rest and peace for France. Ravaged by revolution, wars, and dictatorship, the nation known as the "Eldest Daughter of the Church" drew a deep breath. Yet beneath the surface, the forces of revolution were engaged in a ruthless duel for power with those of the reaction. The conflict, played out in salons and boudoirs, in newspapers, novels and pamphlets, was nevertheless a fight to the death, from which one party would emerge the conqueror, while the other would sink into the oubliette of exile or imprisonment. The Left had many weapons: the international connections of freemasonry, the wit and connivance of Talleyrand, the charm and popularity of Louis-Philippe; not to speak of periodic bread shortages and high unemployment rates.

As for the reactionaries, they possessed mediocre, frail or aged princes, with followers whose religious convictions were sometimes prone to be superficial or bigoted. They had, however, one weapon, and that weapon was a woman, a woman who embodied in herself the tradition of legitimacy, of a heritage reaching far back into the mists of the early centuries of Christianity, to when the first King of the Franks was baptized and anointed at Rheims. Orphan and exile, she seemed to incarnate the collective guilt and collective pain of the nation. Consumed by a quest, wrestling with demons, her greatest strength and her fatal flaw was a refusal to compromise principles for politics. Of cold demeanor with a heart of fire; of bitter aspect, with an unfailing generosity, her undying faith and zealous devotion to God, His Church, and the poor led her to be the heroine and defender of the idea of the Christian state. Daughter of a martyred king and queen, she was Marie-Thérèse-Charlotte of France, the Duchesse d'Angoulême, who from childhood had been called "Madame Royale."

LIST OF CHARACTERS

Louis XVII, King of France and Navarre. (Born 1785) *The child king, son of Louis XVI and Marie-Antoinette, said to have died in the Temple prison on June 8, 1795. Called "Charles" by his family.*

Louis XVIII, King of France and Navarre. (Born 1755) *Christened Louis Stanislaus Xavier and formerly known as "Comte de Provence." Brother of the slain Louis XVI, and uncle of Louis XVII.*

Marie-Joséphine, Queen of France and Navarre. (Born 1753) *Wife of Louis XVIII.*

Charles, Comte d'Artois. (Born 1757) *Younger brother of Louis XVIII. Later King Charles X of France.*

Louis-Antoine, Duc d'Angoulême. (Born 1775) *Elder son of Artois.*

Marie-Thérèse-Charlotte de France (Madame Royale), the Duchesse d'Angoulême. (Born 1778) *Daughter of Louis XVI and Marie-Antoinette. Wife of Angoulême.*

Charles-Ferdinand, Duc de Berry. (Born 1778) *Younger son of Artois.*

Louis-Philippe, Duc d'Orléans. *Formerly Duc de Chartres. Son of Philippe Egalité.*

Mademoiselle Adelaïde d'Orléans. *Sister of Louis Philippe.*

Marie-Amélie of Sicily. *Wife of Louis Philippe. Daughter of the King of Naples and niece of Queen Marie Antoinette.*

Marie-Caroline of Sicily. (Born 1799) *Niece of Marie Amélie and granddaughter of the King of Naples. Becomes Duchesse de Berry in 1816.*

Marie-Thérèse-Louise d'Artois. (Born 1819) *Daughter of the Duc and Duchesse de Berry. Also called "Louise de Berry."*

Henri, Duc de Bordeaux. (Born 1820) *Son of the Duc and Duchesse de Berry. Later known as "Comte de Chambord."*

Monseigneur de Quélen. *Archbishop of Paris.*

Abbé Latil. *Confessor to Artois.*

Comte Pierre de Blacas. *Later "Duc de Blacas." Master of the Wardrobe in the King's household.*

Auguste de la Ferronnays. *Gentleman-in-waiting to the Duc de Berry.*

Madame de Narbonne. *A lady of the French Court.*

Comtesse du Cayla. *Favorite of Louis XVIII.*

Count Axel von Fersen. *A Swedish nobleman.*

Ladies in waiting to Madame Royale:

Madame de Sérent

Madame d'Agoult

Madame de Damas

Madame de Béarn, *née Pauline de Tourzel; daughter of the governess of Louis XVII.*

Madame de Genlis. *Former governess of Louis Philippe.*

Madame de Mackau. *Former governess of Madame Royale.*

Mathieu de Montmorency. *Grand Master of the Knights of the Faith. Later gentleman in waiting to Madame Royale.*

Madame de Gontaut. *Governess of the Children of France.*

Madame de Boigne. *A lady of Paris society and a gossip.*

Baron de Vitrolles. *A Minister of Louis XVIII.*

Jules de Polignac. *A friend of Artois and later Prime Minister.*

Joseph Fouché. *Former priest, revolutionary and regicide. Minister of Police under Napoleon Bonaparte.*

Elie Decazes. *Minister of Police and confidant of Louis XVIII.*

Prince Charles Maurice de Talleyrand du Périgard. *Former Bishop of Autun. Foreign Minister to Louis XVIII.*

Dorothée de Courlande, Duchesse de Dino. *Talleyrand's nephew's wife.*

Vicomte René de Chateaubriand. *Famous author and statesman.*

Madame Juliette Récamier. *A friend of Chateaubriand.*

Madame de Staël. *Renowned authoress.*

General Decaen. *Commander of the Royal Troops at Bordeaux in 1815.*

Count Hector Lucchesi-Palli. *A Neapolitan nobleman.*

George, Prince of Wales. *Regent of England and eldest son of King George III.*

Alexander I, Tsar of Russia.

Napoleon Bonaparte. *A Corsican usurper and claimant of title "Emperor of the French." Referred to in Royalist circles as "Buonaparte."*

Joséphine de Beauharnais. *His wife.*

Marie-Louise, Archduchess of Austria. *Cousin of Madame Royale and second wife of N. Bonaparte.*

Archduke Karl von Habsburg. *Austrian Field Marshal, brother of Emperor Franz. Former suitor of Madame Royale.*

Archduchess Sophie. *Mother of young Emperor Franz Josef of Austria.*

Lady Charlotte Atkyns. *A former actress, who attempted the rescue of Louis XVII.*

Madame Hue. *Reader to Madame Royale.*

Amy Brown. *Mistress of the Duc de Berry.*

Madame Elisabeth Vigée Lebrun. *An artist.*

Sister Lucie. *A Sister of Charity at the Hôpital des Incurables.*

Sister Catherine Zoé Labouré. *A novice of the Sisters of Charity at the Motherhouse on the Rue de Bac.*

Naundorff. *A watchmaker.*

Jean-Marie Hervagault. *Son of a Norman tailor; claimed to be Louis XVII.*

Madame Nicole Hervagault. *Mother of Jean-Marie Hervagault and former mistress of the Prince of Monaco.*

Lazare Williams. *A French Canadian boy of mysterious origins.*

Baron de Richemont, alias Claude Perrein. *Claimant of the identity of Louis XVII.*

Jeanne Simon. *Widow of Simon the cobbler, caretaker of Louis XVII in prison. A patient at Les Incurables.*

PLACES

Tuileries. *The royal palace in Paris.*

Palais Royal. *The palace of the Orléans family in Paris.*

Little Trianon. *Marie-Antoinette's country villa.*

Versailles. *The principal residence of the Kings of France until October of 1789.*

Bagatelle. *Country villa of the Comte d'Artois.*

Villeneuve l'Étang. *Country home of the Angoulêmes.*

Rosny. *Country estate of the Berry family.*

PROLOGUE:

Midnight at the Palais Royal
Passiontide, 1789

"He, therefore, having received the morsel, went out immediately. And it was night." St. John 13:30

"And what are you writing in your memoirs, my dear?" asked the Duc d'Orléans of Madame de Genlis. They had just finished an intimate supper in a secluded, upper chamber of the Palais Royal. From an open window came sounds of merriment regardless of the season of Passiontide. The cafés and theaters of the Duc d'Orléans' palace courtyard were teaming with soldiers, streetwalkers, forgers, pickpockets, artisans and aristocrats. A footman and a waiting woman were quietly clearing away the crystal and porcelain from the linen-draped table, above which floated a chandelier shaped like Montgolfier's balloon.

The Duc lounged in a brocaded chair; on the wall behind him hung a life-size portrait of himself in the full regalia of a Knight of the Holy Spirit, complete with velvet mantle, diamond cross, and powdered wig. The man who sat beneath the painting, sipping cognac from a crystal snifter, his wig hanging over the back of the chair, was a study in contrasts with his own image. With untied cravat, wrinkled, partially unbuttoned shirt, and tousled sandy hair, he looked breezy and unkempt in spite of his striped vest, yellow coat of oriental silk, and high English riding boots. Only his aquiline Bourbon nose gave a certain doubtful dignity to his acne-scarred face, lined with self-indulgence.

On the opposite wall, gazing rather sadly at the portrait of the Duc, was a Vigée-Lebrun original of a lady who bore a marked resemblance to Louis XIV. In Turkish dress, her high, frizzled coiffure artfully stuffed into a turban with long, dark ringlets flowing to her waist, the lady's face glowed with a quiet resignation, shadowed only by the melancholy sweetness of her smile. Beneath the lady's portrait, scribbling in a large book, sat another woman, a truly altogether different woman. Although she was similarly dressed in Ottoman-inspired costume, with long, straight auburn tendrils falling out of a silk turban, her face, lacking both powder and rouge, was illumined by her alert, darting, dark eyes. She wore no jewels except for her wedding-band; notwithstanding her deliberately loose, corset-less and windblown appearance, she sat very erect, her pen scratching vigorously along.

"I am not writing about you, Philippe," replied Madame de Genlis, her small, thin mouth smiling daintily. "As surprising as it may be, you are not my entire preoccupation. I am describing an incident in my youth when my sister and I collected pails and pails of milk from all the cows on our estate, so as to bathe in it, mixed with rose petals. There was so much, we could actually swim in it! How desperately we wanted to be beautiful!"

"How decadent you were, Félicité," commented Philippe, Duc d'Orléans. His countenance brightened. "Perhaps that is something we can accuse Antoinette of doing! It is easy enough to start circulating rumors with all my connections."

""You are terrible, Monseigneur," sighed Madame de Genlis in half-admiration.

"The rumor I like the best," continued the Duc, is "the one about the Queen's bedclothes being of black satin, and how she burns thousands of black candles every night in her bedchamber. It is amusing how many people believed it." He paused. "Be sure, Félicité, to write in your memoirs of everything that the Austrian Woman has done to humiliate the House of Orléans."

Madame de Genlis' eyebrows arched. "What exactly would Your Serene Highness have me write?"

The Duc took a generous sip of cognac. "You need ask? First of all, the Queen destroyed my naval career. I was to have been Lord High Admiral of the royal fleet. But Antoinette believed the story about how I hid in the hold during a battle."

"Well, did you?"

"Of course. But I had good cause to do so. Nevertheless, she insulted our family. She did so again when she insisted that we, first Princes of the Blood, go to Versailles to wait upon her half-wit of a brother, Max. Naturally, we refused to do so."

Madame de Genlis calmly nodded. "And what else has the wicked Antoinette done to Monseigneur?" Her voice purred, half-soothingly and half-teasingly.

"How can you forget the exile to Villers-Cotterets? What an ordeal to be buried alive on my country estate!"

"Your wife, your children and I enjoyed the change of scene. But what else, Monseigneur?"

"Well, the worst thing of all, Madame. She is trying to pressure Artois into breaking off his son's betrothal to my Adelaïde. Antoinette wants her own daughter, the little Madame Royale, to marry the Duc d'Angoulême, for he will be closer to the throne if anything should happen to the Dauphin, and his brother Normandie. The Daupin Louis-Joseph is dying, as everyone knows. Antoinette wants the crown for at least one of her children, and she is determined that Madame Royale will marry Angoulême. She even rejected an offer from the Crown Prince of Naples." He sighed. "And I so wanted Madame Royale for our young Chartres. What a striking couple they would make! But Antoinette will not hear of it. She behaves as if our household is not respectable."

"Indeed?" asked his mistress, without taking her eyes from her writing. "I know that neither of Their Majesties approve of my being the governess of your children. They just do not understand that your wife and I are such good friends." She glanced upward at the portrait behind her. "And that Madame la Duchesse is wise enough to turn a blind eye to our ... arrangement." Her lively eyes looked fixedly into those of the Duc, who poured himself more brandy from a crystal and gold decanter.

"Ah, there is no one like you, Félicité. You will make my children to be just as I want them – natural, affable, and democratic. But I do wish you would not dress them in such coarse clothes, and force them to eat such plain and rugged food."

Madame de Genlis' small, pointed chin could be quite stubborn. "It is good for them, Philippe. After all, we want them to become virtuous republicans, not decadent aristocrats. You will be pleased when you see how tall and strong Louis-Philippe is getting to be. It is because of the armloads of firewood I make him carry every day, besides the weights he must lift, and the lessons in carpentry. It is an education worthy of Rousseau's Emile."

The Duc sighed again. "That is all very well for the boys. But what of my Adelaïde? What will become of her, if her betrothal to Angoulême is broken?"

Madame de Genlis beamed. "Mademoiselle Adelaïde will nevertheless be a truly democratic princess, who will be able to hold her own in the new world order that is about to be born. If only she learns to stop making personal remarks." She stopped writing. "It is Louis-Philippe who troubles me more."

The Duc's features hardened. "Please refer to my son by his title, Félicité. These democratic ideas can be carried too far."

"Very well, Monseigneur. 'Monsieur le Duc de Chartres' it shall be. He tells me that I am an Albigensian."

"That you are a *what*?"

"An Albigensian, Monseigneur. A *manichée*. Merely because I emphasize the New Testament over the Old! Making them read and reread it, while pointing out to them how democratic the gospels are, and how the ideas of liberty and freedom are based upon them. As for the Old Testament, it is cruel and violent, and has been done away with. I told them so. Young Chartres replied that that is exactly what the Albigensians believed. I also try to emphasize the spiritual and disembodied over the carnal and material, since physical love is to be despised!"

18

The Duc stared with incredulity at the notorious courtesan whom he had brought into his household, amazed that she apparently scorned the very desires she illicitly enjoyed. Likewise, he himself was often bored with his pleasures, and always restlessly seeking new ones. He yawned.

"Such matters you must discuss sometime with Talleyrand. He understands metaphysics, even though he does not practice any of it. Incidentally, he is paying us a brief visit this evening, and will probably bring Mirabeau. I also expect Gerardin to come by with some new sketches– his most audacious yet, I am told! How fun it is to plot an insurrection!"

"You sound as if it were a horse race," said Madame de Genlis. "Let us hope, Monseigneur, that you are not overwhelmed by forces larger than yourself. Truly, we want liberty and equality, a new age of the People, when the government will be by them and for them. But are you certain, Philippe, that you are not just a tool, to be thrown away when the brethren are finished with you?"

The Duc ignored her question. "When the old order is swept away, then a prince who is enlightened, who is democratic, shall reign. Why should it not be I, or one of my sons? At any rate, the upcoming Estates-General is tremendously exciting to prepare for. What else would I have to do during this infernal Lent? No opera balls! And how I miss the theater!"

"The theater! But, Philippe, you go every evening to one of your private theaters here at the Palais Royal!"

"Alas!" exclaimed the Duc, "it is not the same! There is nothing to be compared with my box at the opera. Thank heaven, this tiresome penitential season is about to end! Talleyrand has returned from his diocese at Autun, not only as their bishop, but as their newly-elected deputy for the First Estate! The Estates-General is soon to open; the operas will begin, and the uprising, too! Not to mention the races in the Bois de Boulogne! What a spring and summer we will have!"

"Poor Talleyrand!" Madame de Genlis pushed a thick lock of her studiedly messy hair out of her face. "I remember meeting him at the archepiscopal palace at Rheims, before he entered the seminary at Saint-Sulpice. How miserable he was! How he hated the idea of becoming a priest. He was taking Holy Orders only to please his family. And then his parents did not even attend his ordination! He rebelled by going to meet Voltaire, which appalled poor, old Archbishop Beaumont. 'I will make them regret that they ordained me,' I once heard him declare. He has at least kept *that* promise. Truly, he is to be pitied, though. If it were not for his crippled leg, he would have inherited his ancestral title and lands."

"Pitied!" exclaimed the Duc. "With a woman like Madame de Flahaut as his mistress?! And so many others who chase him, in spite of his limp. Now that Talleyrand has become a bishop they seem to flock to him all the more. Even your name has been linked with his, dear Félicité."

"You yourself should know better than anyone else not to believe every rumor, Philippe," retorted Madame de Genlis, "especially since you begin so many false ones about other people."

There was a scratching at the door and an elderly retainer entered. Bowing, he announced the arrival of the Bishop of Autun and the Marquis de Mirabeau. In limped Talleyrand, with his turned-up nose, meticulously powdered hair, and elegant silk suit. Nothing indicated his episcopal dignity, except for a large, jeweled ring on his finger. Talleyrand's companion, who towered above him, was not a sight for the fainthearted, with a wild mane of hair and a deeply pocked countenance. Mirabeau's vast, bulky form was attired in a suit of the richest velvet. Both gentlemen profoundly inclined to the Duc, who nodded. Approaching Madame de Genlis, they bowed again, but not as reverently, although each of them kissed her hand. She rose ever so slightly, giving a half-curtsy, while bestowing her most pleasing smile upon Bishop Talleyrand.

"Your journey from Autun was uneventful, Monseigneur?" asked Madame de Genlis.

"Quite uneventful, Madame," replied Talleyrand, in his deep, caressing voice. "I was delighted to get away before Easter. The rubrics for the Mass of the Resurrection would have annihilated me. And behold, I am the deputy for the First Estate from Autun."

"So we heard, dear Talleyrand!" exclaimed the Duc. "Tell us, however did you manage to get elected?"

"I preached to the seminarians on the value of prayer; I gave lectures on morality; I reformed and reorganized the diocese. I may not care to practice Christianity, but I do not begrudge others their right to do so. When the clergy saw that I was making every effort to be a good bishop, they elected me. And just in time, too."

"I have been elected a deputy of the Second Estate," boomed Mirabeau. "We nobles must lead the way to freedom!"

"Truly, Monsieur le Marquis," agreed the Duc. "That is why, as an elected deputy for the Third Estate, I plan to wear a plain black suit and march with the representatives of the people in the procession at Versailles on May 4." They gazed at him with awe, for Philippe Duc d'Orléans outranked everyone in France, except for the Royal Family.

"When I was in Prussia, I had the honor of meeting many Illuminati, including our founder, the great 'Spartacus' Weishaupt," related Mirabeau. "The brethren emphasized many things to me. This revolution is only the beginning and will lead to greater revolutions, until Mankind is transformed, deified, and entirely liberated."

"And I, as Grand Master of the Grand Orient Lodge, am aware of the deeper implications of our plans," announced the Duc. "The monarchy must be transformed from an archaic, medieval institution into a modern one which better serves the purposes of the Sect."

"We will have a constitutional monarchy like England," said Mirabeau. "Is everything in readiness for July 14?"

"All is prepared," replied the Duc. "The cannon in my gardens will give the signal. All we need is the rabble rousers, whom I am paying quite generously, to make it look like a spontaneous uprising of the populace. They will march to the Bastille to take the munitions stored there. One thing will lead to another and, as I am assured by those in the know, the Bastille will fall, and its fall will be the symbol of Liberty. As for the colors of the revolution, they have already been decided upon: my racing colors of red, white, and blue. Green was almost chosen, but quickly rejected, for it is the color the Comte d'Artois."

What of the Comte de Provence?" asked Mirabeau. "Is he willing to march at the head of the people?"

"I do not know," said the Duc. "Provence has done much work for us at Versailles. His secret printing press is responsible for pamphlets on the Queen that are worse than anything I have dared to distribute. His wife easily spreads libels. Both of them have circulated the story that all of Antoinette's children are illegitimate, and that Count von Fersen is her lover. Being the brother of the King and his sister-in-law, everyone thinks they speak the truth."

"Then Provence is on our side?" asked Mirabeau.

"Provence is on the side of Provence. He will play his hand stealthily, and will stay at the side of the King until the most opportune moment arrives. Perhaps he is most useful to us there, next to the throne. As for Artois ..." Orléans made a dismissive gesture. "He is more royal than the King. He is against all reform, and will probably leave the country as soon as things prove to be beyond his control. What else can you expect of someone whose hero is Louis XV?"

A hint of displeasure played upon the usually immobile and serene face of Talleyrand. "With all due respect, Monsieur le Duc, Monsieur le Comte d'Artois is my friend ... perhaps my best friend. If he departs, I shall be desolate."

They all silently realized that Talleyrand was not being witty, but was absolutely serious. Orléans bowed in apology. "At any rate," he continued, "if the King were as old-fashioned as Artois, our work would be easy. But the King is such a liberal in so many ways. He is so open to reform."

"The people," pronounced Mirabeau, "positively worship the King. During the last harsh winter, did they not build a statue of him made of snow, in gratitude for the many ways he sought to relieve the famine?"

"Indeed they did," conceded the Duc. "But they also built a statue of me. Did not word get out that I sold many of my most prized paintings to purchase bread for the starving masses?"

"Yes, Monsieur le Duc," agreed Mirabeau. "You are loved by the Parisians. But we must remember that we do not want to destroy the monarchy, or the people's love for the King. We only want to put an end to absolutism."

The Duc did not reply.

Talleyrand spoke. "I do not think any of us have considered what to do with the deficit once our glorious revolution is under way. It will not just disappear."

"What suggestions have you, Monseigneur de Talleyrand?" asked Orléans.

"Perhaps the Church will pay the debts of the Nation."

"The Church?" asked Mirabeau.

"Yes, the Church, as you know, has enormous lands. All the leaders of the people have to do is declare the nationalization of the Church lands. Then they can be sold and...no more deficit." Talleyrand spoke with a flourish of his hand. The episcopal ring sparkled in the candlelight.

"Sell the Church lands?" asked the giant Mirabeau. "King Louis XVI would never agree to it."

"Of course he never would. But by the time our plans mature, he will have signed away most of his prerogatives. It is an excellent idea, Monseigneur de Talleyrand." The Duc glowed approvingly.

Talleyrand bowed. "Monseigneur, we beg you to excuse us. We are expected at a small gathering, *chez* Madame de Staël. Madame hopes Your Highness and Madame de Genlis will also honor her salon with your presences tonight."

"Very good! Very good!" exclaimed the Duc. "I hope, then, gentlemen, to see you again there." They both bade *adieu* to Madame de Genlis, who had been sitting wide-eyed and tight-lipped, and took their leave. As Orléans turned rapturously to her, saying, "Come, Félicité, let us go!" there came another scratch at the door. The footman entered, announcing Monsieur Girardin, the engraver. A small, eager man with beady eyes came briskly into the salon.

"Ah, Girardin! I have been awaiting the latest results of your diligent efforts to recreate the image of our Queen in the eyes of her subjects." Orléans opened Girardin's portfolio and began to laugh heartily. "Excellent! Marvelous! Félicité, look at these sketches!! Are they not masterpieces? And drawn right at Versailles! Look, my love!" He held out a drawing for Madame de Genlis to appreciate. Woman of the world that she was, her white face drained even whiter, then flushed red, as she rapidly averted her eyes.

"Really, Philippe, you go too far!" she gasped. "How obscene!"

"Oh, come now, Félicité. Do not recoil. I am doing this for my children, to save them from despotism!"

Madame de Genlis choked in response. "Who is the man supposed to be?"

"Why, Artois, of course."

"Artois! You had better not let Talleyrand see those pictures. You know how fond he is of Artois."

"Nonsense! Just because they chased women together and paid each other's gambling debts! Artois and Talleyrand each stand for entirely opposite points of view, like it or not. Such friendships must be sacrificed to a higher cause." With a nod he dismissed Girardin, not before slipping a bag of coins into his hand. Then he asked the footman to bring him his hat, gloves, and cane, which were promptly delivered. The Duc buttoned his shirt, tied his cravat, and put on his wig. Donning his high-crowned, English-style hat, and drawing on gloves of the softest chamois, he addressed Madame de Genlis rather coldly. "Well, are you going to accompany me to Madame de Staël's soirée?"

"I think not," replied the lady. "I am tired and I could not bear to hear Madame de Staël jabbering all night."

"Suit yourself. I am going. Madame de Staël is a Protestant, and does not keep Lent the way we do."

"When have you ever kept Lent, Philippe?"

"I had fish tonight for supper, did I not? And have I not been deprived of the opera every Lent of my life?"

"I doubt," parried his mistress, "that Madame de Staël is any example of a Protestant. If John Calvin were alive, he would have her deported from Geneva for lewd conduct."

"Perhaps. But her *fêtes* are amusing. Goodnight, Félicité." Before leaving, he turned to the portrait of his wife and raised his glass to her image before draining it.

"Sleep well, my angel," he said, softly and wistfully to the sad-eyed picture of his Duchesse.

"I doubt that she sleeps," said Félicité. "She is downstairs in the chapel praying for your soul – and for mine."

"She no longer reminds me about saying my Office of the Holy Spirit. She goes ahead and says it herself in my place." The Duc faced Madame de Genlis. "It is very important for a prince to have a virtuous wife. That is one thing which I hope you have instilled in my sons."

"Someday, she will leave you." Madame de Genlis' usually musical voice came to him like an icy wave. "And someday, perhaps, so will I."

"The mother of my children will never leave me," replied the Duc. And neither will their governess." He may have been against despotism, but he could sound dictatorial when he chose. He started for the door, but suddenly spun around and flashed her his most charming smile, his features handsome and seemingly benign.

"*Now*, Félicité. *Now* it begins."

"Now it begins," she echoed him in hollow tones. "But where will it end?" And she gazed with unseeing eyes out of the window into the depths of the night.

Part I: ANTIGONE

Chapter One:

The Emigrants

Summer 1809

"Woe is me, that my sojourning is prolonged!" Psalm 119:5

On Pentecost Sunday 1809, a group of *émigrés* were filing out of the Catholic chapel on Little George Street. High Mass had just ended, and the sun was as bright as could be expected in London. There emerged from the chapel a tall, slender lady, with a thick, much-mended veil over a worn straw bonnet; a thin gray shoulder cape over a patched, gray poplin, high-waisted gown. In spite of the attempted anonymity of her hidden countenance, the *émigrés* clustered around her and fell to their knees, grasping, if they could, one of her begloved hands to kiss. Hearing the soft, rapid French, astonished passersby paused, wondering who on earth the foreign lady might be.

Then one or two more knowledgeable citizens began whispering to their fellows in the street: "It must be the Princess, the daughter of Louis XVI and Marie-Antoinette! It is Marie-Thérèse of France!" The princess nodded to her countrymen as she swiftly moved away from them. She walked down the street with a stiff, slightly jerky gait, two ladies and a gentleman following in attendance.

Often when she awoke in the mornings, Thérèse would for a moment forget that she was in exile in England, and imagine that she was home in her room at Little Trianon or Versailles. Especially in the glow of spring dawns, when the birds chanted lauds outside of her window, the intervening years were wiped from her mind, and she expected at any instant to hear Madame de Mackau's gentle footstep, her mother's "good morning", or her little brother's mischievous laughter. The illusion lasted only a few heartbeats, until the reality of her life would come crashing in upon her. The remembrance that her parents and beloved aunt had been guillotined, that her brother had been tormented to madness or death or both, that her childhood home was gone forever, her country far away, and that she was trapped in a hollow, childless marriage engulfed her. She longed to stay in bed, turn her face to the wall, and die. It was only the knowledge that soon the candles in the chapel would be lit for Mass, and the chaplain would be awaiting her presence before beginning, which helped her to resolve once again to go on with living.

Pushing back the curtains, she would climb out of the high, four poster bed, put on her dimity wrapper and kindle a fire in the grate. That morning she had arisen especially early so as to attend High Mass in London, which had become her custom on feastdays. Accompanied only by Madame Hue, Monsieur and Madame de Sérent, members of her private suite, she was glad to escape from Hartwell and the bickering and the intrigue of the court for at least part of a day.

Turning a corner, they were surrounded by the throngs on the busy street, and stopped in front of a narrow row house. Monsieur de Sérent bowed and continued walking, while the ladies entered a side door. After ascending three or four flights of a rickety staircase, they reached a low garret door. Madame de Sérent, a middle-aged dowager with an ethereal expression, knocked.

"Who is there?" came the faint voice of an elderly French lady.

Madame de Sérent, being partially deaf, knocked again, and announced: "Her Royal Highness the Duchesse d'Angoulême is here to see you, Madame la Marquise!"

"Come in, please."

Madame de Sérent had not heard the response, but being nudged by her mistress, she opened the door, entered the room, and curtsied profoundly as Thérèse passed. Behind Thérèse came Madame Hue, a petite brown bird of a woman, carrying a covered wicker basket. In the cramped, dingy attic chamber a frail, old lady was lying on a musty cot. Thérèse hurried to her side, knelt beside her and took her hand.

"Madame la Marquise, I promised you I would visit next time I was in London," she said, as her husky, rasping voice rang through the room.

The little lady started, "Oh, Madame Royale, it is you. Please, *ma princesse*, let me see you."

Thérèse slowly lifted her veil, revealing her penetrating gaze, which flickered from sapphire to agate according to the light, deep set in classic features like a stern Athena. It was a face in which energy strove with sorrow, like fire with rain. With the weather-beaten complexion of one who spends hours a day in the open air, her countenance was more noble than beautiful. The bitter droop of the mouth, set in the stubborn Hadsburg jaw, seemed to have put every hint of beauty to flight, and yet one felt compelled to search for it in fascinated futility when gazing upon her.

"Are you all alone, Madame?" asked Thérèse, trying to make her harsh voice as gentle as possible. It was rumored among the *émigrés* that the princess' voice had been irreparably damaged from lack of use during her long years of imprisonment as an adolescent. Thérèse herself did not know. She remembered that at times during the Revolution she had been struck with dumbness by the terrible sights she had witnessed. At the moment her dear Papa was taken away to die, an agony had seemed to freeze her vocal chords. Her mother had tried to help by teaching Thérèse to sing in prison. But soon her mother was also led to the scaffold. Whatever the reasons, Thérèse had to be careful of the unpleasant timbre of her voice, which often unwittingly caused a kind remark to be misconstrued as an insult.

"My daughter was at Mass, but she will soon return."

"We have brought you some good, nourishing soup," said Thérèse. "It is seasoned with herbs from the little kitchen garden we keep on the roof of Hartwell House. Also, some cheese made at our dairy, and good fresh bread, baked this morning." As Thérèse spoke, Madame Hue stoked up the fire in the tiny stove where she heated the soup, in addition to boiling water for tea.

"Oh, Madame," the old Marquise was at a loss for words. "Thank you."

"Nonsense," said Thérèse. "It is the least we can do for a fellow Frenchwoman in distress. But if you wish to thank us, then pray that my uncle will someday be restored to the throne of France."

"Yes, Madame, I will. But oh …!"

Taking a broom, Thérèse had begun to sweep and tidy the attic chamber. "Do not fret, Madame," she laughed, seeing the old lady's consternation," I was raised to work with my hands." Her mother, the Queen, had abhorred idleness of any kind.

"Yes, *ma princesse*," said the old lady. "Everyone knows how in your prison, you daily swept your cell and made the bed."

Thérèse made it a rule never to mention her years of imprisonment, or her family's tragedy if she could help it. In spite of her efforts, her ordeal as "the Orphan of the Temple" had become legendary in *émigré* circles.

"It was good exercise," she curtly replied to the old Marquise. When the soup and tea were ready, she and Madame de Sérent fed the poor creature from some of the cracked crockery in the attic. Then it was time to depart.

"We must go now," said Thérèse. "Madame Hue has fetched you some fresh water. I will leave you a bottle of wine, and this…." She put a bag of coins in the venerable lady's hand. "Perhaps you and your daughter can secure better lodgings. God bless you." She kissed her on the forehead and hurried out the door.

"Adieu, Madame Royale! Merci! Merci! Adieu!" The lady's voice faded away as they descended the stairs, to where Monsieur de Sérent was awaiting them with the coach. He had been making some brief calls on behalf of Thérèse's uncle, King Louis XVIII, with whom she dwelt in the country manor of Hartwell House, about forty miles northwest of London, in Buckinghamshire. Even with a small, light coach and a team of six, it would take most of the afternoon to make their return journey, if they wanted to be at Hartwell in time for dinner. As they began to rumble out of London, they had a simple repast of bread, cheese, sausage and wine. The city and its suburbs gradually dropped behind, and as the coach broke in upon the green English countryside, Monsieur and Madame de Sérent fell to conversing softly, as Thérèse indicated that she preferred to peruse the London gazettes which Monsieur had purchased in town. Madame Hue read silently also, but soon lapsed into a doze.

Thérèse's mind wandered from the doings of the British parliament. It seemed to her that from around the time of her marriage ten years earlier she fell prey to distractions whenever she attempted to read, or pray, or in any other way apply her mind. Not prison or the Terror, not threat of death or even the loss of her entire family had been able to rattle her steel-trap mind. All the sorrows were suddenly catching up with her, like hounds closing in upon their game. After a decade of maintaining a day by day façade of marital contentment, of suppressing her emotions of betrayal and disappointment, of fighting envy of women with children, of trying to build the confidence of a man whose soul was scarred almost beyond repair, she felt she had lost her former self-possession and was scrambling to cling to every vestige of peace and sanity that remained to her.

Often, when closing her eyes, she vividly saw her mother's face as at the moment when the guards had come to take the Queen to the Conciergerie. Then she would see the alabaster skin, the large, blue eyes blood-shot from weeping, the face framed by the black mourning veil.

"Do not let this crush you," brave Maman had said. "You have faith. It will sustain you." Only her faith had sustained her over the years and provided her with moments of joy and consolation. She clung to prayer, to daily Mass, to spiritual reading with an unflinching resolve. She made frequent acts of faith and hope whenever she felt that God had abandoned her. She made acts of charity even though her heart seemed to have withered up, like an unloved garden. She clung to the sage advice of her confessor, Abbé Edgeworth, who had once risked his life to accompany her father King Louis XVI to the scaffold. Abbé Edgeworth had always told her to offer everything she suffered to the Sacred Heart of Jesus in reparation for sins. She offered, with every fiber of her being, weighed upon by the pain of intrusive memory.

Her spiritual guide had been dead for two years, and how Thérèse missed him. After burying the Abbé at Mitau in Courland, the exiled French Court had been forced to seek refuge elsewhere. The new Tsar Alexander sought to please Buonaparte, and so no longer wanted to harbor the Bourbons. Their wanderings had at length brought them to England, where the British government granted them asylum on the condition that Thérèse's uncle Louis XVIII entered the country as a private citizen, under the alias of "Comte de Lille." Until last spring they had been guests of the Marquis of Buckingham at Gosworth Hall. The numbers of dependents and hangers-on who surrounded the person of Louis XVIII required a larger establishment, so the King had rented Hartwell House at 600 pounds a year.

After several hours, the coach lurched its way through Buckinghamshire, into the Vale of Aylesbury, where the meadows and woodlands were resplendent with summer. Driving through the lush, sunlit greenness, Thérèse was overwhelmed by a faint but poignant glimmer of eternity, as if she were for an instant outside of time. It seemed impossible that such a day, so tranquil and fragrant, could pass into another yesterday. The illusion of never-ending summer mirrored for her, to an infinitely lesser degree, the reality of the Kingdom which is forever and ever.

"'And grant us endless length of days in our true native land with Thee,'" she quoted to herself from the *O Salutaris Hostia*. She thought of her earthly homeland, her beloved France. She always maintained that she would prefer to live in the poorest house in France to the most magnificent palace of any other country.

Because she was the daughter of a king, she could not enter her own country. She hoped, at least, that when she died she would be buried in France.

Finally, they turned off the main road, through the rusticated arch, and onto the long, lime avenue of Hartwell House. In a few minutes the horses were clattering across the stone bridge, gracefully extending across the lake, from whence one could see on either side two little islands, ideal places for rowing and for picnics. What a romantic place for a young couple on their honeymoon, Thérèse often thought bitterly. She strove to push the idea away; Abbé Edgeworth had warned her about nourishing any bitterness. Looming before them was the northern, Jacobean façade of Hartwell, the rectangular, light brownstone mansion. The drive circled around an equestrian statue of the late Prince of Wales, father of the mad king, George III, now gloriously reigning. Hartwell House had the distinction of combining within itself the Jacobean style with the Georgian. (The south side of the mansion was Georgian.) The entire house was surrounded by improvised stalls, where impoverished noblewomen of France sold articles they had either made or acquired: wax flowers, embroidered handkerchiefs, straw hats, and memorabilia of Versailles. Money was one commodity which was scarce at Hartwell House. It was Sunday, so the makeshift shops were closed.

Footmen in faded, patched livery ran up to the door of the coach and helped them climb down. Thérèse entered the arched portal, her weary retinue trailing in behind. She marched through the echoing, stately gothic hall, up the wide, elaborately carved staircase, bearing on its banisters the most fantastic figures in full armor. Portraits of her uncle Louis XVIII and his wife Queen Marie-Joséphine, as they had been in their distant youth, hung on the wall over the staircase; her uncle smiled down craftily, while her aunt emanated a sullen audacity even from the oils. Both of the halls and most of the rooms of Hartwell House were partitioned by screens and curtains, in order to provide offices and living space for all the members of the royal household. Louis XVIII, though an impoverished exile, insisted on maintaining the strictest etiquette from the old days at Versailles, just what Thérèse's mother had fought against.

Thérèse disliked the constant formality of ever being in some ceremonial situation, but her uncle had explained his reasons. "It was the flouting of etiquette that brought on the Revolution. People lost respect for the sovereign, and for the royal authority, when the atmosphere at Versailles became too relaxed." It was one of his ways of blaming his sister-in-law, Queen Marie Antoinette, for everything that had gone wrong. Therefore, as she walked to her chamber, every courtier and every servant she passed made the customary gestures of obeisance, while Thérèse nodded to each in acknowledgment.

Her chamber was a moderately spacious one, with room enough for her *sécrétaire* and *prie-dieu*. The Duchesse de Damas was in attendance and, with the *femme de chambre*, Madame Blanchard, helped Thérèse to change into a worn gown of green brocade, in the sheath-like, classical mode, with short, puffed sleeves and an open neckline. It was slightly outdated, but it was the best she had, and she saved it for high feast days such as Pentecost. The ladies uncoiled and rearranged her thick chestnut mane, fluffing out the side curls. Many of the court ladies continued to dress their hair in the antiquated bouffant style, and many gentlemen as well as ladies still wore wigs. Thérèse chose the modern, Grecian fashion, and while leaving her hair unpowdered, she used face powder and rouge when appearing before the entire court, a tradition which had been mandatory at Versailles. She put on a pearl necklace and earrings, some of the only jewels she had not pawned in order to pay their many debts.

She briefly glanced at herself in a full-length mirror. Thérèse had not inherited Marie-Antoinette's grace or charm, but she had the same swan-like neck, sculpted shoulders, slender arms and beautiful hands with long tapering fingers. She had retained her youthful figure, if not her once superb complexion. She was only thirty, but how her features had coarsened! Thérèse went to join the household in the drawing room, where they customarily gathered to play cards and billiards before going in to dinner. She descended the outlandish staircase, accompanied by her ladies-in-waiting: charming Madame de Damas, clever Madame d'Agoult, a close friend of her youth, and dear, deaf Madame de Sérent, former attendant of Thérèse's beloved Tante Babette. They went through the bright, spacious Georgian hall and the rococo morning room.

At last they approached the drawing room, with its magnificent chandelier, like a mingling of ice and fire, sparkling in the center above the Savonnerie carpets. The court was gathered around a billiard table and several smaller card tables. As she stepped through the doorway, she heard her uncles and her husband discussing their favorite topic of "Why-the-Revolution-happened-and-what-could-have-prevented-it." As usual, her uncle Artois, who was also her father-in-law, was expounding at great length on the Revolution, although he knew the least about the actual events, having left France in July 1789 after the storming of the Bastille. On the other hand, Louis XVIII, whom she once called "Uncle Provence," said the least about the upheavals, although he possessed intimate knowledge of the causes and a thorough comprehension of the results. Artois' son, Thérèse's husband Louis-Antoine, the Duc d'Angoulême, interjected an occasional comment; his knowledge of the cataclysmic occurrences being limited to information he had gleaned from prodigious reading, from his days in Condé's royalist army, and from Thérèse herself.

"It all began with the Assembly of Notables in '87," Artois was saying. As was his custom, he was impeccably attired in a meticulously tailored English suit, simple but of the latest cut, with high starched collar, striped silk cravat and pearly waistcoat. Not tall, but of a slender, well-knit physique, the Comte d'Artois remained as debonair and dashing in his fifties as he had been as a rakish young prince at Versailles. His silvery hair was trimmed in the classical mode, his wide, brown eyes and tanned, noble face combined to make him handsomer than in his youth.

However, a rake he was no longer. During his Scottish sojourn, his mistress Louise de Polastrion, had perished from consumption. With her dying breath, after having been reconciled to the Church by Abbé Latil, she called out to Artois: "Be God's! Be all God's!" He immediately repented of his transgressions, made his confession, and resolved to live a chaste life. After the death of his estranged wife in 1805, he had sought neither wife nor mistress; his private life was above reproach. Artois' new-found religious fervor had not, unfortunately, quite delivered him from his love of cards. He had many debts, and was always short of funds. Although he preferred to live in London, he was often forced to retreat to the country in order to escape his creditors.

"The Assembly of Notables merely paved the way for the explosion of 1789. Going to the people was a big mistake," said Artois.

Louis XVIII shook his head. "It was," he proclaimed in his deep, musical voice, "the dissoluteness and extravagance of the court, and the manner in which etiquette was mocked and disregarded by those whose place it was to uphold our traditions." He disregarded the fact that his personal expenditures at Versailles had been higher than those of anyone else in the Royal Family. "Respect for the monarchy crumbled as a result."

Louis XVIII sat majestically in a velvet armchair, his rotund form dignified yet slightly grotesque, since he was practically squeezed into the blue uniform with the red collar that he had prescribed for all the gentlemen of his court. He was never without his sword, the distinguishing mark of a noble, for as King of France he was first nobleman of Europe. His aquiline nose and sly, full mouth gave an air of distinction to the otherwise fleshy and smooth countenance, while his enigmatic, pale blue eyes saw everything and betrayed nothing. His hair was long, powdered and tied with a black ribbon at the nape of the neck in the eighteenth century fashion. His swollen, gouty legs made movement painful and difficult, but the immobility worked to his advantage, for it gave him the exotic, hybrid aura of an oriental potentate, to be always obeyed and never questioned.

"It was the freemasons, Sire," put in Angoulême. "It was all the fault of the freemasons. Going back to Voltaire, d'Alembert and Frederick of Prussia. They plotted the entire debacle. Read it for yourself in Abbé Barruel's book."

The King did not like to discuss conspiracies, since he himself had been involved in so many. He was, however, fond of Angoulême. "I have read it, nephew," he said crisply and benignly. "It is a masterpiece."

Thérèse's husband, the Duc d'Angoulême, was awkwardly perched on the edge of his chair at the royal card table, eyes blinking and shoulders twitching. At age thirty-four, he resembled a monkey even more than at age twenty-four, when he had married Thérèse. With cropped, brown hair, a Bourbon nose too large for his sallow, pitted face, hairy hands, a short torso, and unnaturally long, thin legs, he stood a head beneath his wife and appeared to be overwhelmed by his own awkwardness. Devoted to books of theology and military or historical treatises, he loved uniforms and parades almost as much as ornate, religious ceremonies, yet he himself could be extremely temperamental and stubborn. Amid the splendors of Versailles, he had been given to the servants to raise; they had neglected to nourish him properly. Others whispered that he had been born with a disease inherited from the early excesses of his father, the Comte d'Artois. His parents had barely tolerated each other. They had eventually separated, thereby engulfing both of their sons in their own lovelessness and with a bizarre combination of over-indulgence and neglect. Thérèse pitied him, for her childhood had not been that way at all. If only he were not so ridiculous, if only he would be a man and a prince and the strong arm she needed to lean on.

They broke off their conversation as they saw her. The courtiers rose, sinking into appropriate postures of homage. What a motley collection of worn velvet, shiny serges, frayed brocades, wilted, skimpy ostrich plumes, and faded gold braid! Surely such an assortment had never existed before; yet the dignified and grave faces of the *émigrés*, many of whom had sacrificed homes and fortunes in order to be near he whom they held to be their lawful sovereign, kept the court from being a hapless sideshow.

Thérèse curtsied to the King; he took her hand, kissed it, and raised her from the ground. "We have been awaiting you, Madame. Let us proceed in to dinner." With great difficulty and the help of Angoulême, the King rose from his chair, then leaning on Thérèse's arm and his cane, he led the procession into the dining room. Thérèse sat at the King's right and Artois on his left. The Grand Almoner, Cardinal de Montmorency, asked the blessing, and then the first course was served.

"The latest act of revolution," said the king, continuing the conversation they had been having in the drawing room, "which threatens the security of Europe, occurred five years ago when Buonaparte placed the imperial crown upon his own head. Now any parvenu, any clever general or wily politician with an army behind him, can in a single stroke declare himself to be a new Charlemagne. Within a mere span of years, any popular hero or genius can sweep aside the tradition of centuries, and become a dictator, with the fate of millions dependent upon his every whim. Well," he continued, after pausing to take a spoonful of soup, "it may all work to our advantage in the long run. 'What the discordant harmony of circumstances would and could effect'." He delighted in quoting his favorite author, Horace.

The soup was thin and watery; the mutton, when it came, was tough; the vegetables were wooden and almost unpalatable. How ironic that the former Comte de Provence, who once employed the best chefs in France and whose table had been equal to none, now, as King, could only provide his household with such poor and meager fare. He began to discuss the writings of Mr. Gibbon with Angoulême, who was helping him to translate *The History of the Decline and Fall of the Roman Empire* into French. Thérèse's husband noisily slurped his soup and actually scratched his head at the table. Thérèse cringed, not daring to glance over to see if he was using the correct utensils; she knew he probably was not.

Madame de Damas and Madame de Narbonne were wittily sharing anecdotes about the Prince of Wales, his wife Mrs. Fitzherbert, and his daughter Princess Charlotte. The doings of the British royal family were a favorite topic of conversation at Hartwell. Madame de Narbonne began to tread in dangerous waters when she brought up the subject of the Princess of Wales, whom Thérèse thought to be a dissolute woman, and not an appropriate subject for discussion at meals. As Madame de Narbonne began to describe the Princess of Wales' antics in Italy, Thérèse's flashed her a look of displeasure, and the lady gracefully changed the topic. The court knew never to say anything that even bordered on being off-color when Thérèse was present. Even the King had to wait until she and her ladies retired for the evening before indulging in some ribald humor.

"The Princess is displeased," said her husband, who had been watching her out of the corner of his eye. His efforts at teasing never failed to irritate her.

Thérèse ate little. Lately, she had become more and more tense at family meals. She was glad when dinner ended at last, and they proceeded back into the drawing room for coffee, cards and conversation. Most of the ladies embroidered; on Sundays only the most dainty and delicate needlework was permitted. They usually discussed literature in the evenings, but for some reason the King wanted to talk about Napoleon Bonaparte.

"The usurper, of course, once begged me to renounce my legitimate claims. 'No, never,' I wrote to him. 'I may have lost my country, I may have lost my possessions, but I still have my honor, and with it I will die.' In this century," he paused dramatically, making certain that every ear was attuned to him, "it is more glorious to merit a scepter, than to wield it."

"I wonder," mused Artois prosaically, the momentous utterance completely lost on him, "I only wonder what Buonaparte has done to my Bagatelle. The roses that grew there were incomparable." Sighing for his lost villa, he leaned over a candelabrum and lit a cigar. He had acquired the British custom during his exile. Thérèse understood why English ladies took their recreation separately from the gentlemen.

"Buonaparte has probably given your house to one of his numerous relations," said the King, inhaling the bouquet from his glass of cognac. He was too urbane to show how annoyed he was with his younger brother at that moment. "As for your roses, Monsieur, Buonaparte's wife, Joséphine, is said to adore them. I am certain she will protect them from any callous *nouveaux-riches.*

"I thought Buonaparte was planning to rid himself of Joséphine," said Artois, puffing blithely away. "Does he not plan to have Joséphine annulled, and marry the Tsar's sister or perhaps…" he glanced at Thérèse, "even Madame's cousin, the Archduchess Marie-Louise?"

Thérèse was fond of her cousin Marie-Louise, with whom she had played during her three years in Vienna. She could not imagine any of her relatives being married to the brigand from Corsica.

At that moment, a very different "Joséphine" from the one whom they had been discussing appeared in the doorway of the drawing room. It was the Queen. Marie-Joséphine, formerly Madame la Comtesse de Provence, was a specter with a red nose in a puffy, wrinkled face, along with glazed eyes, a crooked nightcap and a much-mended brocade dressing gown. Swaying into the salon, she pointed at her husband, her speech so slurred as to be incoherent.

"Provence…" she uttered, after the manner of the Delphic oracle.

"She found the key to the wine cellar again," Angoulême whispered to no one in particular, but loud enough so that everyone heard him.

Thérèse jumped up and dashed forward. Then she paused, for she had almost forgotten to curtsy to the King, and to withdraw walking backwards, according to etiquette.

"The Princess is disturbed," proclaimed her husband. Everyone else looked down or away in embarrassment, as Thérèse guided her slightly deranged aunt from the room.

"He is not the true King!" muttered the intoxicated lady, with an extravagant gesture towards Louis XVIII. "I refuse to walk backwards for Provence! He has much to answer for!"

Thérèse motioned to Madame de Narbonne, whose sweet tones and light-hearted manner often helped to soothe the Queen on her bad days. They started to ascend the carved staircase. Marie-Joséphine halted so quickly, she almost knocked Thérèse backwards.

"Look!" she cried, trembling and gesturing towards one of the statues on the banister. "There is Antoinette!"

"No, no, Madame," said Thérèse, as gently as possible with her cavernous voice. "That is not my mother. It is a statue of a soldier."

The Queen ignored her. "Antoinette is staring at me! Her eyes, they burn me!"

"No, *ma tante*," Thérèse finally persuaded her to pass the statues. She was glad when they got her up the stairs and down the gallery to her own chamber, where they tucked her into bed. Thérèse directed one of the maids to boil water for tea.

"Antoinette is dead," the old Queen said flatly and faintly. "Is she not?"

"Yes, Madame," said Thérèse, her hand trembling slightly as she took the dried meadowsweet that she kept in a tin canister in the Queen's room, crushed it, and put it in a blue and white Chinese tea pot. She always tried to keep generous quantities of the herb on hand, since it was a cure for her aunt's dropsy, as well as for her uncle's gout. She added a pinch of winter marjoram and a teaspoon of sweet woodruff, both of which she also kept there. Soon the water in the big kettle in the fireplace was boiling, and with the maid's help, she poured the water into the pot.

"And Louis-Auguste?" asked the Queen.

"Yes," Thérèse gasped.

"And Babette?" Thérèse could only nod.

"And little Charles… is he dead?" asked the Queen, tipsily scrutinizing her niece's face.

"Yes," said Thérèse, in a near whisper. "He is."

The pungent smell of the herbs filled the room as they steeped. Thérèse poured her aunt a cup of tea. "Sip slowly, *ma chère tante*. It is quite hot."

The old Queen did not seem to hear. "Is he? Is he? Is he?" She kept repeating the question, each time sounding more agonized. "Is Charles dead? Is he?"

At last they got her to sip the tea, and after a few minutes she quieted down. In her elegant diction, Madame de Narbonne read aloud from an Italian novel that the Queen favored. Thérèse sat in a chair by the bed, holding her aunt's hand until the latter began to snore. The Queen's question continued to echo in her heart. "Is Charles dead?" If only she knew.

Chapter Two:

The Dream

Summer 1809

"I will be mindful and remember, and my soul shall languish within me." Lamentations 3:20

Thérèse was beginning to feel the weariness of the long day. She gave directions to Madame de Narbonne, who had offered to sit with the Queen for a while. She glanced at her watch, one of the few rescued treasures which had belonged to her mother. There was an hour or so before Benediction. She decided to rest in her room, but at the end of the gallery she saw her "Papa" Artois. He was motioning to her, as if he wanted to speak to her.

"Come walk with me in the garden, my dear child," said Artois. "It is still daylight, and I want to see the roses."

"Yes, Papa." Somehow the word "Papa" sounded so different when applied to her father-in-law than when she had used it for her own beloved father. They went downstairs, through the Georgian hall, and out the French doors onto the terrace. There were others abroad in the deepening shadows of dusk, either watering the plants, or strolling. Inside, the lamps and candles were being lit. The sky was the deepest azure, except for the gold and scarlet which clung to the hills of the horizon. Artois stopped to examine the roses, the clematis, his beloved syringa, and the King's prized camellias. They ambled across the lawn and down to the pond, where a few hardy lilies were beginning to close for the night.

"My daughter," said Artois, "I wish to address you concerning a matter of great import. Your gowns – you must have some new ones. The dignity of the House of Bourbon requires it."

"But Papa, the money!" protested Thérèse. "So many of our people dwell in miserable hovels and garrets. I prefer that any available funds be given to them!"

"It does not help our people if their princess, a Daughter of France, goes about dressed like a governess, to the scorn of the English aristocracy. Your clothes are at least five years behind the styles, my dear. Let me give you something for a few new gowns." Artois liked for the women around him to be fashionably dressed. "And as for the money," he continued, his voice falling to a near whisper, "I lately won a very large sum at cards."

"Oh, Papa, you are decadent!" cried Thérèse.

He regarded her with a bemused sadness, as if pitying her for having such a prudish, bourgeois outlook on life, brought on by the many losses she had sustained.

"Nonsense, child," he said, with the winsome smile that had melted many a feminine scruple. "Decadent! It would only have been decadent if I had lost!"

"Whom," asked Thérèse, "did you defeat this time?"

"The Duke of Kent, the Earl of Sandwich and…" he hesitated a moment, "the young Duc d'Orléans."

"Orléans! Papa, you associate with him, with Louis-Philippe?!" She referred to the former Duc de Chartres, who had assumed the title of Duc d'Orléans when his father, the notorious Philippe "Egalité," was guillotined during the very Revolution he had done so much to promote. It was the late Duc who, as a member of the Legislative Assembly, had cast the deciding vote which sent Thérèse's father, King Louis XVI, to his execution.

"Come now, daughter," said Artois. "We must forgive and forget the past. Young Louis-Philippe d'Orléans has retracted the political errors of his revolutionary days. He hopes to marry your cousin, Princess Marie-Amélie of Naples, a most pious maiden. He longs to be received here at Hartwell."

Thérèse remembered the last time she had seen her cousin Louis-Philippe. He had been making a courtesy call at the Tuileries before leaving for the war. Her parents had received him coldly; it was known that he frequented the Jacobin Club. In the bloom of his youth and in his brand-new uniform he had cut a dashing figure. How Thérèse and her friend Pauline de Tourzel had whispered about him afterwards; they had never before seen anyone who was at the same time a revolutionary and a prince, wicked yet, by all accounts, virtuous in his private life. How solemn his face had been, how fired with revolutionary zeal! Nevertheless, he had kissed her hand as gently as if she had been a porcelain doll. Almost twenty years later, she had almost forgotten that he had once been a suitor for her hand in marriage.

"I shall never receive Louis-Philippe!" she blurted so brusquely that Artois looked startled. She suddenly felt annoyed with her father-in-law. For a distinguished man with white hair, he sometimes behaved like a naïve schoolboy.

"But, daughter," pleaded Artois, "Louis-Philippe saved non-juring priests from certain death during the September days. He has lost his father and brothers. Only his mother, his sister Adelaïde, and his governess Madame de Genlis are all that remain of his family. We must be family to him. Receive him, I implore you, at least out of courtesy for his future bride."

Thérèse's face was set in its most stubborn cast. "Princess Marie-Amélie is my friend as well as my cousin. I write to her. But I cannot play hostess to the son of Philippe Egalité."

"You do not realize, Marie-Thérèse, what a difficult time he has had. He worked as a tutor in America! Imagine! He suffered from hunger, humiliations and so many family troubles."

Thérèse was well aware of the separation of Louis-Philippe's parents during the Revolution. She thought it much sadder than if they had been parted by death alone. Nevertheless, she said nothing.

"He was a brave soldier," continued Artois.

She spun to glare at him, eyes flaming. "Papa, he fought for the Revolution!"

It was Artois' turn to become annoyed. "Louis-Philippe is as charming a gentleman as one could hope to meet, every inch a prince, well-spoken and affable. He is liked by everyone in Europe. Indeed, he is someone we should have on our side." He hoped to appeal to her well-developed sense of dynastic expediency.

She was silent for a few moments. "It is for the King to decide," she said. Artois knew he had won.

"But please, Papa," she continued. "Promise me you will not gamble for high stakes ever again. We really cannot afford it."

Artois kissed her hand. "We cannot afford *not* to gamble, my dear. But as you will. On my word as a prince and a gentleman."

They walked back to the house. Pausing on the terrace, they enjoyed for a moment the fragrant dusk, the fireflies, and a nightingale's lament. Then, through the open windows came the sounds of shouting.

"Oh, no," said Artois. "Berry has arrived." He was referring to his younger son, Charles-Ferdinand, Duc de Berry. Thérèse and her father-in-law hurried to the library, which Louis XVIII used as his combined audience chamber and study. The carved paneling and shelves were lined with what the King had salvaged from his once extensive library at Versailles. Louis XVIII's corpulent form was ensconced in a big, leather armchair, in which he spent so much of the day that it almost seemed to be a part of him. He sat at his desk, with books, ink, quills, blotter and snuff box arranged most precisely, reflecting his own orderly mind. Angoulême stood behind the King's chair, like a pallid and nervous shadow.

Stamping with rage upon the red, black and gray Savonnerie carpet was a broad-shouldered, stocky young man in the prescribed blue uniform of the Court. His black curls were more than usually unruly, his dark, slightly bulbous eyes flashed, but the charm of his countenance was not disfigured by his apparent wrath, nor by the long, pointed nose inherited from his Piedmontese mother. Except for his clean-shaven jaw, he was a living portrait of the first Bourbon king, Henri IV.

"And why," he demanded with another stamp of his booted foot, "why will you not receive my wife?!" The Duc de Berry was addressing his sovereign and uncle, whose placid countenance was beginning to redden with outrage. Thérèse hated family quarrels, which always erupted when her brother-in-law visited from London. She felt a piercing headache coming on.

"How many times have I told you," said Louis XVIII, in a cold, seething voice," that you have no wife. Miss Amy Brown is not your wife. She is your mistress, and she may not come to Hartwell."

Berry crumpled and twisted his kid gloves, flinging them to the carpet. "My marriage to Amy is completely legal, and fully recognized by the laws of England!"

"You are third in line, after your father and brother, to inherit the throne of France," declared the King. "You were married without the permission of your sovereign, and in a Protestant ceremony. Such a union is considered illicit by your Church and by your King."

Berry shook his fists and Thérèse feared he might do violence to either himself or to their uncle. "You old hypocrite!" he shouted. "You only care about the Church as long as she fits into your schemes!"

"Son!" burst in Artois. "My son! You forget yourself in the presence of His Majesty!"

"Majesty! *Sacré bleu!*" Berry was in the habit of using much coarser oaths, but he managed to realize that Thérèse was in the room. "He sits in this rented house with ragged courtiers, who flatter him all the day long, and consequently imagines himself to be a king! Ha!"

Artois rolled his eyes heavenward in despair. The King mopped his brow with a handkerchief.

"Nephew," he said, with the firmness and composure that were his usual hallmark. "Nephew, I will try to forget what I have just heard you utter, if you will try to remember the manners becoming to your rank. Miss Brown is a commoner, and even if it were in my power to welcome her and her children to Hartwell, neither I nor any earthly monarch could make those of our retinue accept her. She would be very unhappy with the court."

"She would be snubbed," added Angoulême from behind the King's chair.

Berry's response was to pick up a porcelain figurine from the King's desk and raise it as if planning to smash it.

"Please do not, Berry!" pleaded Thérèse. "These things do not belong to us!" She was concerned for the rented furniture, which might suffer from flying pieces of porcelain. Berry restrained his hand, and put the statuette down.

"How do we know for certain that he is the king," he fumed, pointing at the former Comte de Provence. "How do we know that little Charles is dead? Even the British government says that there is not proof enough!"

"Berry!" Artois and Angoulême exclaimed at once. There was one subject which Louis XVIII did not care to ever hear discussed, that being the fate of his nephew and predecessor, Louis XVII, Thérèse's brother. As for Thérèse, the mention of her brother, and the thought of the intense sufferings of his imprisonment, made her ill, even after fifteen years. Her head was pounding.

"Your Majesty, I beg to be excused," she said to her uncle. "Please excuse me also from Benediction." She quickly kissed his hand and retreated backwards from the room, thinking foremost of the refuge of her chamber. She rang for her ladies and waiting-woman. She really did not need any help, as her toilette was simple, but they would have been hurt if she did not summon them. Madame de Damas and Madame d'Agoult were not on speaking terms, but one would never have guessed from the gracious manner in which they nodded to each other, handing one another articles of clothing in order of precedence. Neither of them was speaking to Madame de Sérent, who was genuinely oblivious of being the object of their rancor; her deafness mercifully protected her from a great deal of petty intrigue. She serenely brushed Thérèse's magnificent chestnut hair, as abundant as in her girlhood, when people had whispered that Madame Royale must be wearing a wig.

She remembered her Vienna days, and how she would often visit the convent school which bordered the gardens of the Belvedere Palace. The girls at the convent would beg to brush her hair. They would, on occasion, pull out a single strand to keep as a souvenir, and Thérèse would pretend not to notice. How she had longed to remain in the tranquil surroundings of the convent. Perhaps she should have become a nun, especially after being jilted by Archduke Karl von Habsburg.

"Perhaps Madame Royale has a religious vocation?" a Carmelite nun had once wondered aloud to Marie-Antoinette, when the Queen and her daughter were visiting Louis XVI's aunt, Mother Thérèse of St. Augustine, at the parlor grate. The nuns were genuinely impressed by the obedient and well-behaved little princess.

"I should be very much gratified," Marie-Antoinette had replied. Thérèse had begged the nuns to remember her in their prayers, but she had never seriously considered embracing their way of life, for she had always wanted to be a wife and a mother. Motherhood, however, was denied to her, for her marriage with Angoulême existed in name only.

Her hair was braided and tucked into a nightcap. Once in her nightgown, she climbed into bed. Usually, Thérèse and her ladies recited Compline together, but her head ached too fiercely. After taking a spoonful of vinegar of roses, soothing to headaches, she blessed herself with holy water, and managed to sleep for a while.

In her repose, she began to hear the sound of knocking. It grew louder, and more demanding, as if someone was about to break down the door. The knocking was accompanied by harsh laughter, the laughter of those who are either drunk or possessed. Thérèse felt trapped and hemmed in by mixed emotions of shame and terror. The phantom laughter became more raucous and more threatening, and then there came the all too hauntingly familiar sounds of a bolt being drawn back, as the door creaked open. She tried to scream, but her throat was paralyzed. With a gasp, she awoke, sitting up in bed, covered with perspiration. There was no knocking; everything was silent, except for the singing of the crickets and the pollywogs outside.

Thérèse fell asleep again. The nightmarish laughter was gone, and instead she dreamed that the door of her room was open, but she was unafraid, because there was only a little boy. It was Charles. He was as he had been before being given over to the degradations of Simon the cobbler. He stood at the foot of her bed, vivid with the innocent beauty of a seven-year-old. Large, roguish eyes, arched eyebrows, blonde curls, button nose, and mischievous grin; he was too real to be a dream. Suddenly, his expression became grave.

"Sister," he asked, "when are you coming to find me? When are we going home?"

"Soon, Charles," she heard herself saying. "As soon as I hear from Count Fersen. As soon as we are restored to France."

"Sister, I want to go home now. I am the King. It is my throne. Papa and Maman wanted you to take care of me."

She reached out her hand to him. "I will, Charles, I will, I will."

She awoke. Tears were streaming down her face, but her headache was vanished. She sat up. No one was there. The only movement was the votive candle which flickered in front of the small statue of the Virgin. The only sound was that of the crickets, and a gentle rain which had begun to fall. She trembled.

"Charles, where are you?!" she called into the night.

Thérèse went to her *prie-dieu* in front of the statue, and found her rosary. Climbing back into bed she prayed, and after a few *Aves*, drifted into a deep and dreamless sleep.

Chapter Three:

The Mystery

Summer 1809

"For nothing is covered that shall not be revealed; nor hid, that shall not be known." St. Matthew 10:26

The following morning, Thérèse was on the roof of Hartwell House, bending over the wooden tubs of rosemary, winter savory, sweet woodruff, horehound and sage. In a wide-brimmed, old-fashioned straw hat, such as Marie-Antoinette would have worn at Trianon, she weeded and cultivated the kitchen garden. Among the tubs of herbs and vegetables were cages with rabbits and chickens. The various birds in her husband's aviary sang and warbled. The roof was, after the chapel, Thérèse's favorite haunt at Hartwell House, where she could seize a few moments of solitude. As she worked, she tried to say the little prayer Tante Babette used to say in the Temple prison.

"What will happen to me today, O my God? I know not; all that I know is that nothing will happen which Thou hast not foreseen, willed and ordained from all eternity. That suffices me..."

She was supposed to be in her chamber having her rouge applied and her hair dressed, but she had wanted to visit the herb garden before changing from her white dimity dressing gown into a daytime dress.

"I adore Thy eternal and impenetrable designs; I submit to them with all my heart for love of Thee."

Thérèse found it especially difficult to concentrate on her prayers that morning. Even at Mass, her mind kept turning to the dream of Charles. She had arisen with pangs of hunger, having missed supper the night before due to her headache, and was happy when the coffee and *brioche* were brought to her chamber after Mass.

Even then, the picture of little Charles, at breakfast in the Temple, intruded. The blonde boy sat in the big chair, swinging his legs and saying, "Maman, I found a cupboard for this *brioche*."

"And where, young man, might that be?" Marie-Antoinette had asked.

"Right here," said Charles, as he popped the pastry into his mouth.

"I will all, I accept all." Thérèse turned her mind from the distant scene and back to her prayer. "I make a sacrifice to Thee of all, and I unite this sacrifice to that of my Divine Saviour."

After finishing her coffee and brioche that morning, Thérèse had slipped down to the library to return a book. The other night, she had raged at her poor Reader, Madame Hue, over a trifle. To make up for the distress she had caused the faithful friend and servant, she thought she would exchange the book they had been reading, *Le Roman de la Rose*, for *La Princesse de Clèves*, which Madame Hue might like better. She hoped to find the library empty, since the King and his retinue would be at the royal *lever*, his official rising from bed. Louis XVIII insisted upon maintaining the ancient ceremony as if they were at Versailles. The library was not deserted, however. Her husband sat at a table, reading a thick tome of Bossuet's Sermons, a candelabrum lit in front of him.

"Angoulême!" Thérèse exclaimed, blowing out the candles. "What a waste! Even tallow candles cost money! Why do you not read outside in the sunshine of the garden on a morning as clear and fair?"

"The air makes me wheeze," said Angoulême, petulantly. He was having one of his sullen and taciturn fits.

"Well, then, at least sit by the window with your book. Anyway, why are you not at the King's *lever*?"

"I am not well." He would not look up from his Bossuet, as he shifted to a chair by the window.

"Antoine, can I get you anything?" asked Thérèse.

"No." His voice was hard and blunt, as he refused to raise his eyes from his book.

She left him, wondering how someone so pious could be so difficult. She realized that many people thought the same thing about herself. She was relieved to put on an apron and climb the stairs to the roof. Gardening and prayer were serene companions, and there was no time like early morning for weeding. The dew sparkled on the herbs, and she breathed in their mingling fragrances. One of the rabbits scurried about in his cage, kicking his hind legs. It reminded her of little Charles, playing with his pet rabbits at the Tuileries. She recalled the day when one of them scratched him above his lip, and he had called it a "dirty aristocrat." How distressed his governess Madame de Tourzel had been to discover that her young charge had overheard one of the many revolutionary slogans.

Thérèse finished her prayer. "I ask Thee in His Name and by His infinite merits for patience in my afflictions, and the perfect submission that is due to Thee for all Thou willest or permittest. Amen."

She decided to climb up into the small, colonnaded window's watch, which was the highest point of Hartwell House. She found the wind in her face to be refreshing, for it dispersed her sensation of claustrophobia, as did seeing the expanse of the surrounding countryside. Coming down the drive were carts, wheelbarrows, and pack mules belonging to various local tradesmen and craftsmen, who came up in the mornings from Aylesbury, hoping to sell their wares. She gazed beyond the grounds of Hartwell, as far as she could see to the southeast, knowing that if she were a bird she would be flying in the direction of France. Looking to the north, she thought of the rest of the counties of England, and beyond them the wilds of Scotland, home of her Stuart ancestors. It would be wonderful to be a private person, to get on her horse and ride far away from the court and from her suffocating existence. What nonsense! No lady could just go riding away from her family and her duties! What dishonor!

Thérèse noticed a large coach coming down the drive. She wished she had the telescope her Papa had kept on the roof of Versailles for looking at the stars. The coach was too grand to belong to any of their fellow countrymen. All of the French people in her acquaintance were too poor to rent such a vehicle. Horrors! Thérèse hoped it was not Madame de Staël, but no, the notorious Germaine was rumored to be on the continent. Then it dawned on her who it might be.

"Count von Fersen!" she exclaimed to herself.

She hurried from the widow's watch, and through the rooftop garden. She flew down the staircase to the gothic hall, in spite of her patched dimity wrapper, and the ruffled cap into which her hair was stuffed, under the floppy straw hat.

"Count von Fersen!" she called, as she ran to meet the dearest friend of her parents, who during the dark days of the Revolution had been one of the only people they could completely trust. He had been a link with their ally, the King of Sweden, and other European monarchs, whose help they had hoped to receive as the violence escalated, and the royal authority waned. He was climbing down from his coach, still every inch the tall, distinguished Swede, now well into middle age. His dark blonde hair was worn long, in the style of the last century, and gold rings gleamed in his ears, but his blue eyes were tinged with sadness; melancholy lined his kindly face. The fine thin nostrils of his straight nose betokened his precise discriminating tastes. As he leaned on a copper-tipped cane, his elegant simplicity of dress complemented the noble and unaffected manner in which he removed one of his chamois gloves, took Thérèse's outstretched hand and brought it to his lips.

There flickered through Axel von Fersen's heavily lashed eyes an expression of dismay at her appearance; it shone there for the briefest moment, to be replaced by a half-paternal, half-deferential demeanor. Thérèse was suddenly aware of how she must have altered since the last time he had seen her – on her wedding day. Her once superb, translucent complexion had succumbed to hours and years of gardening, riding, and traveling in the harsh northern climates of her exile; her features bore the hardness of many wearisome struggles.

"Count von Fersen!" she exclaimed again. "Words cannot express my happiness at your presence!"

"Your Royal Highness, it has been many years," said the Count.

"I shall always be 'Madame Royale' to you, Monsieur le Comte, true friend of my family. Perhaps I shall call you 'Monsieur Rignon!' That was your alias, was it not?"

"I have tried to prove myself worthy of the trust Your Highness's illustrious parents placed in me. I bring you … news."

"We will speak later." Her heart fluttered. She hoped perhaps he had heard something about Charles. "I am sure you want to pay your respects to the King. He is in his chamber, and shall be delighted to see you."

At that moment her father-in-law Artois came to the door.

"Fersen, Fersen!" He greeted his old crony with a British handshake. "How excellent it is that you have come to see us! I hope you still know how to lose at whist!"

Fersen clicked his heels together and bowed. "At your service, Monsieur."

"Of course, of course you do!" continued Artois. "Come, let me take you to the King! Excuse us, my dear."

Thérèse hurried upstairs to finish her toilette. While having her hair dressed and her rouge applied, she received petitioners, mostly poor widows and impoverished nobles, begging for money or a place at court for themselves or a family member. She did her best to accommodate them all, denying herself in order to give to others. Everyone withdrew except for her ladies, when it was time for her to dress. She then went with Madame Hue with a basket of food and medicines to visit the tenant farmers on the estate. The rest of the morning and early afternoon she spent writing letters, going over household accounts, and settling disputes between courtiers. She hoped to have a private interview with Count von Fersen after dinner.

That afternoon, Count von Fersen entertained them at dinner with stories of the Buonaparte family, with which Europe was buzzing. News from the continent was always welcome at Hartwell House, and Count von Fersen seemed to be cognizant of everything.

"Joseph Buonaparte has decided that he does not want to be King of Spain," related the Count. "The Spanish hate him. He distributes alms in Madrid, and the people leave the money lying in the streets. They want their own King restored to them."

"Ah, this is hopeful for us," said Louis XVIII.

"Joseph wants to be King of Naples again," continued Count Fersen, "but Buonaparte has already given Naples to his sister Caroline and her husband Joachim Murat."

"What of the Spanish Royal Family, our cousins?" asked Thérèse.

"Most of them are being kept under house arrest at Talleyrand's country place," answered Count Fersen.

"Aha! Talleyrand!" laughed Artois, in fond remembrance of his old friend. "Talleyrand! Always in a compromising situation, just like the old days!"

"What of that rascal Jérome?" asked Berry. "Did he ever go back to his American wife?"

"No, he did not, Monseigneur," replied Count Fersen, politely pretending to enjoy the tough roast beef on which they were all feeding. "He has abandoned her, and married a German princess, even though the Pope refused to nullify his first marriage."

"Bigamy!" exclaimed Angoulême, furtively glancing at his brother.

"How very sad for Elizabeth Patterson," said "Thérèse, "and for her little son."

"Elisa Buonaparte Bacciochi has been given Lucca by Napoléon, part of which she has torn down in order to build a magnificent palace, the principal purpose of which seems to be that of housing an enormous statue of herself as a classical goddess."

"*Sacré bleu!*" exclaimed Berry, chasing down his amazement with a glass of Bordeaux.

"What of Lucien?" asked the King. "He seems to be the only member of the clan with any brains and sanity, besides the usurper himself."

"Lucien has continued to refuse cooperation with Napoléon, who has occupied Rome, and is threatening to throw his own brother into prison, as well as Lucien's wife and children."

"What barbarism," commented Artois.

"Joséphine, who is Buonaparte's wife, at least for the present," said Count Fersen, "orders hundreds of dresses a year, and almost as many hats."

"All at the expense of the French people, I presume," commented Thérèse.

"Indeed, yes," said Count Fersen. "At her chateau of Malmaison, Joséphine keeps a menagerie of rare and exotic animals, including gazelles, kangaroos, an ostrich, a vulture, and an eagle, not to mention the usual domestic livestock." Thérèse silently wondered how people could have dared to complain about her mother's Petit Trianon. Yet the majority of the French were said to be fond of Joséphine, and tolerated in her the same faults which had been repugnant to them in Austrian-born Marie-Antoinette, although they existed in a lesser degree.

Count von Fersen would not even mention Napoléon's beautiful sister, Pauline Borghese, knowing Thérèse as well as he did. The scandalous Pauline would not be considered an acceptable topic for polite conversation, and everyone else, including the King, knew better than to ask about her. The conversation, in the meantime, was more satisfying than the actual food. In the drawing room Count Fersen joined Artois, Angoulême and Berry for a game of whist, while Thérèse embroidered with the ladies. She wanted to ask the Count about his search for Charles, as well as other things that she could discuss only with him.

"Pig!" shouted Artois at Berry. "You cheated!" He was always every inch a prince and a gentleman except when he lost at cards.

"Honestly, Papa, I did not," Berry meekly protested.

Artois threw down his hand, fuming. He sipped the aromatic port that Count von Fersen had brought from London. It was a welcome change from the cheap brandy they had been drinking. Then he lit up a cigar for consolation, after first offering one to Axel, who declined. He did not think it proper to smoke in the presence of ladies.

Axel turned to the King. "Your Majesty, may I have the honor of asking Her Royal Highness to show me the gardens?"

Louis XVIII nodded in assent. "And while you are there, Monsieur le Comte, could you be so kind as to pick some camellias for the Queen. She delights so much in them." In exile, he had become a more attentive husband than in the days of his prosperity.

Thérèse and Count von Fersen went out onto the terrace. "It is amazing, Madame!" he sighed.

"What amazes you, Monsieur?"

"So many French lords and ladies, crammed into one house, eating tough beef and drinking bad brandy, and no one has been murdered."

"Monsieur le Comte, they are overflowing the house. Some camp in the outbuildings, including the gazebo over there. The gentleman who inhabits the gazebo has painted the inside with cartoons of the Buonaparte clan. They really are quite amusing, and you should stop in and see them sometime while you are here."

"Still, the place is very crowded. How does the King support them all?" asked Axel.

"With difficulty," she replied. "Uncle has repeatedly urged them to return to France and find positions in Buonaparte's regime. Most of them refuse. They prefer to live in penury with their true sovereign."

"There is a streak of nobility in the French character which exerts itself in truly awe-inspiring ways," observed Axel.

They had begun to pick the camellias. "There is so much I wish to ask you, Monsieur le Comte," she said.

"And I to tell you, Madame. But, begging your leave, this moment is not the time." He lowered his voice. "Even the shrubbery has ears."

She realized that with the clipped hedges of the garden, someone could be hiding nearby, listening to them. They were not far from the house, and she thought she saw a movement at one of the windows, but perhaps it was only the breeze shaking the curtains. She could tell by a sudden intake of his breath that Count Fersen had seen it, too. Now Thérèse knew why her crafty uncle had asked them to pick camellias.

"Let me show you the pond, Count Fersen," said Thérèse. They began strolling away from the house, but Axel sank into silence, as if the beauty of the June evening plunged him into sadness.

"June is a difficult month for me, Madame." He was referring to the abortive royal escape attempt which he had planned so carefully in June of 1791. Thérèse would never forget the nightmare of her family's recognition and capture at Varennes, and the violence of the long, slow ride back to Paris.

"If only I had accompanied your coach..." he began. She interrupted him.

"No, Monsieur le Comte. It is past. Please do not reproach yourself. You would have been imprisoned and guillotined if you had been captured with us. And then where would I be now in my search for...." She stopped before uttering the name of Charles, for an idea came to her.

"We have a few horses, Monsieur. Perhaps you would like to go riding tomorrow?"

"And ruin your reputation, *ma princesse*? The way I ruined your sainted mother's reputation when I rode with her in the park of Versailles, within view of a thousand eyes? Yet the Comte de Saint-Priest spread malicious rumors about the Queen and myself which persist to this day. I would wager that it was he who was watching us just now from the window. Believe me, Madame, he is not above starting such stories about us, even though I am old enough to be your father. He has always been my enemy...." He sighed."Some people never change. They only grow old, and become more themselves than ever before."

Thérèse was aware that Count Fersen had taken some indiscreet liberties with the wife of Monsieur de Saint-Priest, causing the latter to have an undying grudge.

"What if I bring with me a mature lady of known virtue, who also happens to be deaf?" She referred to Madame de Sérent.

"Excellent, Your Highness. It shall give me pleasure to see the estate with you tomorrow."

The camellias were beginning to show the need for water, so they circled the pond and started back towards the house. Axel reminisced about his first visit to Versailles. "I had just come from England, where I was snubbed by a young lady. How touched and surprised I was to be remembered by the Queen of France, who had only briefly conversed with me once before at the Opera Ball. 'Here is an old acquaintance!' Her Majesty said. What kindness! I never forgot it."

Suddenly Thérèse blurted out a question, as if the weight of years at that moment became too heavy, and pushed it from her.

"Monsieur Fersen, were you in love with my mother?"

Count Fersen smiled into her eyes, his own full of tears and understanding, as if he had long expected the question, and long welcomed it. He gestured towards the moon, which was rising through the trees like an unpolished opal in the soft, azure, summer sky.

"Is it possible not to love the moon? And such a moon, which gleams at the edge of darkness, so proud, yet so alone and so hauntingly vulnerable. One cannot possess it, nor would one want to. Is it possible not to love the evening star, in all its jewel-like warmth and fire and enchantment? One cannot help loving it, but to possess it would mean being consumed and destroyed. No, one can love the moon, the evening star, and even the nightingale which serenades them, but they belong to another realm, and it behooves the onlooker to love, and to pass on."

Thérèse nodded and understood.

The next morning found them cantering across the green park of Hartwell on passable mounts, with Madame de Sérent, proper as a governess, following at a discreet distance on a decrepit old nag. Thérèse could not help thinking of her uncle's superb collection of saddle horses at Versailles; he who could not even ride on account of his bad hips. In their humbled circumstances, they were grateful for the motley array of horses which peopled the stables of Hartwell.

"You ride like one of our Norse Valkyries, *ma princesse*," said the Count, his dapper riding apparel greatly contrasting with her hopelessly old-fashioned habit and shovel hat. Thérèse flashed one of her rare, child-like smiles. She felt endowed with a gracefulness on horseback that deserted her on every other occasion. The sky was overcast and there was a light drizzle. They slowed to a walk.

"Now, Monsieur, please tell me of my brother," said Thérèse.

"I visited Lady Charlotte Atkyns in London," related Count Fersen. "She is convinced that Louis XVII is not dead."

"Lady Atkyns? You mean the former actress, who smuggled aristocratic children out of France during the Reign of Terror?"

"Yes, Madame. She was known before her marriage as 'Mrs. Walpole' and she specialized in playing the part of boys on the London stage. She became a spy for the British government, known as 'the Little Sailor' because it was disguised as one that she traveled back and forth across the channel. The French police knew her as 'Mrs. Williams of Liverpool', but they were never able to capture her. She claims that she infiltrated both the Temple prison and the Conciergerie, dressed in the uniform of the National Guard, and twice spoke with the Queen, your mother, who begged her to rescue her son Louis XVII. After her husband's death in 1794, Lady Atkyns began to expend a great deal of money in an attempt to deliver the young king from his captors. A journalist in London put her in touch with a circle of French *émigrés*, who furnished her with contacts in Paris. She became entangled in such a web of espionage and counter-espionage, beyond anything she had ever imagined, all with the little King at the center, the startling conclusions of which she has only begun to discern, as she ties up all the loose ends."

He broke off for a moment. They had come to a beech grove, a spot of such singular, summer beauty, that it made the dark nature of their conversation all the more unreal. Thérèse wondered once again for the thousandth time in her life: "How could it all have happened?"

"Madame," Count Fersen turned towards her in the saddle, the lines in his face deeper than ever. "Madame, there are many things which are shadowed from me. I can only guess how difficult the very mention of those sad days is for you. And yet, if we are to find Charles, the picture must be made as clear as possible for me. May I ask…?"

Thérèse interrupted him. "Count Fersen, my faithful friend and true friend of my parents, you may ask me whatever you think to be necessary."

"Could Your Highness tell me of the state of your brother's health during the first months of captivity in the Temple tower?"

Thérèse's eyes darkened to agate, as she drew aside the curtains of her mind, and stared into the past. "When we were incarcerated in the Temple tower in August of 1792, my brother the Dauphin enjoyed the most robust state of health. He was seven years old; always running, jumping, laughing and playing soldier with his toy sword; proud of his National Guard uniform. He loved to cry, 'Bayard, without fear or reproach!' the motto of the knight of old. By the time spring came, he had fallen ill, due to the unnatural confinement of prison life, and the limited amount of fresh air he was allowed to take, he who was accustomed to being so often outdoors. The first time he became ill, it was probably from worms, due to the unsanitary conditions of the tower. Also, our family was suffering the loss of my father. In May, Charles began to have a pain in his side, and headaches. Maman was anxious, remembering our Louis-Joseph, who had died at seven years old. When summer came, Charles recovered, and soon that gloomy place rang once more with his laughter, his teasing, his games.

"Then, in June, he injured himself on a stick he was using as a hobby horse. Maman asked the guards to summon a physician at once, which they did, a Doctor Pipelet, who carefully examined him, scrupulously recording the cause of the accident. As you may recall, the accident was twisted by Hébert, and used against Maman in the most vicious way. A few weeks later, Charles was forcibly removed from us. Maman never saw him again, except from a distance. It almost destroyed her."

Thérèse's hands quivered on the reins. It took but a moment to gain command of herself again, so used was she to suppressing her more violent feelings.

"The last time Your Highness saw the little King," began Count Fersen, almost hesitantly, "was it not in the council room of the Temple in the autumn of 1793?"

"Yes." Thérèse's voice, in cold tones more raspy than usual, fell from her lips as if her mind was far away. "Yes, Monsieur. He sat in a big chair, swinging his legs, reciting in the most unnatural manner, almost like an automaton, the most atrocious calumnies against Maman and Tante Babette. His eyes were bloodshot. He started to weep, and took my hand. Then they led him away. At the time, I did not fully understand what they were making him say about my mother and my aunt. Now I do."

They were both quiet. Then Axel spoke. "I do not believe such an infamy was the work of the Dauphin's keeper, Simon the cobbler. He was a coarse and brutal man, but I do not think he had the wit to conjure up that kind of a libel. Hébert and Chaumette planned all of it. Both men were so vile in their personal habits, they could not see beyond the mire of their own minds. They deliberately plotted to destroy the mind and morals of your brother, to degrade him in every possible way, and instructed Simon accordingly."

"Yes," agreed Thérèse, sadly. "Simon gave my brother too much wine to drink. It made Charles sick by the end of the summer. He was kept on the second floor. Tante Babette and I were on the floor immediately above; we could hear Charles swearing and blaspheming, singing the *Marseillaise*, the *Carmagnole*, and a thousand other horrible things with Simon every day. Simon struck my brother, and made him fetch and carry for him. He had been told to make 'Charles Capet' lose all idea of his rank; to democratize him. Nevertheless, Simon's wife made Charles' bed and kept him clean. She was not a bad soul, just very common and extremely ignorant. She took care that Charles ate properly. Much of this I discovered later, from my companion Rennette, from Gomin the jailor, and from our governess, Madame de Tourzel, who made her own inquiries. At the time, Tante Babette and I could only guess what was going on by what noises we heard coming through to the third floor."

"And your own situation, Madame, and that of Madame Elisabeth, was becoming more difficult?" asked the Count.

"Indeed, it was. Maman, of course, had been taken to the Conciergerie. The guards often came into our prison to search us. By November of 1793, they were searching us three times a day, once for three and a half hours. It was...a nightmare. Four drunken guards, amidst the coarsest oaths and most filthy insinuations, addressing us in a familiar manner. It pained me to see my beloved aunt, so modest and pure, the victim of their indignities. She suffered similar agonies on my behalf."

Count Fersen hesitated. Thérèse knew that there were things which he could never ask, and which she could never tell.

"When was it, Madame, that you stopped hearing any sounds of your brother in the rooms below?" he asked after a period of silence.

"On January 19, 1794, my aunt and I looked out the window, and saw packages being carried from the tower. The packages were placed in a cart filled with linen, which belonged to Simon and his wife. They were leaving the Temple that day, and we assumed that my brother was going with them, perhaps smuggled out beneath the linen in the cart, for it suddenly grew very quiet on the floor below. We thought Charles had been replaced with a quiet prisoner, whom we nicknamed 'Melchisedec.' After January 20, I heard nothing to indicate that my noisy, naughty, blaspheming, little brother was living in the tower. As I later discovered, a poor, miserable child was living in Charles' rooms, sick and solitary. Whether the boy was Charles I do not know for certain, because I was never permitted to see him, or to communicate with him in any way."

"Are you aware, Madame, that no one saw the prisoner for over six months? His food was put in a small window, that is all. Hébert and Chaumette were accused of being involved in a royalist plot and were guillotined. All of the former servants at the Temple, everyone who had known Charles before January 20, 1794, were sent away and replaced, except for Monsieur Tison. Tison was walled up in an isolated cell and not permitted to see or speak to anyone."

"Then Simon did take Charles away, and left another boy in his place?" asked Thérèse.

"Perhaps. There are still many connections which I hesitate to make, which I almost dread to make."

Thérèse was afraid to ask what he meant. Axel continued. "When was Madame Elisabeth taken away?"

"On May 9, 1794. She was guillotined the following morning. I was alone in the tower, except for the mysterious prisoner, and the guards. One night, I had a visitor – an officious man in a nankeen suit, powdered wig, and steel spectacles. I demanded a doctor for my brother, but he said nothing. He just stared at me, and left."

"Do you realize, Madame, that it was Robespièrre himself who came to see you? He was overthrown shortly afterwards, in July of '94, by Barras, Tallien, and the other 'Thermidoreans.' The Terror had ended, but many continued to die in the war, and in other horrors. France was in chaos until Buonaparte came to power in 1799. Families were broken up, children lost, homes burned, bandits terrorized the countryside. The years of the Directory under Barras were those of turmoil, in which the strange and unexpected were mundane occurrences."

"It pained me to leave my country when I was finally released from prison," said Thérèse. "People would stand under my window and serenade me. On my journey to Austria, the peasants, when they recognized me, ran weeping to my coach, begging me to remain. How I loved them! How I love the French people – my people, who have suffered beyond all imagining."

They had come to the lime avenue. The drizzle had stopped, the sun broke through, and the leaves sparkled. Axel gazed admiringly upon Thérèse and her devotion to country, which no adversity could shake. He decided it was time to plunge headlong into a new revelation, even though it would bring her more distress.

"It was in the chaos of 1794 that Lady Atkyns and her agents became deeply involved in trying to rescue the child in the Temple tower, whom they believed to be your brother. Among her agents were many scoundrels, with the exception of the Comte de Frotté, a dedicated royalist. In her capacity as a spy, Lady Atkyns uncovered several royalist plots. It does not seem possible, Madame, but Hébert and Chaumette may have been in contact with your uncle, the former Comte de Provence."

"What!"

"They planned to restore the monarchy, with Charles as a puppet king, and Provence as the regent. Anyone could see that France had descended into anarchy, what with the foreign war and the civil war in the Vendée. They needed a figurehead to unite the country. Their plan failed, but a similar one was taken up by Robespierre."

"Robespierre! A monarchist!" exclaimed Thérèse.

"Robespierre, like every dictator and tyrant, was consumed by fear. His solution was to eliminate all political opponents – hence the Terror. One of the members of his inner circle on the Committee of Public Safety was a spy for the British. It may have been Barère, who later took part in the coup of Thermidor. The spy uncovered evidence that Robespierre was corresponding with your uncle the Comte de Provence. Robespierre was planning to use the child-king as a pawn for bargaining purposes with either the foreign powers or with the royalist army of the Vendée. He was considering a restoration of the monarchy, with himself as regent, or Provence. There is even talk that Robespierre was planning to marry you, Madame."

"That is absurd!"

"Remember, Madame, the saying before the Revolution that was applied to Provence, now Louis XVIII: 'As treacherous as Monsieur.' I am afraid it is highly likely that your uncle plotted with the revolutionary leaders the fate of young Louis XVII... and the fate of yourself."

Thérèse remember how her mother had always mistrusted her brother-in-law, Provence. What she was hearing did not surprise her. It only rubbed the salt of the reality of her situation into her deeply wounded happiness.

"After the Thermidorians guillotined Robespierre," continued Count Fersen, "their leader Barras, who has been described as having the soul of a louse, visited the Temple, and appointed the young Creole Christophe Laurent to take charge of Your Highness and the mysterious child prisoner."

"I remember Laurent," said Thérèse. "He was polite to me. He said that he cleaned my brother's cell, and got rid of the lice."

"Or so he claimed," remarked Count Fersen. "I doubt that he cleaned it immediately. Lady Atkyns' agent refers to Laurent as 'the Black Devil.' I suppose he was a double agent. He never allowed you to see your brother, did he?"

"No, Monsieur, he did not."

"Nor did he call a doctor for the sick child prisoner, or allow him out of his cell to get some fresh air, as Barras had instructed. I am sorry, Madame, but Laurent was no good. There were many 'counter-revolutionary' plots against Barras' government, on the part of various factions, with various agendas. In November, Gomin was sent to the Temple. A pleasant man, I believe."

"Why, yes. He was very kind to me. He brought me matches, and said he was taking good care of Charles."

"I see." The Count sounded doubtful. "Then I wonder at the report of Harmand, the chief of the metropolitan police, who visited the little prisoner in December. He found a dumb boy with rickets, covered with tumors, but still able to walk, and obviously able to obey simple commands. He later described him as having long, chestnut hair."

"Charles' hair was pale gold, the color of straw!" exclaimed Thérèse. "Surely, the boy was not he!"

"He was not Louis XVII. Unless, as some claim, the Dauphin had been so brutalized and denatured under Robespierre's regime that he was no longer himself. He had been deliberately corrupted so that even if a rescue occurred he would never be able to reign, but be only a puppet. It could be that the little King had been driven into a state of melancholy by his tormentors, by the neglect, and by his many illnesses. Or it could be he had been replaced by another boy."

"Replaced... by whom?"

"I am not certain... yet. I know that at the end of March 1795, Laurent was sent away from the Temple, to be replaced by Lasne. It was Lasne who at last summoned a physician for the unfortunate boy. Meanwhile, Lady Atkyns' agent, Monsieur de Frotté, wrote to her that he was convinced that Louis XVII had been replaced by another boy, and that the French government wished to do away with the replacement, who was becoming an embarrassment. You see, Madame, both the Spanish government and Charette, the leader of the Royal and Catholic army of the Vendée, were demanding the release and safe delivery of yourself and your brother, in exchange for peace. The Directoire of Barras badly needed peace from both its external and internal foes, but would not surrender Your Highness until the child in the room below had died on June 8, 1795."

"It was only then that I was allowed to leave my prison cell, and go down into the garden," recalled Thérèse. "As for the boy who died, I was told he was my brother, but I was not permitted to care for him in his illness, to pray at his deathbed, or even to identify his corpse. It was only when he was safely buried that I was able to leave."

"*Ma princesse*," said Count Fersen, "Lady Atkyns does not believe that the boy who died on June 8 was Louis XVII. Her agents believe that Your Highness' brother was murdered by Robespierre's henchmen, possibly by Simon, and then replaced by another boy. Lady Atkyns merely says 'a higher power than mine took possession of him.' She believes he is still alive."

"But who, Count Fersen? Who has him? Where is he?"

The thudding of horses' hooves kept the Count from replying. They both glanced at the broad-shouldered young gentleman cantering up behind them. It was Berry.

Chapter Four:

A Predicament

Summer 1809

"Save me, O God, for the waters are come in even unto my soul. I stick fast in the mire of the deep, and there is no sure standing." Psalm 68: 2, 3

"Berry!" exclaimed Thérèse. "What are you doing here?!"

Berry doffed his hat. "Madame my sister; Madame de Sérent; Monsieur Fersen," he said, nodding to each in turn. "I came to share your secret counsels concerning the fate of Louis XVII. I have a deeper interest in this matter than you may think. I have been making inquiries of my own, and have reason to believe that he yet lives."

Thérèse gasped. "How, Monseigneur, did you know...?"

Berry's laugh interrupted her. "Why else would you go riding so far afield? To escape Monsieur de Saint-Priest, and Uncle's other spies. I am acquainted with Lady Atkyns, and am aware of her search, and of yours, Monsieur Fersen."

Count Fersen bowed in the saddle. "Monseigneur de Berry," said Axel in firm tones, "you understand that if our young

King still lives, his safety will depend entirely upon our conversation not reaching certain ears."

"And I know whose ears, too," blurted the prince. "Provence! I know that he bargained with the revolutionaries. He tried to bargain with Buonaparte. Why, he would bargain with the devil himself, and probably already has!"

"Berry!" Thérèse was horrified at her brother-in-law's words. Yet it would be a help for her to have someone else in the family in her confidence. "Very well. You may ride with us, Berry. But you must behave, and you must be discreet."

"How much do you know, Monseigneur?" asked Axel.

"I know that the boy who died on June 8, 1795 in the Temple prison, and was buried in the Sainte Marguerite cemetery, was not Louis XVII. Whether my little cousin was murdered earlier or smuggled out, I do not know for certain. There are many mysteries surrounding this case, including the Petitval massacre. I do know that there lives in France, even as we speak, a young man whom many people regard as their rightful king. He goes by the name of Jean-Marie Hervagault."

"Ah, yes, Hervagault," said the Count, nodding. "May I ask, how does Your Highness know of him?"

"I am acquainted with many people in London, with *émigrés*, who get news from the continent. I also have many English friends, some of whom have been involved in this affair in one way or another, or are familiar with others that have. I ask questions here and there," explained Berry.

"Tell me, Berry, what is the Petitval massacre that you mentioned?" asked Thérèse.

"Perhaps, Monsieur Fersen can tell of it better than I," said Berry, with a look at Axel.

"At Vitry-sur-Seine there lived a wealthy royalist banker named Petitval," began the Count, "who oversaw many of Your Highness' parents' personal financial affairs. In exchange for money to help overthrow Robespierre, Barras was to deliver young Louis XVII safely to Petitval. In August of 1794, Barras sent a boy of about nine years to Petitval's estate at Vitry. Lady Atkyns thinks he sent a decoy, a false Dauphin, and that Petitval soon discovered that he had been deceived. One morning, every soul at Vitry-sur-Seine was found murdered, everyone from Petitval's aged mother to his servants, their throats cut. Lying on the front lawn was Petitval himself, his skull crushed. Nothing was stolen from the house, but all of Petitval's papers were gone, as was the mysterious child."

"What a dreadful tale!" cried Thérèse.

"Unfortunately, my sister, such stories became commonplace in revolutionary France," said Berry. "But the connection with Louis XVII makes the Petitval massacre unique."

"What do you know about Hervagault, Berry?" asked Thérèse.

"Only that he appeared on the road to Châlons in 1796, a charming, well-mannered little beggar of about eleven years old. He was brimming with fanciful tales, calling himself a 'Prince of Monaco,' then saying he was 'a Norman'. The citizens of Châlons immediately assumed him to be of noble birth, especially when he displayed a familiarity with our intricate family tree— one which I myself find difficult at times. The identity of Louis XVII was soon pinned upon him, and he did not deny it. He was showered with money and gifts by peasants, shopkeepers and aristocrats alike. The police arrested him for vagrancy and swindling, although no one had complained of being swindled. He was sent home to his 'parents' in Saint Lo, the tailor René Hervagault and his wife Nicole, *née* Bigot. Jean-Marie Hervagault ran away from home again and again; each time the people flocked to him as to their sovereign.

"In 1798, the High Police became involved. They summoned René Hervagault to formally depose in court that the lad was indeed his son, Jean-Marie. The only problem was that the young 'swindler' did not look a day over thirteen, whereas, according to the baptismal records Jean-Marie Hervagault was eighteen years old. And there is yet another, more bizarre twist to this situation. René's wife Nicole, had before their marriage been the mistress of the Duc de Valentinois, Prince of Monaco, and the real Jean-Marie was not the tailor's son at all, but the natural son of Valentinois. There are those who say that the boy who died in the Temple in June of '95 looked much older than ten, but was rather well into adolescence."

72

"You mean …" said Thérèse.

"I mean that perhaps the real Jean-Marie Hervagault was exchanged for our Charles, who was sent to live hidden away at St. Lo with the tailor. Or, perhaps the boy sent to Saint Lo was not Charles, but a decoy, maybe even the same one who was sent to Vitry-sur-Seine. Whoever he is, it would have been safer for him if he had stayed in the obscurity of the tailor's shop, but he kept trying to make his way west and south, as if headed for the Vendée."

"I, too, have heard of the Hervagault affair," said Thérèse. "In December of 1798, while residing in Vienna, I received a letter from Abbot Lestrange of the Trappists in Munich. It was told to him by a Carmelite nun, a distant relation of ours, who was travelling through Châlons on her way from Paris to Germany, that a Sister Delorme, superior of the nursing sisters of Châlons, possessed vital information concerning the pretender Hervagault. In the opinion of Sister Delorme, Jean-Marie Hervagault, whom she frequently visited, was indubitably and without question King Louis XVII. I was seized with terror."

"With terror?" asked Berry. "Whatever for?"

"Because if the boy was my brother, any attention or recognition from me would be his doom, especially as long as he remained in France. There were many dark forces at work. I wrote to Uncle Provence saying that I guessed it to be an idle story, which I half-supposed it to be. Cardinal de la Fare, who was supervising my correspondence at the time, wrote on my behalf to the Abbot, who was offering to be a means of sending money to Hervagault for an escape from prison, which Sister Delorme would arrange. The Abbot was urged to drop the matter."

"You acted wisely, my sister," said Berry. "If you had displayed the least interest in the claimant, Uncle would have heard of it, and Hervagault, whoever he might be, would have become more inextricably caught in the web than he already is. Now, there is hope for him, if he is our Charles. He has been in and out of prison, and the last I heard, he had joined Buonaparte's army– a safe hiding place for an aspiring Bourbon prince."

"But Hervagault is not the only claimant," said Count von Fersen. "In March of 1794, there appeared in Albany, New York a

Monsieur and Madame Jardin. Monsieur Jardin was a former valet of the Comte de Provence."

"And Madame Jardin had been one of Maman's maids!" cried Thérèse.

"Yes, indeed, *ma princesse,*" said the Count. "Both of the Jardins were intimate with the royal family. They had with them their own daughter, Louise, and a boy of about nine."

"The exact age of Charles!" exclaimed Thérèse.

"They left the boy with a half-breed Iroquois family named Williams," continued Axel.

"I do not believe the boy was Charles," said Berry. "Not if he had anything to do with Uncle Provence. I am convinced that Uncle has been sending out boys as decoys, just to cause confusion, and make it more difficult for the real Louis XVII, if he lives. There is word of such a rascal in Normandy, a French boy planted by Uncle Provence to stir up trouble for Buonaparte... and for the Louis XVII."

"That may be true, Monseigneur," said Fersen, "but we must be certain. We must follow every lead, even if it brings us to a cul-de-sac." He inclined his head towards Thérèse. "The parents of Madame would have wished it so. You see, there are other claimants in America. In a village by the name of Greenwich, outside of New York City, there dwells an enigmatic young gentleman who calls himself 'Mr. LeRoy.' The villagers insist that he is Louis XVII. In Quebec, there is a man named 'Louis-Charles Lebel,' also known as 'Olivier Lebel," who was brought to Canada by the Jesuits. Many believe him to be the lost King of France. In Brewster, Massachusetts there is a sea captain, a Captain Nickerson, who says he was in Paris during the Revolution, and brought away with him the Dauphin, who sails with him under the name of 'René Rousseau.' In Louisiana there is a young Creole gentleman called 'Jean-Jacques Audobon', a brilliant artist and ornithologist, who, it is rumored is, in actuality, Louis XVII."

"Oh, Count Fersen! The whole thing is mad! It makes my head spin. So much audacity! So many claiming to be someone they are not!" Thérèse shook her head.

"If there is the chance that one of them *is* your brother, Madame, then we must find him," explained Axel. "I plan to make a lengthy journey to America within the next year or so. I have duties in Sweden that must be attended to first." He was, after all, Lord High Steward of the realm. "And then I shall go."

"Oh, Count Fersen, if one of those young men is Charles, you will recognize him. You would know him at once," said Thérèse.

"Yes, Madame," he replied, softly and sadly. "I would recognize him. And I am already familiar with America, having fought there with the French army. It will be a long search, but, God willing, a fruitful one."

"We will pray that it will be so, Monsieur le Comte," said Thérèse.

"I, for one, hope that Charles is found," declared Berry. "If he is restored to his rightful place someday, I will be further from the throne, and free to be with my Amy."

"What will we do if my brother is mentally incapacitated?" asked Thérèse. "He went through such an unspeakable ordeal. Simon did everything to corrupt him. What kind of morals will he have? Would he even be capable of ruling?"

That, *ma princesse*, is a question which your family must resolve," said Count Fersen. "If we do find him, and he has been so traumatized by his sad past and brutal treatment so that it would be cruel to bring him back into the world of rank and royalty, from which he has been removed for so long, then perhaps in the end it would be most merciful to leave him in obscurity, safe and well-provided for, of course."

Thérèse started to weep. "What a dreadful predicament! What a bitter chalice, to search for one who perhaps is better left unfound! But … it is my duty; I shall not swerve from it– and perhaps he can be reclaimed."

"I shall help you. And Angoulême, too," said Berry, trying to comfort her.

"Since the burden of this matter is so heavy, Madame," said Count Fersen, "you should confide in your husband."

"Oh, no!" Thérèse protested. "Angoulême believes Charles died in the Temple. He will hear of no other theory."

"We should take him into our confidence," said Berry, "at least to a degree. Otherwise, if he discovers that he has been left out, he would go to Uncle and tell everything."

Thérèse agreed. Berry burst into a sudden torrent of angry words. "How can you stay with Uncle, Marie-Thérèse?! How can you and Angoulême keep living under the same roof with him, after all the evil he has perpetrated on your parents, on your brother…and on you?!"

"Berry, be silent!" Thérèse pleaded.

"It is true! He plotted against your parents, libeling them at every turn. He plotted your brother's destruction with the revolutionaries. He tricked you into marrying Angoulême, just so that he could control you and have you on his side, so the *émigrés* would support him!"

"Oh, Berry!" She restrained herself from galloping away, and faced her brother-in-law. "Berry, hear me. Louis XVIII is my King. For now, he is my lawful sovereign. He is the King of France. Oh, Berry, my brother and cousin, I believe in France, in her destiny as Eldest Daughter of the Church. As she has led other nations into revolution, war and chaos, so someday she will lead them back to the fullness of truth, to Christian unity in the Holy Apostolic Catholic faith. I believe in her heritage, in the martyrdom of so many of her children, and in their prayers. I will stay at the side of my King, for to serve him is to serve my beloved France."

Berry's dark eyes widened as if, for an instant, he stepped beyond his own world of pleasure, into a world of self-sacrifice and devotion to family, to country, and to God, the world of Thérèse.

"Gentlemen," she said, "it is time to dress for dinner. Come, I will race you back to the stables!"

They sprang forward, with Madame de Sérent primly cantering behind at a discreet distance, across the meadow to the green lawns of Hartwell.

Chapter Five:

Secrets

Autumn 1810

"But I say unto you, that every idle word that men shall speak, they shall render an account for it in the Day of Judgment." St. Matthew 12:36

The wind moaned around Hartwell, swirling the russet and gold leaves, luminous in the grayish afternoon of rain and turbulence, against the windows of the Queen's chamber. Thérèse sat at her aunt's bedside, watching Marie-Joséphine's belabored breathing. The sooty brows and reddish nose were the only points of color in the aged lady's pallid, sunken countenance. The stale smell of sickness and death lingered in the room, unconcealed by bowls of potpourri. The chamber was swathed in shadows, except for the innocuous little fire in the grate, and the single blessed candle Thérèse had lit near the bed, since her aunt was approaching the end.

In the last year Marie-Joséphine had become increasingly demented, suffering from violent tremors, living almost entirely on soup, tea, and milk laced with brandy. Yet as her body weakened, her mind seemed to reclaim its lucidity at closer intervals, so that she occasionally made startling and acutely honest observations. Thérèse practically lived in her aunt's sickroom, personally tending to her every need. No one could take the place of one's own family when one was deathly ill – no servants, doctors, or courtiers would suffice. When she was sick as a child, her mother never left her side; both of her parents had sat up with her all night. Taking care of the dying Queen was an almost welcome distraction from the gaping wound of loss which bled anew inside of her. Last June, Count von Fersen had died.

He had spent a great deal of the summer of 1809 with them. Every time he had made ready to go, her uncle the King would beg him to sty a little while longer at Hartwell, and the Count would comply. His cheerfulness and colorful anecdotes lightened the conversation at table; every member of the family glowed in the sun of his wit and warmth. He and the King would discuss politics while picking camellias for the Queen; Artois loved him for losing so gracefully at whist; he delighted Berry with his knowledge of art and music; he broke Angoulême's most morose moods by talk of military strategy and war experiences in America. When Axel's many duties summoned him back to Sweden, they all missed him deeply. Troubles in Sweden prevented him from making the trip to America as soon as he had planned.

Then one day, almost a year after Axel's departure from Hartwell, Angoulême came to Thérèse while she was working in the garden, his hands trembling; the letter in one fell to the ground. She picked it up, read a few lines, and it was only Angoulême's unsteady arm around her shoulders which kept her from fainting. "Varennes!" she gasped. "It was on the anniversary of our capture at Varennes – the twentieth of June – the infamous day! O God, have mercy!" She choked on her sobs. "He died as Maman had so dreaded to die – at the hands of the mob!"

Count Fersen's enemies had blamed him for the sudden, mysterious demise of Sweden's Crown Prince, whom he was unjustly accused of poisoning. During a procession in Stockholm in his robes of state, he was dragged from his coach by an angry mob, who kicked and pummeled him, tearing out his earrings. He escaped into a house, only to be thrown out of a window, after which his lifeless body was stripped and mutilated. A cloud of horror enveloped Thérèse, filling her with a stifling, sickening, aching grief and dread such as she had not known since the days of the Terror. It was almost like losing her father all over again.

Who now could help her to find Charles? No one else had such international connections, combined with sympathy for her family. Who else could she trust as much? Berry was too impetuous; Angoulême refused to countenance the idea that little Charles was anywhere but in the Sainte Marguerite cemetery. She dared not broach the matter with her uncles.

Thérèse was dragged from her thoughts by the black eyes of Marie-Joséphine, which had popped open and were riveted upon her. Thérèse braced herself, knowing that one of the Queen's disconcerting spells of coherency had come.

"How you have changed since you came to us, my dear," mumbled the Queen. "How lovely you were– even Madame Vigée-Lebrun could scarcely capture it."

Thérèse flinched at the reminder of the Vigée-Lebrun portrait of herself as a young girl that hung in the library. Someone had managed to salvage it from the wreck of the monarchy; she almost wished they had not, since the sweet, florid beauty of adolescent Madame Royale had long ceased to be hers, and gazed at her forlornly like a child of her own that she had lost.

"What have we done to you to transform you so?" sighed Marie-Joséphine.

Thérèse retreated into mute rigidity. "Are you ready for some hot milk, Madame?" she asked stiffly after several moments.

The Queen ignored her query. "You have no secrets from me, Marie-Thérèse-Charlotte. I know what you have suffered: the ordeal of a marriage that exists in name only." The Queen coughed and sputtered.

"Aunt!" exclaimed Thérèse, as horrified to hear her unspoken sorrow put into words as if her nakedness had suddenly been uncovered. "Aunt! I pray you, do not speak of it!" She was immensely relieved that they were alone. Mercifully, not even a chambermaid was present.

"I shall speak of it!" Marie-Joséphine's glazed eyes flashed blearily into her own. "They call you 'The French Antigone' and it is true. Like Antigone, you have been buried alive! You have no marriage! Everyone knows about Angoulême!"

"Please, Madame, I beg you…" said Thérèse.

The Queen relentlessly continued. "Your…union with Angoulême is null and void. You were tricked into marrying him. Believe me, I know. Provence tricked you. Remember the saying, before the Revolution: 'As treacherous as Monsieur.' He may not tell me his connivances, but I find him out. My husband is not the only one who has spies. He himself wrote those love letters to you in Vienna that were supposed to be from Angoulême, in order to persuade you to come to Mitau and marry that pathetic excuse of a man, your cousin."

"It was the desire of my parents that I marry Angoulême, said Thérèse, bristling, while trying to hide her inner struggle. "I wanted to be obedient to their last wishes for me."

"Piffle!" exclaimed the Queen. "When your parents planned to marry you to Angoulême, you were both children. They little dreamed how he would turn out. They would never have wanted to deny you motherhood. Alas, you should have wed Louis-Philippe." She coughed and wheezed, then allowed herself to be given a few spoonfuls of hot milk laced with brandy. "I implore you, my child. When I die, leave this place. Go to Rome, present your case before the Holy Father. He will not deny you a decree of nullity. You certainly have grounds." Marie-Joséphine was unaware that the Pope was being held in France as Napoléon's prisoner. "Then marry Louis-Philippe."

Hot tears streamed down Thérèse's face. "He is already married, to my cousin Marie-Amélie." She choked on the words, startled at her sudden gale of feeling.

"Then marry Napoléon himself, for Heaven's sake. But no, I forgot that Provence once plotted to get you wedded to Buonaparte, but the Corsican already has a wife."

"A wife, indeed!" cried Thérèse, through her sniffling. "He is now in a bigamous union with my cousin Marie-Louise of

Austria. Poor Joséphine! He sent her away somewhere. As if I could have married such a brigand!"

"At least he is a man," sighed the Queen.

"A man! He is an antichrist! He sought to be a Constantine by reuniting the Church in France with Rome, but he has quickly become a Constantius, for now he persecutes the Holy Father for not permitting his whims. At any rate, he is a social climber par excellence, as is every member of his rapacious clan." She hoped the subject of the Buonapartes would distract Marie-Joséphine from the topic they had been discussing, but in vain.

"Promise me, Marie-Thérèse, that you will go away from here after they bury me. Go to Scotland, to that castle where Artois once stayed. That is the way! Go to Scotland, and then to Rome. You can say you are going north for your health, and then − to the coast, and a ship for Italy. I have some jewels hidden away that you can pawn. Get an annulment. Find a good husband. What happened to that Archduke who courted you in Vienna? Do not tell me he also is married."

"Yes, he is." Thérèse's voice was cold, but her tears had ceased. The thought of the blue eyes and rugged face of Karl von Habsburg froze her, so painful was the memory of the evening at the ball in Vienna when her fears were confirmed, and the glasses were raised to toast the new Field Marshal, who had won his commission by sacrificing his orphaned princess. She had thrown down her glass of champagne and run from the palace. Standing on the bridge, gazing longingly at the river, she had wanted to plunge herself into its forgetfulness. What had stopped her? A hand upon her shoulder, the familiar, kindly voice of one of her Papa's former servants. Her great love for Karl, coming on the heels of tragedy, died a slow death; part of herself died and was buried with it.

"No, *ma chère tante*. I could never leave Angoulême. I could never humiliate him and dishonor him so. He would be destroyed. What a scandal, what …!"

"Do not let human respect deter you," said the Queen. "That was my mistake. Human respect, and the longing for a phantom crown. Ha! I am Marie-Joséphine, Queen of France! What a joke! How Antoinette would have laughed!"

Thérèse flinched at the flippant mention of her mother's name, but steeled herself. "I will not abandon my husband. He may yet change. And I will not leave my King. My place is at the side of Louis XVIII, and at Angoulême's side. It is here I am needed. I believe it to be the will of God for me, no matter what the cost." The resolution, often made privately, was reinforced by long-practiced resignation.

There was a long silence. Marie-Joséphine shook her head in a gesture of surrender. "You are right, my child. Anyway, even if you left, Provence would find some way of bringing you back, just as he found a way to bring me back into his clutches, after I had gotten away and was living my own life happily far away from him. But he needed me here to chaperone you, when you first came to us in all your loveliness. *O mon Dieu*! You no longer require a chaperone!"

"Of course not, Madame. I am almost thirty-two years old." Thérèse ignored the unflattering implications of the Queen's final remark. Marie-Joséphine did not seem to hear her last words. She closed her eyes and appeared to have fallen into a doze, except that she began to moan as if in deep pain.

"Aunt, what is the matter?" asked Thérèse, anxiously taking the old Queen's hand.

Marie-Joséphine's eyes shot open again; the pupils were dilated. "Do you not see it?" she groaned.

"What, *ma chère tante*? What should I see?"

"The blade! The blade of the guillotine, dripping red!"

Thérèse dropped her aunt's hand, as a shudder swept her being from head to toe. "I only see it at night," she replied, "in my dreams."

"In your nightmares, you mean. My entire existence, waking or sleeping, has become a nightmare. Not even my precious brandy can stop the dread worm of remorse which gnaws at my vitals, or the inextinguishable fire which burns my soul."

"You must speak with Abbé Latil, Madame. Please let me summon him." Thérèse had been hoping for such an opportune moment. It was time for her aunt to see a priest, and sooner was better than later. She started to rise. The Queen grasped at her sleeve.

"I want first to speak to you, Marie-Thérèse. Death eludes me, or rather it plays with me, like a cat with a mouse. I am not yet at the door of eternity, although it begins to open. Oh, mercy, mercy!" She moaned excruciatingly.

"What do you need to tell me?" asked Thérèse, sheer dread making her voice hoarser than usual.

"About your mother. About Antoinette. I killed her."

"Nonsense. The revolutionaries did so. You were far away in Germany, remember?"

"I was far away, but I killed her all the same. My hatred murdered her."

"What had she done to you that you should hate her so?" Thérèse asked, as a gentle calm enfolded her.

The Queen's eyes glared into days gone by. "She was everything I was not. Witty, charming, beautiful. Men loved her. Most of all, her husband loved her. She had children, she was beloved. She was Queen. From my earliest childhood, I was told I was going to marry the heir to the throne of France. But the first two heirs died. Then, Choiseul and La Pompadour plotted the Austrian alliance– to get the Dauphin Louis-Auguste married to an Austrian Archduchess– your mother. So she became Queen– and I had to be contented, or rather, discontented, as Comtesse de Provence. How I resented Antoinette! How I mocked and calumniated her behind her back, all the while priding myself on being so proper and pious, while Antoinette danced and gambled with her set. Oh! The best, most subtle form of calumny is not the blatant, outrageous lie; rather it is a raised eyebrow, a grimace, a glance and an innuendo. The shaded meaning which screams like a bright, painted sign, shooting like a dart from ear to ear, from mind to mind, until the slander was planted in every heart and everyone looked at Antoinette with new eyes, as if each were nourishing a secret knowledge of her, like some bloated louse. The seemingly good and virtuous can wreak far more damage when they set out to shred the reputation of another than a handful of hired pamphleteers. Provence thought he was subtle and secretive when he spread outrageous stories about Antoinette. I was far more subtle, and a thousand times more dangerous than even he. Alas, how I suffer now! It is far, far better to die in innocence, than to live in guilt."

Thérèse, trembling with pity for the tormented woman, took her limp, blotchy hand and kissed it. What she had long suspected was revealed at last. "My mother forgave you, Aunt, before she died. I know she did. She forgave everyone who had done her any harm. My father forgave you. And I ... I forgive you."

A tear trickled out of the corner of Marie-Joséphine's eye. "Oh, my child, all you need to go to heaven is a pair of wings!" And Thérèse sent for Abbé Latil.

Chapter Six:

The Banquet

Summer 1811

"It is better to go to the house of mourning, than to the house of feasting: for in that we are put in mind of the end of all, and the living thinketh what is to come." Ecclesiastes 7:3

Even at the moment of being handed out of her coach in the courtyard of Carlton House, and ascending the steps of the Corinthian portico to the triumphant strains of the military band, Thérèse could hardly believe it was really happening. The entire Bourbon family had been invited to the Prince of Wales' garden party and banquet. Thérèse, as the only surviving child of the murdered King Louis XVI, was the guest of honor. Her uncle, Louis XVIII, was ecstatic. It was the first time a member of a ruling house had given him anything even bordering on official recognition. The fact that he was not going as "Louis XVIII, King of France" but as the "Comte de Lisle," the only title he was allowed to publicly assume in England, bothered him not in the least. It was only the first step back into the limelight, and Thérèse was his ticket, just as he had planned. For it was Madame Royale, the tragic and legendary Orphan of the Temple, that British high society wanted to see and to meet.

The household of Hartwell was in a flurry of excitement when the invitation came, and the date finally fixed for June 19. The death of Queen Marie-Joséphine the previous November had plunged the court into motley and makeshift mourning. They had all trooped down to London for a state funeral, which the newly appointed Regent, the Prince of Wales, had allowed to take place in Westminster Abbey. Louis XVIII had taken his wife's death much harder than anyone would ever have dreamed. Thérèse would never forget the sight of him weeping beside the still-warm corpse of the woman whom he had driven to drink for over forty years. He hobbled beside her up the steps of Carlton House on his gouty, tree-stump legs, squeezed into new silk breeches. The invitation from the Prince of Wales had been enough to extend his credit, and that of his court. Everyone scurried to get necklaces, bracelets, and tiaras, as well as bejeweled canes, snuff boxes, buttons and buckles out of hock, as a cortege of dressmakers and tailors carved deep wheel ruts in the road between London and Hartwell all throughout the first weeks of June 1811.

As for Thérèse, the long-cherished wish of Artois was fulfilled, for she consented to purchase a new gown for the occasion. In the dawn glow of her chamber at Hartwell, her ladies had breathed forth their admiration at seeing this princess swathed in softly shimmering folds of oriental silk, a flowing, voile shawl trimmed with silk tassels, high kid gloves and satin slippers, all in purest white. The double band of pearls which bound her head and chestnut coils, the white plumes, the ivory fan, and the nosegay of camellias, accented the simple elegance, modest grandeur, and self-effacing majesty of her slender form.

Crossing the threshold of Carlton House, Thérèse was overwhelmed with gratitude for her uncle, who had insisted on maintaining the most stringent etiquette at Hartwell. Surrounded by the highest ranking nobility of England, she felt not in the least afraid. The press of bejeweled personages was almost overwhelming for any exile. It was rumored that nearly two thousand invitations had been issued, and she believed it. She was ushered into a hall hung with blue silk and gold fleur-de-lys, and it echoed with the chamberlain's booming voice.

"Her Royal Highness, the Duchesse of Angoulême!"

The great ladies swept into profound curtsies, while all the great lords bowed. Thérèse returned the curtsey, as her mother would have done. She heard the rest of her family being announced, beginning with the "Comte de Lisle," and ending with her distant cousins, the Prince de Condé and the Duc de Bourbon. Towering in front of her was a plump, heavily rouged, pasted and pomaded middle-aged man with light brown hair, long side whiskers, and watery gray eyes. His gargantuan form was corseted within an inch of his life into a gold-embroidered field marshal's uniform, the Order of the Garter gleaming on his chest. It was the Prince of Wales. Before she could complete her courtsey he was raising her up, his lips brushing her hand, his still handsome face breaking into wrinkles of affability and humor.

"Madame la Duchesse," he said in near perfect French. "*Enfin.* At last."

She nodded as graciously as possible, suddenly speechless and shy to be confronted with so famous a person as the Prince of Wales. He greeted her uncles, husband and cousins with sincere and overflowing courtesy.

"The Queen my mother regrets that due to the King's indisposition, she cannot be at my side to greet Your Royal Highnesses." He made no mention of his illegal but canonically valid Catholic wife, Maria Fitzherbert, or his legal but invalid Protestant wife, Caroline of Brunswick, or his daughter Princess Charlotte, all of whom he was currently keeping conveniently out of the way. He escorted Thérèse through his house, pausing to introduce his brothers and their wives, as well as other distinguished Britishers, while asking polite questions regarding life at Hartwell. Thérèse was awed by the opulence of the prince's residence, by the vastness of his private art collection, by the elegant furnishings, tastefully but lavishly displayed, and by the elaborate flower arrangements everywhere she went. With effort she managed not to look like a wide-eyed, gaping country lass, who had never seen a palace before. The Prince obviously delighted in entertaining. A host par excellence, he knew how to set people at ease. He had a bantering word or a light jest for every guest, each of whom he gave the impression of being intimately acquainted with, while squiring her through the gilded rooms as if she were a rare trophy which he held in the most profound reverence.

Thérèse nodded and smiled at everyone, trying to remember the names of those to whom she was being introduced, while simultaneously staying aware of how the male members of her family were deporting themselves at the *fête*. Occasionally, she would glance about to see. Her uncle and father-in-law were beaming as they received the homage of the émigrés, emanating the dignity and charm for which they were both famous. She could hear Angoulême sniffing, and out of the corner of her eye she saw him nervously twitching; she uttered a short, silent prayer that he would remember to use his handkerchief if he needed to wipe his nose. Berry was surrounded by young ladies; Thérèse hoped he would not drink too much, because when he did he forgot to suppress the oaths and obscenities which often came out of his mouth. She knew the stiff Prince de Condé and the Duc de Bourbon were behaving themselves and had no worries on their account. As for herself, she only dreaded the inevitable meeting with Louis-Philippe, Duc d'Orleans.

She hoped she would not react as she had last spring, when Louis-Philippe first came to call on them at Hartwell House. On that Sunday morning, Thérèse had been coming out of the chapel after Mass, followed by the entire court. As she was crossing the hall, there loomed up before her a tall gentleman in travelling garb, his cape confidently thrown back over one broad shoulder, hat in hand. Dark curls and fashionable side whiskers framed his noble features, shy but determined. Of proud and manly bearing; courteous and bold; jaunty, yet every inch a prince, his intense gaze met hers. It flashed into her mind like a bolt of electricity who he was– the son of Philippe Egalité! His father had cast the deciding vote which sent her Papa to the guillotine. He was now married to Marie-Amélie of Sicily and they already had one or two little children.

She heard her aunt's voice call her as if from the netherworld: "You should have married Louis-Philippe." Her knees began to tremble, her throat froze, and perspiration broke out on her forehead, while the room whirled and swam. Louis-Philippe dashed forward to catch her. The only clear, conscious thought in her head was that he must not touch her, so that just as his arm began to go around her shoulders, she pushed him away. Her ladies helped her into a chair until she recovered enough to be half-carried upstairs to her chamber. She was later told with what difficulty her uncle the King persuaded Louis-Philippe to stay for dinner, so distressed and offended was the Duc over Thérèse's reaction to the sight of him. She had heartily apologized that same day, and hoped to do so again at Carlton House.

"Ah, Monsieur le Duc!" exclaimed the Prince of Wales.

Thérèse turned, and there was Orléans, already bowing low. She gave him her hand to kiss, saying, "Monsieur d'Orléans, my good cousin, what a great pleasure to see you again. You honor us by your presence here today." Her rough voice fell flat.

"I wanted once more to pay my respects to one of the greatest ladies in Europe," said Louis-Philippe. An English uniform heightened his martial bearing. "I hope that the memory of past sorrows will not blight this meeting of long-estranged cousins."

"It is your wife, Monseigneur, who is one of the greatest ladies in Europe. For her sake, I long to repair the discourtesy shown to Your Serene Highness when last we met." Her response sounded blunt and harsh, although she wanted to be charming.

"Very good, Madame. Then, with our royal host's leave, and that of Monseigneur d'Angoulême, would Madame do me the honor of walking with me?"

The Prince of Wales smiled as he relinquished her hand. Angoulême, fumbling with his handkerchief, bowed stiffly and coldly to Louis-Philippe. The eyes of the throng were upon Thérèse as she slowly took the proffered arm of the son of the most unrelenting nemesis of Louis XVI and Marie-Antoinette. A momentary hush crept through the gallery where they were standing, as ears strained to hear any words of forgiveness that might fall from either of their lips. With the first few steps of their promenade, the crowd began to buzz again.

"What a beautiful house it is," said Thérèse. "I have never seen such opulence."

"It is incredible, Madame, that you should say that," said Louis-Philippe. "You who once lived in the most splendid palace on earth!"

"You were deceived by the mere surface of things, Monseigneur. Versailles was a veritable ruin. The drains were broken. The stench was horrific, especially in the summer. The repairs that were required were so extensive that the entire court would have had to move to another palace for quite a length of time, which is why my father bought the château of Saint Cloud." She knew her parents had been greatly criticized for the purchase, because few had known the true reason for it, and that it had been paid for by another crown property sold in the south of France. "There were still not enough funds for the repairs needed, so the project had to be given up. Truly, cousin, I have never seen a mansion such as this, where everything is so new, so spotless, and furnished with incomparable magnificence."

"This English opulence makes me long for French elegance," said Louis-Philippe. "If ever I should return to the Palais-Royal, I shall kiss the very steps of the place. It is strange that I should think of it as my home, when most of my boyhood days were spent at La Belle Chasse, under the tutelage of Madame de Genlis. But the Palais-Royal is where my mother always stayed. It is the home which calls to me in my exile."

"Your mother, she is well?" asked Thérèse.

"Yes. After a long sojourn in Paris, she now lives quietly in Spain. The Bonapartes leave her alone, so greatly is she reverenced by the people for her charity and piety."

Thérèse fell into the silence of cold anger. There were others who had been just as charitable and pious, such as Princesse de Lamballe and Tante Babette, yet the Revolution had turned on them with a merciless fury. Certainly, the Duchesse d'Orléans was devout, but Thérèse was convinced it was the late Duc's masonic connections that had protected her during the last twenty, turbulent years.

"I have heard of Madame de Genlis' unusual methods of education." Her voice cut like a lathe through metal. "Making you and your brothers carry pitchers of water through the center of town. What a spectacle! What democracy!"

The Duc smiled. "We were also made to go up and down steps with weights on our backs, and to sleep upon a paillaise on rough planks."

"Very monastic and edifying," Thérèse sniffed. "Unfortunately, piety is not what Madame de Genlis is known for...." She trailed off sarcastically.

Orléans bristled. It was said that he was devoted to Madame de Genlis, almost as much as he simultaneously despised her, for she had divided his parents, and would have abandoned his own sick sister when fleeing the armies of the Revolution, if Louis-Philippe had not himself carried the girl out to the carriage.

"The life of Madame de Genlis has been quite transformed," he said, crisply. "She lives in Paris, quite religious and respectable."

"I am glad to hear of it," said Thérèse.

"As for unusual methods of education," continued the Duc, "did I not hear of little Madame Royale waiting on peasant children at the table, and even mingling with them in her games?"

"So you actually heard something good about us! It rejoices my heart to know it," said Thérèse, dryly.

They had come to a large window, whence one had a splendid view of the gardens. There, the Prince of Wales had ordered the construction of galleries and promenades out of flower-covered trellises, with woven mats laid down upon the turf to protect the ladies' high heels, and linen-covered tables set up under pavillons to accommodate the overflow of dinner guests. As they stood in the embrasure, Louis-Philippe turned and faced her, earnestly looking into her eyes, leaning so close that his aquiline Bourbon nose almost touched her own. She realized how almost identical his features were to those of their mutual ancestor, Louis XIV.

"Madame," he said, "we have both suffered, losing fathers, homes, and country. Let there be peace between us, as we work and pray for the happiness of France."

"There is, perhaps, some difference between us as to what that happiness might be," replied Thérèse. "I, Monseigneur, know of your past refusal to don the white cockade of Henri IV. Yet you adorned yourself with the tricolor ribbon eagerly enough when you fought for the Revolution."

"It was France that I fought for, and her liberty," restored Louis-Philippe. "Madame, *ma cousine*, I do not believe, even if France is restored to a monarchical system, that we can ever return to the days before the Revolution. Nor would we want to do so. The world and France have moved forward, indeed, all humanity is step by step advancing to forms of government in which the voice of the common man will be heard. The peoples of the earth will direct their own destiny! It is for us, the privileged classes, the descendants of kings, to be the principal guides of the people in their journey to freedom."

Thérèse's eyes blazed like blue steel. "The people of France, *mon cher cousin*, have always been free. They have been free from the day when St. Rémi baptized and anointed Clovis as King, and the Frankish nation was reborn from the night of idolatry into the light of Christ. Night has descended upon the French once again, because of those like Voltaire, d'Alembert, Talleyrand, and Robespierre. Now, they are nothing but the chattel of Napoléon Buonaparte. No, Monseigneur, as the people of the world march farther from the Cross, as they move step by step away from the Gospel of Christ and the guidance of His Church, they walk blindly into slavery, slavery to any and every dictator who knows how to twist words, command armies, and organize a network of spying secret police. The ideas of which you speak are the seeds of antichrist. I will fight those ideas, for they mean slavery and destruction to my people."

"But, Madame, there is the new republic in America!" protested Orléans. "I have lived there! The people are very pious, very strait-laced. Democracy works there. Did not Your Royal Highness' father give support to the American Revolution?"

Thérèse gave him a terrible look. She did not like her father to be spoken of or referred to lightly. "Truly, my father gave generously to the American rebels, never asking to be repaid. He had his reasons for doing so. Within one hundred years, I sadly predict, America will know civil war and upheaval, and in two hundred years, complete anarchy. It took France many centuries to descend into anarchy, and that is because the True Faith was abandoned for Voltaire, Rousseau, and freemasonry. Furthermore, in America there exists slavery! It is actually legal! This much-vaunted liberty exists only for a few. Money is the king, or so I have been told."

"Madame," said Louis-Philippe, "in the new world that is coming of age around us, money is everything. Someday, rank will mean nothing, that is, one's birth and bloodline will count for less than nothing. The change is inevitable. But let us speak of France. The name of Bourbon has been practically forgotten. The star of Napoléon, however, is beginning to set. His ambition will destroy him, either his ambition or his rapacious relatives. Oceans of French blood have been shed since 1789, fertilizing fields all over Europe. If Buonaparte falls, then France will be open to the restoration of a legitimate regime. I heard the Austrian ambassador say, as you passed by him, Madame, 'Will the feeble hand of a woman lift up anew someday the social edifice that is drenched in blood?' You, *ma cousine*, will perhaps be the instrument through which peace will be restored to France, and to the world."

Thérèse's eyes stared keenly into his. "If that day comes, in God's time, I pray that my family will be worthy to enter again into our heritage. We will want you with us. But you must realize, Monseigneur, that you cannot be a prince and a republican! You have Jacobin notions, and I warn you, with such notions, I shall never compromise. I say to you, Louis-Philippe d'Orléans, that I am an adversary who gives no quarter!"

"And I say to you, Marie-Thérèse-Charlotte de France, that I shall always do what is in the best interests of our country, but neither you nor I can stop the tides of destiny."

The steel of her eyes softened for a moment, and became peacefully radiant. "It is all in the hands of God. His will is what matters, and now..." she abruptly turned from his gaze, "Monseigneur, I must return to my husband's side."

Louis-Philippe kissed her hand and escorted her to where Louis XVIII was receiving the homage of his exiled countrymen, in front of a tapestry of blue velvet embroidered with gold *fleur-de-lys*.

Angoulême, fumbling with his handkerchief, looked relieved to see her approach. Thérèse asked one of her ladies to bring her a cold glass of champagne, which she found almost impossible to sip, because of having to continually extend her hand to be kissed by the hundreds who wished to be presented to her. Giddy from hunger, thirst, and emotion, she was glad when the royal chamberlain finally announced that dinner was served.

Thérèse and the Prince of Wales headed the procession of two hundred lords and ladies who were to dine in the fan-vaulted, gothic conservatory; the other guests dined in the gardens. Thérèse would have preferred dining out-of-doors, for to do so always reminded her of Trianon, but as she walked into the splendor of the conservatory she realized that the charm and freshness of the gardens were rivaled by the spectacle before her. Flowers and greenery were clustered and entwined everywhere. In front of the center of the head table, where she was seated beside the Prince, was a water garden, complete with fountain, water lilies, irises, gold and silver fish (some of which, unfortunately, had died), bordered by mossy banks. The pond was surrounded by urns, emitting puffs of exotic, oriental incense. Over her head was an illuminated crown with the letters "GR" for "George Rex." Behind the head table were stands draped with hot soups, roasts, and other succulent fare, every dish prepared to perfection. The tables themselves were laden with peaches, grapes, apples, pineapples, and oranges, with champagne on ice every three or four persons. All the dishes, plates, soup tureens and platters were silver gilt, and caught the glitter of the ladies' jewels, as well as the gleam of the innumerable crystal glasses and goblets, five at every place. Thérèse had never dined at such an exotic meal, and one so efficiently served, as if in a private home.

With every bite she thought of her brother Charles. Was he starving somewhere, as she enjoyed such luxury? What of the French people, and the thousands who had starved and died in the last twenty-five years? The grandeur of her surroundings instantly seemed to be tinsel and glass, easily crushed and broken, so fleeting and dreamlike. "O God," she silently prayed, "there is only heaven." Nevertheless, her anguish veiled, she smiled benevolently on all, as the Prince's conversation sparkled, and course after course was served.

Chapter Seven:
The Knight
Spring 1812

"For we are saved by hope. But hope that is seen is not hope. For what a man seeth, why doth he hope for? But if we hope for that which we see not, we wait for it with patience." Romans 8:24-25

One spring night, through the drumming of an endless rain, Thérèse was awakened by a gentle but persistent scratching at her door, and a piercingly whispered: "Madame! Madame!"

She recognized the voice of the Comte de Blacas, Pierre de Blacas d'Aulps, the King's secretary. He had been with them for about a year, and she often wondered how they had ever managed without him. He kept both the household accounts and the King's papers in order; he listened to the exiled monarch's long stories of the halcyon days at Versailles, anecdotes which everyone else had heard at least five hundred times; he tended the obese sovereign through his numerous indispositions and bouts of gout.

"Madame! Madame!"

"Is the King sick?" asked Thérèse sleepily, sitting upright in bed. Often she had to rise in the night to help tend her uncle; when he was in a great deal of pain from his swollen legs, he usually sent for her. She always feared a repeat assassination attempt on his life as there had been on the continent a few years before. She threw on her wrapper and went to the door, opening it a crack, enough to discern the lofty brow and aristocratic mien of Blacas, illumined by a candle in his hand.

"No, Madame." Blacas' voice was kind and gentle, albeit stiff. In spite of his proud features, his was the humblest and most genuinely self-effacing of souls. "His Majesty requested that Your Royal Highness join him in the library." Unfortunately, the fondness of the King for Blacas stirred up the jealousies of the other courtiers, resulting in their subtle but never-ending persecutions of the man.

"The library? At this hour, Monsieur?"

"Yes, Madame. There is a visitor."

"I am coming." She hastily straightened her nightcap, and then followed Blacas down the corridor.

Ever since the Prince of Wales' banquet, life at Hartwell had dragged on as before. Louis XVIII had decided to buy the house as his own, for Buonaparte seemed more firmly entrenched than ever on the throne of France, especially since Thérèse's cousin Marie-Louise had given him a son and heir. There seemed little hope of a restoration in spite of the regard lavished on them by the Prince of Wales. Louis-Philippe had returned to his wife and children in Sicily. In London, Berry had settled into domestic bliss with Amy Brown. They did not see much of him, or of Artois, who also spent most of his time in London, gambling and holding small receptions. Neither father nor son were good at letter writing, although Artois occasionally sent gifts and feast day greetings. Angoulême hid from her behind a fortress of books, sullen and remote. With resignation, Thérèse continued to embrace her childless existence, throwing herself passionately and energetically into corporal works of mercy. Prayer remained her only solace and refuge.

In the library a single candle was lit, and beyond its circle of light was a void of darkness. Sitting in his big leather armchair, near the candle on his desk, was Louis XVIII, and beside him stood Angoulême. The dressing gown of the King was brocade and velvet, old but in fairly good condition, except for a few stains of coffee and snuff; his tasseled nightcap matched it perfectly. Angoulême, on the other hand, wore a tattered, moth-eaten dressing gown; his stocking cap had such large holes that tufts of his hair stuck through. Thérèse blushed for him, but how could she have known that his nightclothes were in such a lamentable state? She must somehow devise a way to retrieve the nightclothes from him so she could mend them.

Blacas bowed to the King, and as he raised himself, the light from his candle fell upon the shadowy form of a stranger. In the dimness, it took a few seconds for Thérèse to discern that it was a travel-stained gentleman, the high collar of his cloak partially concealing his face. His hat was currently under his arm, but from the look of his matted dark hair and the red crease on his forehead, it had been pulled down to his eyebrows. An expression of well-tested courage dominated his chiseled features almost as much as his large, dark eyes, bright with intelligence and alertness.

"Madame," said the King, "this brave and extraordinary gentleman is one of our countrymen. He has just arrived from France, with news which I am sure will please you." As the King spoke, the Frenchman threw himself at her feet, kissing the hem of her dressing gown.

"Oh, Madame, *ma princesse*!" he cried. "At last, I am at your feet, in your service … forever!"

"What is your name, Monsieur?" asked Thérèse, trying to raise him.

"I am Mathieu de Montmorency, Madame."

"Monsieur de Montmorency, please get up. You must be exhausted. Your Majesty, I beg your permission to allow this poor man to sit in your presence, and have a sip of brandy."

Louis XVIII nodded and waved his hand at Blacas, who poured Mathieu a glass of brandy.

"Merci, Monsieur," he said, sitting on a tabouret. "I am too honored." He sipped from the glass. "But no! I will not sit in the presence of my King." Taking a final sip, he handed the glass back to Blacas, and stood up.

"Monsieur de Montmorency," said Louis XVIII, "you come from a great family and an ancient one. Please tell Madame, as you have been relating to us, of the noble enterprise to which you have devoted your energies, following the tradition of your family and their services to the Crown."

"Willingly, Sire. I come on behalf of the Knights of the Faith, of whom I am the unworthy Grand Master."

"The Knights of the Faith?" queried Thérèse. "I have not heard of them."

"Madame, we are a chivalric order in service of the Altar and the Throne, founded two years ago by Ferdinand de Bertier and his brother, Bénigne-Louis. They are the sons of the Monsieur de Bertier who was lynched by the mob during the storming of the Bastille."

"Ah, yes," said Thérèse, recalling those tense, bloody days.

Mathieu continued. "Ferdinand de Bertier and myself were members of the lay order known as the Congregation of the Virgin, which met regularly for prayer and catechetical instruction. In 1809, we secretly circulated the papal bull which proclaimed the excommunication of Buonaparte. We saw the need for a well-organized, underground society of Catholic laymen, uniting in a strong concerted effort to overthrow Buonaparte's régime, and restore the ancient monarchy. Years of planning by the masonic lodges produced the Revolution. What great good, then could Christian knights, fighting in union with the angels, bring about if only we would unite and organize! The Bertier brothers infiltrated a masonic lodge to study their methods of propaganda and organization. Why cannot the children of light use the same weapons as the children of darkness, but for a noble and just cause?"

"They can and they should," put in Angoulême, empathetically.

"Pray continue, Monsieur de Montmorency," said Louis XVIII.

"And so we organized 'banners' to rival the 'lodges' of freemasonry. The lower grades are employed in charitable works, in the propagation of Christian and monarchical ideals. Gradually, we reveal to them the secret of the restoration of knighthood, and they enter the grade of squire. Eventually, they are knighted, and in a magnificent ceremony they receive a blessed ring with the word *caritas* inscribed inside. The knights hospitaller are devoted to work in prisons and hospitals, and their insignia is a rosary with an ebony cross. The highest rank, who alone know the whole extent of the order, and the dual political and religious agendas, are the Knights of the Faith. Our insignia is this...." He held up a black rosary with a silver crucifix. "We govern the society with a high council of nine members. Enrolled in our society are men from all walks of life. One of our members even enrolls the porters of the grain markets throughout Paris. We have found that among most of the younger generation the very name of 'Bourbon' is unknown or forgotten. In the state schools founded by Napoléon, which can only be described as vestibules of hell, the facts of history are altered and abridged. The Bourbon kings who succeeded Louis XIV are not spoken of at all. And yet...." He turned to Thérèse whose face was blanched in a mixture of horror and tense expectation. "'The Orphan of the Temple' is well-known among the people. You, Madame, have become a legend. All the French people cherish the story of the captive princess, alone in the Temple tower, courageous and bereft, who somehow became lost to them. Alas, Madame, no intellectual freedom exists in France. We cannot openly tell the truth of your life to the people, although we distribute pamphlets in secret whenever we can. It is very dangerous. Fouché and his secret police constantly dog our path. Spies are everywhere."

"How good it is that you instruct the people in their religion," said Thérèse. "Is their faith growing strong and vigorous?"

"The True Faith has almost become lost in some sectors of society. Many churches are empty. There are few religious to teach the children, except for some Lazarists and Christian Brothers, who are permitted to function. Religious orders, as you know, were abolished. The dirty work of the Revolution has blossomed with the current generation. Family life is in ruins. Vice reigns in the sanctity of the home. Civil marriages, as you know, were the law until Buonaparte's concordat with Rome. Divorces are increasing. Buonaparte's taxes are bleeding the country. People are growing very dissatisfied with the imperial regime, especially in the south.

They are tired of endless, wanton wars. They long for peace at any price. Censorship is extended even to our great classics, to the works of Corneille and Racine. The economy is in shambles; work houses are full, and in some provinces women and children are left alone to labor in the fields, since all the men have been taken by the Army, even seminarians! But there are pockets of faithful and devout people everywhere, who teach their children at home, who cling to their Catholic faith no matter what. All is not lost...."

Thérèse's eyes streamed with tears to hear the misery of her people. And yet, how ironic that once many of them had actually called her bon Papa a "tyrant." She longed to ask Mathieu if he had any news of Charles, but she could not do so in front of the King and Angoulême. Her mind began racing to seek a way.

The King was watching her. "My dear, you must agree that this is the best news we have heard in quite some time. We thank you, Monsieur de Montmorency, for risking your life to come to us. We must begin to plan our next move. As Horace said, 'In peace, as a wise man, he should make suitable preparation for war.' We need only one good defeat for Buonaparte, and one victory for England and her allies. Perhaps the English will help us."

"But, Sire," said Angoulême, "as my father has often maintained, it is the French people who must recall us. A restoration must come from within."

"Angoulême, you speak the truth," agreed the King, "and we see how such a movement is in action. But I fear the princess is tired.... Madame, I give you leave to go."

Thérèse curtsied. "I hope I may have another interview with Monsieur de Montmorency tomorrow?"

"Unfortunately not, Madame," said the King. "Monsieur has explained to me that it would be unsafe for him to tarry at Hartwell for any length of time. He begs leave to depart at daybreak. He will not have many hours of sleep, I fear."

Thérèse took a candle from the candelabrum and lit it from the burning one on the King's desk. She turned to leave.

"Your Majesty!" cried Mathieu, "I beg to present Madame with this small token of our loyalty and devotion." He held up to the King's gaze what appeared to be a snuff box. Louis XVIII nodded, although a flicker of displeasure touched his brow. Mathieu knelt and presented his gift to Thérèse. It was a tiny box of white, green, and gold enamel. On the lid was a picture of the royal navy yard at Cherbourg, with the year "1785" graven beneath, an obvious commemoration of the famous visit of King Louis XVI to his fleet. At Cherbourg in 1785, the crowds had lined the road and cheered, "Long live the King!" while Louis XVI had shouted, "Long live my people!" 1785 was also the year of Charles' birth.

"Thank you, Monsieur," said Thérèse. "God bless you! May Our Lady protect you!"

Clutching the snuff box, she made her way through the shadowed halls and corridors, candle held aloft. 1785! She wondered if Mathieu de Montmorency was using his gift to convey to her some news of Charles! Alone in her chamber, she quickly opened the box to see if it contained a written message. It was empty. She examined it closely for any more inscriptions. There were none. She gingerly pressed the bottom of the box; such articles were known sometimes to have false bottoms. Sure enough! The inner gold lining of the box popped open, and there was a much folded piece of paper. She unfolded it until she held in her hand a letter-sized sheet with nothing on it but some lines of poetry from Corneille's *Le Cid*:

> *Immolez, non á moi, mais á votre couronne;*
>
> *Mais á votre grandeur, mais á votre personne;*
>
> *Immolez, dis-je, Sire, au bien de tout l'Etat ….*

"Immolation?" She wondered to herself. "What can this mean? Someone is immolated for someone else's crown and grandeur? Is he referring to Charles?"

Thérèse pondered the lines over and over again. Perhaps it had nothing at all to do with Charles. She was exhausted and overwrought by all the excitement. Her imagination was running wild. Blowing out her candle, she climbed back into bed. She coughed. She had been coughing more frequently in the last day or so. She had asked Madame Hue to prepare her some hot gingerroot tea with sliced lemon. She looked into the pot by her bed. There was enough tea left for a cup, although it was tepid. She poured a cup and squeezed one of the small wedges of lemon into it.

"Lemon juice!" She almost dropped the teacup, while springing out of bed. Taking the mysterious letter, she went over to the small votive light she kept burning in front of the statue of the Virgin. Holding the paper close to the glass, the heat caused words written in lemon juice to glow. The invisible sentences were crowded in between the verses of poetry. She herself had used lemon juice so often in past, secret correspondences. How could it have taken her so long to realize it was being used here? She soon deciphered the fiery message, which read as follows:

Madame—

In the Bicetre prison there is a young man, very sick and at the point of death. His name is Jean-Marie Hervagault, but many people believe him in actuality to be your brother, King Louis XVII. A few days ago, a priest came to confess him and bring him Holy Viaticum. In the presence of the Sacred Host, the Abbé begged him to renounce his 'fraud' and to confess his true identity. The dying gentleman firmly asserted that he is the son of Louis XVI and Marie-Antoinette. He then turned his face to the wall and would say no more. The warden, who witnessed the scene, is a member of our society. Madame, we pray with you for him. Long live the true King!"

M. de M.

Thérèse burned the paper in the fireplace. Trembling, she climbed into bed and lay there thinking and praying. Was the prisoner Charles? Was Charles dying, alone and forsaken? Why was she always far away when death came for those she most loved? At dawn, the rain stopped, and amid the birdsong, she heard a horse galloping away from Hartwell House.

Chapter Eight:

The Triumph

Spring 1814

"The Lord hath blessed thee by his power, because by thee he hath brought our enemies to naught ... for thou has not spared thy life, by reason of the distress and tribulation of thy people, but hast prevented our ruin in the presence of God." Judith 13:22, 25

On March 25, 1814, Thérèse knelt beside the chair of the King in the chapel at Mass, praying for her husband, her father-in-law, and her brother-in-law. The cardinal was chanting the Collect: *"Deus qui de beatae Mariae Virginis utero Verbum tuam...."* (O God, who didst will that Thy Word should be made flesh in the womb of the Blessed Virgin Mary....") It was the Mass of the Annunciation. Thérèse herself had decorated the altar with greenery and paper flowers.

"Please, Most Holy Virgin," she prayed in her heart, "do not let them be captured and shot by Buonaparte." If they were killed, it would be Thérèse's fault, for it was she who had insisted that they join the fight against Napoléon. Ever since the Corsican usurper's defeat at the Battle of Liepzig in 1813, the Bourbons had been on pins and needles, trying to decide the wisest course of action. Thérèse had spent her Lent in intensive fasting and supplication.

How many Frenchmen had frozen to death in the snows of Russia? How many soldiers of Napoléon's Grand Army had been sacrificed on the altar of his ambition? France and Western Europe had not sated his lust for power. No, he had to be the ruler of the Russian Empire as well. Buonaparte's failure to obtain his goal cost hundreds of thousands of French and Russian lives, not to mention the great destruction of farms, villages and entire cities. To Thérèse, it was so unbelievably appalling that anyone could continue to support the man and that they could fail to acknowledge him and his works as fruits of the same Revolution which had destroyed her family.

The makeshift choir of courtiers was chanting the various propers of the feast day. Thérèse tried to immerse herself in the immolation of the Saviour. "O Lord, was I right to beg Artois, Berry and Angoulême to go to France?"

As Napoléon's power tottered, word came to them that the Allied leaders were trying to decide on a candidate for the French throne. Among the names under consideration the most favored were Napoléon's little son and Louis-Philippe, Duc d'Orléans. Louis XVIII was held in extremely low regard by the monarchy of Europe, with the exception of the Prince of Wales. Artois and Berry were hastily summoned from London for a family council. They talked for hours around the fireplace in the library.

"O, messieurs," pleaded Thérèse with the men of her family. "England, Prussia, Austria and Russia have united to dethrone Buonaparte. Would you have them replace him with Louis-Philippe, or with Marie-Louise's son? Now is the hour, now is the moment for boldness, for valor!" It had been many years since they had seen her so animated. Her eyes sparkled with an almost electric blueness; her cheeks glowed with color.

"But my dear," said her uncle the King, "I have tried to get support from the Allies for the past fifteen years. I have been ignored by all except the good Prince of Wales."

"The Allies despise us," said Artois. "I could not tell you how many letters I have written to Tsar Alexander, and how many rude replies I have received, or else received no reply at all."

"They do not like us, I tell you," chimed in Angoulême.

"If any of us set a foot on the continent, we will be shot," insisted Berry. "Just like our cousin Enghien. Kidnapped by Napoléon's men, he was, dragged into France and marched before the firing squad. And he was not even an heir to the throne!"

"The Knights of the Faith have been working for us in France," said Thérèse, "and I tell you, the mood of the country has changed. There have been pamphlets distributed in our favor, written by the Vicomte de Chateaubriand. Madame de Staël herself has launched a fierce literary attack on Buonaparte. The people want the peace and order that they knew before the Revolution. We have only to show that we, the authentic Royal Family of France, are willing to fight our own battles to rally the French, and perhaps even the Allies, to our side."

Artois nodded. "And we do have one other powerful ally. It is none other than the Bishop of Autun."

"The Bishop of Autun? You mean Talleyrand?!" exclaimed Thérèse.

"Yes, my child. Talleyrand and I have been corresponding for some time. He had a great falling out with Buonaparte several years ago, after Buonaparte publicly insulted him, calling him, 'a silk stocking filled with…!'" He paused a moment. "'With mud.' He has promised to support our cause when the first opportunity arises."

"But Talleyrand! Oh, Papa! Oh, Uncle, he is an apostate bishop!" protested Thérèse. "A revolutionary! Did he not marry an actress?! Does he not permit his 'wife' to wear his pectoral cross as an adornment at dinner parties?! I would rather do without the help of such a man!"

"I am afraid that we cannot do without such help, Madame," said Louis XVIII. "Did not the Knights of the Faith try to plot an Anglo-Royalist invasion of Brittany? Was it not a miserable failure?"

Thérèse remained adamant. "If we go ourselves, in person, I believe we can rally the French people. For the nation's sake, we must attempt it! We must try! Oh, if I were a man, I would gladly go, even if it meant prison and death!" As one who had spent several years in prison and who had come very close to death, her words had an edge which cut away their fear.

In the middle of January 1814, Artois and his sons left England for the continent. When Thérèse parted with Angoulême in his oversized military coat, she felt she was sending to the wars not her husband, but her son, and she wondered what on earth would become of him. It was not that he had never before been involved with the military, because he had. He had even fought in battles, but when he was much younger, and slightly more resilient.

Thérèse stood for the Gospel of the Annunciation, chanted by Cardinal de Montmorency. *"In illo tempore missus est Angelus Gabriel a Deo...."* ("The Angel Gabriel was sent from God....")

"Be it done to me according to thy word." Thérèse echoed in her heart the response of the Most Holy Virgin. News of her menfolk had gradually drifted to her at Hartwell. "Papa" Artois had gone first to Holland. After much meandering and many games of whist, he journeyed to Switzerland with the Austrian army. The Austrian High Command treated him insultingly, and tried to deny him the permission to enter French territory with them, but he insisted that he did not need the permission of foreigners to enter his own country. He arrived in the Franche-Comté subject to many humiliations at the hands of the Allied troops, forbidden to wear a uniform, bear arms, or make any attempt to further the Bourbon cause.

Berry had landed on the isle of Jersey, planning to take a ship from there to Normandy, where he hoped to stir up a revolt against Buonaparte. Then he heard that the police were awaiting him on the Norman coast in order to promptly arrest him if he dared to set foot on French soil. Thérèse was grateful to be spared the tantrums Berry must be throwing in his frustration.

As for Angoulême, he had somehow managed to get as far as the south of France, where he tried to join the British army. The Duke of Wellington would not have him, for he despised the Bourbons, and made Angoulême go to the rear of the army with the baggage train. He was safe enough there, for the army of the "Iron Duke" was practically invincible, but what an ignoble situation for a prince of France to be in.

Thérèse received Holy Communion as was her custom on feasts of Our Lady. *"Ecce Virgo concipit..."* chanted the choir. ("Behold a virgin shall conceive, and bear a Son, and His Name shall be called Emmanuel.") She pushed all earthly anxieties from her mind, and adored the Word made flesh, the Incarnate God. For a few moments she was enveloped in deepest joy. She did not even hear the commotion in the hall outside the chapel, the flurry among the servants, and the murmuring of courtiers. She did not see Comte de Blacas whisper something in the King's ear.

As Thérèse came out of the chapel on the King's arm, they were met by several men, some in French army uniforms, some in civilian clothes, and all obviously having just traveled far and hastily. They carried with them the white and gold lily banner of Royal France. They bore white cockades on their lapels and on their hats, the latter having been respectfully doffed and held under their arms. At the sight of Louis XVIII and Thérèse, they all bowed low. One of the men stepped forward and went down on one knee before the King.

"Sire, we are men of Bordeaux. We bring you joyful tidings." He spoke in a southern accent, which reminded Thérèse of the Comte de Blacas or one of the Polignacs. "Here are dispatches from the most noble and puissant prince, His Royal Highness, the Duc d'Angoulême." He handed the letters, bearing Angoulême's seal, to the Comte de Blacas, who in turn gave them to the King. "Our city of Bordeaux has the great honor of being the first among all the towns and cities of France to openly declare its loyalty to Your Majesty. Other towns are now throwing off the shackles of Buonaparte. In the Vendée an uprising against the Corsican is being prepared. The Duke of Wellington and other Allied commanders have invited His Royal Highness Monsieur le Comte d'Artois to treaty negotiations in Your Majesty's behalf. Events are moving so quickly that perhaps, even as we speak, the imperial eagle falls, to be replaced by the lilies."

As the herald spoke Thérèse's spirits rose so quickly it was as if she were numb with elation, and everything around her seemed twice as vivid, as if bathed in unreality. Her uncle, his plump face beaming, clasped her in his arms, kissing her cheeks. She, in turn, began to embrace the ladies of her household. Within seconds the entire court, which had filed out of the chapel, was embracing amid tears of joy and exclamations of gratitude to the Good God. The King put into her hands a letter from Angoulême, addressed to herself. Breaking the seal, she began greedily to read her husband's familiar scrawl.

March 12, 1814

Madame, my very dear wife,

It is with trembling hand that I attempt to relate the events of this most joyous day to you, my esteemed princess. So hopeless did our cause appear that until a few short days ago it had been my intention to return to England. Divine Providence willed otherwise, for there were sent to me two Knights of the Faith. For the last year, Monsieur Ferdinand de Bertier has resided in Bordeaux, actively building support for our cause. He has done so without great difficulty because of the enormous dissatisfaction that the Bordelais have with Buonaparte's government. The Knights of the Faith informed me that the Bonapartist troops under General Soult, after much pillaging and rapine, had withdrawn from Bordeaux and its environs. The Duke of Wellington was persuaded to send to Bordeaux a small corps of English and Portuguese troops under the command of General Beresford. Many faithful and loyal Frenchmen and I accompanied them, albeit we were made to stay with the rearguard.

As Beresford and his troops arrived, the mayor of Bordeaux publicly tore off his tricolor sash, and donning the white cockade, shouted, 'Long live the King! Long live the Bourbons!' By the time our party reached the city gates, the word had spread that I, the husband of the Orphan of the Temple, had come, and we received a most enthusiastic welcome from the crowd. I waved my hat and shouted: 'No more wars! No more conscription! No more vexatious taxes!' I cannot describe the joyous reception as I rode through the streets to the Cathedral, where the good Archbishop d'Avian greeted me, and escorted me into the nave for Benediction and the *Te Deum*. Monseigneur d'Avian has assisted us in organizing a provisional royal government. It is my deepest prayer that soon I will have the pleasure of welcoming the King and you, my princess, home to our beloved fatherland.

Your affectionate husband,

Louis-Antoine

At dinner, Thérèse listened in awe as the herald recounted the story of Angoulême's triumphal entry into Bordeaux, of how he was hailed as a hero for braving so many dangers to return to his country; of how they loved him simply because he was her husband. So the good French people had not forgotten her! They loved her as she loved them! She wanted to hear the story over and over again. So unused was she to being happy that the surge of emotions overwhelmed her, and the next day she was prostrate as if from extreme exhaustion.

The following night, March 27, she was awakened by an insistent knocking on her door. Throwing on her wrapper, she opened the door, and to her supreme astonishment, saw that it was her uncle in his dressing gown and nightcap, standing on his swollen legs without support.

"Madame! My dear child! What news! A messenger from the Prince of Wales!"

Thérèse felt almost frightened because Louis XVIII did not look like himself at all. His usual coolness had fled; he was like a kettle about to whistle, bubbling and incoherent. He emanated an aura not of joy or happiness but of frothing obsession; of one whose all-encompassing, consuming desire for a singular object was realized at last.

"Oh, Madame, Buonaparte has been captured! Paris has fallen; Marie-Louise and her son have fled! The Allies have asked for our return to the throne of France!"

"Oh, *mon uncle!*" She kissed his fat hand. "Then we will be returning to France!"

"Indeed, yes! As soon as possible!"

"Oh, France! France!" Thérèse exclaimed like a child. "We are going to France! We are going home!" And in her heart she called to Charles, with an intensity of feeling and thought that surely it reached across the miles. "Oh, Charles, wherever you are, living or dead, I shall find you, for at last, I am coming home!"

Chapter Nine:

The Return

Spring 1814

"And the redeemed of the Lord shall return, and shall come into Sion with praise ... they shall obtain joy and gladness, and sorrow and mourning shall flee away." Isaias 35:10

All the bells in the city of Calais were pealing with joyful abandon, punctuated by salvos of artillery, as there sailed into view the English ship *Royal Sovereign*. While the winds and tide pulled the ship closer and closer into the harbor, the multitude, which crammed the piers, sang royalist anthems such as *Vive Henri IV* amid the plaudits, erupting spontaneously for anyone or anything connected with the illustrious persons whom they were waiting to receive. Soon the great ship glided into port, its cannons reverberating in salute, its banners waving among the billowing sails which caressed the cloudless sky.

The cheering swelled like the roar of waves, drowning the cries of the seagulls, as the eyes of the crowd fell upon the bridge of the ship, where there stood a corpulent old gentleman. He raised his plumed, tricorner hat, then, extending his arms, cried: "My children! My children! Heaven restores my children to me!" He placed one hand on his heart, holding out the other to a young woman in white, who suddenly appeared at his side from somewhere on the ship. "It is Madame! It is Madame Royale!" shouted several people in the crowd, which from that moment went from ecstasy to delirium, mingling sobs of happiness with other sounds of welcome.

Thérèse was amazed at her uncle's sense of drama as he held out his arms to the multitude in a gesture of embrace. She was too blissful to be annoyed by his theatrics. She had spent the entire voyage across the channel on deck, breathlessly awaiting her first glimpse of France in almost twenty years. How wonderful to stand still for even a few hours during a whirlwind of activity.

After receiving the good tidings, they had to postpone their departure from England for several weeks due to a brutal attack of gout suffered by the King. It was providential in the long run, for it gave Thérèse and Comte de Blacas more time to supervise the extensive packing of the household, and to resolve their business affairs in England. Meanwhile, they had received effusive letters from Artois, describing his triumphal entry into Paris on Easter Sunday, April 12, and the enthusiasm of the city's inhabitants as he pranced through the streets on his white steed in his elegant new uniform. To his great delight, his old friend Talleyrand, former Bishop of Autun, had met him at the gates of the city. He wrote of how he wept during the solemn *Te Deum* at Notre Dame Cathedral, and how he almost fainted with joy on the main staircase of the Tuileries Palace, only recently vacated by the Buonaparte family.

"It was the first day of happiness I have had in thirty years," Artois penned in his bold, sensual script. "I heard a hundred times as a youth at Versailles that in the Tuileries there was not enough room, and that it consisted primarily of garrets and holes. Much to my surprise I find the rooms to be large and magnificent! Buonaparte, albeit a scoundrel, is a man of refined taste. The great salons and galleries of the Tuileries are furnished with supreme elegance; everything is gilded, polished and superbly restored!" Thérèse was glad that the Buonapartes had been careful to preserve for posterity the beauties of the past. If only they had been as zealous for the cause of religion. She had heard that there were many churches in ruins. At any rate, the clan was scattered, with Napoleon in exile on the isle of Elba.

Thérèse and the King departed from Hartwell on April 20. The Prince Regent himself met them halfway to London and accompanied them as they entered the city, which hailed the royal party with great rejoicing. Hyde Park and Piccadilly were teeming with an immense populace. The houses were hung with white bunting. The English people saw the restoration of the King of France to his throne as the beginning of peace for their own country. The Prince of Wales held another grand reception for them at Carlton House, where he and Louis XVIII, who entered as a king and not as an incognito "Comte de Lille," outdid each other with long, flattering speeches, exchanging decorations, and ignoring the fact that such persons as the Tsar of Russia and Talleyrand had helped to bring about the downfall of Buonaparte.

After three days of feasting in London, the Prince accompanied the Bourbons to Dover. The road to the port city was lined with jubilant citizens, and Dover harbor filled with vessels, all flying the white banners of royal France. Guns saluted them as they boarded the *Royal Sovereign*, and continued to thunder as the white cliffs receded. The sound of English cannon had barely faded when they began to hear an echoing roar on the French shore. The closer the coast of her homeland came to her, the more the rush of tears seized Thérèse. After past weepings, she was certain that no tears could be left, but she seemed to possess within her a bottomless reservoir. The moment had come at last. There she was, in a high-crowned, beplumed hat, and tailored white dress with a shoulder cape, at her uncle's side on the ship's bridge, looking at the throng who had come to greet them. They were her own people, for whom she felt an overwhelming maternal love that would risk anything for their benefit.

The moment of disembarkation had arrived. With the King leaning upon her arm, they went forth from the ship, to be met by the local clergy and worthies of Calais. What joy to be surrounded by ordinary citizens, all of whom spoke her native tongue. "Oh how happy I am to be among my good French people!" she exclaimed. The first to bend the knee was an old priest, who had once been exiled for refusing the constitutional oath.

"Monsieur le curé," said King Louis XVIII, "after more than twenty years of absence, Heaven gives my children back to me, and me back to my children. Come, let us thank God in His Temple!" They climbed into a carriage which sixteen of the most distinguished citizens of Calais themselves pulled through the streets, strewn with flowers and hung with white lily banners, to the cathedral where the *Te Deum* was sung. After the service, the King addressed several delegations in turn. To a group of Christian Brothers he said: "Make good Christians, and you will make good Frenchmen."

His words enflamed Thérèse's heart, for in that instant she saw her vocation, the reason why her life had been spared and why she had married Angoulême. In a flash, many puzzles were solved. She had lived when everyone else of her immediate family had died, and had married a French prince, all for the day when she could return to France to help rebuild the Church. She vowed in her deepest soul to use any influence she possessed to reestablish monasteries, to aid missionaries, both domestic and foreign, and to endow Church schools. Ancient churches, such as the great Basilica of Saint Martin in Tours had been destroyed. Others, like Sainte Geneviève's in Paris, had been converted into secular buildings. So many relics and tombs of saints had been desecrated. An army of sisters was needed to run hospitals and orphanages, to instruct the poor and care for the blind and the lame. She felt as if she could not wait to begin her work.

That evening, the ancient tradition of dining in public was revived by Louis XVIII, as they ate in the city hall surrounded by curious onlookers. The next day, accompanied by their cousin the Prince de Condé and his son the Duc de Bourbon, called "Chouchou," who was, in turn, father of the young Duc d'Enghien, murdered by Buonaparte, they began their triumphal progress to Paris. Everywhere they were greeted by all ranks of society, waving white flags and handkerchiefs, throwing flowers and crying: "Long live the King! Long live Madame!" In the town of Amiens, Thérèse was approached by several young girls, all dressed in white, who sang for her the famous chorus from Gluck's *Iphigénie*: "Let us praise and celebrate our Queen," so often sung for Marie-Antoinette in days gone by.

The closer they got to Paris, the more Thérèse noticed the signs of war and heavy taxation. For one thing, the roads were deeply rutted and in desperate need of repair. Buonaparte had apparently only maintained the principal highways so as to move his armies, letting the lesser thoroughfares fall into rack and ruin. Even the road from Calais to Paris was a jolting experience to traverse. In the reign of Thérèse's father, King Louis XVI, the roads in France had been the envy of Europe. Now everything had deteriorated. She began to notice burned and deserted farms, untilled fields, maimed or crippled soldiers limping home. In spite of the desolation, as the royal cavalcade jostled along through the fields of Picardy, fragrant with spring, Thérèse could not help thinking that France was the most beautiful country in the world.

At length they arrived in the town of Compiégne, not far from the outskirts of Paris. There was much planning to be done before their entrance into the capital. It was near sunset when they finally alighted in the courtyard of the château of Compiégne. The full-throated chorus of birds singing as they only do on a spring evening was drowned by the ceremonial beating of drums. There assembled were the Marshals of France of Napoléon's Empire, and soldiers of what was left of the Grand Army. "Long live the King!" they cried. Thérèse wondered how such proud men would be able to change allegiance from the cult of Buonaparte to their legitimate sovereign. She could hardly believe that the mere fear of losing position and rank could influence such a quick transition. Could it be that people were so hard and cynical? It had surprised her that they did not wish to follow Buonaparte into exile, as so many old courtiers had followed the King, for Napoléon had raised them from nothingness into dignitaries of the Empire.

As soon as the King entered the palace and settled himself in a chair in the royal apartments, he received the Marshals, including Ney, dubbed the "bravest of the brave."

Marshal Bertier, hat in hand, addressed the King on behalf of all: "Sire, after twenty-five years of uncertainty and storm, the French people have again delivered the care of their welfare to that dynasty which eight centuries of glory have consecrated in the history of the world as the most ancient in existence. As soldiers and as citizens, the Marshals of France have seconded this outburst of the national will. Absolute confidence in the future, admiration for greatness in misfortune...." The eyes of the rugged old soldier went to Thérèse, who stood by the King's chair. "… All concur to excite in our warriors, the upholders of the glory of France, the transports Your Majesty has witnessed on your journey."

The King waited a few moments before responding. His plump but well-shaped head slowly turned, as he calmly and majestically surveyed the assembly. The Marshals of Napoléon seemed to unblinkingly wait with baited breath. Then Louis XVIII spoke in his deep, firm, honeyed tones, which asked for no favors, but made the hearers feel the honor of being in the presence of the heir of St. Louis.

"It pleases me to meet you, gentlemen. I rely upon the sentiments of affection and fidelity which you express toward me in the name of the French army. I am happy to find myself amongst you." He paused, his pale blue gaze again meeting every eye that was riveted on him. "Happy, happy and proud."

The Marshals stared as if enchanted. They were used to being shouted at by Napoléon. The King addressed each one individually.

"You, Marshal Mortier, I shall never forget the esteem you once showed for the Queen, my wife. And you, Marshal Marmont, did you not come near to losing an arm in Spain?"

"Yes, Sire," replied the Marshal. "But I have found it again in Your Majesty's service."

As her uncle was speaking to the marshals, Thérèse noticed in the back of the salon a short, slender middle-aged gentleman with unruly black curls, a gentle, melancholy expression in his handsome face, with self-mocking, mischievous eyes, dark and observant. She wondered who he might be. Suddenly, without aid, the King rose from his chair and hobbled forward on his unsteady legs. Two of the nobles of his personal escort hastened to help, but before they could, Louis XVIII had taken the arms of Marshals Ney and Berthier.

"It is on you, Marshals, that I always desire to lean," said the King. "Come and surround me; you have always been true Frenchmen. By serving France, you have served your King. I hope France will have no further need of your swords. But if ever – God forbid– we are forced to draw them, gouty as I am, I will march with you!"

The Marshals were visibly moved. "Sire, let Your Majesty consider us the pillars of the throne!" one of them cried. "We will be its firmest supports."

That night they all supped together in magnificence, the King and the marshals ceaselessly complimenting each other. The very soldiers who had fought at the side of Napoléon and often ate at his table appeared deeply flattered and awed at the attentions paid to them by a fat, bloated, sickly man of fifty-nine years, newly returned from exile. Thérèse was amazed at her uncle's ability to master and manipulate every and any situation. During the meal there was presented to her the man with the melancholy face whom she had seen earlier.

"Madame," said the King, "here is a gentleman whose writings have greatly furthered our cause and the cause of France. Monsieur le Vicomte de Chateaubriand."

"My compliments and my gratitude, Monsieur le Vicomte," said Thérèse. "I have read *Les Martyrs* and the *Génie du Christianisme*." Her voice grated more gruffly than usual. She was aware that the words of Chateaubriand had done much to make the jaded free-thinkers take Christianity seriously again, and yet she had heard that the author's scandalous private life did not rise to the level of his vaunted religious principles. Such divergence between thought and behavior were incomprehensible to Thérèse, and she naturally mistrusted persons who said one thing but did another. It was alien to her, whose principles and beliefs always dictated her every word and act.

Chateaubriand replied, "The kingship of legitimate monarchs has slumbered for twenty years, but their rights, like their virtues, were indestructible, for they live in your person, Madame. This fair land of France bears lilies spontaneously; they will grow more beautiful than ever, since they have been sprinkled with the blood of the Martyr-King and the tears of Madame Royale."

Thérèse had been determined to remain unmoved by the surpassing Breton eloquence of Chateaubriand; she did not want to be affected by his spell as other women were. Tears sprang to her eyes, and she extended her hand to him, which he raised to his lips.

During the next two days, Thérèse received many persons, both famous and infamous, who came flocking to Compiégne to see the King. There came early in the morning the notorious Talleyrand, former bishop and revolutionary. She was spared the ordeal of having to spend any time in his company, for Talleyrand and the King remained closeted for hours. She recalled the fourteenth of July, 1791, on the Champs de Mars, the day her Papa was forced to sign the new constitution which stripped him of most of his authority. Talleyrand had celebrated the Mass, stumbling over the rubrics. He had, of course, taken the dreadful oath which denied the Pope's authority, even though it was said that he rescued priests who refused it. On that account, and because it was he who had laid the diplomatic groundwork for the Restoration, did Thérèse agree to receive him at all. His hair was powdered in the old style; his clothes rich in their simple elegance; his complexion grayish and corpselike. She winced as he bent to kiss her hand. She could not fathom why he had such a reputation with the ladies; she assumed they pitied his limp, or were touched by his gentle baritone voice and quiet dignity.

Later the same day, Artois and Berry arrived, each with a large entourage. Artois' retinue was comprised of mature, ultra-royalist noblemen like himself. Berry, on the other hand, was surrounded by young whippersnappers. Father and son strolled with Thérèse in the gardens of the château. Angoulême remained in the south, organizing that region in the name of the King. Artois talked of the splendors of the Tuileries and how polite the Allied monarchs were now behaving towards him. He had joyfully repossessed his beloved Bagatelle, a villa near the Bois de Boulogne. Berry raved about the wonders of Paris, which he had been too young to appreciate when he fled in 1789. He extolled the beauty and elegance of the ladies, and the reams of invitations he had been receiving to lavish balls and receptions.

The Court was officially reconstituted that afternoon. Among the nobles that came to seek royal favor were Madame de Boigne and her mother Madame d'Osmond. Thérèse remembered Adéle de Boigne.

"As a child she had sometimes been allowed to play at Trianon," she murmured to Berry, as Madame de Boigne made her way through the crowd of courtiers. "Do you remember?"

"Yes, indeed," replied her brother-in-law, under his breath. "And what a disagreeable girl she was even then. Twenty-five years later, they say there exists no more critical or gossiping woman.... Enjoy!"

Thérèse placed her open fan over her lips to hide a smile, as Madame de Boigne made a deep curtsy. Plump and pretty, her fair curls and blue eyes softened her air of shrewd condescension.

"Why, it is Adéle!" Thérèse exclaimed, her voice sounding gruff because of her concerted effort not to laugh.

Madame de Boigne begged to be allowed to design a gown for the entry into Paris. Thérèse accepted the offer; within twenty-four hours Mesdames de Boigne and d'Osmond presented her with a white silk and silver lamé gown, cut in the most fashionable Parisian mode, with a ruff collar and a rather fantastic headdress that resembled a toque with white ostrich plumes. Thérèse much preferred her simple English costumes, but realized it was not good politics to make a public appearance in foreign garb.

Finally, the Tsar arrived, a red-headed giant of a man who had wanted Louis-Philippe to be king. He heartily disliked Thérèse's family; she remembered how he had them evicted from the Mitau palace in Courland. Louis XVIII startled everyone by taking precedence over the "Sultan of the Tartars," as the Tsar was nicknamed, by making him sit in a chair inferior to his own. Tsar Alexander, known for his liberal politics, was enough of an autocrat to take offense. However, there was nothing he could do about it, for everyone's thoughts and energies were focused on preparing for the triumphal entry into Paris.

Chapter Ten:

The Lilies

Spring 1814

> *"My beloved to me and I to him, who feedeth among the lilies."*
> *Canticle of Canticles 2:16*

The vast square in front of the gothic façade of Notre Dame Cathedral was filled with cheering citizens. Their mood contrasted with the grim-faced cordons of soldiers, who lined the route of the royal cavalcade. They looked with suspicion upon the obese gentleman with powdered hair, tricorner hat, and boots of velvet because his swollen legs could not fit into leather ones. Beside him in the open carriage drawn by eight horses was a stiff woman in white, half-concealed by a parasol. Her cold, repellent expression was interpreted by some to be one of disdain. She greatly contrasted with the King, who beamed and nodded to the waving multitudes. Facing them in the carriage were the Prince de Condé in his powdered wig and Cousin Chouchou. Artois and Berry rode on horseback nearby. People seemed to be spilling out of the houses which bordered the square; each building was hung with white bunting and garlands of flowers and greenery. It was a festive scene except for the obvious discomfiture of the princess, the legendary "Orphan of the Temple" and "French Antigone," a glimpse of whom nevertheless caused certain emotional persons to faint.

Thérèse clutched the basket of white and yellow irises, the *fleur-de-lys* that a small child had handed to her a few moments before in the Market of the Innocents. The angelic, golden-haired child had reminded her of a certain small boy, who every summer morning would hurry out to the garden to pick flowers for his Maman, to place on her dressing table before she awoke. They had no sooner passed through the Porte Saint Denis into the capital of her ancestors than Thérèse became bathed in a cold perspiration, and seized by a wild and nameless fear. She stiffened herself to keep from visibly trembling.

Thérèse could not understand what was happening to her. Everything had been going so smoothly. They had stopped at Saint Ouen the day before, where Louis XVIII had granted a Charter, a sort of constitution by which he was to govern France. It maintained that all taxes were to be approved by elected representatives; civil and personal liberties were assured; freedom of the press was guaranteed, except for precautions necessary to preserve the peace, as well as freedom of religion; private property was declared inviolable; all the pensions, ranks and military honors of the Napoleonic regime were retained, including the Legion of Honor. The document was deemed to be a great cause for rejoicing, for it blotted out all past treasons, and manifested the King's desire to give everyone, as well as himself, a fresh start. Thérèse had a few doubts over it, fearing human nature would find loopholes and abuse the King's liberalism, yet her heart had been glad; she had looked forward to all the work which awaited her in Paris.

With a blare of trumpets, the carriage slowed to a halt in front of the ancient, arched doorways of Notre Dame. Thérèse was pleased to see that the magnificent carvings on the huge portals had been repaired, after suffering defacement during the Revolution. She rejoiced to see the stone patriarchs, prophets, and saints looking down upon her once more, along with the granite kings and queens of the Franks.

The rector of the Cathedral came forward and addressed the King: "Sire, one of the illustrious ancestors of Your Majesty here poured out at the foot of the altar of our august Patroness his prayers, and to him was granted the birth of a son, Louis XIV. For many long years we, too, in silence, have laid our prayers and tears upon the same altar, and today Heaven gives us back our father, Louis XVIII. The God of St. Louis has raised your throne; you will strengthen His altars."

The King stood up in the carriage and replied in a loud voice: "Upon entering my good city of Paris, my first concern is to come to thank God and His Holy Mother, the powerful Protectress of France, for the marvels that have ended my misfortunes. I, the Son of St. Louis, will imitate his virtues."

He then climbed into what resembled a sedan chair, and was borne into the Cathedral by four Augustinian canons. Artois walked on his right, Thérèse at his left; they were followed by Berry, the Prince de Condé, and Cousin Chouchou. As Thérèse entered the Cathedral, she recalled how the venerable building had been desecrated by the enthronement of the goddess of Reason during the Revolution, and then by Buonaparte's insult to the Pope at the moment he formally usurped the crown of France. Then the strains of the organ and the polyphony of the choir sounded in her ears, and all thoughts fled from her mind, except the realization of being in the house of Our Lady. As the choir launched into a rendition of "*Salva festa dies*" "Hail to thee, festival day", for it was the Paschal season, her eyes fell upon the statue of the Virgin; the Mother of God was welcoming her home. She felt surrounded by the angels and the saints; among the just were many of her ancestors. Through the music and peeling of the bells, they seemed to cry out to her from Heaven: "Do not forsake the lilies."

So transfixed was Thérèse that she felt pulled into another dimension, and was barely conscious of those around her. She did not see her uncle on his portable throne, looking straight ahead, absorbed in his own majestic aura. Neither did she see Artois and Berry, solemn as acolytes, eyes upon the altar. She did not notice the Tsar of Russia, bursting with annoyance, or Chateaubriand, whose face was illuminated by the stained glass windows, the light of the candles, and the near luminous whiteness of the lily banners that streamed from the vaulted arches. He was enraptured, as if the glory and splendor of the middle ages had returned for one afternoon, and the Catholic faith was indubitably shown to be the most beautiful of all religions, even as he, Chateaubriand had written of it.

As the royal family reached the foot of the altar, the choir burst into a polyphonic chant: *"Domine salvum fac Regem Ludovicus!"* "The Lord save King Louis!" Louis XVIII with great difficulty ascended the altar and was helped to his *prie-dieu*. The new Grand Almoner of France, Cardinal Talleyrand du Périgord, pious uncle of Talleyrand the Apostate, handed the King his prayer book. Thérèse fell to her knees beside the King. In the surpassing ecstasy of the moment, she was completely unaware of the tears on impious Talleyrand's countenance, washing away the half-bored, half-amused expression he usually assumed at religious ceremonies. As Thérèse went on her knees before the Virgin, everyone wept, from the Tsar to former revolutionaries and regicides, like Joseph Fouché.

The *Te Deum* was intoned. *"Te Deum laudamus; Te Deum confitemur."* "We praise Thee, O God; we acknowledge Thee to be the Lord." She joined her raspy voice to the others, asking the Mother of God to supply with her praise and fervor for what was lacking in Thérèse's. The fragrance of the lilies that adorned the altar filled her nostrils, and in a moment that seemed outside of time, she felt the love of the Holy Virgin envelope her like a mantle.

"Te martyrum candidatus laudat exercitus." "The white-robed army of Martyrs praises Thee."

She was blessed, not cursed to be the child of martyrs, of a King and Queen so disdained by the worldly wise that few understood them, or what they had suffered and sacrificed.

"Te ergo quaesumus tuis famulis subveni, quos pretioso sanguine redemisti. Aeterna fac cum Sanctis tuis in gloria numerari." "We beseech Thee to help Thy servants whom Thou hast redeemed with Thy Precious Blood. Make them to be numbered with Thy Saints in glory everlasting."

It was as if her father, her mother and Tante Babette were there, closer to her than ever, now that she had returned to the places where they had died, and where somewhere their bodies were buried.

After solemn Benediction, the royal party climbed back into their carriage and onto their horses for the procession to the Tuileries. The entire route from the Cathedral to the Pont Neuf was lined by a regiment of Buonaparte's Old Guard. Their faces radiated anger and indignation at having to present arms in salute to an overfed man who had never fought in a battle. Thérèse was blind to their hostile expressions. She was entirely focused on trying to overcome the icy hand of terror that was gripping her throat; she was beginning to have some difficulty breathing.

They passed the Palais de Justice, where Marie-Antoinette had been sentenced to death. The gothic spire of the Sainte-Chapelle pierced the Heavens. The Crown of Thorns had been housed there. She saw in her mind her Papa, donning the bonnet rouge of the Revolution in order to placate the mob. She saw not happy citizens and resentful soldiers but rather a sea of faces from the past, seething with hatred, shouting: "Down with the Fat Pig!" and "Death to the Austrian whore!" There were the towers of the Conciergerie, where both Maman and Tante Babette had been imprisoned before being taken to the scaffold.

As they approached the Pont Neuf, she pictured her mother sitting in the garbage cart, behind the horses' tails to show the people that she was nothing but dung, in her white wrapper and cropped hair, hands tightly tied behind her back. Two prostitutes were guillotined, one before and one after Marie-Antoinette, for in the eyes of the Revolution the Queen was just one more harlot. The scene of her Maman at the scaffold rose before her although Thérèse had not been there, but they said she climbed the steps with her usual dignity and grace, displaying the nimble eagerness of a young girl at her first dance, for she had known that those steps led beyond the guillotine and into eternity.

"I beg your pardon, Monsieur. I did not do it on purpose," were the Queen's last words, spoken to her executioner when she accidentally stepped on his hand. Three individuals had rushed forward to dip their handkerchiefs in her blood, and were promptly arrested by the authorities.

Pain began to surge through Thérèse's mind and body, a pain that transcended mere physical pain, which she could master or ignore. She could only compare it to the fires of purgation in the after life, for she was burning, and in searing mental agony, without help. Her eyes rolled heavenward, and she began to slip into unconsciousness. As she slumped over, the King's arm went behind her back and upheld her, while Cousin Chouchou, no stranger to tragedy, kindly leaned forward and began gently patting her hand. The breeze from the Seine fanned her face; she forced herself back into the present.

The procession halted for a moment, to watch an actress ascend in a balloon, while some singers gave yet another rendition of *Vive Henri IV* around a statue of that monarch, the first of the Bourbon kings. Thérèse could not applaud, or even smile or bow, but she sat in a stony half-stupor. It required all her strength to keep from bursting into loud sobs and wails. As the carriage neared the Tuileries, the sharp waves of pain began to sweep over her again. She had the sense of drowning, or of suffocation. She gazed upon the very spot where the guillotine had stood, and the street down which her family had been taken in October of 1789, with the bloody hands of their Swiss guards carried ahead on pikes. She drew into her mind the image of the Saviour, scourged and mocked. The executioners tore off His robe, re-opening all the earlier lacerations. "O Jesus, help me and save me!" she murmured.

Then the Tuileries Palace arose in front of her, with its large Renaissance pavillions, and the magnificent clock tower in the center. Buonaparte had certainly cleaned the exterior. How much scrubbing had it taken to remove the bloodstains from the massacre on August 10, 1792? It was on that dread day that Thérèse had last seen the place, when her family had hastened out the back entrance through the gardens to the National Assembly, and Charles had carelessly skipped about in the leaves which had fallen so early that year. Princesse de Lamballe had been with them, she who within the month was to be torn to pieces by a mob.

Thérèse was helped down from the carriage, and slowly and stiffly began to ascend the wide steps. In front of her were two hundred women arrayed in white, each holding a bundle of lilies. They knelt down, as one of them cried, "Daughter of Louis XVI, grant us your blessing!" There loomed before her inner eye the image of her Papa, crystal clear, as he had been at the very last moment she had seen him on earth. His expression was compassionate as he looked sadly down at her, for he knew it was farewell. As a girl of fourteen, she had imagined those dear eyes lifeless, the lips purple, the head severed from the body. At age thirty-five, she reacted as she had as a girl; redness tinged her vision and a flashing of colored lights, then the roaring in her ears. Thérèse collapsed. She never knew how they half-carried, half-dragged her into the palace.

When Thérèse woke up, she was surrounded by her ladies, who were fanning her, rubbing rose water into her wrists, and holding a vial of smelling salts to her nose. At first she did not know where she was. The room looked vaguely familiar. She realized it was her Tante Babette's former bedchamber in the Pavillon de Flore, although most of the original furnishings had been altered. Emblems of bees and eagles adorned the walls and ceilings. What struck her was how totally clean everything was. She had never known a palace to be so clean, so thoroughly dusted and polished. And yet the Buonapartes had actually lived there. It was unbelievable.

"The King awaits Your Highness on the balcony." Madame de Damas whispered to her. Thérèse staggered through the rooms and corridors to the great balcony on the Pavillon d'Horloge. She was quickly remembering how to get from place to place. Like a sleepwalker, she stepped on to the balcony with the rest of the royal family. The King embraced her, and placed a crown of white lilies and roses on her head. The crowd below exploded into paeans of praise.

The King waved to them, and as he did so, he muttered under his breath, "Scoundrels! Jacobins! Monsters!" Thérèse began to laugh, softly at first, but soon uncontrollably, mixed with sobs. From the distance, the people perceived only that she was smiling, and applauded, thinking that their Princess was happy at last.

Chapter Eleven:
The Opera
Spring 1814

"But she with a rosy color in her face, and with gracious and bright eyes, hid a mind full of anguish, and exceeding great fear." Esther 15:3

Inside the Opera house, lights were already ablaze, as carriage after carriage halted before the entrance, where mingled wealthy bourgeois with aristocrats and foreigners, all in their finery. It was the evening of May 17, and Paris was in bloom. The City of Light had become a city of flowers. The balconies and window boxes of houses, the shrubberies in the parks and gardens, were laden with blossoms. The leaves of the chestnuts which lined the boulevards glimmered in the soft dusk. Along the Rue de Richelieu vendors were selling lithographs portraying Madame d'Angoulême with her uncle Louis XVIII, trudging through the snows of Lithuania.

She had long been dubbed "The French Antigone," faithful in adversity like the princess of the Greek myth. The opera about to be presented, Gluck's *Oedipe à Colonne*, was meant to honor the long-suffering daughter of Louis XVI and Marie-Antoinette, lately returned to her country and her people after years of wandering. There had been some doubt as to whether the princess would actually attend the gala event, since she had already shown herself to prefer hospitals and orphanages to the ballroom and the opera box. When the word spread that she was indeed to be at the King's side for the performance, every last ticket was sold.

The interior of the theatre was bedecked from top to bottom with garlands of white spring flowers; the heady scent of lilacs, lilies and lilies-of-the-valley caused many persons to sniffle and sneeze. Whispering beneath the glitter of chandeliers, the ladies, vested in white, wore no diamonds, but instead were adorned with wreaths, corsages, and nosegays of snowy flowers. Most of the gentlemen were in uniform; those who were not actually in the military had gone to extraordinary lengths in order to beg, borrow or steal the befitting martial attire.

In one strategically located box, whence the royal box and the stage could be viewed with equal clarity, there was placed the coat-of-arms of the House of Talleyrand du Périgord. From behind a curtain in the depths of the box, there limped to the forefront a slender, mature gentleman with powdered hair. On his satin coat were a few discreet decorations recently received from the crowned heads of Europe.

At the sight of him, an exclamation went up from the assembly: "The Prince! It is the Prince!" Prince Maurice de Talleyrand du Périgord, former Bishop of Autun, gave a slight bow and a flourish of his hand in acknowledgment, gracefully discouraging any further, tasteless attention to himself. There appeared at his side a young lady, hardly out of her teens. Once she was seated, the Prince took his own chair. The girl picked up her pearly opera glasses and scanned the house, oblivious that all eyes were riveted upon her. White lilacs rested against her clouds of black hair, with a corsage of the same on the bodice of her chiffon gown. Her beauty was foreign and unconventional, high cheekbones betraying her Baltic ancestry. In her thin, pointed face sparkled gray eyes, witty and intelligent.

"Uncle," she asked, "who is that tall lady with the turban, who waves at you from the other side of the theatre?"

"I have no doubt," replied Talleyrand, "that it is Madame de Staël. I am grateful to you, my dear Dorothée, for warning me. I shall take care not to look in that direction." He glanced instead at his niece-by-marriage, a casual yet lingering glance. Anyone who knew Talleyrand well would have noticed the ardent nature of his look, deliberately offhand as it was. A plump, handsome lady in her mid-thirties with tight ringlets and ostrich plumes, who sat on the other side of Dorothée, did notice. There were few things which Madame la Comtesse de Boigne failed to observe. For this reason, Talleyrand had invited her to sit in his box, for he wanted information. From her conversation he could glean what was going on at the Tuileries without paying the usual spies. Madame de Boigne was party to all the gossip concerning the Royal Family, and in exchange he would permit a few speculations on her part concerning his relationship with his nephew's wife.

For that matter, all Paris was talking about Talleyrand and "La Dino" almost as much as about the Duc de Berry's escapades. Already Dorothée was being referred to as "La Dino," even though the title "Duchesse de Dino" had not yet been formally bestowed upon her by the King. Talleyrand had originally been offered the title himself, but he preferred to be a prince, and so passed the dukedom on to Edmond, his worthless nephew. Talleyrand had very conveniently exiled the Princesse de Talleyrand to the country. His wife's never-ending *faux pas* and ceaseless vulgarity had been tolerated by the Buonapartes but would be unendurable to the Bourbons. It was a further embarrassment to Talleyrand that he had a wife at all, since he was a bishop, anointed and consecrated. The very fact of a Princesse de Talleyrand would keep him from being received at the Tuileries as often as he would like. As if being an excommunicated apostate was not reason enough.

"Why, Uncle," asked Dorothée, "do you not care for Madame de Staël? Was it not she who enabled you to return to France after your exile?"

"Indeed, it was she," Talleyrand sighed. "Madame de Staël has only one fault: she is unbearable. Furthermore, she never does anything in the proper way, but constantly abandons herself to exaggeration and sentiment."

"But, Uncle, I thought it was considered elegant to be sentimental." Dorothée opened her gauzy white fan. It was hot, as usual, in the theater.

"Dorothée," responded Talleyrand, "Madame de Staël lacks simplicity and consequently fails to be elegant. You must realize that the union of simplicity and elegance is the measure of nobility in every case and in every person." He gave another furtive glance in her direction. He planned to take the exquisite and exotic creature with him to the Congress of Vienna. As the newly-appointed Minister of Foreign Affairs, he would represent the King of France among the Allied powers who were meeting to decide the course of post-Napoleonic Europe. Half the work of the Congress would be carried out in the social entertainments of the evenings. He would be obliged to give balls and receptions at the French embassy in Vienna. It was indispensable, therefore, that he have a hostess with the tact, discretion, grace and wit necessary to preside over such momentous functions. The wife of his dissipated nephew Edmond du Périgard would fit the role to perfection.

Monsieur Edmond despised and neglected Dorothée. Talleyrand had already been compelled to expel him from the house several times for his loutish behavior. It was an insult to Talleyrand, who had gone to the trouble of choosing such a refined and well-connected young lady to be Edmond's wife. Dorothée de Courlande was intimate with the Russian Imperial Family, and other grand personages throughout the continent. At any rate, Talleyrand need not bother about taking Edmond to the Congress, for he was currently indulging in a spending spree in the *demi-monde* of Paris.

Talleyrand motioned to the scene before them – the white gowns and flowers. "*Voila*! How the simplicity of this sight contrasts with the bombastic preferences of the *nouveaux-riches* Bonapartes!"

"Oh, yes, Uncle." Dorothée had taken up her opera glasses again. "Why, Madame de Staël is no longer waving at you. She is conversing with a rather vehement-looking gentleman."

"Undoubtedly, it is Benjamin Constant. They were united in their literary efforts to destroy Bonaparte. Among other things."

"There is a very beautiful lady with them. Why, I believe it is Madame Récamier! There is a Prussian officer at her side."

"That is not surprising," commented Madame de Boigne. "You know that Prince Augustus of Prussia once desired to marry her."

"Oh? Why did he not?" asked Dorothée.

"Because Madame Récamier's husband talked her out of an annulment," said Talleyrand, "which she had every cause to seek."

"An English general is joining them," said Dorothée. "Ah, it is the Duc of Wellington! He is kissing Madame Récamier's hand!"

"Well, he shall not get anywhere with her," said Talleyrand, dryly. "No one *ever* does. The Tsar is also smitten with Madame Récamier. Dorothée, do you see Tsar Alexander?"

"Why, yes. His box is beside the one reserved for the Royal Family, near the center of the first tier. He is surrounded by all his Russians, and looks quite sulky."

"That does not surprise me," observed Talleyrand. "He has had many reasons to be so. For one thing, he wanted Louis-Philippe to be King."

"I know, Uncle. The Tsar told me so himself, just yesterday. He despises the Bourbons. 'They never learn anything,' he said."

"Nevertheless," responded Talleyrand, "Louis XVIII always conducts his affairs in the proper manner. Everything about the Restoration has been conducted with the utmost taste."

"You were very moved at the Cathedral, Monsieur de Talleyrand," said Madame de Boigne. "As were we all, when Madame d'Angoulême fell to her knees at the altar."

"And I thought you were an atheist, *mon oncle*," teased Dorothée, waving her fan.

"My dear child," said Talleyrand, looking quite offended. "There is no sentiment less aristocratic than that of nonbelief." Few persons were aware of the generous donations he discreetly bestowed upon many impoverished religious houses.

A ripple of excitement swept through the multitude. The Royal Family had finally arrived. It seemed they were having some difficulty getting the King up the staircase to the royal box. The musicians began tuning their instruments.

"They say many of the citizens of Paris were disappointed on May 3. What have you heard, Madame de Boigne?" inquired Talleyrand.

"Monsieur le Prince, people expected to see in Madame a resemblance to the beautiful Marie-Antoinette. Instead, she is so stiff, so morose, so plain. And yet they say the Archduke Karl was wildly in love with her."

"When I used to see Madame d'Angoulême at Mitau, she was exquisitely lovely," said Dorothée. "I was present at her wedding, you know. I was quite small, but I shall never forget the vision of Madame Royale coming into the hall in her bridal gown, her fair hair on her shoulders beneath the wreath of lilies. She came often to our house, and was very kind to me." By "our house," Dorothée meant one of the large palaces owned by her handsome, dissolute and wealthy mother, the Duchesse de Courland, where she had grown up with her equally handsome and dissolute sisters. "She hoped that I would someday wed the Duc de Berry."

"He is too old for you," said Talleyrand, "and far too decadent."

"It is said that Madame prefers charitable work to dancing? Is that so, Madame de Boigne?" asked Dorothée.

"It is, Madame. When at home in the palace, she wears the same ugly frocks she had in England. She refuses to take an interest in clothes except, of course, the official costume to be worn by ladies of the court."

"Is it true that she wants to bring back hoops and wide panniers?" asked Dorothée.

"Yes," said Madame de Boigne, "but we were able to talk her out of it. She refuses to be a queen of fashion like Marie-Antoinette. Of course, she faints at the mention of Louis XVI's name. Neither will she allow her coachman to drive past the spot where the guillotine stood."

There was a flourish of trumpets, as the heavy red velvet curtain opened, revealing a pastoral scene. The entire audience stood, and faced the back of the theater, where the King appeared in the royal box, leaning on the arm of Madame d'Angoulême, with Berry on their left and Artois on the right. A mystic hush fell upon the vast assembly at the sight of the princess, as if something holy had just come into the Opera house. Then cries of "Long live the

King! Long live Madame!" echoed in the heights of the ceiling. The princess glittered from afar.

"She wears white satin covered with diamonds," said Dorothée from behind her opera glasses. "High plumes and a gold filigree tiara, covered with gems."

"Her necklace and earrings...surely they are Marie-Antoinette's own diamonds," said Madame de Boigne, looking through her own glasses. "The tiara is new...it is in the Merovingian style. Well, she is certainly a princess of whom France need not be ashamed before the world."

The Royal Family sat down. Their box was decorated with white and gold banners, and large bouquets of lilies. From the orchestra pit there came the cacophony that proceeds any performance. The opera commenced. The music of Gluck, so loved by Marie-Antoinette, rose and fell through the vast hall.

Thou august victim of mischance and woe

That thou alone shalt be our liege and love

Our zealous care, that of Antigone.

As the singer mentioned "Antigone" a round of applause shook the theater, punctuated with cries of "Madame! Long live Madame!" Madame d'Angoulême rose and curtsied to the multitude.

"A marvellous gesture!" exclaimed Talleyrand. "Few young ladies today know the proper way in which to curtsey. Madame was obviously taught by her mother." The plaudits gradually subsided after Madame was seated again, but broke out once more during the aria which began:

On me she lavished her tenderness and care....

The house was in a tumult, which increased as the King drew Madame d'Angoulême into his arms at the lines:

Come, my faithful guide, as your father waits to press you to his heart.

"How strange!" whispered Dorothée. "Madame's expression remains one of sadness and melancholy. She hardly smiles at this moment of glory. Any other woman would be glowing!"

"She is no ordinary woman," whispered Madame de Boigne from behind her ostrich plume fan. "You know, they say she suffered terrible outrages in the Temple prison. Why, there is a woman going about today who claims to be the daughter of the Duchesse d'Angoulême, begotten during the long incarceration. They also say that some of the officials who escorted her to the Austrian border after her release attempted to molest her."

Dorothée's eyes widened in horror. "Oh, no!" Her lips formed a silent exclamation.

"She is positively haunted by phantoms at the Tuileries," continued Madame de Boigne. "Every room holds some troubling memory. Madame weeps and weeps...and yet she ransacks the palace for mementos of her childhood. She sent for the old piano tuner, Monsieur Dubois, to ask what had become of her pianoforte. He tried in vain to convince her of the superiority of the pianofortes left there by Empress Marie-Louise, but no, Madame wanted *her own*, which she had played as a girl."

Talleyrand motioned for the ladies to be quiet. He seemed absorbed in the opera and in his thoughts. The sight of the princess moved him deeply, as she had that day in Notre Dame. Purity and innocence often touched him, yet they had been willfully tossed from his being long before his hands were anointed at his ordination. Nevertheless, a lost memory was plumbed at the appearance of Madame d'Angoulême, the memory of himself as a small boy, sitting in his little chair at Mass next to his beloved great-grandmother, and the intensity of love and peace surrounding him in a homey yet supernatural splendor. And then the piercing sorrow of being torn from his grandmother's arms, of never seeing her again, of never being loved so much by anyone else in the world, that pain never left him. He had sought and sought, all in vain. Perhaps he had been wrong about a few things. Alas, his course was set; he was inextricably caught, and all he could do was snatch whatever happiness he could in his own way.

It was the *entr'acte* and a ballet was performed to the strains of *Vive Henri IV*. The audience sang with the chorus.

"How often must they play *Vive Henri IV*!" sighed Dorothée. "I am glad we shall soon be departing from Paris." She waved her fan as she spoke, in an effort to draw Talleyrand's attention back to herself.

"Oh, you young people," mused Talleyrand. "You do not know how sweet life was before the Revolution."

"Then, why, *mon uncle*, did you become a revolutionary?" asked Dorothée.

"Because I thought the world would improve. But it has not. Before the Revolution, there was wickedness, but there was also elegance. There was malice, but there was also wit. Today there is mostly tasteless wickedness, and the malice of stupidity." He sighed. "I do not know what will become of the world. What I do see is that nothing is being replaced. Once something ends, it is finished. What has been lost is the only thing that one sees clearly."

"Oh, Monsieur le Prince, if it is up to Madame d'Angoulême, *everything* will be just as it was before," said Madame de Boigne. "The King, of course, is a liberal. Already it is Monsieur d'Artois and Madame ranged against Louis XVIII in matters of policy. As for the palace, why, it has been transformed overnight. How I am reminded of Versailles! Everywhere, the smells of cooking, slops left in odd places, beggars and tradesmen in the corridors, dust on the high mouldings! Exactly like the old days! And the quarrels over uniforms – every gentleman wants one, even if he never saw a single battle in his life. Buonaparte's old soldiers are furious! All the former *émigrés* and impoverished, loyal aristocrats are demanding places at Court!"

"A rather desperate situation," commented Talleyrand. He was beginning again to be preoccupied with Dorothée's allurements. Long ago, he had lost, along with his innocence, the ability to put certain distractions from his mind. Madame de Boigne chattered on.

"Madame has insulted many of the Marshal's wives with her blunt manner and harsh voice. Madame Ney went away in tears, for she thought that Madame's use of her Christian name was a reference to the fact that her mother had been a maid of Queen Marie-Antoinette, and that her low origins were being thrown in her face. Not at all the case, I assure you, but what a furor it caused!"

"Goodness!" exclaimed Talleyrand, picking up Dorothée's handkerchief which had somehow fallen on the floor.

"In the meantime," continued Madame de Boigne, "Madame's new gentleman-in-waiting, Mathieu de Montmorency, accompanies her when she visits hospitals. They say he is making many inquiries on her behalf. She appears to be seeking someone."

"Whom does she seek?" asked Dorothée, coyly receiving her handkerchief back from Talleyrand. Their gloved hands touched as he gave it to her, relinquishing it in a slow, caressing gesture. Madame de Boigne did not fail to notice, and she longed to tell her friends that another victim was about to succumb to Talleyrand's lust.

"Whom do you think?" asked the former Bishop of Autun, his eyes intent upon Dorothée. It was easier for him to despoil innocence than admire it, since the thrusting away of actual grace had become second nature to him.

"For Louis XVII?" asked Madame de Boigne. "Is he not dead?"

"No," said Talleyrand. "He is not. During my sojourn in New York in the mid-nineties, I was told by the French ambassador, Monsieur Genet himself. Louis XVII is living in the wilds of America with the Indians."

"Well, you should tell the princess!" exclaimed Dorothée.

"She will soon discover the truth for herself, and find that Louis XVII is better off left in the wilderness." And then he fell silent, for the second act of the opera had begun.

Part II: THE QUEST

Chapter Twelve:
The Grave
Summer 1814

"He hath set me in dark places as those that are dead forever."
Lamentations 3:6

In the Pavillon de Flore of the Tuileries palace, Thérèse glanced from her knitting to the window. She tried as usual to avert her eyes from the long avenue of trees which opened onto the Place de la Révolution, where the guillotine had stood. She was watching for Berry, who had promised to join her for tea. She sat in a chair which had once belonged to the Buonaparte family, while Imperial eagles and bees still glowered down at her from the gilded mouldings and carvings which adorned her boudoir. Golden *fleur-de-lys* had been stamped upon the bees in the carpet. Her eldest friend, Madame Pauline de Béarn, *née* Tourzel, had been regaling her with tales of the vulgarities of the Bonapartist ladies.

"So I offended Madame Junot," said Thérèse. "I am sorry to hear of it." She had accidentally ruffled the feathers of many *grandes dames* of Napoléon's court.

"Madame Junot is deeply slighted if anyone refers to her as 'Madame la Maréchale' instead of 'Madame la Duchesse.' When

Your Royal Highness addressed her as plain 'Madame Junot,' she was horrified," explained Pauline. Pauline de Béarn, with her kind blue eyes like those of her mother, Madame de Tourzel, retained the soft albeit faded loveliness of her youth, as well as a certain cheerful shrewdness. Little Charles had loved to call her "my Pauline." Pauline and Madame de Tourzel had been imprisoned in La Force with Princesse de Lamballe, and miraculously managed to escape the September massacres in which the latter suffered a gruesome death. Pauline had been permitted to visit Thérèse in the Temple in 1795 before the princess was sent to Vienna, and had begged to accompany her, but had been forbidden to do so by the authorities. The two old friends were happily united again, and Thérèse had given Pauline's husband the Comte de Béarn a place in her household, making Pauline one of her ladies-in-waiting and almost constant companion.

The ladies, clad in light afternoon dresses and beribboned lace caps, sat by a large silver tea tray which crowned a small table. Thérèse took the silver teapot and poured the piping stream of tea into a delicate Sévres cup. There was a scratching at the door.

"*Entrez*," said Thérèse. The Duc de Sérent, a grave and imposing older gentleman, entered and bowed low.

"Monseigneur le Duc de Berry," he announced. He bowed again, as Berry came whisking in with Mathieu de Montmorency at his heels.

"Monsieur le Duc de Montmorency," announced Monsieur de Sérent almost as an afterthought, before he himself withdrew. Mathieu de Montmorency, the Grand Master of the Knights of the Faith, had become indispensable to Thérèse during her first weeks in France, especially in her search for Charles.

"Forgive me for being late, Madame." Berry strode forward, kissing Thérèse's hand in the casual, lackadaisical fashion which caused many in Paris to comment upon his lack of manners. It was bad enough that he had brought Amy Brown and her children over from England, and established them in a house on the Rue des Mathurins. His chasseur uniform made his head seem too small for his broad shoulders.

"I am glad that Monsieur de Montmorency found you before the tea became cold," said Thérèse, passing him a cup. "Please sit down, gentlemen. I am eager to hear Montmorency's tidings."

"As am I, my sister," said Berry, noisily stirring sugar into his tea. "But first I must tell you that they still have not located the 'legal' grave of Louis XVII at the Sainte Marguerite cemetery."

Thérèse shuddered. She handed a cup to Mathieu. "I know. The little patch of dust in the old Temple garden is the only spot where I have to grieve." She referred to the mysterious grave discovered in the moat thirteen years earlier but not uncovered since. In 1811, Joseph Fouché, the nefarious Chief of Police, had persuaded Buonaparte to demolish the Temple tower. Latent with secrets and guilt, the medieval fortress had begun to attract the pious, who paused to pray at the place where the Royal Family, and the child-king in particular, had suffered.

Thérèse often went with Pauline to pray there at the Temple site, and at one special corner of the old garden she often lingered. About ten feet from the ancient east wall, Thérèse had planted a weeping willow tree and some cypresses, in what had formerly been the moat. It had been revealed that a certain royalist leader, Comte d'Andigné, on his recent deathbed had breathed forth a startling tale. Andigné, during his lengthy imprisonment in the Temple, had undertaken the cultivation of a vegetable garden in the dried-up moat, and while digging there in 1801, had come across the skeleton of a child. He guessed the child to have been about seven or eight years old, not dead longer than a decade. He had quickly reburied the remains and told no one of it until his deathbed.

Berry had heard the story through Lady Atkyns. Where the moat had once been, there now stood the Hotel de Ville for the Third Arondissement, and it was impossible to find the exact location of the body. Nevertheless, Thérèse would kneel in mourning and supplication near the weeping willow for the child who might be Charles. She already had the plans drawn up for a chapel and a monastery of Benedictine nuns of Perpetual Adoration of the Blessed Sacrament to live a life of prayer and reparation on the site of so many horrors.

Meanwhile, she had launched a search for Charles' "legal" grave in the Sainte Marguerite cemetery, without success. The bodies of her parents, however, had been found. A royalist had bought the land where their decapitated corpses had been dumped, in order to safeguard them. A state funeral was being planned for January. The body of Madame Elisabeth could unfortunately not be recovered.

"Comte d'Andigné's discovery," said Berry, "confirms the sad belief that continues to grow in my mind. The forlorn little prisoner who died on June 8, 1795 under the care of Dr. Pelletan was not our Charles. I... I do fear that Charles was secretly done to death much earlier, perhaps the winter of '94, by poison or strangulation, to be secretly buried in the moat by Simon, before the cobbler left the Temple for good. Gomin the jailor, whom I have found and with whom I have spoken, shares my opinion."

"Gomin showed kindness to me in prison," said Thérèse, remembering how he had brought her candles and shoes. "I have no reason to doubt his word, although dear Count Fersen (God rest his soul) did not entirely trust his veracity. On my visit to the Hotel Dieu, I was able to speak with Dr. Pelletan, and invited him to the Tuileries for an interview. He, an ardent revolutionary, had performed the autopsy on the mysterious little prisoner. Convinced the child was my brother, he preserved the heart in a special reliquary. But he had never seen Charles in his better days and neither, for that matter, had Gomin."

"Which brings us to Montmorency's discovery," said Berry. "Tell us, Monsieur. Madame says you have found important papers concerning the pretender Hervagault." He set down his cup and saucer with a clatter.

"Yes, Monseigneur. First, I sought Hervagault himself, but he eluded me."

"You mean, he has died, as we thought?" asked Thérèse.

"Perhaps, Madame. There are rumors that he escaped from the Bicêtre prison, in spite of his grievous illness. No grave or body of his could I find, only a death certificate in the prison records for one 'Jean-Marie Hervagault,' dated May 8, 1812, with the names of his parents left blank. I present to you, Madame, a notarized copy."

Mathieu handed a paper to Thérèse, which he had drawn from inside of his coat, along with some other documents. "These papers here are of great value to you, Madame. They came into my possession through the network provided by our Order, and the Congregation of the Virgin. They are copies of the papers of the late Charles Lafont-Savine, ex-Bishop of Viviers. The originals were confiscated by the police."

"Was he not the apostate bishop who recognized Hervagault to be my brother?" asked Thérèse.

"Yes, Madame. Bishop Lafont-Savine was frequently at Versailles before the Revolution, as Your Royal Highness may recall. In 1790 he took the constitutional oath and joined the Revolution. He then worked in the Arsenal library where he had access to many hidden archives and secret documents. In 1795, he researched the matter of Louis XVII and, guessing him to be still alive, he went to visit Hervagault when the boy-pretender began holding court in Châlons. The bishop, having often seen the little Dauphin in the days before the Revolution, became convinced that Hervagault was he. He became Hervagault's mentor and guide. His papers reveal several provocative reflections concerning the boy he believed to be his king." Mathieu hesitated a moment.

"You are not drinking your tea, Monsieur," said Thérèse. "Please do so, then tell us what the bishop wrote of Hervagault."

Montmorency sipped his tea, his distinguished and genteel manner greatly contrasting with Berry's boorishness. "The young lad Hervagault," he continued, "displayed innate nobility, a profound sense of *noblesse oblige* which won for him the hearts of many. However, as Lafont-Savine discovered, beneath the veneer of courtesy and charm was a tormented soul, addicted to liquor and pornographic books, and given to ungovernable fits of rage. He bragged that Hébert had bribed him with a special toy, in order to make the infamous false testimony against the Queen. The bishop writes here that the lad, aged about thirteen at the time, had obviously endured such degrading treatment at the hands of his keepers that his mind had become warped and so debased that, in the bishop's own words, 'he could be neither saved nor recognized.'"

"Alas, how true that would have been in the case of our Charles, if he did survive," lamented Thérèse. "Yet I can hardly believe he could be so easily bribed. Except for his imprisonment, my brother would have been a great man; he had great courage, an exceptional character, and deep love for his country. Is there no record of what Hervagault looked like?"

"Here is a copy of a description of him, Madame," said Mathieu, "set down while Hervagault was in prison at Vire in September, 1800, in order to be sent to Madame de Béarn's mother, Madame de Tourzel, the Dauphin's governess."

"Indeed, yes, Monsieur," said Pauline de Béarn. "My mother received the description and she sought to see Hervagault for herself, even though she has always remained convinced that the young King perished in the Temple. The police, however, never permitted us to visit Hervagault, and when he was released from Bicêtre for the first time, we were ordered to leave Paris."

"'Description of Louis-Charles de France set down in the prison of Vire, September 10, 1800,'" read Montmorency. "'Age about fifteen; height about five feet; light chestnut hair; large, well-formed eyes; arched eyebrows, darker than hair; prominent, bright and very beautiful eyes; well-formed nose; average forehead and mouth; small, dimpled chin; a mole at the corner of the right ear; a scar between the nose and upper lip; on the middle of the right leg, a shield-like impression bearing three *fleur-de-lys* above the royal crown and around them the initials of the names of the Dauphin, his illustrious parents, and noble aunt, Madame Elisabeth. Face slightly marked with small pox.'"

"I do not know anything about the tattoo," remarked Thérèse. "Otherwise, the description sounds rather like our Charles, especially the eyes, and the scar on the upper lip. Charles was once scratched by a rabbit, and bore such a scar. Also, he had been inoculated for smallpox, which left a few slight pockmarks, barely noticeable. Charles had an ill-formed ear lobe. Any such detailed description of him would surely have mentioned it, as well as the marks of the inoculation itself, on his arm. Perhaps, then, Hervagault was not he. What else, Monsieur de Montmorency, does the Bishop write?"

"He writes very guardedly of an 'international sect,'" quoted Montmorency. "'A power superior to all others and which governs Europe today, a power which the Dauphin would not escape if ever he appeared to resume his flight towards his first destiny. I even fear that this terrible power, which has eyes and ears everywhere, possesses spies in its pay who watch over this child and allow him to live only on the condition that he is lost in nothingness and disdain.'"

"It is as I long suspected," sighed Thérèse. "Those lines confirm to me the deep forebodings of my heart. If my brother lives, he is hounded by the Illuminati sect, and any interest or attention upon the true Charles by myself or anyone connected with our family would mean, or perhaps already has meant for him, his doom."

Montmorency nodded in sad agreement. "Madame, I fear that you speak truly. The bishop begged Hervagault to stay in obscurity, for his own safety. In the meantime he, Lafont-Savine, was harassed by the police for his friendship with Hervagault. They threw the frail, penitent, old ecclesiastic into prison, and later into an insane asylum. He died a holy death, worn out from austerities and penances, completely reconciled with the Church, and adamant that Hervagault was Louis XVII. As for Hervagault himself, there are whispers that he is not dead, but has been spirited away by his supporters and is in hiding somewhere."

"What of Hervagault's alleged parents, René and Nicole Hervagault?" asked Thérèse.

Hervagault *pére* is dead," said Montmorency. "His widow has left their native village, and no one knows where she has gone. Remember, one of the police commissioners who often visited the Temple was one Rémy Bigot. 'Bigot' was Nicole Hervagault's maiden name. She may have had ties to Paris."

"To speak to her is necessary," said Thérèse. "She should be sought for."

"Indeed," said Berry.

"I will seek for her," said Montmorency. "Permit me, nevertheless, to caution Your Royal Highness. We need to watch and wait. And now I beg leave to bring in Captain Artain."

"Captain Artain? The adventurer you have found to search for Charles in America?" asked Thérèse. "Yes, bring him in. It is to my everlasting regret that our dear Count Fersen was prevented from making the journey by his untimely demise."

Montmorency bowed and left the room for an instant, returning with a tall, dark, robust gentleman in a worn white, green and gold uniform of the Catholic and Royal Army of the Vendée, complete with white and green feathers in his jaunty hat, which he swept from his head. He had longish hair, a thick moustache with thicker eyebrows over keen, penetrating eyes. His was a scarred visage, his bearing, fearless, with a pistol through his green sash. He drew his sword, laying it at Thérèse's feet.

"Captain Artain, at your service, Madame *ma princesse*," he proclaimed in a rugged, southwestern accent. She extended her hand; he fell to one knee and embraced it.

Monsieur *mon capitain*," said Thérèse, her voice raspy with emotion at the sight of such unabashed devotion, "Monsieur de Montmorency will provide you with the finances and information necessary for this venture, including what names, places, and dates are available to us. If only we had Count Fersen's papers; he had much information that is now lost, and so we must begin almost from scratch. After so many years, it will be difficult to pick up the threads of so many long-lost claimants. We are asking you to journey over rough seas, across wild rivers and through notoriously savage Indian country. You will report on your findings personally to me. Please do not send dispatches, lest they should fall into the wrong hands. You will likely not return for many months. Are you willing, Monsieur?"

"I am willing to risk all for my princess," said the hardy soldier. "And I will seek high and low for our young king. I will go to New York, then to Canada, and to the West, seeking Lazu Williams, for a start."

"Then my eternal gratitude is yours. We shall continue to make enquiries here as our duties permit. Monsieur de Sérent will see to your comfort and well-being before your departure. May the good God go with you."

Captain Artain kissed her hand again, slid his sword into his scaffold, and withdrew backwards, hat still beneath his arm. Thérèse lapsed into a pensive silence.

"Simon the cobbler," she murmured at last. "The infamous Simon. My brother's keeper, who so terribly abused him. He is dead, is he not?"

"Yes, my sister," said Berry. "He perished on the scaffold."

"What of his wife?" asked Thérèse. "Perhaps she is still living. If she is, we must find her."

"Madame, I will search Paris for her myself," said Montmorency.

"She was one of the last persons to have seen my brother alive and in his right mind. Whatever the truth of this mystery is, I believe Madame Simon to be at the heart of it." Thérèse looked out of the window for a long time before finishing her tea. Then she noticed a plump, tall, overdressed young man blithely strolling through the Palace gates as if he owned the place.

"Berry, who is that man?" she asked.

Berry came to her side and peered out. "That," he said, "is Decazes. He is Fouché's assistant."

"Fouché!" Thérèse exclaimed. "What a dreadful calamity to have that regicide at Court. So this Decazes is his creature?"

"He is indeed. What is more, Uncle is fond of him. Why, he is probably going to visit Uncle right now."

Thérèse sighed. "No good will come of it."

Chapter Thirteen:

Ghosts

Summer 1814

"Who will give water to my head and a fountain of tears to my eyes? And I will weep day and night for the slain of the daughter of my people." Jeremias 9:1

      Thérèse's carriage jolted down the western highroad from Paris. It was a halcyon summer afternoon and she was going to Versailles. The warm stillness of the August day gave the upheavals of the past twenty-five years the semblance of being mere illusions of night or phantoms of the imagination, and in reality, Papa, Maman, Tante Babette and Charles were all waiting for her somewhere in the palaces or the gardens of Versailles. What a summer it had been! After long, peaceful years at Hartwell, she had plunged into a constant flurry of activity. Being the first lady of the Court of France was no small undertaking. Restoring dignity and standards of morality to court life was an imposing and unpopular task. She was a great disappointment to those who longed for her to gossip and dance until dawn. Thérèse cared next to nothing for what people thought or said about her. She did what she perceived to be her duty, no matter what the cost.

What a range of emotions the last six months had doled out to her! After her debut at the Opera in May, Angoulême had come to Paris at last. She had not seen him since the previous winter, when he left England for the south of France. Apparently, he had been a great success among the common people, but a dismal failure among the nobles, who were put off by his gross manners, his jerky bows, and his tendency to ask, "What is that one's name?" whenever a stranger approached him. Yet his kindly ways and innate decency touched the hearts of the simple folk. His gauche behavior was due to his shyness and abysmal lack of early training. Nevertheless, Thérèse was proud of him for having taken the risk, for having dared to raise the royal standard at Bordeaux.

Thérèse and Berry rode outside the city to meet the returning hero. They were accompanied by a large number of troopers, including the National Guard, as well as gendarmes and citizens of Paris, lining both sides of the road. When Thérèse first glimpsed Angoulême on his horse in his martial attire, whether it was the spring sunshine, she did not know, but for a flash he looked like the prince of her dreams. She remembered how during their secret betrothal she had innocently referred to him as her "lover." She had not yet seen him as an adult, but read and reread his passionate love letters, which she later discovered had been written for him by Louis XVIII. After their disastrous wedding night, she never again applied the word "lover" to Angoulême.

Now, at the head of an army, he had a confidence and a poise that she had not seen before. He cantered up to her carriage and dismounted. She, in turn, alighted and went to his side. The multitude cheered as Angoulême kissed her hand. She suddenly felt speechless and shy. She wanted to thank him for risking his life and going to Bordeaux. "At Bordeaux…" she began.

He clasped both her hands between his. "It was for you, all for you, that I did it." And as he brought both her hands to his lips, they were dampened by his tears. Her face beamed with the radiance of a moment of purest joy, a joy which makes long years of suffering seem as transient as mist on a morning lake in summer. Amid the waving throngs, he helped her back into the carriage and trotted beside her on his horse all the way to the palace.

Another prince to return to Paris after years of exile was Louis-Philippe d'Orléans. Thérèse wondered at the audacity which brought him home to France now that the fighting was over. She was proud of her menfolk who had been willing to risk their lives while Orléans had been enjoying the sunshine in Sicily. Thérèse was not present when Louis-Philippe kissed the steps of the Palais-Royal, which he took possession of, along with the other vast Orléans estates, restored to him by royal decree. The King, however, was suspicious of the son of Philippe Egalité.

"Do not trust him," Louis XVIII confided to her. "But do you not agree, my dear, that while keeping him at arm's length, we must not overtly offend him?" The King generally consulted Thérèse about such matters.

"Yes, Sire. Then should I accept the Duc's invitation to view his gardens at Monceaux?"

The King urged her to do so, although she dreaded another encounter with Louis-Philippe. She was not certain why she so disliked being with him, except that he reminded her of his father's regicide. Nevertheless, the Duc welcomed her with utmost courtesy. His gardens were sublime, filled with roses and splashing fountains, almost as enchanting as Artois' Bagatelle or Maman's Trianon. An outdoor repast was prepared beneath a small, almost intimate pavilion, with few attendants, so that the meal was casual and delightful. They conversed about their mutual relatives, and after the dessert, she strolled through the June splendor with him, listening to his anecdotes of the small children he had left behind in Sicily with his wife. She discerned that his mind was on something else and he kept regarding her as if he wanted to ask her something: she could not fathom what.

Thérèse found herself combatting subtle feelings of jealousy towards Marie-Amélie, as the complete picture rose before her of what a superb husband and father Louis-Philippe must be, in spite of his leftist political convictions. She realized she was confused, not only by his charm, but by his questioning dark eyes. Annoyance flashed through her. After all, an abyss lay between them, and the shadow of the English. She broke off their conversation rather abruptly, asking for her carriage to be sent for, leaving Louis-Philippe befuddled and offended. She departed rather ungraciously, after coldly consenting to be the godmother of the new Orléans baby, expected in September.

Midsummer commenced with the Corpus Christi procession, the first to take place in Paris for many years. By royal proclamation, every house along the route was decorated with garlands and banners. Every member of the Royal Family and their mutual households walked on foot, tapers in hand, behind the monstrance. All the ancient and glorious hymns to the Blessed Sacrament were sung in both Latin and the vernacular. Those of the older generation remembered and joined in, but few of the younger people knew any of the words. Thérèse longed for the voice of an angel in which to fittingly express the near rapture she experienced at seeing the Savior given public homage in the very streets where so many sacrileges had occurred. Not only Paris, but the provincial towns had witnessed scenes of desecration, such as donkeys dressed in vestments and mitres and led through the streets, the destruction of relics of the saints, the smashing of stained glass windows, the confiscation of bells and sacred vessels by the revolutionary government.

In July, Thérèse journeyed to the spa at Vichy for what was intended as a time of rest. However, as the news spread that Madame d'Angoulême was taking the waters, people began to flock there. Instead of relaxing in the baths as much as her inclination warranted, she spent hours receiving delegations from various towns, as well as petitioners: old royalist soldiers, crippled for their king; impoverished nobles, who had lost everything in the Revolution. She went on foot and on horseback into the neighboring villages to visit the needy and the sick.

Everywhere she was greeted with emotion. One man was so overcome he threw himself at her feet in sobs. "Madame, forgive me! My voice fails me! I cannot deliver the speech intended for Your Highness."

"Rise, Monsieur," she bade him. "Why do you regret you cannot speak to me? What better can you say?"

From the Vendée came the hero La Rochejacquelein and other leaders of the *chouannerie* who had survived. She heard endless stories of atrocities perpetrated by the revolutionary soldiers, called *les bleus*, on those faithful to the Church and the crown in the

1790's. There was the "meadow of howling" where two hundred peasant men, women and children had their tongues ripped out and their fingers, ears and noses cut off as they died in agony. She had been told of the infamous "Republican marriages," in which a man and woman would be tied together naked and drowned, but she had not heard of the mass murders at Gonnard, where two women and thirty children were buried alive in a pit. (Some of the revolutionary leaders had a strong dislike of children.)

In early August, Thérèse and her entourage departed from Vichy along the flower-strewn road to the silk-manufacturing city of Lyons, long-suffering, faithful Lyons. Crowds lined the road as she passed. Often the royal progress was halted so Thérèse could receive the greetings of the multitudes. She was profoundly humbled by the rising adulation and could only attribute it to the fact that the people realized that she had suffered even as they had suffered. In their eyes she was the embodiment of the sorrows of the nation.

The continued accounts of what her countrymen had endured deluged her heart so that her own griefs were flooded out of it. Rumors had come to her for years; finally all the details were spilled at her feet. Never could she wash from her mind the images which now lurked there. She was haunted as if by a thousand ghosts.

At Le Mans, where *les bleus* discovered the women and children who had been hiding from them, they ripped off their clothes using bayonets and sabres, and after violating and killing them, the corpses were bound together in various grotesque poses. In other towns, the weak and innocent were roasted in baking ovens while their homes were being burned to the ground. Some people were burned to death in their churches.

In the Vendée, it was a popular pastime among the soldiers of liberty to throw children out of windows and catch them on bayonets. "There is no more Vendée!" bragged General Westermann to the Welfare Committee in Paris, after weeks of committing atrocities on civilians. In the end, the victory belonged to those who had fought for the altar and the throne, for the Revolution had consumed itself, at least for the time being.

The feast of the Transfiguration brought Thérèse to the triumphal arch erected at the gates of Lyons. Thousands had been massacred there for resisting the paganism of the Revolution. The citizens of Lyons outdid themselves, and perhaps everyone else in France, in their efforts to welcome her warmly. Daughters of the most distinguished families, dressed all in white, presented her with flowers. She asked them their names; one petite, dark Mademoiselle Pauline Juricot seemed particularly eager to do all the talking for the others. Thérèse drove through the city in an open carriage. Over one of the bridges was a large Ionic temple bearing the words: "Love to Madame." There were fireworks and an illumination of the city. The next day, she assisted at a solemn High Mass in the cathedral. After a cruise on the river and an evening at the theater she arose early on the morning of August 8 to review the troops on the plain of Brotteaux, the site of mass executions in the days of the Terror at the direct order of Fouché and his henchman. Among the banners and martial emblems was a standard proclaiming: "Our blood has flowed for the King" and another: "The siege maintained for sixty-three days in the year 1793."

"*Vive le Roi!*" "Long live the King!" "*Vive Madame!*" "Long live Madame!" the soldiers deliriously shouted as she passed through their ranks.

After several days at Lyons, Thérèse departed for Paris and the great procession of August 15. Napoléon Buonaparte had set aside that day, which happened to be his birthday, as the celebration of his own cult of personality. In the *ancien régime*, the feast of the Assumption of the Blessed Virgin Mary was the patronal celebration of all France. Louis XIII had vowed to make a procession in honor of Our Lady on every August 15, in supplication and later in thanksgiving for a son and heir, which heaven granted to him in the person of Louis XIV. How joyful was Thérèse to see the custom renewed, as she and her family led the populace in giving public homage to the Queen of Heaven and earth. During the procession, Thérèse decided that she was ready to see Versailles again. Two days later, she went there.

She had not laid eyes upon her childhood home since the rainy, bloody day of October 6, 1789, when with her parents, aunt and brother, they left the great château through churning mud and a howling mob. It surprised her how little everything had actually changed. Some fine old trees were gone; those that remained were taller and wider. The magnificent statues and fountains showed little alteration. Apollo still drove his chariot through the pond. At the fountains of Latona, the frogs, which had so fascinated her as a child, had not ceased to squirt water from their mouths. Buonaparte had been planning to remodel Versailles for his own megalomaniac purposes, and therefore the gardens had been maintained after a fashion. The daunting cost of repairs was too much even for Napoléon, who preferred to instead spend money on his conquest of Europe.

Thérèse went accompanied by Pauline, Mathieu de Montmorency and a few others of her household, who lagged behind at a discreet distance so she could wander freely and alone. She went first to Petit Trianon. The sight of the familiar square façade quickly blurred for her as she walked through the wrought-iron, brass-tipped gate. The simplicity of the neo-classical, colonnaded house was as she remembered, yet the silence almost screamed at her from the floor-length rectangular windows, once full of music, singing and children's laughter. Entering the front door, she climbed the winding staircase with the elaborate iron balustrade, bearing the entwining initials of "M.A." On the main floor, she saw that much of the original furniture remained intact. The house had been used as an inn for many years, until Buonaparte bestowed the property upon his favorite, most decadent sister, Pauline Borghese. Thérèse shuddered to think of such a lewd woman sitting in her mother's chairs, playing on the Queen's pianoforte.

While the infamous Pauline had left hardly a trace of herself at Trianon, Thérèse could almost hear Marie-Antoinette's voice coming from the grand salon, raised in an aria from Gluck's *Orpheus and Eurydice*. Did she hear the nearly audible strains of Maman's harp, playing the "Dance of the blessed spirits"? No, it was the breeze swaying the chestnuts in the park. She did not linger in the house, but went out the south side doors to the wide terrace, the lawns and gardens spreading before her. It was whispered that several people had seen ghosts at Trianon, particularly the form of a woman in a flowing white dress and plumed straw hat, gliding amongst the trees in the moonlight, or sitting motionless on the terrace in dusky twilights. Thérèse had lived in many places, but there were none so haunted as Trianon, or as vibrant with memory. Its haunting was a wistful and compelling call to linger, as if the murmuring poplars and cedars entreated one to stay forever. The soul seemed drawn into an enchanted realm where time itself dallied. She breathed in the scented air. No one would ever live there for long in peace; no one could ever again make it a dwelling place, for the person who had enlivened Trianon with her own spontaneous magic was gone from the world.

Thérèse picked one of the Fantin-Latour roses which blossomed in the arbors as in days of yesteryear. The copses and paths were heavy with their fragrance. She strolled to the Temple of Love, where Cupid still carved a bow from Hercules' club. She passed the Belvedere, peeking for a moment into the *papier-mâché* miniature theater, where a dashing, young Artois had played the part of "Figaro." She sat for awhile in the grotto, then visited the *hameau*. The cottages where the Queen had housed several destitute families remained, but all was deserted. The cows Blanchette and Brunette had left no heirs; all the livestock were gone. But the orangerie was pruned and orderly, and fish leaped in the pond. She wandered by the rose-gold Grand Trianon, where Baby Sophie had died. A melancholy swept Thérèse; it was time to visit the main palace.

The vast rooms echoed with her every footstep and movement, those salons once filled with ladies in wide-panniered skirts and gentlemen in silk embroidered coats. No one was living in any of the principal rooms of the château; only a few impoverished *émigrés* had timidly moved into the less exalted quarters. All the furnishings were gone, either burned, stolen, or sold. They could never afford to live there again, even though her uncle toyed with the idea from time to time. Buonaparte had decided to store part of his art collection at Versailles; there were plenty of paintings on the walls, pillaged from palaces all over Europe, but not much else. Some of the gold leaf on the mouldings and carvings remained but most had been stripped off.

Maman's bedchamber, where Thérèse and her brothers and sister had been born, was completely bare. Gone were the embroidered, canopied bed, the wall hangings, mirrors and the other furnishings. She went through the *petits-appartements*, down the narrow back passage leading to her father's bedchamber, the same passage down which Maman had fled in the night the fishwives had burst into her room and hacked her bed to pieces.

Papa's apartment was also empty. What had become of his portrait of Erasmus, his maps and globes, his astrolabe and telescope? She paused by the window where Maman had picked up Charles and held him up in front of Papa, saying, "I beg you, for the sake of this child, and for your own, let us escape the next time the opportunity arises!"

"Oh, Papa, why, why…?" Thérèse moaned aloud to the empty bookcases in his beloved library. She stepped onto the balcony where she had stood with Maman, facing the mob. Maman's hair had fallen out of her nightcap, sticking to Thérèse's tear-stained face. Thérèse wondered if it was at that moment that her vocal chords froze, as if strained by the scream that rose within her, but never fled forth.

Before leaving Versailles, she prayed long in the chapel where she had been baptized, praying for the souls of her parents and her own. She had failed to find Charles, to find any solid proof even of his death. There could not even be a public requiem Mass, although, of course, many churches had held private Masses for him. What a bitter chalice, which she had only begun to drain. In a moment of manifestation, Thérèse saw in the tormented child-king all the lost children of France.

Chapter Fourteen:

The Hospital

Advent 1814

"For behold my witness is in heaven, and He that knoweth my conscience is on high." Job 16:20

A modest coach bearing the royal coat-of-arms rumbled through the sewage-filled, garbage strewn boulevards of Paris. Other vehicles moved aside, as pasersby pressed themselves against buildings or stepped into doorways in order to avoid being hit. A few scattered cheers arose from those citizens who happened to notice that Madame's own arms also adorned the vehicle's doors. The citizens of Paris had become accustomed to seeing Madame la Duchesse d'Angoulême making her rounds of the various and sundry charitable institutions. It had been her intentions to make a complete tour of all such houses at the beginning of the Restoration, but she was being constantly interrupted by her own obligations.

On that particular December day, accompanied by Pauline and Mathieu, she was planning to visit the Hôpital des Incurables run by the Daughters of Charity of Saint Vincent de Paul. Her visit had a double purpose, for Simon's widow had been found. The superior of Les Incurables, a Sister Lucie, had written to Thérèse concerning one of the patients, an elderly woman called "Mother

Simon." Mère Simon incessantly spoke to the other inmates of her days as governess of the Dauphin, maintaining that Charles was still alive, and that she had seen him.

"I wish to speak to Sister Lucie first before confronting Madame Simon," she said to her companions. "Is it not odd that we should finally receive word of Widow Simon, after hearing what Madame Hue had to tell?" Thérèse's Reader, Madame Hue, had been receiving visits at the Tuileries from a peasant woman of the Vendée, Françoise Desperez. Madame Desperez was quite a heroine in her own right for during the Revolution she had worked as an agent for the Royal and Catholic army, risking her life on several occasions by journeying into Paris on secret missions. At present she was happily receiving a royal pension and living comfortably at the Hôtel des Trois Moillets in the Rue Montgoreuil. She confided to Madame Hue that in June of 1795, some royalist leaders (she would not say who) met her with a carriage at a particular street corner near the Temple. After climbing into the carriage, a beautiful boy of about ten years old was brought to her. It was Louis XVII himself, she claimed. She dressed him as a girl, and took him by coach to Fontenai, where she delivered him safely to the Vendéan leader Charette. What had become of him after that she did not know, for Charette was killed, and the Royal army eventually dispersed.

It was a gray afternoon, expectant with Advent stillness. The drive from the Tuileries to the hospital on the Rue de Sèvres was short. The hospital staff was lined up outside to meet her, mostly Daughters of Charity in their blue habits and white starched cornets, which caused the Ottomans to refer to them as the "Swallows of Allah." They curtsied as Thérèse climbed out of the coach. A sister in her mid-thirties, perhaps (it was difficult to tell for certain), with a fresh, bright face and a firm, determined manner stepped forward. Mathieu briefly spoke with her before introducing her to Thérèse. She was Sr. Lucie, the superior of the Hôpital des Incurables. As they entered the hospital, Thérèse asked Sr. Lucie how many beds they had, were the medical supplies adequate, were the patients able to attend daily Mass and the other questions she generally proffered on her visitations. The hospital was scrubbed from the floors to the ceilings; the sisters, cheerful and diligent; the patients, serene and even happy. Every room had a crucifix;

pictures and statues of the Virgin and the saints added a sublime serenity to the corridors and wards. Thérèse was well-satisfied, and thanked the Good God for the nursing sisters. In Protestant countries like England, the sick poor suffered terribly without them. After visiting a few wards, and speaking to many of the patients, they paused in the sisters' parlor, where Sister Lucie offered them some tea.

"My good Sister Lucie, you wrote to me of Madame Simon," said Thérèse. "How long has she been here?"

"For twenty years, Madame," replied the sister. "She came here after her husband's execution, sick and destitute. As Your Highness is aware, the sisters were not in residence then." The hospital had only recently been restored to the care of the Daughters of Charity. "When the other patients discovered who she was, they were angry with her, the Dauphin's sufferings being well-known. Mère Simon had asserted over and over again to everyone at the hospital that on the day she left the Temple in January of 1794, the Dauphin was carried away in a cart filled with dirty linen and another child was left in his place."

Thérèse nodded. She herself had seen the cart filled with linen from the window of her prison on that January 19 so long ago. Sister Lucie continued.

"Simon had a wicker hamper with a double bottom brought to the Temple, as well as a pasteboard horse and several toys. From the horse, which was hollow inside, they took a rickety boy and left him in the Dauphin's room, while they put the Dauphin in the hamper, then covered him with soiled linen. When the guards tried to examine the hamper in the cart, Simon began shouting at them to keep their hands off his dirty linen. Needless to say, they let him pass unhindered."

"Where did he take my brother?" asked Thérèse.

"I do not know, Madame. But Mère Simon has often said to me: 'You are young. You will see him on the throne, but I, I am old. I shall not see him.' I can truly say that even though her body is frail from chronic asthma, her mind is quite sound. She is a woman of sense, not given to superstitions, neither does she drink and, overall, she has proven herself to be an honest soul. There has been no variation in any of her statements in the time that I have been acquainted with her. I cannot imagine that she has been influenced by outsiders to fabricate such a story."

"She is a Catholic?" asked Thérèse.

"Yes, Madame, she practices our Faith. She receives Holy Communion at least five or six times a year."

Thérèse thought for a moment. "Sister, we will finish our tour of the hospital, but please, I do not wish for Madame Simon to see me. I will return later this afternoon to speak with her. I will come incognito."

"Yes, Madame. I will see that Mère Simon stays in her room."

After finishing the visitation, Thérèse hastened back to the Tuileries to change into simple clothes, and told Pauline and Montmorency to do the same. She exchanged her velvet dress, ermine-lined shoulder cape and muff for a worn maroon serge gown and mantle, a black felt bonnet over which she draped a thick crêpe veil, so that she resembled a poor but genteel widow. She had decided to leave the Tuileries through an obscure, back entrance, and had directed her retinue to wait for her there. She remembered that there was a hidden passage, formerly used by their confessors during the dark days of the Revolution, which Count von Fersen would also take when he would come to visit her parents.

She slipped into the antechamber of her apartments and from there she need only get to the small door in the corridor which led to the passage. Everything was quiet since most of the Court were finishing their afternoon naps. She opened the door of her antechamber, having earlier sent away the page whose duty it was to open doors, and was startled to see her husband. He leaned against the wide lintel, his right hand tucked inside his vest, like a bizarre caricature of Napoléon Buonaparte.

"Angoulême!" she exclaimed. "I thought you were with your regiment today."

"I know where you are going," said Angoulême. "I know, Princess. You have been seeking Charles." His left shoulder twitched with his usual nervous tic, but his amber eyes were adamant. "I am well-informed of all of your movements."

160

Thérèsa's eyes blazed with defiance. "I scorn you and your despicable spies! It is my duty to seek my brother! My sacred duty! Nothing will deter me!" She tried to walk past him. He grabbed her wrist and held her back. She was shocked at the gesture, as well as at the strength that came from his deceptively puny frame.

"I warn you, Marie-Thérèse!" said Angoulême, sternly. "Uncle knows. He does not like it. The police are watching you, too. I implore you to leave this matter alone."

"How can I?" She tried to wrest herself free. "Charles may be alive!"

"Charles is dead," he stated slowly and deliberately. "You are not accepting the facts because in your heart you want him to be alive. You want to pretend that he escaped, but he did not. He died of mistreatment and neglect in the Temple. The autopsy of two physicians confirmed it. He died, his nails grown long like a beast's, his hair unkempt and stuck to his ulcers and sores, his bed linen crawling with lice, his arms and legs unnaturally distended from consumption and rickets, alone and cold and afraid! That is the truth of the case, Thérèse, and you must acknowledge it!"

He finally let go of her wrist, as she covered her veiled face with her hands and trembled. "You are my husband," she said after several moments. "If you forbid me to seek further, I will obey, although I do believe all the facts are not yet known."

He stepped away from her and sadness swept his face. "I do not forbid you, *ma princesse*. How could I? I have forfeited such a right. But I plead with you, I warn you, be aware of the danger in which you are placing yourself... and others."

"You have forfeited nothing," replied Thérèse. "A wife is bound to obey her husband."

"Go...go..." he said, averting his eyes from her face, "if that is what you think is best." He abruptly turned and quickly walked in the direction of his own apartments. Without sparing a second, Thérèse whisked down the corridor to the small door hidden in the panelling, which opened on to the narrow passage. The passage was fairly clean and obviously being used by the servants. She descended a winding, spiral stone staircase to the ground floor, and another door leading to a side entrance of the palace where her coach awaited her, a plain coach without arms. Pauline and Mathieu were already inside.

Within a few minutes they were once more at the Rue de Sévres. Sister Lucie met them at the door, and led them to a small parlor, where a frail old woman sat alone by a stove. She was in a wheelchair, a white linen cap on her head, a shawl around her shoulders and a blanket across her legs. She was tatting in the fading December light streaming in through a window.

"Mère Simon, some people are here to visit you," said Sister Lucie. She withdrew without curtsying, as Thérèse had asked her. Lifting her veil, Thérèse approached the cobbler's widow. Her eyes met the steel gray ones in the withered face. It was a hard visage, as hard as she had ever remembered it to be, but not evil. She stared keenly at Thérèse for several seconds before looking down again at her tatting.

"Sit down, Madame," said Widow Simon, gesturing to a chair. Thérèse sat down; Pauline and Mathieu remained standing by the door. "You have heard, I suppose, that I was once the governess of the Dauphin. People talk of nothing but the Dauphin nowadays. Everyone wants to know about him, and I tell them everything I can recall."

"Yes, Madame Simon," said Thérèse, trying to soften her grating voice. "I would like to hear about the Dauphin. They say he was a handsome child."

"Handsome!" exclaimed Mère Simon. "Ah, *mon Dieu*, he was like an angel with his golden curls and thick eyelashes! Both of my little Bourbons were beautiful children. Yes, his sister was a lovely girl, too." She furtively glanced at Thérèse. "A proud lass, but lovely. *Oh, la la*, but my Charles was a naughty rascal."

"You took care of him, did you not?"

"Indeed, yes, Madame." The old widow stopped tatting and closed her eyes. "I made certain he ate all the food on his plate. I swept his chamber every day and mended his clothes. I changed his bed linen often. Those tales about lice – well, not while I, Jeanne Simon, resided at the Temple. My Charles loved me and I loved him. He wanted to come with us when we left."

"Your husband," asked Thérèse, hesitantly, "did he love Charles?"

Madame Simon's eyebrows arched defiantly. "I do not care what stories you may have heard, but Simon did not hit Charles all that often. Why, he only hit him when he was drunk, and then he would hit me, too, for that matter. And Charles was a rascal – all those princely airs and graces, those fine manners and book-learning, why, it just made Simon as mad as can be. He had to beat it all out of him, and knock some sense into his head. He would have done the same to a boy of our own. But he never hit him with an iron poker, knocking him half-dead. That's an evil lie. And he never broke his toys, or killed his pet birds. Not Simon. As for the guards – well, that's another story altogether. They would wake the little fellow up every few hours a night, when they let him sleep at all, to make certain he was still there. 'Capet, are you awake? Show yourself, you whelp!' they would call. It angered me, I must say. Simon did no such thing. He even brought Charles a dog, which was given to the boy's sister after he left."

"Yes," said Thérèse, remembering little Coco. "So I have heard. But tell me, did you take the Dauphin away with you?"

"We did, indeed. Simon smuggled him out in a hamper of dirty linen. Hiding the likes of Monsieur Charles was no easy task, let me tell you. Then Simon took him to some place called Vitry. Afterwards, Simon was killed. I did not see the Dauphin again for many years."

Thérèse suppressed a small gasp. "You saw him, Madame? When?"

The old woman's eyes brightened and her face glowed. "My Charles came to see me in 1802. He stood right here in this room."

Thérèse felt her pulses pounding, as she hid her emotion. "From the tower of the Temple until 1802 is a long time," she said lightly. "How were you able to recognize him?"

"By the scar on his upper lip, where the rabbit scratched him." The hard mouth softened into a sly smile. "Madame, I recognize you quite well, notwithstanding your disguise, although I have not seen you for very much longer….You are Madame Marie-Thérèse!"

Thérèse stood up and almost bolted from the room, followed by her friends. So overcome was she by the interview that she hardly remembered leaving the hospital and driving back to the Tuileries. She sent a message to Berry to come as soon as possible. She doubted he would visit that night, since he always spent the evenings gallivanting about the city. He called the next morning while Thérèse was having her hair dressed. She sent her hairdresser and ladies away, while she recounted to Berry the events of the previous day. He was skeptical.

"Thérèse, Madame Simon is an old woman with a guilty conscience. She knows that Charles was murdered probably by Simon himself, and secretly buried in the moat. She has obviously read the penny novel *The Madeleine Cemetery* by Regnault-Warin. Most of the details of the hamper story are directly from that book, and she, in her anguish, has made them true in her mind. Forget what she has said."

"But what of her mention of 'Vitry.' Do you think she is referring to Vitry-sur-Seine, Monsieur Petitval's estate, where the massacre took place? Did not Petitval ask to be given Charles in exchange for money? Do you think Simon was in league with Barras?"

"I doubt it," he replied to her last inquiry. "Perhaps I should speak to Barras all the same. If you like, I will also go and question Madame Simon myself, if I can get to her before the police do."

"The police?" exclaimed Thérèse.

"Yes. Uncle does not like anyone to talk about Louis XVII's fate. He wants no attention drawn to it at all, which is why he has allowed no solemn requiem Mass for the boy to take place, or monument in his honor to be planned. Oh yes, he wrote an epitaph for him, but I doubt that you shall ever see it anywhere…which points all the more to who the *real* murderer is!" And Berry stomped from the room without another word.

A few days later, the police raided Les Incurables and threatened Madame Simon and the sisters, making them promise to allow the widow no visitors in the future. When Berry visited with his entourage, including an armed bodyguard, he was given access to the patient, but Madame Simon denied that she had seen Charles in 1802. She was obviously terrified.

Chapter Fifteen:
The Salon
January 1815

"But the souls of the just are in the hand of God, and the torment of death shall not touch them. In the sight of the unwise they seemed to die, and this departure was taken for misery…but they are in peace." Wisdom 3:1-3

In an elegant mansion on the Rue de Mont Blanc, a lady of surpassing loveliness reclined on a Grecian sofa, just as the artist David had immortalized her on canvas a decade and a half earlier. She had altered little since those mad, blithe days of the Directoire and Consulate when she, Madame Récamier, had reigned as queen of Parisian society, draped in white, Hellenistic robes in which she would perform her legendary "Shawl Dance" like a graceful dryad. Her once unruly brown curls were neatly arranged in orderly ringlets at the temples; the rest of her long tresses were braided into a crown at the top of her head. She exuded the charm and wistfulness of one who lived in an eternal spring, full of possibilities, always in blossom, yet never ripening into reality and fulfillment.

Her usual white had been exchanged for black chiffon, for she had that day been to the funeral of King Louis XVI and Queen Marie-Antoinette. As a child of ten, while watching the Royal

Family at one of the public dinners at Versailles, she had been noticed by the Queen, who invited her to Trianon to play with Madame Royale. The Court had marvelled at the contrasting beauty of the dark haired girl with the blond princess, and Julie had been a legend ever since. In the Récamier drawing room were gathered an assortment of friends, eager to discuss the funeral, for hers was one of the most interesting and distinguished salons in Paris, where the conversation always promised to be provocative, as well as gratifying.

Madame Récamier's had been one of the many strange marriages that occurred during, and immediately after, the Revolution, when the chaos of the times and the upheaval of the Church and society had led, at least in her circle of acquaintances, to either divorce or to unions which existed in name only. Hers was in the latter category. During the days of the Terror in her native Lyons, fifteen-year-old Julie Bernard, through a legal ceremony, was bound to the wealthy banker Récamier, old enough to be her grandfather. There were some that whispered that Julie was actually Récamier's secret, illegitimate daughter, and that the proceedings were more of an adoption than a marriage, in which the middle-aged bachelor sought to safeguard the lovely maiden in those most unstable and dangerous times. He whisked her away from Lyons to the relative security of Paris, where the revolutionaries left him alone because of his financial expertise and the fact that he made an effort to be present at the public executions. He cherished Julie as only the most doting and indulgent of fathers can, allowing her to pursue her love of art and music. As soon as the Terror ended, she quickly began to rival Joséphine Buonaparte and Thérèse Tallien as one of the most radiant hostesses in Paris. She, in turn, loved Monsieur Récamier as a daughter, saying to him more than once: "Every happiness I have known in this life is due to you." Through the most decadent of times she retained her virtue. Many nobles, princes, and parvenus sought to make her their mistress or bride, but she would give herself to no one.

In 1798, she became acquainted with the witty Madame de Staël, notorious for the lack of virtue in her personal life, but oddly enough the two very different women grew to be close friends and confidantes. Madame de Staël dubbed her "Juliette," which was how she was known ever after. Monsieur Récamier's financial reverses, Juliette's banishment from Paris by Napoléon, and her own virginal integrity, seemed to attract people rather than vice versa. Unfortunately, she was a devastating flirt; her greatest sin was that she had carelessly caused many good and decent men to fall in love with her by a thousand imprudent smiles and looks, by long, gushy letters and prolonged *tête-à-têtes*. Not greatly educated or exceptionally clever, Juliette Récamier was an entrancing listener; she enchanted her guests with the gentle gaze of wonder and attention she bestowed upon every speaker. With jaded or lonely men, this unwittingly worked like a magic tonic, causing the number of her devoted and ardent admirers to increase in spite of herself.

Perhaps the most devoted among her many friends was the upright and noble Mathieu de Montmorency. He sat on a *tabouret* across from the fireplace in Madame Récamier's drawing room. The dancing fire and candles illuminated the room in an amber glow, reflecting in the embossed gold on the rows of leather-bound books and in the crystal prisms of the chandelier and candelabra. Near him were Juliette's harp and pianoforte, which usually she deigned to play for her guests. Behind him was a large portrait by Elisabeth Vigée-Lebrun of Madame de Staël as "Corinne," a character in one of the latter's novels. The portrait was one of the attractions of the evening, along with the famous artist herself. Madame Vigée-Lebrun was in Paris for the winter, having come out of her customary seclusion for the funeral of her good friend, Marie-Antoinette. Mathieu was describing to the gathered company the entire drama of the funeral procession, which he, as a member of the royal household, had been privileged to witness.

"Under the tent on the Rue d'Anjou, the site of the future expiatory chapel, the coffins of the Martyr-King and the Martyr-Queen reposed in state. At eight o'clock this morning, Their Royal Highnesses Monsieur le Comte d'Artois, the Duc d'Angoulême and the Duc de Berry kneeled by the coffins and prayed for an hour. The proceeding began at nine. What a vast crowd it was!"

"It is remarkable how many stood along the streets!" exclaimed Juliette. "And with such intense cold! I pitied the soldiers who lined the route to Saint-Denis. They appeared to be none too pleased."

Nodding, Montmorency continued. "The remains of the King and Queen were carried by the Scottish company of the bodyguards, followed by rank upon rank of gendarmes, grenadiers, hussars, light infantry, and the National Guard. Then came the carriage of Monsieur and his sons with the rest of the Court in their wake."

Leaning against the marble mantelpiece, a melancholic and far-away expression in his dark Breton eyes, was René de Chateaubriand. He listened intently to his friend Mathieu, who had persuaded him to come to Madame Récamier's house. He preferred the ultra-royalist salon of the Duchesse de Duras, shunning at all costs the liberal salon of Madame de Staël and the Bonapartist salon of Queen Hortense. Madame Récamier's gatherings were known to be a mix of all parties. He was not surprised then to see Madame de Genlis, former mistress of Philippe Egalité, knitting quietly in a corner in her widow's weeds. He had not known her in the old days, when she shocked Paris by going to a ball at the Palais Royal in an afternoon frock, sans powder or rouge, but he had heard of it, and so regarded with curiosity the once infamous courtesan, now a writer of devout novels with prim, pursed lips.

"What of Madame d'Angoulême?" asked Madame de Genlis, her voice as purring and musical as in her tarnished youth. Her face was still unpowdered and there was no rouge on her lips or cheeks. With her hair hidden by the crêpe veils, she was the image of respectability.

"Her Royal Highness spent the day at the Tuileries, secluded in her private oratory," said Mathieu. "The same oratory which had been Madame Elizabeth's."

"It is customary after all for a daughter to refrain from attending the funeral of her parents," commented a brunette with lively features and snapping eyes. Her accent betrayed her occitan origins; regardless of her thin diamond circle and title of Crown Princess of Sweden, she remained plain Désirée Clary, the silk merchant's daughter of Marseilles. Her husband, the great Marshal Jean-Baptiste Bernadette, a general of Napoléon's, had been adopted by the King of Sweden as his heir, thus becoming Buonaparte's implacable foe. Désirée, weary of the stiff, court protocol and northern snows, had begged her husband to allow her to return to Paris for a time. She was often to be found at Madame Récamier's, where happily everyone forgot that she had become a princess.

"I thought the muffled drum rolls every few moments to be quite effective, especially in emphasizing the sense of loss," said she.

"Oh, yes, Madame," agreed Juliette. "And the music, oh, the music of Cherubini in the Basilica of Saint-Denis! What thought you of the music, Monsieur de Chateaubriand?"

Chateaubriand sipped from his glass of sweetened almond milk, the most popular beverage at such affairs. "Ah, Madame," he replied, "tears would have been wrung from a stone."

"The homily," said Mathieu, "surely evoked much lamentation. I thought the words of the Bishop of Troyes to be sublime when he spoke of the Martyr-King: 'You trampled under foot his earthly crown, and you circled his brow with a crown of immortality. When you bound his anointed hands, you showed that they alone were worthy to bear the scepter. In irons, Saint Louis was a king; Louis XVI was a king on the scaffold.'"

"I was not present when the Office of the Dead was recited in the crypt," said Madame de Genlis. She referred to the very crypt where the kings and queens of France had traditionally been buried, which was so hideously desecrated in 1793, when the graves were opened and the corpses made sport of by the revolutionaries. "I only saw the old Comte de Suzannet carried out in a faint."

"Yes," said Mathieu. "Monsieur de Suzannet, who fought in the Royal and Catholic Army of the Vendée, was particularly moved during the Office, as were others, especially when Monsieur and the Ducs d'Angoulême and de Berry prostrated themselves before the sepulchres of Louis XVI and Marie-Antoinette who have, at last, received a Christian burial after twenty-two years."

Madame Récamier was watching Chateaubriand. "Monsieur de Chateaubriand, I am eager to hear your impressions. What felt you in the burial place of so many kings?"

Chateaubriand raised his eyes as if to heaven. "I will tell you, Madame," he said, after a sufficiently dramatic pause. "I will tell you. Yesterday I went alone to the empty Basilica, and the thought of death oppressed me like a nightmare. I was overwhelmed by the vanity of human greatness. I wanted to cry to the vaulted arches which centuries and tumults have not shaken: 'Is there nothing in this nothingness?! Are there no thoughts in the dust?!' All who were buried there, who were destined to rest there, the king who hunted and the queen who danced, everything they dreamed, believed, and hoped – have all things become but phantoms like them, and like them, been swallowed up in the abyss? Is life but a moment? Yes! It is! But heaven is the reward of the victorious! Let us, then, close our eyes upon this world, and fill the maddening abyss of life with the grand and mysterious words of the martyr: 'I am a Christian.'"

Madame Récamier beamed with scintillating appreciation. She had never heard such high oratory in her own drawing room, not even from her friend Germaine de Staël. The other ladies were moved as well, and Montmorency was glad to have found a person other than himself who would instill Christian ideals into his friend Juliette.

There was a commotion at the front door and suddenly into the drawing room swept a tall, plump woman draped in an outlandish black and silver brocade gown with a matching turban, better suited to a Turkish seraglio than a Parisian salon. Long black ringlets trailed onto her bare shoulders. Her green eyes kept searching the ceiling, as her full lips gaped slightly apart. She held out her thick arms to Madame Récamier.

"Juliette!" she exclaimed, as if she had not seen her friend for many years, when in actuality they had taken tea together that afternoon.

"Germaine!" called Madame Récamier in her serene, bell-like voice. "At last you join us! Come, warm yourself by the fire. We have been discussing the funeral."

A Louis-Seize chair was pulled close to the fire for Madame de Staël by Chateaubriand; she flopped herself into it. "Merci, René," she said. "What an occasion! No one could see without emotion the obsequies of Louis XVI and Marie-Antoinette! My heart turned to the sufferings of their august daughter the princess, who has returned to the palaces of her ancestors, not to enjoy their splendor, but to honor the dead."

"Yes, too true, Madame," purred Madame de Genlis, hiding her dislike. While the two women were literary rivals, Germaine's political and philosophic novels were more celebrated. Madame de Genlis had in the past retaliated by spying on her for Napoléon.

Madame de Genlis turned to Mathieu de Montmorency. "Monsieur, it is said that Madame d'Angoulême received poor old Madame Campan most harshly, simply because Madame Campan taught the Buonaparte princesses at her school."

"I cannot say, Madame la Comtesse," replied Mathieu evasively. "I was not present when Her Royal Highness received Madame Campan."

"Is it true," asked the Crown Princess of Sweden, who once adorned Napoléon's court, "that Madame d'Angoulême, when receiving the Comtesse de Chastenay, was almost what one would call rude when the Comtesse told her of her father's death on the guillotine? They say that Madame visibly shuddered, sent the Comtesse away, and has not spoken to her since."

"Her Highness cannot bear to hear anything having to do with the Terror or the Revolution," explained Mathieu. "The very word 'guillotine' has been known to cause the princess...great distress." It was considered bad form for a courtier to speak of the health of a member of the Royal Family without express permission to do so, therefore he could not mention the several fainting fits he had witnessed in the last few months, when some poignant memory was evoked without warning in the presence of the princess. Neither could he tell of how Madame d'Angoulême jumped whenever there was a sudden noise, especially if it sounded like a bolt being drawn and a prison door creaking open.

"I question the wisdom of Her Royal Highness returning so soon to Paris," sniffed Madame de Genlis. She was well aware that the Tsar had wanted her beloved Louis-Philippe to be king, and she would have preferred to have had all the Bourbons of the senior branch stay in England. "There are many indeed," she continued, "who question even the wisdom of a public funeral especially on such a lavish scale. Was not the cry *à la lanterne* raised when part of the funeral car became caught on a lamp post?! It is a political miscalculation, for it is rubbing salt in the wounds of those who were on the other side during the Revolution." With freedom of speech restored again by the advent of King Louis XVIII, Madame de Genlis could speak critically of the regime in a manner never dared when Buonaparte ruled from the Tuileries.

"Have pity!" came a clear and gentle voice. Madame Elisabeth Vigée-Lebrun was wiping her eyes with a handkerchief. On the delicate white lace fichu at her neck was a cameo profile of Marie-Antoinette. Her black velvet gown was adorned with the Order of St. Catherine, received from the Tsar during her years in Saint Petersburg. Beneath her small turban and crêpe veil, her dark curls were tinged with silver.

"Have pity," said the artist, as pretty as in the days when she was Court portrait painter, "on the daughter of many kings, on the Orphan of the Temple. Should she be deprived of her beloved homeland, where she herself was a victim of numerous ordeals, simply because the memory of so many horrors continues to haunt her? I think not. Neither should she be deprived of at last being able to give her parents the burial befitting their rank and religion, due to the disturbance in the hearts of the assassins who remain alive and free in the France they sought to enslave with godless principles."

Madame de Genlis was silenced but a moment by this speech. "Well said, Madame Vigée-Lebrun. There is a rumor, however, that the bodies buried today were not truly those of the King and Queen, whose remains, according to one police report, were burned, and the ashes scattered in the Montmartre sewer."

"Nonsense. I myself was present at the exhumation," declared Chateaubriand, "and I was convinced of their identity, especially upon close examination of the Queen's jaw. I was reminded of the time I stood in the Hall of Mirrors at Versailles, and saw Her Majesty smile as she passed. She appeared to be enchanted with life!"

"I believe her to have been one of the worthiest persons to have occupied the throne of France," proclaimed Madame de Staël, "as well as the tenderest of mothers. When the Dauphin was torn from the arms of Marie-Antoinette, and her motherhood was outraged, the motherhood of every woman was threatened. All women were immolated in her ordeal by fire. Alas, extraordinary women are fated to be unhappy!" Her eyes closed for a brief moment, as if reflecting upon personal experience. Then they rolled ceiling-ward again. "I will never forget July 14, 1792, when the King took the oath to uphold the Constitution for the second and last time. When he ascended the steps to the altar, it was as if a holy victim were offering himself voluntarily to be sacrificed. From that day, the people did not see him again except on the scaffold."

"I must confess," said Mathieu, "that as a young man I was exhilarated by the ideas of liberty and equality as presented by the Revolution. I wholeheartedly joined what I thought to be the march of progress, the triumph of the rights of man. But when I saw my brother's lifeless corpse, my brother the priest, who had never harmed anyone, but worked tirelessly for good...when he was murdered by the mob, I saw the Revolution for what it was, a manifestation of Antichrist. I broke with it, and repented."

"I, too, so eagerly embraced the Revolution," said Germaine de Staël. "I remember watching the procession which opened the Estates-General from a window at Versailles. Madame de Montmorin, the wife of the Foreign Minister, said to me: 'You make a mistake in rejoicing. Great disasters will come of this, both for France and for us.' How true were her words! She and all her family perished on the scaffold! Six months after that procession, the Royal Family was being dragged to Paris with the heads of their bodyguards carried before them on pikes. I wonder how Madame d'Angoulême can endure to live in the Tuileries, to pass through the room where her father was humiliated and forced to don the red cap of liberty. I could not endure it if it had been done to my father."

"But where, we must ask, is her companion in adversity?" asked Chateaubriand. "Where is Louis XVII? He was not mentioned in the obsequies of today. Never did the crown press so heavily on the forehead of Louis XVI, as the badge of innocence weighed upon the brow of Louis XVII amid that life of suffering in the fortress."

Madame Récamier smiled upon Chateaubriand as she dabbed her big, brown eyes. At that moment the candles flickered, as a cold draft invaded the salon, along with a broad-shouldered gentleman in a dark suit, black cape, and wild shock of curls. It was the Duc de Berry, accompanied by his aide-de-camp, the Marquis de la Ferronnays. Everyone who had been sitting was standing in an instant. Madame Récamier left her couch and glided forward.

"Your Royal Highness honors us," she said, curtsying. Berry raised her up, kissing her hand, and motioned for the company to sit again.

"Madame, it is not my intention to disrupt the harmony of this gathering. I come to pay my respects to the great artist whose paintings grace the palaces and salons of Europe." Berry kissed Madame Vigée-Lebrun's hand even as she curtsied, as a chair was brought in from the dining room and placed next to her for him. Berry was incongruous in a drawing room, and never failed to act as if he were in an army camp. There was frozen mud on his boots, the melting remnants of which were now on Madame Récamier's carpet. Nevertheless, he could be charming when he made the effort. He praised the portrait of Madame de Staël as "Corinne."

"Oh, Monseigneur," said Germaine de Staël, "you are proving yourself to be a connoisseur as well as a soldier!"

"Ah, soldier indeed, *sacré bleu!*" laughed Berry, slapping his thigh. "Did you not hear? I was reviewing the troops and they called out: 'Long live Napoléon!' 'You liked him very much, I see!' said I. 'He led us to victory!' shouted one bold fellow. 'Of course he did, with soldiers like you!' I shouted back. Now they say 'Long live the King!' But under their breath they add: '... of Rome and his Papa!' No," he added soberly, "in spite of the demonstrations of loyalty today, we have not quite succeeded in winning the army."

"His Majesty has dealt quite benevolently with the Bonapartists," said Chateaubriand. "Even though it was Buonaparte who brought foreign armies upon us. Yet the Bonapartists and *nouveaux-riches* liberals continue to take offense at the slightest infractions."

"Yes, Monsieur," said the Crown Princess. "Many were offended by the King's banquet on August 25. The etiquette was quite formidable, and the so-called *nouveaux-riches* did not like being made to feel ridiculous and gauche when they did not know what to do."

"Yes, Madame" agreed Berry. "I admit the ceremonial was quite byzantine. Unfortunately, my sister-in-law does not permit people to enjoy themselves in their own way."

"There are too many pious, aristocratic ladies who are of sour and bitter aspect, I think," said Madame de Genlis.

"Christians must radiate joy," said Berry, "which is why, Madame Lebrun, I have longed to discuss your work with you. You have succeeded in capturing the inner radiance of soul of so many of your subjects. For instance, the famous 1787 portrait of my aunt, the Queen, with my three cousins. There is something quite spiritual about that painting, in my view, and yet it is of an entirely mundane scene."

"Mundane, Monseigneur?" asked the artist. "Mundane? I do not wish to contradict Your Highness but motherhood, while being of this world, has a strong supernatural dimension. The Queen, in the painting, sits near her jewel box, yet she wears few jewels, for her children are her most precious jewels. Joyful expectation of a new baby suffuses her face and brightens the scene. For there is a glory and sublimity in everyday life, a blessedness in our human situations, which is there for us to rejoice in, if we could but see it."

"And it is for artists like yourself, Madame Lebrun, to help us to see," said Berry, kissing her hand again. His round dark eyes shone like a child's, like the innocent child he had once been, the little boy who had loved beauty in all its forms.

"Art!" cried Madame de Staël. "Ah, but is not politics the pursuit of art, religion, morality and poetry all in one?"

"I think not, Madame," said Chateaubriand. "Politics is definitely of this world, although religion must play a part. The throne of Saint Louis without the religion of Saint Louis is an absurdity, and descends into gross tyranny when separated from true belief. Buonaparte forced religion to serve the state; now, the crown is at the service of the Church. The Altar is supported by the Throne."

"Talleyrand has done great things with politics in Vienna," said Madame de Genlis. "French prestige has been restored among the nations. It seems we have truly seen the last of dictators."

"I hope so," said Madame de Staël. "Yet a constant dread holds possession of my mind. In the evening, when the fine buildings of the city are illumined by the moonlight, it seems as though my happiness and that of France are like a sick friend whose smile is sweeter as the time of separation draws near."

"They are passing bunches of violets in the cafés," said the Crown Princess of Sweden. "Violets are Napoléon's emblem. I fear we have not seen the last of him. He can never be trusted or underestimated. Believe me, I know." In her youth Désirée Clary had been betrothed to Buonaparte, but he had broken faith with her. "I am afraid that Louis XVIII does not sleep securely at the Tuileries." She sighed.

"I believe that I shall sleep, if we do not have some music," said Juliette Récamier. "Come, Monsieur de Chateaubriand. Please join me in a duet." And the evening ended in a burst of song, as the voices of Chateaubriand and Madame Récamier mingled in a tremulous unison.

Chapter Sixteen:
The Heroine
Spring 1815

"For thou hast done manfully, and thy heart has been strengthened, because thou hast loved chastity ... therefore also the hand of the Lord hath strengthened thee, and ... thou shalt be blessed forever." Judith 15:11

Thérèse stood before a large mirror, as with her ladies she completed her toilette for the ball. It was a mild, damp evening in the south of France, one of those evenings when it is certain that winter is about to be defeated. Thérèse and her husband had gone to Bordeaux to celebrate the first anniversary of the day the white flag of royal France was raised by the citizens there because of Angoulême's presence. After a triumphal journey to the south, they had glided down the Gironde river in a huge gondola, to be greeted by enthusiastic Bordelais. Their carriage had been drawn through the streets by young men and maidens in white, as the chorus from *Iphigénie*, "Let us praise and celebrate our queen," was sung.

For a week and a half, the royal pair had been taken from festivity to festivity. Thérèse worried how shy, retiring Antoine would endure the constant public scrutiny, but he held up admirably. He was his usual awkward but kindly self, and the citizens of Bordeaux gave him their hearts. The ball that evening was sponsored by all the merchants of the great wine city, and was to be the climax of their visit.

Madame de Sérent was securing Thérèse's ostrich plumes and jewelled tiara, which rested on the tight curls and ringlets of her coiffure. A veil of *point d'Alençon* lace trailed almost to the hem of the stiff, white satin, gold-embroidered gown.

"Would Your Royal Highness like us to attach the train?" asked Madame de Sérent, hopefully. Thérèse rarely wore a train, much to the horror of her ladies-in-waiting who, like all the ladies of the Court, were required to wear one themselves.

"No, thank you, Madame," said Thérèse. She felt awkward enough whenever there was to be dancing without having to worry about tripping over a train. Madame de Sérent hid her dismay, as she motioned for Thérèse's gloves to be passed. Pauline de Béarn took them from a dressing table and handed them to Madame d'Agoult, who in turn gave the gloves to Madame de Sérent. She helped Thérèse to draw them on, with great difficulty, for they reached above the elbows, and had many tiny buttons. Thérèse was startled when, glancing up, she saw her husband standing in the middle of her bedchamber.

"Depart, all of you!" he cried, gesturing to her ladies. "I need to speak to Madame alone." His face was drained of color and eyes as bright as if he were feverish. Curtsying hurriedly, the *mesdames* rustled from the room. Thérèse nearly dropped her ostrich plume fan.

"Antoine, what is the trouble?" she asked.

He held up a packet of letters. "These despatches have just arrived from Paris. Buonaparte has escaped from Elba! He has landed on the coast of Provence, near Cannes, and is raising an army!"

Thérèse stood as one paralyzed, gazing mutely at Angoulême. He handed her the letters, and she gingerly began to glance at their contents.

"I am commanded by Uncle to go post-haste to Nîmes," said Angoulême, "where as lieutenant-general of the southern provinces I am to gather all loyal troops in the region of the Rhône, in an effort to cut off Buonaparte's progress towards Paris. They say he is already perhaps as far as Grenoble, and the soldiers are going over to him like wild fire!"

Thérèse at last found her voice. "O, that this strife may not cost rivers of French blood!" Then she began pacing back and forth, opening and closing her fan without seeming to notice what she was doing. "We shall fight until the bitter end!" she suddenly exclaimed, turning to Angoulême.

"We shall certainly fight as long as we can," he said. "I must go to Nîmes on the morrow. Uncle wants you to stay here to rouse support among the local troops. As for the ball tonight, there is no reason why we should disappoint the good citizens of Bordeaux."

"We will go very calmly, and betraying no anxiety," said Thérèse, more to herself than to him. She stopped pacing and drew a deep breath. "General Decaen is certain to be at the ball. He is commander of the regular troops at Bordeaux. He has made many declarations of loyalty to the King, but this evening we should be able to better discern his mood and intentions."

Smiling and serene, they went to the ball, which they opened by leading a *colonne anglaise*. Mercifully, they did not trip over each other's feet, and Thérèse was grateful that the scandalous new dance called the *valse*, which was said to be the rage at the Congress of Vienna, had not yet drifted as far west as Bordeaux. She had not learned to do it; Antoine surely had not, and looking ridiculous together was the last thing they needed. Alas, for the Congress of Vienna! Such great concessions were being won for France by Talleyrand and thus Thérèse felt doubly furious with Buonaparte, because with his coming, France would again be looked upon as a rogue nation.

General Decaen was at the ball and Thérèse almost caused her ladies to faint when she half-flirtatiously tapped the stern warrior on the arm with her fan, asking in her throaty voice, "Monsieur le Général, will you not dance?"

He sheepishly kissed her extended hand and led her into the midst of the ballroom for a quadrille. She smiled and attempted to make small talk, not one of her finer talents, and at the end of the dance, asked the bemused general to escort her over to the punch bowl. He had obviously not heard the news about Buonaparte.

"Your soldiers, they are devoted to the King?" she asked, lightly.

"Madame, each man of the 11th military division has sworn a sacred oath to defend His Majesty's crown and protect the personnages of Your Royal Highness, whatever the cost. The garrison of Bourdeaux has mingled with the public joy on the occasion of the visit of the worthy scions of the best kings of whom France can boast."

"I am happy to hear of it, Monsieur," she replied. "Your strong arm is one on which the King will be pleased to rely." She usually retired early from a ball, but that night she was so agitated that sleep would be impossible. When the ball ended, it would be a morning of doubts and fears.

Thérèse and Angoulême stayed until four o'clock in the morning with the good bourgeois of Bordeaux. They left in time for her husband to change from his dress uniform into battle garb and a warm military cape. Thérèse was still in her ball gown as she walked with him down to the courtyard of the palace where a mail coach was waiting to take him to Nîmes. Gleaming in the turquoise dawn was the morning star. Angoulême put his arms around her neck and waist and kissed both her cheeks several times, as well as her lips and forehead.

"He does love me," she thought. "If only ..." He traced the sign of the cross on her brow.

"*Au revoir, ma princesse*," he said, and with a single aide-de-camp he jumped into the coach, which sped away.

"May God go with you, Antoine!" she called after him. "Adieu!" His blessing and embrace caused her to be tremblingly renewed. People were saying that she was not really the Duchesse d'Angoulême, but that she was an imposter who had been exchanged in the Temple for Madame Royale. Sometimes she wondered herself. Was she the same brave girl who, when about to be released from prison, had exclaimed to her former governess: "As for me, these bitter years have not been unfruitful; I have had time to reflect before God and with my own self. I am stronger against evil."

Standing alone in the chilly morn, with a few adventurous birds calling upon the sun, she reflected within herself once again. "I am stronger against evil. I will not surrender to Buonaparte, at least not without taking a stand."

In the days that rapidly succeeded, Thérèse plunged into preparing a counter-attack. By noon of March 10, everyone in Bordeaux had heard the news of Napoléon's return. The strongly royalist citizens rallied to her side with enthusiasm, but of the army she had many doubts, although they warmly applauded her at the great banquet of the anniversary fête. Presiding at the town council, she gathered volunteers, held reviews, and made all the soldiers renew their oaths of loyalty to the Crown. How ironic that Angoulême could not be there for the festivities, but was again in danger because of Buonaparte, the rapacious eagle!

A few months before, when seeing a painting of Science and Art bestowing France upon Napoléon, she had remarked: "It was not necessary to make the gift; he was able to take it for himself." He was now trying to recover what did not belong to him. Unfortunately, some of the Marshals of France were helping him, forgetting that they had pledged fidelity to Louis XVIII. Even Marshal Ney, the "bravest of the brave," after marching to do battle with Buonaparte, declaring that he would bring the Corsican back to Paris "in a cage," ended by joining his former comrade-at-arms.

With such a major defection, the King's cause was as good as lost, and Paris was open to capture. In the meantime, Thérèse had heard no word of Angoulême, except that he had made it safely to Nîmes, where he was endeavoring to raise an army before Napoléon's troops overran the entire Rhône Valley. Amid her busy schedule, her husband often came to mind. Thérèse was saddened at how, because of his shyness, nervous tics, and habit of saying, "1...2, 1...2," when he walked, few people were aware of his profound courage and other virtues, but saw only the surface eccentricities.

Two weeks sped by and one morning after Mass Thérèse was praying in the small salon of the palace that she used as an oratory, as was her custom before attending to the business of the day. The young hussar who was acting as her adjutant could be heard walking through the several consecutive salons to the one where she knelt. Someone was with him. She raised her head, as the aide announced: "Monsieur le Baron de Vitrolles!"

Thérèse rose and turned to face one of the most distinguished ministers of her uncle, long a faithful servant of the family and an old friend of Artois'. His usually urbane features displayed a profound distress he could hardly conceal.

"Monsieur le Baron!" she exclaimed, anxiously extending her hand, which he duly kissed. "What brings you to Bordeaux?" He handed her a letter affixed with Louis XVIII's seal. She numbly glanced at the few lines penned in the King's meticulous script.

> Madame, our very dear daughter, as we inscribe this sad message, Buonaparte is at the gates of Paris. It was our desire to stay in the Tuileries and be captured, rather than flee the usurper. The fear that our presence would cause our loyal subjects to fight on our behalf and perhaps forfeit their lives has compelled us to leave the château of our ancestors for safety in a foreign land. Monsieur de Vitrolles has been granted full powers to advise you in your adverse circumstances. As your Sovereign, we invest you and our nephew Angoulême with the authority to act in our name and in our behalf.
>
> Your affectionate Uncle,
>
> Louis

Thérèse looked at Vitrolles with unseeing eyes. Distraught at the sight of her fallen and pale countenance, the helpless Baron spoke slowly and gently.

"Madame, Paris has fallen. His Majesty bade me to convey to you these words: 'Hold Bordeaux as long as you can, then do as I am doing.'"

"Where is the King now?" she asked. "And the rest of my family?"

"The King, the princes, and the Court have removed themselves to Ghent, except for the Duc de Bourbon, who is in the

Vendée with a small army, and Monseigneur d'Angoulême, who is known to be in the vicinity of Nîmes. But all is not hopeless, Madame. There are enough royalist troops to hold the left bank of the Loire. If our forces are concentrated, we may be able to hold the southern and western provinces for the King, with the administration in Toulouse. That is what we shall endeavor to accomplish, though probably too late."

"Why do you that?" asked Thérèse.

"Because it is too late, Madame, replied the Baron. "Paris is no longer ours, and its influence will paralyze our efforts. Because...."

"Do not say it!" interrupted Thérèse, with a sudden fierceness. "What is well-conceived is already successfully executed. The troops here, while not appearing overzealous, have at least the semblance of loyalty; the officers have renewed their oaths between my own hands. General Decaen, their commander, is said by some to be incompetent or even treacherous. He has pledged his faith, however, and I have been given no reason to doubt his sincerity." As she spoke, she paced back and forth, as if thinking aloud. "As for the National Guard, they would unquestionably fight to the last man for the King, which I hope they are not called upon to do. As for me, I prefer death to flight and exile! The position of the King afflicts me greatly, and I am sorry to be separated from him during these hardships. My only consolation is that perhaps my presence here may be of service to him. Come, Monsieur, we shall consult with General Decaen and his staff."

The afternoon was spent in consultation with General Decaen, who suggested writing to the Spanish and the English for help. Thérèse wrote to her uncle's ambassadors in those countries, although it pained her to ask for foreign aid. The thought of alien troops on French soil was unbearable. She had no sooner done so, than the word came that Napoléon's forces, under the command of General Clausel were marching on Bordeaux. The local troops were thrown into a state of unrest, and ripped the *fleur-de-lys* from their shakos, crying, "Long live the Emperor!"

On March 30, General Decaen begged Thérèse to leave. "Madame, General Clausel is now at the castle of Saint André de Cubzac on the right bank of the Dordogne. His cannon are aimed at the city. On the left bank are some five hundred royalist volunteers whose resistance will be useless.General Clausel is demanding that the city gates be opened to him, and he gives Your Royal Highness twenty-four hours in which to take your leave of Bordeaux."

"I refuse to leave," she replied. "Can you not make your troops fight?"

"They cannot be trusted, Madame," said the General. "And Bordeaux is not Saragossa. The citizens here are unwilling to have their fine city blown to pieces by cannon."

Thérèse spent the entire night in prayer. The sun found her still on her knees, her heart full of resignation and peace, for she knew what she must do, leaving the outcome to God. Her resolution was strengthened by a courier bringing news of Angoulême. After many difficulties, he had succeeded in raising an army of six thousand men at Nîmes, which he led to the town of Pont Saint-Esprit, occupied by the enemy. During the reconnaissance of the town, when warned that he might be captured if he went any closer, he declared: "I am near-sighted. I like to see the enemy at close range." His courage brought about the capture of Pont Saint-Esprit, and he was said to be presently marching boldly towards Valence. If he was successful again, the road to Lyons would be open to the royalist forces. He was, however, greatly outnumbered by Buonaparte's men and his danger was great.

Thérèse was determined to buy him some time. She remained firmly planted in Bordeaux when the twenty-four hours expired. General Clausel had not dared to fire upon the city. On the morning of April 1, she summoned General Decaen, whose agitation was evident.

"Your Royal Highness, I beg you to escape while you can. General Clausel has granted you another twenty-four hours in which to depart. He esteems Your Highness' person, as do I, and he is aware of how greatly you are loved by the Bordelais, but he will not wait any longer."

Thérèse's eyes flashed like steel. Decaen was beginning to sound more like Clausel's messenger boy than a general of the

King. "According to you, Monsieur le Général," she retorted, "those troops which I have been reviewing, and who have been swearing fidelity to the King, are ready to pass over to the enemy. Can you not maintain order?"

"I do not think so, Madame," he meekly replied.

"Then I shall endeavor to do so," she announced. "I wish the troops to assemble at once in their barracks. I will go and see them."

"Madame," said the General, firmly, "I ask Your Highness' permission to disobey you. I dare not give an order so fraught with dangerous possibilities and consequences ..."

"I alone am answerable, Monsieur. I take full responsibility for any...bad results." She had to discover for herself whether the soldiers were faithful or not, whatever the cost. Otherwise, if she were forced to flee, she would have no peace.

The General was close to tears. "Madame, you indubitably have not realized that ammunition was distributed to the troops this morning, by order of the government."

Thérèse dared not ask which government he was referring to: the King's or Buonaparte's. She realized that General Decaen had capitulated, and that once she was out of town, he would don the tricolor cockade.

"No more arguments!" she said, crisply. "I compel no one to accompany me. Those are my orders. I wish them to be obeyed!" General Decaen knew the matter was closed. She curtly nodded to him in dismissal.

That afternoon, dark and windy, Thérèse drove in an open carriage to the first of the local barracks, Saint Raphael. To her surprise, General Decaen accompanied her on horseback. She prayed to Saint Louis, and to Jeanne d'Arc. She was clad in a uniform with a riding skirt and military hat; her chestnut hair, bound by a simple black ribbon, flowed down her back. She entered the barracks on foot, followed by an escort of officers, volunteers, and National Guards. The soldiers were lined up in two ranks, facing each other. The officers came forward to meet her, their faces grim and unyielding.

Accompanied by General Decaen, she walked twice down the lines. The soldiers stared straight ahead; their very silence was like a shout. In the cold faces, Thérèse perceived that the seeds of the Revolution were planted deep in their souls. After all, they were young men who as children in school had been made to memorize a catechism about the greatness of Napoléon. Most of them had already fought for the tricolor flag, and had been told that it was France's destiny to spread ideals of liberty, equality and fraternity to the unwilling countries of the rest of Europe. Finishing the review, she addressed the officers.

"Messieurs," she said in her husky voice, "a usurper has taken the crown from your King. Bordeaux is threatened and the National Guard is determined to defend the city. Are you willing to assist them? Answer me truthfully, without equivocation. Yes or no – will you fight for the King?" The officers were deathly silent.

She held out her hands, her cheeks flushed. "You do not then remember the oaths you renewed but a short time ago, between these hands of mine?! If there still remain among you some men who do remember them, and are faithful to the cause of the King, let them come out of the ranks! Let them show themselves!"

After a brief pause, a few officers stepped forward, to Thérèse's amazement. "There are very few of you!" she called to the others. "It does not matter. At least I know who is dependable!"

"Your Royal Highness may count upon us to defend her person and watch over her safety," replied the officer commanding the battalion.

"The question is not my safety, but the service of the King!" she retorted. "Will you serve him, or will you not?"

"We have no desire for civil war! We will not fight our brothers," said the same officer.

"No, never!" they all exclaimed. "We will not shed the blood of our brothers!"

"Your brothers!" she cried. "You forget that they are rebels!" Turning her back on them, she swept from the barracks and drove to the next one, where she was met with rudeness and hostile shouts of "*Vive l'empereur!*" "Long live the Emperor!"

She gazed at them with silent, pleading dignity, then withdrew. "Now we shall go to review the troops at Château-Trompette," she said, calmly.

"Madame, I beg you," pleaded the weary General Decaen as he handed her into the carriage. "Do not go to Château-Trompette. They love Napoléon there, too. They will receive Your Highness with hostility and rudeness. It is too dangerous! Please escape from Bordeaux before General Clausel puts a cannon ball through the city gates. Furthermore, he has orders from Napoléon to arrest you."

"Monsieur le Général, you are impertinent," she said, as the carriage rolled forward. "I will go to Château-Trompette. My own Angoulême regiment is there."

At the gates of the fortress, sentries barred her carriage from entering. A non-commissioned officer was waiting to inform her that she could not enter with her escort, but if she entered it must be alone.

"No matter," she said. "I will go in alone." Her officers and attendants paled with fright, but said nothing. General Decaen insisted on accompanying her. She strode into the barracks where the soldiers were lined up in battle formation. The commander presented himself before her with a reluctant salute.

"What is your reason for refusing admittance to my escort?" she demanded of him.

The surly man replied in sarcastic tones. "I hold my commission from the King and I can take no orders but the King's."

"Do you intend to fight for the King's cause?" she asked.

"No, Madame," sneered the officer. "Circumstances are changed. Besides, our soldiers will not fight against Frenchmen."

"Monsieur, you are insolent." She faced the other officers, who had gathered around her. "If that is the reason that prevents you from doing your duty, promise me at least to remain neutral, and allow the National Guards and the royal volunteers to defend themselves."

"No, Madame!" cried the commander. "If the National Guard attacks, we will throw ourselves upon it!"

Thérèse almost choked on the tears that were rising to her eyes. "Then you no longer regard as Frenchmen those who remain faithful to their honor. Do you all think as your commander does?!" she cried.

"Yes!" they shouted, but one officer stepped from the ranks and presented her with his sword.

"Your Royal Highness, I am Captain Cosseron de Villenoisy and I will not increase the number of traitors. Rather, I will die for the King than be false to my oath."

The other soldiers grew disorderly and threatening. Fumbling with their swords and muskets, they shouted, "*Vive l'Empereur!*"

"If only you would reflect for a moment, you would follow my example!" Captain Villenoisy called back at them. They shouted all the louder. "*Vive l'Empereur! Vive Napoléon!*"

"Madame," whispered General Decaen, "please let us depart."

Thérèse glared at the soldiers who were insulting her with the same look she gave Berry when he swore and Angoulême when he slurped his soup. One by one, they fell silent. She quietly walked over to the Angoulême regiment.

"Do you not know me? Is it possible that I appeal to the *régiment d'Angoulême* in vain?" Her pleading was met with hostile silence. "Have you forgotten your Prince, and me, whom you called your Princess?"

Tears began to stream down her face. "Oh, God! It is cruel! After twenty years of exile and sorrow, to be exiled once more! I have never ceased to love France! I am French! But you are no longer children of France! Begone from my sight!"

As she started to slowly walk towards the gate, they began to play a long drum roll in salute. She was not certain whether they were actually saluting her or mocking her. Captain Villenoisy followed protectively. General Decaen's face showed great relief when they exited the fortress and she was once more in her carriage. It would have been a terrible humiliation for him if one of the officers had decided to arrest the Princess in the name of the Emperor. The Bordelais would have never forgiven him.

"It is all over," Thérèse said to General Decaen, who trotted beside her. "The troops have definitely refused to fight. I thank God for that, because if they had promised me their loyalty, they would not have kept their word, and Bordeaux would have been the victim of my mistaken confidence."

"Will Your Royal Highness now consent to depart?" asked the General.

"I will leave Bordeaux tonight. Tell General Clausel he may enter the city in the morning. I must first say farewell to our loyal National Guards and royal volunteers."

A review of the faithful troops was held, in full view of General Clausel's cannons. Standing up in her carriage, in spite of their protests, she made them promise not to fight so that they would not all be killed. They began to shout, "Death to Decaen!" and a riot almost erupted. General Decaen had disappeared. Thérèse went up onto the balcony of the palace. Her presence and her words restored calmness and order to the disappointed soldiers and citizens.

"Gentlemen!" she called to the loyal officers. "You answer to me for the safety of the town! Keep your troops in line, and preserve Bordeaux from all disorder! From this moment, it is in your hands!"

"We swear it!"

"Ah!" cried Thérèse. "More oaths! I have heard enough of them. I want to hear no more. The niece of your King gives you her last command. Obey it!"

Thérèse and her entourage left Bordeaux in a swirling rain shower, darkness, and mud. And yet the voices of the saints seemed to pierce the curtain of rain. There was always hope. If only she knew if her husband was safe. They traveled all night, their coaches slipping and bumping along in the blackness. By morning they reached Pauillac, with its port and the ship which would take them away from France.

Thérèse hardly thought about where they were going. She heard Mass in the parish church, then went to board an English ship called *The Wanderer*. Her military escort assembled on the pier to bid her farewell, as the rain continued to pour. Where were the vast crowds? Where were those who had flung themselves weeping at her feet? Never again would she lavish a single, splintering thought on human honor and praise. It was all less than nothing. The faithful few begged for some tokens, and she gave them the feathers from her bonnet, and the green and white ribbons which bound her hair.

"Bring them back to me in better days!" she cried, the wind and rain blowing around her. "And Marie-Thérèse will show you that she has a good memory, and that she has not forgotten her friends at Bordeaux!"

The vessel carried Thérèse over stormy waters to Spain, and then across the treacherous channel to England. It was a rough and tumultuous crossing; most of her ladies were morbidly seasick, besides being distressed over their belongings left behind at the Tuileries for the Buonaparte clan. When Thérèse and her party finally arrived at the royal French embassy in London, she was greeted with the news that the Duc d'Angoulême had been captured, and was a prisoner of Napoléon Buonaparte.

Chapter Seventeen:

The Retribution

Summer 1815

"To what shall I compare thee? Or to what shall I liken thee, O daughter of Jerusalem? To what shall I equal thee, that I may comfort thee, O virgin daughter of Sion? For great as the sea is thy destruction: who shall heal thee?" Lamentations 2:13

The shutters were closed in the rooms of Madame in the Pavillon de Flore of the Tuileries palace, as was the custom during the hottest, sleepiest time of the day. The indolent, afternoon glow illumined the boudoir in spite of itself. Madame sat stiffly on her favorite sofa by the window, alone and swathed from head to toe in black crêpe and sooty voile. Scarcely a month had passed since the battle at a village called Waterloo in Flanders. Thousands of Frenchmen had died and foreign armies overran France, pillaging, looting and terrorizing the citizens. While Buonaparte had been soundly defeated by Wellington, it was the French nation which bore the weight of retribution. A heavy tribute had been levied and territories had been confiscated. As for the Duchesse d'Angoulême, her heart was sundered; all earthly happiness had fled.

Thérèse was waiting for a certain illustrious visitor who had asked to call on her that afternoon. Tsar Alexander himself was coming to beg her intervention in the case of the first general who had betrayed his oath to the King and joined with Buonaparte. General Labédoyère's defection had created a domino effect in the army; one by one many of the marshals and commanders had gone over to the enemy. The peace which France had begun to enjoy was shattered; one of the bloodiest battles in history had raged, and the Bourbons were restored to Paris behind four thousand foreign troops. One of the foreign leaders had been known to openly brag to Madame de Staël: "France is our prey." The British and Russians remained more or less under control, but the Austrians and Prussians were behaving dreadfully. The Prussians threatened to blow up the Iéna Bridge, until Louis XVIII declared that he would come over and sit on it.

Worst of all were the royalists who had stayed faithful to the King, risking exile and death. They triumphed over the defeated Bonapartists, demanding the execution of their leaders. The respectable ladies of the Faubourg Saint-Germain were the most bloodthirsty and vengeful of all. France was hideously divided. While Thérèse had already intervened for many traitors, she could not save every single one.

The King and his family once again inhabited the Tuileries, hastily vacated by the Buonaparte clan, just as the Bourbons had hastily vacated it a hundred days before. The Buonapartes had ripped the *fleur-de-lys* off the bees on the carpets; everything had been scrubbed, dusted and polished within an inch of its life. Since the King's return, the dust was settling again; the inefficiency of the cumbersome and overstaffed royal household was generating its usual dirt and grime. Thérèse, however, felt less at home than ever before in the Tuileries, like a poor pensioner in a public hotel with an irate landlord who might throw her into the street at any time. Someday she must find some other place to live.

In England, she had been plunged into mortal anguish for Antoine's safety. By all accounts, he had conducted himself very bravely. His small, determined army had valiantly fought against the superior rebel forces, so that even among his adversaries there were those who admired his valor. Surrounded by the enemy, Antoine decided to surrender in order to spare his followers, on the condition that his men would be allowed to go their way unmolested. General Gilly agreed to the terms, as long as the Duc would take a ship for Spain. Antoine journeyed as far as Pont Saint-Esprit, where he was arrested by the imperialist General de Grouchy, who imprisoned him in a house, soon to be surrounded by a Bonapartist mob clamoring for the Duc d'Angoulême's life. Antoine wrote to Louis XVIII: "I am resigned and worry only about those whom I hold dear. I fear neither death nor imprisonment, and shall willingly accept at the hands of God whatever may come."

Louis XVIII had ordered Thérèse to stay in England rather than join him in Ghent. He wanted her to keep an eye on Louis-Philippe, who was residing in London with his family, contrary to the specific command of the King. Louis-Philippe, extremely haughty in his disobedience, had proclaimed that he, as first Prince of the Blood, was not to be capriciously ordered away from the safety of London so as to be a "figure in a procession or in a drawing room," which was his disdainful description of the refugee Court at Ghent.

"His London residence has become the center for all royalists who are dissatisfied with Louis XVIII," said Mathieu de Montmorency to her one day at the French embassy, where she was staying.

"I know it," said Thérèse, "but the Palais Royal had become that even before Buonaparte's return. The Duc and Duchesse d'Orléans give many lively parties, with a complete disregard for proper etiquette, and they will receive almost anyone. So, of course, they are very popular with the malcontents among the *nouveaux-riches*. I do not blame Madame d'Orléans, but rather Mademoiselle Adelaïde d'Orléans, Louis-Philippe's sister. She takes very much after her father, Philippe Egalité."

Thérèse remembered, although she did not mention it to Mathieu, how Adelaïde had once practically been betrothed to Angoulême, but the Revolution prevented the marriage. Besides, she Thérèse had been privately betrothed to him at her mother's insistence. If Adelaïde had married Angoulême, then she would be first lady of the Court of France, instead of a middle-aged woman living with her brother's family.

If Thérèse had married Louis-Philippe, then perhaps she would now be the mother of the plump, rosy-cheeked, delightful Orléans children whom she saw at the christening ceremony at Notre Dame Cathedral last September. As she held her squirming little godson, the Duc de Nemours, over the sacred font, she felt within her heart dueling emotions of religious fervor and human sorrow at her barrenness. She ignored the condescending glances of Adelaïde, whose insolent expression seemed to say: "You may appear to be married, but you are really just an old maid, and everyone knows of it." Devotion suffused Louis-Philippe's and Marie-Amélie's every gesture and look with regard to each other. What a contrast to her bleak marriage with Angoulême!

Marie-Amélie of Naples was the daughter of Queen Maria Carolina, Marie-Antoinette's sister. Marie-Amélie was as blond and fair as any Habsburg, although her father was a Bourbon, just like Thérèse's father. She was quiet, simple, and pious, and Thérèse longed to be her friend, but a barrier of politics prohibited such amity. Furthermore, Louis-Philippe's presence always made Thérèse ill at ease. She avoided him as much as possible in London, even though she was supposed to be spying on him.

"There are some of the Allies, such as the Tsar, who continue to push for Louis-Philippe to be made King of France," Thérèse said to Mathieu de Montmorency.

"Madame's presence in London, specifically in Your Highness's dealings with the House of Orléans, will show to all that the Duc is not viewed as a foe, nor considered to be a rival for the crown," advised Mathieu. So Thérèse visited a few times with the Orléans family, and the encounters would have been unbearably awkward if not for Marie-Amélie's sweetness. Louis-Philippe was often present. As at Monceaux, she sometimes caught him looking at her as if he wanted to ask her something, but did not dare. The Duke of Wellington favored Louis XVIII, so he was restored a second time to the throne.

Word finally arrived that Angoulême's life had been spared. Napoléon ordered him to be released, as if not considering him a great enough threat to send before the firing squad, while, remarking that the Duchesse d'Angoulême was the "only man in her family." Antoine sailed to Spain and made his way to Madrid.

To his overwhelming distress, his loyal soldiers were brutally massacred by Protestants in the Cévennes region.

Then news arrived of Waterloo; one by one the Bourbons were reunited at the Tuileries. Artois continued his former receptions in the Pavillon de Marsan, replete with delicate pastries and luscious ices, and the ultra-royalists flocked to him. Berry reestablished his mistress and her children on the Rue des Mathurins.

Thérèse hoped that the reunion with her husband would mark a new beginning for them, but after an initial flush of ardor he retired most evenings to his own apartments as before, and she would not see him again until he joined her for breakfast, when they fell to arguing over politics. To avoid such unpleasant scenes, Thérèse began inviting various cabinet members and courtiers to breakfast with them, so that often fifteen places were laid at the table. Angoulême favored the liberal politics of Louis XVIII, that of maintaining revolutionary institutions with the veneer of royalty and tradition, while Artois, Berry, and Thérèse urged, in varying degrees, a return to the structures of the *ancien-régime* as much as was possible.

A scratching at the door signalled that the Tsar had arrived. The Duc de Sérent entered and announced in solemn tones: "His Imperial Majesty, Alexander, Tsar of all the Russias!"

In walked a red-haired giant with keen blue eyes and an oval face, similar to that of his grandmother, Catherine the Great, the empress whose name Marie-Antoinette would not permit anyone to mention in her presence. He was the son of Tsar Paul, to whom Thérèse had said as a little girl at Trianon: "You are a nice man." He had also been a mercurial man; his son deposed him and, it was rumored, may have plotted his murder. The Tsar made a partial inclination to Thérèse; she returned it with a half curtsy. She could not help remembering how he had twice evicted them from the palace at Mitau in Courland; she and her uncle had trudged through the snows of Lithuania as a result.

"Your Majesty honors me by your visit," said Thérèse politely. "May I offer you some tea? Or sherry perhaps?"

"Thank you, no," said the Tsar. He was well-known for his dislike of the senior branch of the Bourbon dynasty, and had described Thérèse as looking "like a governess." He was, on the other hand, vocal in his admiration of the Bonapartist princesses, especially the late Joséphine, and Joséphine's daughter, Hortense. In Vienna last winter, he had protested the Requiem Mass that Talleyrand had insisted on having for the soul of Louis XVI, branding it as "anti-revolutionary." "I have come, Madame, to beseech Your Highness' clemency, begging you not to make any more widows."

"I myself have almost become a widow in this latest war, in this blatant violation of all treaties, and arrogant breaking of all oaths on the part of Buonaparte and his adherents," replied Thérèse. "I am weary of men who place their personal glory and gain ahead of that of their country. Your Majesty is, of course, referring to the case of Général Comte de Labédoyère, a peer of France?"

"Indeed," affirmed the Tsar. "Labédoyère is a brave man who should not be punished for following his conscience."

"His conscience? Did his conscience tell him to violate his oaths of loyalty to his legitimate monarch?" Her eyes burned with icy intensity. The Tsar would not be so clement to a Russian rebel. "Very well," she said, "but if he is permitted to follow his conscience, then I am compelled to abide by mine."

"Your Highness, where is your heart?" asked the Tsar. "Labédoyère was captured only because he returned to be at the side of his wife, who was about to give birth. His wife implores you, his aged mother implores you, Madame Krudener the holy woman implores you and I, Alexander Pavlovitch, implore you."

Thérèse winced at the mention of the false mystic, Madame Krudener, an eccentric woman who had gained complete ascendancy over the Tsar by her equivocal prophecies, and by calling him "The White Angel" and "Savior of All." She fascinated the salons of Paris with her descriptions of Heaven and pseudo-biblical speeches, which veiled her contorted and warped doctrines.

"Your Majesty," said Thérèse, in the kindest, softest tone possible to her raspy vocal chords, "I forgive the general his treason. I have the deepest pity for Madame la Comtesse de Labédoyère, for her mother-in-law, and for her baby. I have interceded already on behalf of many husbands of such families. You must realize that even the King is limited in these matters, for we have an elected assembly with which to contend, most of whose members are intent upon punishing all traitors. The General in question was the first to abandon the Royal cause and unfurl the tricolor flag, leading to the defection of several others, including Marshal Ney, and the eventual capitulation of the entire Nation to Buonaparte, bringing Your Majesty and other monarchs from your own countries to lose thousands of your subjects in a wasteful and bloody war. No one forced Labédoyère to take an oath of loyalty to the King. Other marshals, like Marmont, have kept their oaths, even at great cost to themselves. I pity Labédoyère's family, but I also pity the families of all the young men who died by reason of one man's ambition and vainglory."

The Tsar took a step forward. His presence seemed to fill the room. "I beg of you, Madame, your indulgence for the Général. Plead for him with the King, who will listen to you."

"I am sorry. It is out of the question," said Thérèse, sadly.

The Tsar paled with anger and consternation. "Why this excessive severity? What good purpose can it serve?"

"Sire," replied Thérèse, "justice requires it. The punishment for treason must be awe-inspiring."

"Madame, if justice claims its rights, so also must charity."

"Charity!" exclaimed the princess. "Charity is not to be distinguished from weakness." She remembered the several times her beloved father, in his compassion and charity for the common people, had refused to allow his guards to fire upon the mob, even when the Royal Family's lives were in danger. There were many who accused him of weakness. Thérèse thought him to be a saint. Who was Alexander Romanov to lecture her on charity?

"You are wrong, Madame," said the Tsar. "Charity wins and melts hearts."

She wrung her hands in a burst of agitation. Her father's charity had been rewarded with martyrdom, but it had melted few hearts. Her mother's goodness and charity had failed to win the hearts of the cruel men who came to drag her little boy from her arms. Yet the mantle of charity had made her parents who they were. She did not reply.

"Madame," said the Tsar. "You are the daughter of a monarch who was renowned for his supernatural clemency and power of forgiving offenses. If he were here…."

Thérèse cut him short, her voice falling like an axe. "It is because of foresworn traitors like Labédoyère that my father is *not* here!"

The Tsar appeared to be troubled. "Very well, Madame," he replied, and the Autocrat of All the Russias gave her a slight, stiff bow, taking his leave.

A week or so later, Thérèse and Antoine travelled to Bordeaux to complete the festivities that had been interrupted by Buonaparte's return. Thérèse was relieved to leave Paris. It was loathsome to her that the ex-priest Fouché, who had voted for her father's death and was responsible for several mass murders, had been forced upon them by the Allies as Minister of Police. It was he who had drawn up the lists of those who were to be executed or exiled for supporting Napoléon. According to rumor, when Fouché took his oath of office to the King, Louis XVIII reminded him of his vote for regicide in 1793, and Fouché whispered: "It was the first service I was able to render Your Majesty." Fouché brought with him his fawning protégé Decazes, who hovered near the person of the King, overflowing with flattery and guile.

The citizens of Bourdeaux hailed the Duc and Duchesse d'Angoulême as a hero and heroine. Portraits of Thérèse, and a few of Antoine and the King, were everywhere in the town, usually surrounded by white bunting trimmed with green for the House of Artois. The Bordelais offered her a magnificent gown, in exchange for the one she was wearing, which she gave to them. They cut it into tiny pieces to distribute as souvenirs. Maidens dressed in white with green sashes and crowned with lily wreaths ran ahead of their carriage, scattering flowers in the street. They were reunited with all their friends in Bordeaux, especially the faithful National Guards and royal volunteers. The Angoulêmes received a similar welcome in other towns and villages throughout the south of France.

Thérèse's heart was too heavy with thoughts of all who had died for her to take pleasure in any of it. Besides, the festivities had a dark side. In some places in the south there were anti-Bonapartist riots, where royalists turned on those officials and personnages who had deserted the King, and many atrocities occurred. Antoine had to again leave celebrations in his honor for the restoration of law and order, particularly along the Spanish border, which the Spanish army was raiding. The "White Terror," as the vengeful demonstrations were called, horrified both of the Angoulêmes. Meanwhile, General Labédoyère had been shot, and in the minds of many the Bourbon Restoration became forever linked with reactionary heartlessness. Other executions came in the months that followed, including that of Marshal Ney, the "bravest of the brave."

"When will blood cease to flow on French soil?" Thérèse sighed to Heaven.

In September, when she returned to Paris from her southern tour, Berry met her with the most urgent and astonishing tidings. A young man, calling himself "Charles de Navarre," had been found in Brittany. He claimed to be none other than Louis XVII, King of France.

Chapter Eighteen:

The Stranger

Spring 1816

"Be not silent: for I am a stranger with thee, and a sojourner as all my fathers were. O forgive me, that I may be refreshed, before I go hence, and be no more." Psalm 38: 13-14

"But I tell you, I am old enough to be her father!" ranted Berry in exasperation. "She is only seventeen, and I am thirty-eight!"

"Thirty-eight! Do you think that you are not old enough to be settling down with a wife?" asked Thérèse, sarcastically.

"I am settled down!" Berry stamped on the cobblestone square in front of the palace of Versailles where they were walking. May-time drifted around them on the breeze from the gardens, laden with hyacinths, narcissus and tulips. Thérèse and her brother-in-law had come to Versailles to inspect the ongoing renovation of the Royal Chapel, which Louis XVIII planned to have reconsecrated, along with several other churches, including Saint Geneviève in Paris. On such a fine day it was a treat to be away from the Tuileries and Paris and relax in the sunshine and verdant air.

It was also refreshing to be away from Decazes' spies and have a conversation out in the open. Thérèse had managed to persuade her uncle to send the nefarious regicide Fouché to Dresden as an ambassador to the Court of Saxony. However, Fouché's unctuous protégé Decazes had taken his place as Minister of Police, and had fleetingly acquired a tremendous influence over Louis XVIII, who treated him almost as a son. Decazes surrounded the King with liberals. Thérèse, Artois, and Berry united against his coterie: Thérèse, in firm, gentle protests; Artois, in none too subtle intrigues; Berry, in displays of temper. Decazes retaliated by making "anti-ultra" speeches of an inflammatory nature.

Berry was even more out of sorts at the fact that he was being pressured by all to forsake Amy Brown and marry Princess Marie-Caroline of Naples, granddaughter of the King of the Two Sicilies. Louis-Philippe's wife Marie-Amélie was her aunt, which would strengthen their ties with the House of Orléans, while Thérèse was her first cousin once removed, so from a dynastic point of view the marriage was highly favorable. Thérèse had her personal doubts concerning the match, for it was said that the princess, after her mother's early demise, had been spoiled by her eccentric, raucous old grandfather the King, who thought it amusing to sell fish on the wharves of Capri and Palermo with little Caroline at his side. As for her grandmother, Queen Maria Carolina, although she was Marie-Antoinette's sister, it was well-known that she had dabbled in freemasonry. Thérèse dared not breathe any of this to Berry, who was angry enough at having a bride foisted upon him.

"Berry, please try to understand that France needs examples of virtue and family life in high places. What with Talleyrand living with La Dino, his nephew's wife, and yourself, living with Amy Brown…no!" She silenced him as he opened his mouth to protest. "You are not married to Amy. It is an illicit union in the eyes of the Church. We have had arguments on this subject for years. It is time you accepted the truth of the matter. Your children can never inherit the Crown and, Berry, France needs an heir. You must beget a son. I … I shall never have one!"

Berry's anger rapidly dissipated in the face of the acute distress of her last statement. His round, brown eyes regarded her with gentle pity, as he considered the hidden sorrow she had borne for so long.

"Well, I suppose I shall have to make the best of it," he said softly, "just as you have."

She ignored his last, near-whispered comment. "The Church and the Nation are both built on stable family life, on the enduring ties of a sacred vow," she said. "There are far too many divorced and separated persons in France for there to be a solid foundation for a happy, thriving populace. Thank God, divorce is being outlawed this year. It is our duty, yours, mine, and Angoulême's, to lead the way by setting a good example."

They had strolled along through the flowery Parterre du Midi, past the orangerie on the south side of the great palace, and were approaching the Parterre d'eau, where fat, bronze children, nymphs, and gods, portraying the twelve months, played or lounged by the water. She realized that if she had not grown up with such statues, she would be quite disconcerted by the pagan aspect of it all. The true results of the so-called "Enlightenment" were neo-paganism and death.

"There is something else I have been wanting to speak to you about," said Thérèse. "Captain Artain has returned from America."

"Did he find Lazare Williams, the Indian chief?" asked Berry.

"Yes, and it is quite extraordinary, and... and disturbing, too, I must say. The man known as 'Lazu Williams' is alleged to have been brought from France as a child of ten by Monsieur and Madame Jardin, and adopted by the Iroquois chief, Thomas Williams. He is now a Protestant minister and lives in a remote wilderness called 'Lake George' in New York state. Can you imagine our Charles as a Protestant minister?"

"He is not Charles," declared Berry, shortly.

"Do not be so ready to dismiss him until you have heard the rest of the story," chided Thérèse. "He is described to me as fair-skinned and greatly resembling the princes of our house, which would almost prove to me that he is an imposter, since Charles greatly resembled Maman, although people do change as they mature. They say he has the Habsburg jaw, as well as the Bourbon ear, large and full at the top with a pointed lobe – like yours."

"Is there a defect in one of the ears, like Charles'?" asked Berry, pulling his ear.

"I do not know. Captain Artain did not mention it in his report. Williams does have a crescent mark from a smallpox vaccination on his arm, and a scar on his forehead, where he was ostensibly struck by Simon."

"Any scar above the lip from the rabbit bite?"

"No."

"There. You see?"

"Perhaps. Whoever he is, he was considered *imbécile*, almost simple-minded, when he first arrived in America. He has fits of insanity in which he scribbles French words and strange numbers. After a head injury his brain became 'clearer,' and he was able to remember portions of his childhood, most of which is blotted out. He has quite forgotten how to speak French. He identified a drawing of Simon the cobbler and claims to have lived in a palace. He receives money on a regular basis from an Indian called Jacob Vanderheyden, who corresponds with none other than Talleyrand."

"Talleyrand!" exclaimed Berry, as they circled the fountains of Latona. "Oh, Thérèse, Talleyrand's involvement in anything should prove to you the unsavory nature of it. I have long suspected that the Williams boy was a decoy sent to America by Uncle or Talleyrand, or some such scheming scoundrel to draw attention away from the more viable pretenders such as Hervagault, or even that new phenomenon, Charles de Navarre. Perhaps Williams is French, perhaps of noble but illegitimate birth, somehow connected with Talleyrand, who sends money for his support. The connection of Talleyrand with the Williams matter is of interest, however, for he and La Dino have become quite intimate of late with Louis-Philippe and Mademoiselle Adelaïde. Did you know that Louis-Philippe has been investigating the fate of Louis XVII?"

Thérèse gasped. The mystery of the questioning gaze of the Duc d'Orléans was thus explained to her. Berry continued.

"Even if Lazare Williams is Charles, he is mentally unfit to reign, and is happier left in the forest with his Indian friends. A Protestant who cannot speak French is truly a King that would please the ladies of the Faubourg Saint-Germain," he sarcastically concluded.

"No, of course not," lamented Thérèse. The mist from the fountains fanned her face as when she was a child; the joyful sound of splashing water soothed her as in the days when Maman scolded her for not being polite enough to people. "But what think you of Charles de Navarre?"

"I think him to be another tool of Decazes, of that fat, lying, odious *parvenu*, in his campaign to make the ultra-royalists look ridiculous. They say the pretender is rude, crazy and vulgar," said Berry, forgetting that there were many who applied similar terms to himself. "I know he is described as looking Austrian, with bright, piercing eyes, and an aquiline, if somewhat twisted, nose. They say he has a prodigious memory and an extensive knowledge of the events of the war in the Vendée. But that does not preclude the fact that he is also a drunken lout, who comes from New Orleans where he worked as a baker, and before that from Brazil, where he was a convict or an adventurer or worse. Nevertheless, Papa is planning on retaining the lawyer Monsieur Méjean for Charles de Navarre's defense, if only in order to annoy Uncle, and Decazes. The King, well, he shouted at Papa the other day, saying, 'You conspired against Louis XVI, you conspire against me, and in the end you will conspire against yourself!'"

"Your father is a rascal, but I am glad he is hiring a lawyer for the poor, lost man," said Thérèse. "I do not believe Charles de Navarre is a tool of Decazes. If he were, why does Decazes try to interfere with my attempts to contact the pretender? Why am I being pressured by Uncle to show no interest in the matter? Anyway, I received a letter from Charles de Navarre. Whoever he is, he has received some upbringing, for his letter was courteous, yet full of inaccuracies about our family. It is reported that he speaks English, Spanish, Italian, German and Russian, and behaves like a prince to his followers, who flock to his side at Rouen, where he has recently been holding court. I will watch from afar how events unfold. I think Decazes will soon clap him into prison, especially after Madame de Tourzel, Charles' governess, wept when she saw him, and held him in her arms."

"Really?" asked Berry, incredulously.

"Yes, that is what I heard, although I have not discussed it with her face to face. I shall watch to see how events unfold, and shall prepare a list of questions for the gentleman. I will try to send them along to him with a brave and trusted servant, like Baron Hue, or Chevalier Turgy."

Berry was silent for a moment. "Has Montmorency found Nicole Hervagault yet?"

"No. It seems she has disappeared, although there are no records of her death and burial to be found anywhere. Mathieu's agents will comb every registry in every parish church in France if they must. So many such records were destroyed during the Revolution and Buonaparte's wars. Furthermore, there is the strange matter of the peasant, Martin 'the Visionary' of Gallardon."

"Is he the crank who claimed to see an angel in a field, wearing a top hat?" asked Berry.

"Yes. I know it sounds absurd, but he insisted he had a heavenly message for the King. He came to the Tuileries and was closeted alone with Uncle. Martin told him of incidents that were known by almost no one but the King himself. Uncle is quite shaken by it, although no one knows exactly what Martin revealed to him. Perhaps it has something to do with my brother's fate. Or perhaps God himself is about to intervene in these matters, especially where Decazes is concerned. Mathieu says that Decazes has Robespierre's papers, papers which prove that Charles escaped from the Temple. Decazes is using the information to control the King."

"No, Thérèse, no," Berry contradicted her. "I do not believe that to be the case. "There… there are things you must know. For one thing, I think Charles de Navarre was Decazes' prod to make Uncle officially declare Louis XVII dead last January. Charles de Navarre, and the secret treaty…."

"Secret treaty!" she exclaimed. "What secret treaty?"

"The treaty Uncle made with the Allies in 1814. It stated that he would for two years be publicly known as 'Louis XVIII,' but in reality he would only be a regent for Louis XVII, until your brother's death could be proven. Even now, they cannot find a

206

patch of dust in the Sainte Marguerite cemetery on which to place a monument. Because he is not there...."

"How did you discover any such treaty?" asked Thérèse.

"Through my own attempts at espionage, by which I also came across a certain letter in my father's papers, a letter from Uncle, exulting over the death of your father, and the inevitable death of your brother!"

They had come to the Grand Canal, where the grass spread as a green carpet between the water and the tall oaks, planted in rows. As a girl she had often watched her Papa canter under those trees, and had ridden beside him as soon as she was old enough. She could not find words to reply to Berry.

"Furthermore, Thérèse, last winter, Barras came to see me. He came to offer information if I would intercede for him, and keep him from being exiled by the law of January 1816, which banishes all regicides from France. I promised to do so. He told me that it is certain that Charles was strangled by Simon on the night of January 18-19, 1794. Simon hastily buried Charles in the moat, without a shroud or coffin, where he was found seven years later by Comte d'Andigné. The Simons left the same day, and Charles was replaced by a sickly, dumb boy; perhaps by several, consecutive boys in the year and a half that followed. Simon committed the foul deed at the behest of Chaumette and Hébert, with Robespierre's approval. Barras knew of it, being in cahoots with Robespierre at the time, and Fouché did too, I daresay. Remember that Fouché hated to walk past the Temple, and begged Buonaparte to tear it down, which he did in 1811. Fouché probably told Decazes of the murder, and also of the fact that the boy's devoted Uncle Provence was corresponding with Robespierre, and may even have encouraged them to do away with Charles. I maintain that it is this knowledge that Decazes is holding over Louis XVIII's head, and thus has all France in his vise, just like... like a dictator." Berry slammed his fist into his palm.

Thérèse soaked in the sun's brightness and the sky's blueness, the scent of lilac and hyacinth, as she attempted to draw a veil between the spring glory around her and the dark turmoil which stormed in her heart.

"I do not trust Barras," she said, when her voice returned. "He is a lying and perverse scoundrel. Anyhow, there are rumors that Joséphine, when she was his mistress, conspired to rescue my brother from the Temple! But it is all ... all rumor!" She trembled and gasped for breath. "Last winter, when they found the lost, last letter of my mother to Tante Babette, hidden by Robespierre in his secret papers...she begged that I help my brother...I have failed, failed miserably. But perhaps he is beyond human aid, except through prayer...O God!"

Berry stroked her hand. "I am your brother now, Thérèse, your own brother, and you are a dear, faithful sister to me."

The trees swayed in the breeze, as the sun disappeared behind some clouds. They walked on, until they were practically at the edge of the canal, far from the palace.

"Well, Berry," said Thérèse, having mastered herself. "If Louis-Philippe is so interested in Charles' fate, it means he is nourishing strong hopes of the succession. If anything were to happen to you or Angoulême, he would be second in line for the throne...and he is such a liberal! What a disaster for France! He would reverse all the good we are trying to accomplish, such as abolishing divorce, restoring ancient orders of chivalry, like the Knights of Molta; the return of the Jesuits, and putting the throne at the service of the altar of God. You must marry Princess Marie-Caroline and have a son, who will be a truly Christian monarch."

At that moment, footsteps crunched on the gravel behind them. Thérèse assumed it was a member of one of their retinues coming to assure their safety. She turned and beheld a gentleman in his early thirties with fair hair. His suit was so worn, it almost could be described as ragged; the innate dignity of the wearer put to flight the notion that he might be a beggar. He was a stranger, yet vaguely familiar. Of medium height, he had a full mouth, with pouting lower lip; large, deep-set blue-grey eyes, an aquiline nose, arched eyebrows, and a high forehead. Rooted to the ground, she felt her hair stand on end. Was he another phantom of her mind? He held out his hand to her.

"Sister, my sister!" he pleaded gently.

Thérèse was surrounded by memory as if by a whirlwind. She saw the distant moment a little blond boy with blood-shot eyes had held his hand out to her, saying "Sister" in the council room of the Temple tower, surrounded by drunken guards and leering officials, where minutes before she had heard him accuse his mother of incest. The pity, horror, confusion, rage and disgust she had known in that hour of darkness returned in a flash, as if the hour were one and the same.

"Go away!" she shouted convulsively to the stranger. "Go away! It is you…you who are the cause of the misfortunes of my family!"

Berry's eyes widened in horror and consternation as his hand flew to his sword, but the stranger had already run into the wood. He soon vanished among the rows of trees. Berry put his arm around Thérèse, who was bent over as if from nausea, and they hurriedly departed from the gardens of Versailles.

Chapter Nineteen:
The Princess of Sicily
Summer 1816

> *"Hearken, O daughter, and see, incline thy ear; and forget thy people and thy father's house ...*
>
> *"Instead of thy fathers, sons are born to thee: thou shalt make them princes over all the earth." Psalm 44: 11, 17*

On June 15, 1816, the Court of France was assembled in the forest of Fontainebleau to await the bride from Naples. The translucent leaves were sparkling with summer. Beneath a cloth of gold canopy, King Louis XVIII sat in a blue velvet armchair, beads of perspiration on his forehead, legs so swollen that standing was impossible. The stocky bridegroom-to-be, in a clean, pressed uniform, glittering with medals and gold braid, wore a solemn expression of resignation and indifference, yet his usually unruly curls were combed and pomaded, and he was manfully trying to hold in his paunch. Artois stood next to his son, beaming and chatting with his ultra-royalist cronies, completely ignoring Decazes, who lounged behind the throne, admiring his well-manicured hands. Thérèse, stiff and rigid on the King's right, stood in full court attire, including towering plumes and a new gown that Artois had talked her into buying. She also ignored Decazes, while trying to disregard her husband's incessant twitching. Angoulême, blinking his eyes and shifting from one foot to another, could not seem to still the muscles in his face and shoulders, but otherwise he looked rather distinguished. The Duc de Blacas was consulting with the Neapolitan ambassador and his staff, going over the various protocols of the ceremonies of the day. Chateaubriand glowered at Talleyrand, whom he had begun to consider his nemesis, as the latter was amusing La Dino with anecdotes of the *ancien-régime*. The Orléans family was lined up next to Talleyrand, the Duchesse nodding graciously to all, while Mademoiselle Adelaïde smirked disdainfully and whispered to Madame de Boigne, who nodded in agreement. Louis-Philippe moved about among the courtiers, shaking hands with everyone, as if on a political campaign.

Nervous anticipation seized Thérèse, for she had longed to have a sister. She remembered Baby Sophie, lying motionless in her cradle like a wax doll. Her adopted sisters, Ernestine and Zoé, had been separated from the family during the Revolution for their safety, and later begged to come into exile with her, but had been forbidden by the revolutionary government. She had searched for them as soon as she returned in 1814, but Ernestine had died a few weeks before, and Zoé was a cloistered Visitandine nun. She tried not to allow her expectations of her new sister-in-law to soar, for she had known disappointment so often.

A flourish of trumpets signalled the approach of the bride. "They say the princess has been well-received throughout France," said Artois to his old friend Talleyrand, who had strolled over to pay his respects. "A truly amiable young lady she is, and the people flock to her in all the towns and villages through which she has passed." He lowered his voice. "Let us hope that she learns to love my son, and that he comes to love her."

"Ah, Monsieur, in a marriage of convenience, as in politics, one must not love too much," replied Talleyrand. "Love confuses. It lessens the clarity of one's vision, which is not to the Nation's advantage. Furthermore, love evaporates at the first sign of trouble."

"Oh, Talleyrand, always the cynic!" said Artois, shaking his head. "I think we usually do not love anyone enough, except perhaps ourselves and then, too much. A loving marriage benefits everyone, but a loveless one sows seeds of sorrow." He knew too well of what he spoke. "And here she is!"

The gilded coach had slowed to a halt. The soldiers who lined the route saluted as Princess Marie-Caroline was helped down. In an instant, a petite, elfin creature, clad in white muslin, came running towards them. Rich lace trailed from the crown of her beplumed bonnet, with streaming, pale blue satin ribbons tied in a bow under her left cheek. Beneath the bonnet were masses of burnished gold ringlets, framing a slender face, dominated by large blue eyes. A pointed, delicate version of the Habsburg jaw gave a determined air to her winsome sweetness, and the mouth would have been a perfect rosebud except for the protruding lower lip of her imperial ancestors.

Thérèse thought that Caroline's eyes were rather shifty and that she carried herself more like an acrobat than a princess, for she danced as she moved, with an air of overflowing exuberance. How different was she from Thérèse at seventeen, who had possessed all the nerves and pensiveness of one newly released from years in the lonely tension of a prison. Artois gazed at the young girl with a far-away expression, as if he were recalling a scene in the distant past.

The King, however, was very much in the present moment. As Caroline curtsied and kissed his hand, he raised her up, embracing her cheeks, and with hand on his heart proclaimed, "Child, I am your father."

He presented her to Berry, whose lips brushed her dainty hand. "This is your husband," said the King, and a broad smile slowly brightened Berry's indifferent demeanor. Caroline returned his smile; her teeth were still pearly and intact. The King placed her hand in Berry's.

"This is your brother," Louis XVIII motioned to Angoulême, who was blowing his nose.

"And this is our angel." Caroline faced Thérèse, who towered over her, looking particularly haughty and unangelic. The two women quietly regarded each other for a few seconds, as battle was joined.

There were those who said afterwards that the Cathedral of Notre Dame de Paris was never as resplendent as at the wedding of Berry and Caroline three days later. Garlands and bouquets of roses and lilies mingled with clouds of incense that ascended to the high, vaulted ceiling. The streaming colored light mingled with the nuptial chants and ethereal chords of the organ. The blond child-bride in her silver gown and pearly diadem which had belonged to Marie-Antoinette, radiated enchantment, like a princess in a fairy-tale. Berry, in his white satin wedding suit and ermine-lined mantle of the Order of the Holy Spirit, was too stout for the rôle of the ideal, storybook prince, but at least he appeared to be relishing the festivities.

The couple spent their honeymoon at the Elysée Palace, which the King had given them for their own. It soon became the center of social life in Paris, upstaging even the Palais Royal, for the Duc and Duchesse de Berry gave brilliant receptions and balls, featuring artists and musicians whom they sponsored. They shared an appreciation for the fine arts, as well as for the theater, and society in general, and many a night they danced until dawn. They danced and entertained through the summer until Martinmas, when Caroline announced, to everyone's overwhelming joy, that she was with child.

Thérèse was glad to see the happiness of her brother-in-law with his young wife. She was, however, appalled at Caroline's disregard of royal etiquette, at her mutilation of French grammar with a thick, persistent Sicilian accent, at her wild gesticulations when she was excited, and, worst of all, at her insistence of walking up and down the Rue de Saint Honoré, while going in and out of shops like a private person. Thérèse, in the manner of an older sister, attempted to explain to Caroline how a Princess of France was supposed to behave. Caroline listened, wide-eyed and pert, only to burst into giggles before Thérèse was out the door, as she watched her ladies mimic Thérèse's ladies and their solemn curtsying.

As for Thérèse's entourage, they incessantly commented upon the deplorable manners of Caroline's household, on their low-cut dresses and transparent stockings. Caroline, in spite of her lack of decorum, or maybe because of it, soon became quite popular among the bourgeoisie of Paris, while people began to refer to Thérèse as "Duchesse Cain," for she had not yet received "Charles de Navarre," whom many believed to be Louis XVII.

Chapter Twenty:

The Assassination

Winter 1820

"Our steps have slipped in the way of our streets, our end draweth near: our days are fulfilled, for our end is come." Lamentations 4:18

By the evening of Quinquegesima Sunday, Carnival was at its height. In the streets and boulevards of Paris, drunken students frolicked and sang, leaping aside to avoid the coaches bearing costumed merrymakers on their way to masquerade balls. In the silent churches, candles illumined the altars where the gold monstrances shown like stars for the Forty Hours devotions that were attended by the pious. In the Tuileries palace, the Duchesse d'Angoulême was putting on her black mantilla before going to join the Forty Hours in the palace chapel. She intended to spend most of the night there in reparation for the sins of Carnival and the Nation, as well as for her personal infidelities and transgressions.

As she arranged her veil in front of the mirror, it struck her how little she had altered since returning to France six years before. At forty-one, she looked much the same as at thirty-one, with a few faint lines around her eyes and mouth, but otherwise her skin was firm and smooth; her neck, swan-like, and her chestnut hair, abundant. While the dewiness of youth had left her due to the hardships she had endured, after a certain point she had ceased to age.

The painter Augustin had portrayed her as another radiant Gabrielle d'Estrées, the beloved of Henri IV, during those few joyful months when Thérèse thought that at last she was expecting a child. Her skin glowed as the symptoms multiplied; she ignored the smirks of the courtiers, who thought that her hopes of motherhood had brought on a hysterical pregnancy. They turned out to be partially correct, although it was the onset of the change of life that made her think that at last she had conceived. In a wave of bitter humiliation, her hopes were crushed, and she doubled her prayers.

Thérèse was not alone in her sorrows. In the royal crypt at Saint-Denis there were two tiny coffins near the sepulchres of Louis XVI and Marie-Antoinette. Caroline had lost two babies, a girl in 1817 and a boy in 1818; all France had wept with her. Last September, however, she had finally given birth to a healthy child, a daughter called "Marie-Thérèse-Louise d'Artois."

"After the girl comes the boy," said Caroline to Berry. The new baby, in the meantime, was the delight of the Bourbon family and their Court, particularly of Artois. She was a serene little angel with thick golden curls, and a shy but enchanting smile. Thérèse loved to embrace her plump cheeks.

Thérèse was about to leave her room when the door opened, and Berry and Caroline came bounding in, both arrayed in rich, evening attire and bursting with child-like joy.

"Caroline is with child once again!" exclaimed Berry. "Oh, my sister, rejoice with us!" He picked up Thérèse and swirled her around.

"Put me down! Oh, Berry, why do you always behave like an idiot!" scolded Thérèse, laughing in spite of herself. "But, these are such happy tidings! I will have much to thank the good God for tonight." She kissed Caroline's cheeks.

"This time, it will be a boy!" said Caroline. "I have been making novenas to Saint Louis. He appeared to me in a dream, and showed me a beautiful son who shall be mine!" She was fervent in her exuberant, Neapolitan way.

"Then, my sister, you must not dance so much," cautioned Thérèse. Last night, she was told, Berry and Caroline were still waltzing at four o'clock in the morning. "Where are you off to this evening?"

"To the Opéra!" said Berry. *Carnival de Venise* is being performed. But we shall not stay for the final act. My little wife needs her sleep. *Bon soir!*"

"*Bon soir!*" And the buoyant pair departed as quickly as they had come.

In moments, Thérèse was kneeling on a *prie-dieu* before the King of Kings, hidden in the Sacred Host exposed on the candle-illumined altar. Pauline de Béarn knelt close by. Thérèse's ladies took turns keeping vigil with her by the hour; few possessed the stamina to pray all night at her side and she did not expect them to do so. On normal days, she usually rose for prayer before anyone else in the morning and therefore kindled the fire in her room, so as not to inconvenience the servants. (Antoine did the same in his apartments.) She prayed for Caroline's unborn child, that he would be the son and heir they needed and that his life would not be tragic like Charles'. She could not help thinking of the pretender, "Charles de Navarre," who was currently imprisoned at Mont Saint Michel in Brittany. She had thought at first that perhaps he was the stranger who had confronted her in the park of Versailles in 1816, but he had been in Normandy at the time.

She had never discovered the identity of the man; he was not the poor lunatic arrested in front of the Tuileries in 1817, ranting that he was Louis XVII. Her every attempt to contact Charles de Navarre was blocked by Decazes; appeals to her uncle the King were in vain. She sent Turgy, a trusted former servant of her father, to Rouen with questions for the pretender, but he was intercepted by the police. Decazes also prevented Françoise Desperez, the heroine of the Vendée, from seeing the alleged prince. Then in the summer of 1817, a certain Vicomtesse de Turpin de Crissé was permitted to see Charles de Navarre, and she recognized him to be none other than Mathurin Bruneau, the son of a cobbler whom she had sheltered in her château of Angrie in 1795, when even as a boy of ten he had pretensions of grandeur.

In September of 1818, Charles de Navarre was put on trial, and while in the witness box behaved like a madman, calling Louis XVIII an "imbecile" and the Duchess d'Angoulême, "Victoire." He was declared insane and incarcerated. His followers claimed that the man who appeared at the trial was not Charles de Navarre, but a police stooge, and that the real pretender had not been given a trial. He was spirited out of the country and sent to a penal colony in America. Some even claimed that Jean-Marie Hervagault and Mathieu Bruneau, alias Charles de Navarre, were one and the same person, using different *nom-de-guerres*. Thérèse engaged a trusted official, the Marquis de Messy, to investigate the matter for her, but even her conversations with him somehow became the subject of police reports, as she later discovered. The lawyer of Charles de Navarre, Monsieur de Méjean, unfortunately was eventually revealed to be a spy of Decazes.

Berry became more convinced that Charles de Navarre was a false Dauphin planted by either Decazes or Louis XVIII to draw attention away from evidence that the former Comte de Provence had conspired with the revolutionaries in 1794 to do away with an inconvenient little nephew. In 1817, a former commissioner at the Temple prison named Damont, came forward with a lock of hair he had taken, or so he claimed, from the sad, young prisoner who died on June 8, 1795. Thérèse was shown the coarse, chestnut lock. It did not belong to Charles, whose hair was blond and fine. It reinforced Berry's belief that Charles had been strangled and replaced with another boy. He began to be less and less discreet in his complaints and accusations against Decazes and the King. However, in June of 1819, Widow Simon died at Les Incurables. On her deathbed, in the presence of the Blessed Sacrament, she reaffirmed her original testimony that the Dauphin had escaped and survived.

In the autumn of 1819, Berry had come to visit Thérèse, visibly distressed. "They have kidnapped Georges!" he cried.

"Georges! Who is Georges?" asked Thérèse.

"My son! Amy's and mine!" Berry collapsed into a chair, weeping. "The police came to the house on the Rue des Mathurins and took Georges away, I do not know where! This is Decazes' way of taking revenge upon me for criticizing him! I will go to Uncle and make him give Georges back, if I have to – to kill him!" Berry ran from the room.

Less than an hour later, the Duc de Blacas came for Thérèse. "Madame, please, the King … I think perhaps he will have a stroke!" Thérèse hurried to the royal apartments, and before she reached them she could hear Berry and her uncle shouting at each other. She entered in time to see the King choke and begin to turn purple, before falling into a fit of unconsciousness. Thérèse thought he had died, but it was only a mild stroke, from which he recovered in a few weeks.

She helped to care for him with the greatest difficulty, for he had abandoned his veneer of charm, and become surly and bitter. One evening, in the presence of the Court, he fainted in his chair. She flew to his side, kissing his hand and patting it.

Suddenly, he regained his senses, and with mysterious strength flung her roughly away, saying, "Hum! Playacting! They hate me! They have come only to make sure I am dead!" Face down on the rug, Thérèse had never missed her beloved Papa so much.

By the last Sunday before Lent, fourteen-year-old Georges had not yet been restored to his mother, and Thérèse prayed desperately for the situation. She was glad that Berry had found happiness with Caroline, especially over their Louise and the new baby on the way, to brighten his mind amid his anxieties over Georges. After about an hour or so of adoration of the Blessed Sacrament, Thérèse heard footsteps behind her. She thought it was Madame d'Agoult coming to relieve Pauline, but then a hand touched her shoulder. Glancing back, she saw her husband. In spite of the dimness of the chapel, she could discern an expression of acute agitation on his face.

"Princess," he whispered. "Come – there has been…an accident."

Thérèse genuflected and followed Angoulême out of the chapel. In the hall was one of Berry's gentlemen-in-waiting, Monsieur de la Ferronnays. He was as pale as death.

"Oh, no," thought Thérèse, "Caroline has had a miscarriage." But then she saw that Angoulême was weeping.

"It is Berry," he choked. "Something bad has happened…. Come, we must go to the Opera house."

Angoulême wrapped his cloak around her and before she could utter a word they were in a carriage driving through the bitter night. Monsieur de la Ferronnays haltingly described to her the events of the preceding hour. After the first act of the ballet, Caroline was overcome with weariness, so Berry had walked her down to the carriage so she could go home. After helping his wife into the carriage, Berry handed in her lady-in-waiting. Out of the darkness there rushed an assassin with a long dagger, which he buried in Berry's heart up to the hilt. Caroline leaped from the carriage, which had not yet driven away, and reached his side as he fell to the ground. Berry pulled the weapon out himself, and a fountain of blood splashed upon his wife and the paving beneath him.

"I am a dead man," he uttered. "A priest…Come, my wife, let me die in your arms!" They carried him back into the opera house, to the small salon behind his box.

When Thérèse and Antoine reached the Opéra, blood still dripped on the steps and carpet of the entrance. The crimson trail led them upstairs to where Berry lay on a sofa, his head on Caroline's lap. His face was gray and damp with perspiration; his lips, purple and foaming, emitted a steady trickle of blood, which Caroline vainly kept wiping away with her handkerchief, already as saturated as her white satin gown. Berry's arms trembled in a sudden spasm.

"Caroline, are you there?" he cried.

Bending over him, she said, softly, "Yes, Charles, I am here. I will never leave you." She gently slipped to her knees beside him so he could see her face.

Artois knelt at his son's feet, his mouth gaping, his brown eyes as wide and uncomprehending as a child's. Next to Artois stood his confessor Abbé Latil, Bishop of Chartres, whose lips moved quietly in prayer. Berry had already confessed his sins, although in the past he had always declared that he could not endure Abbé Latil.

The room was crowded with weeping attendants and whispering physicians, who were deliberating whether or not to bleed the hemorrhaging prince. Through the glass doors between the salon and the box itself, one could see dancers on the stage, and the strains of blithe music rose and fell, as carefree as Berry himself had once been. Everything had happened so fast that the audience and performers were unaware of the disaster, except for Louis-Philippe, Marie-Amélie, and Mademoiselle Adelaïde, who had rushed over from their own box.

Thérèse stumbled to her knees at Berry's side, taking his icy hand.

"My sister," he gasped. "Farewell. Pray for me...."

"Always," she said, kissing his hand. "Have courage, my brother, but if God calls you to Himself, ask my father to pray for France and for us."

"My children..." he said, almost inaudibly. "Amy and my children...I want to say good-bye to my children."

Caroline directed one of her attendants to fetch Berry's children. He quickly departed. It seemed an eternity before he returned with Madame de Gontaut, the royal governess, carrying sleeping Baby Louise in her arms. Caroline took the child, and held her close to Berry for his embrace. The infant continued her serene repose on a cushion nearby.

Standing hesitantly in the entrance of the salon was a lady of exquisite beauty, tendrils of long, fair hair escaping from beneath the hood of her cloak. It was Amy Brown. Seeing Caroline, she took a step back, but the two young girls who were with her ran forward, sobbing, "Papa! Papa!" Artois gazed with sad fondness on the golden-haired granddaughters he had never before seen.

Berry kissed his daughters. "My wife," he said to Caroline. "Please, take care of them."

"Yes…yes," said Caroline, dishevelled and tear-streaked. "I promise you I will be a mother to them."

"We shall adopt them," assured Thérèse. "And we shall find Georges." She glanced back at Amy, who wept in the shadows. Berry's older girls, Charlotte and Louise, kissed Baby Louise with great affection.

"Hear me!" cried Berry, with sudden force. "Hear me, everyone!" The room fell silent. "I ask pardon of all whom I have offended. I beg forgiveness from the people of France for the public scandal I have given. May God have mercy on my soul!"

He closed his eyes, and his breathing became short and shallow. Abbé Latil administered the Sacrament of Extremunction, then began to recite aloud the seven penitential psalms and prayers for the dying. "Go forth, O Christian soul.…" Everyone fell to their knees, but hours passed, and the end had not yet come. His breathing became more labored, as Berry drifted in and out of consciousness, inquiring, in his lucid moments, when the King would arrive, for he had a boon to ask of him. At length his face became pinched, as from his taut lips escaped moans of agony. Caroline's nerves gave way and she screamed. Her ladies led her from the room, but she insisted on returning as soon as she regained her composure. Meanwhile, the police had captured the assassin, a demented maniac. They brought him up for identification and he shook his fist at Berry.

Around five o'clock in the morning, the King lumbered into the salon. Behind him was Decazes. Louis XVIII's face was white and immobile. Berry's eyes flew open.

"Sire," he sputtered, "pardon the man who stabbed me."

The King nodded and embraced him. "We will talk about it by and by. Calm yourself now; you are not as ill as you think."

"O Holy Virgin!" cried Berry, "Intercede for me! O my country! Unhappy France!"

The last hour soon expired. He looked up at his father. "At least I take with me the thought that the blood of a man will not be shed for me after my death," said Berry. Then he was seized by a convulsion. His eyes rolled and as his head jerked back, he breathed forth his soul. The King leaned forward and closed his nephew's eyes. Artois, taking the corpse in his arms, wept inconsolably. Decazes stepped closer to look at the prince's body.

"*Assassino!*" shrieked Caroline. "Take that man away! The sight of him is repulsive to me! Do not let him near my husband! He is the real murderer!" Decazes hastily withdrew as Caroline collapsed.

Thérèse and Madame de Gontaut the governess took Caroline and Baby Louise back to the Elysée Palace. As she regained consciousness, Caroline's hand reached out as if for her husband, and when she could not find him, she insisted on being taken to his room. Kneeling by his bed in her blood-stained dress with Baby Louise in her arms, she wrapped herself in Berry's dressing-gown, and gave herself over to sorrow.

The murderer was a barrel-maker named Pierre Louvel, to whom Berry had once shown a kindness. At his trial, Louvel insisted that he had killed the Duc de Berry at the instigation of Decazes. It was also whispered that he claimed to be Louis XVII. Most people dismissed him as a madman. In spite of Berry's last prayer, he was sentenced and guillotined.

Chapter Twenty-One:
The Miracle Child
Autumn 1820

"I was nursed in saddling clothes, and with great cares. For none of the kings had any other beginning of birth." Wisdom 7:4-5

Georges was found by the Duc de Blacas, he never said where, and returned to his mother, who received a pension. Berry's daughters were ennobled by the King, and brought to live in Caroline's household. As for the young widow, cutting off her lustrous blond locks, she announced her desire to take her little family and return to Sicily.

"I want to go as far as possible from this place where they have killed the only person who could make me happy," she declared. Artois persuaded her not to leave France and, after weeping with her over Berry, urged her instead to go to the country palace of Saint Cloud for a time. Caroline did so, withdrawing into seclusion with Berry's daughters and her attendants. She drew up plans for a memorial chapel at Rosny, her country estate, where she hoped to inter her husband's heart and have perpetual Masses offered for his soul.

After Berry's death, Artois and Thérèse threw themselves at the King's feet, begging him to dismiss Decazes. "Either he goes or I go!" threatened Artois. "I will not continue to live in the Tuileries near that man!"

The King reddened in anger, and burst into a tirade that resounded through the château.

"Sire," sobbed Thérèse. "God has sent our family so much sorrow; permit unity at least to console us. Join with us, and do not deny us this favor." The King relented, and Decazes was sent to London as an ambassador.

At Eastertide, it was thought safer for Caroline to move to the Tuileries for the duration of her pregnancy, so that they could all take care of her. Artois gave her several rooms and a gallery in the Pavillon de Marsan, which she draped entirely with black crêpe, covering even the furniture and the mirror in black cloth and permitting only yellow wax candles. She rarely left the gloomy quarters except to go to Mass, where she prayed for Berry's soul with tear-stained face and shorn head hidden by thick black veils. Yet the safety of the Tuileries proved to be illusory. Caroline had only begun to settle in when gunpowder was exploded underneath the floor of Thérèse's bathroom, which someone mistook for Caroline's. A few days later, an infernal machine exploded beneath Baby Louise's bedchamber. In each case, no one was hurt, the damages were easily repaired, and the perpetrator of both crimes was apprehended. Caroline remained calm and brave in spite of the outrages, and her unborn child was unharmed. However, the royal governess, Madame de Gontaut, a tall, plump motherly lady of courage and character, was shaken at the attempts on the life of her little charge who had not yet seen the light of day. Thérèse, too, was convinced that the forces of evil did not want Caroline's child to be born.

The summer passed without any more disturbances, and the Court was able to repair on occasion to the country air at Saint Cloud. The King did not like to be long away from the Tuileries, because a gypsy fortune-teller in England had once told him that he would "return to the Tuileries but not die there." In September, as the days of Caroline's confinement approached, the Court was once more established at the Tuileries. The official witnesses of the birth were to be the Maréchal Duc de Coigny and the Maréchal Duc d'Albuféra. Their task was to testify that the baby was truly Caroline's and that no imposter had been smuggled in.

In the cool, damp darkness of the morning of the Feast of Saint Michael the Archangel, Thérèse was awakened by the sound of one hundred and one guns being fired from the barracks of the Royal Bodyguards.

"A prince has been born!" she exclaimed. Leaping from her bed, she threw on some clothes, and dashed out of her bedchamber. She ran into Angoulême, who was coming to fetch her, and together they went to Caroline's apartments in the Pavillon de Marsan. The windows were wide opened, for Caroline had fainted, and the yellow candles flickered in the breeze. The room was crowded with doctors, maids, courtiers, and all of Berry's friends and former aides-de-camp. Angoulême and Thérèse led them all into the adjoining antechamber, so Caroline could have the peace in which to recover, and there they found the royal governess with a tiny, sleeping baby in her arms. He was clean and wrapped in a blanket. Madame de Gontaut was so overwhelmed with happiness that she was unaware of being still in her dressing-gown and nightcap, with her petticoats hiked up, revealing her ankles and thick black stockings.

"Oh, Madame," said the governess to Thérèse in a whisper. "Monseigneur came without any warning at all, and the official witnesses could not be found in time. I had to drag in two sentries from their posts. In the meantime, it was all very awkward for Madame de Berry, for she remained attached to the baby, who wailed. Finally, Monsieur le Duc d'Albuféra arrived and the physician was able to cut the cord. It is no wonder that Madame fainted."

"No wonder," echoed Thérèse, amazed, relieved and overjoyed at once, as she gazed upon the pink baby with his fine, downy hair.

"Where is he? Where is my Henri?!" Caroline's voice called from the next room. Madame de Gontaut hurried to her bedside, placing the baby in her arms. Caroline smiled at Thérèse and Angoulême, who stood nearby.

"This is Henri," she sighed in near rapture, flushing with the glowing loveliness that only a young mother can possess. Thérèse was speechless. Angoulême blinked frenetically, then donned his pince-nez spectacles so he could better regard his tiny nephew.

At that moment, the King, Artois and Blacas arrived. Artois embraced his daughter-in-law and new grandson. The Duc de Blacas drew something that sparkled out of a velvet pouch and handed it to the King, who took the child in his big arms, saying, "This is mine."

He handed Caroline a bouquet of diamonds. "This, Madame, is yours." Everyone was silent as Louis XVIII moistened the baby's lips with Jurançon wine, an old tradition of the Bourbon dynasty. "He is the Duc de Bordeaux," announced the King, "in honor of the first city to fly the white banner in 1814." Then Louis XVIII gave Henri to Thérèse. The Duc de Bordeaux was sleeping, but suddenly he awoke. His bleary, baby eyes looked up into hers, and he became her own.

She sensed that someone was leaning over her shoulder in order to better view Henri. She turned her head and saw that it was Louis-Philippe. Behind him was his sister, Mademoiselle Adelaïde. They were the only people in the room who did not appear to be happy.

"I hear that there were no witnesses," said Mademoiselle Adelaïde.

"I beg to differ," said Caroline, who had heard the remark. "Monsieur le Maréchal Duc d'Albuféra was present."

Louis-Philippe turned to the Duc. "Monsieur le Maréchal, I call upon you to declare what you have seen. Is this child really the son of the Duchesse de Berry?"

Thérèse and the royal governess glanced at each other in a moment of shared outrage.

"Tell him, Monsieur le Maréchal!" cried the Duchesse de Gontaut. "Tell him what you saw!"

The old Maréchal Duc d'Albuféra drew himself up and with immense dignity convincingly described how he had found the baby at half past three in the morning, still attached to his mother. "I swear it on my honor! I am more certain that the Duc de Bordeaux here is the child of the Duchesse de Berry than I am that my son is the child of his mother." Orléans was silent. He begrudgingly offered his congratulations to Caroline, and then walked away. As he did so, he muttered something unkind about the baby to one of Caroline's ladies, causing the woman to burst into tears.

"You must pardon my brother," said Mademoiselle Adelaïde to Caroline in barely-veiled acid tones. "One does not easily lose a throne for one's children."

Louis XVIII took Henri and went to the window, where he showed him to the crowds that had gathered beneath Caroline's apartments. The acclamations were deafening. Then he gave word for the entire Paris garrison to enter and meet the new prince, as Thérèse held her nephew, her face so deliriously bright that she was hardly recognizable.

As the day was about to break, the entire court assembled in the chapel for a Mass of Thanksgiving, concluding with a glorious *Te Deum*. "Now it is time for Henri to be greeted by his future subjects," said the King, who carried the little one in his arms once more. With his wobbly legs he stepped onto the balcony of the Pavillon d'Horloge. Thérèse prayed that he would not drop the baby. The plaudits and cheers resounded against the wide façade of the palace. The beams of the rising sun fell upon the King and Henri.

"My children," proclaimed the King in his strong, reverberating voice. "Your joy increases mine a hundredfold. A child is born to us all! He will love you as I and all mine love you!"

The people responded by shouting: "*Vive le Roi! Vive le Duc de Bordeaux! Vive la Duchesse de Berry!*"

At three o'clock in the afternoon, the palace doors were thrown open and 15,000 Parisians trooped in to see the Duc de Bourdeaux. In the evening, the citizens rejoiced in the streets, with revelry, dancing, laughter, and tears, as the wine flowed. Caroline asked that her bed be pushed against the window so she could watch the festivities. The entire garrison of Paris had gathered outside of her window to give her a "bouquet" of fireworks. Leaning out the open window, her short hair curling beneath her frilly nightcap, she clapped at the starbursts which brightened the sky above her. All of Paris was illuminated by torches; it all seemed to be part of some mythical, enchanted kingdom.

The Papal Nuncio, Monseigneur Macchi, had called earlier in the day, and blessing Henri, dubbed him *l'enfant du miracle*, "the miracle child." "This child of sorrows, of regrets, of remembrance is also the child of Europe by the blood of many of its royal families," he solemnly pronounced.

When Henri-Charles-Ferdinand-Marie-Dieudonné d'Artois was christened in the Cathedral of Notre Dame de Paris, the pillars of the venerable building were hung with gold and silver gauze. Artois and Thérèse stood proxy for the godparents, the King of Naples and the Hereditary Princess of Naples, who could not be there. The governess, Madame de Gontaut, in a silver gown and with a long train placed the infant on the high altar, dedicating him to God, then presented him triumphantly to the French people.

The day was not without its shadows. While the carriage in which Thérèse was sitting with the King pulled up in front of the Cathedral, the carriage with Henri, which had already halted, started to jerk forward as the horses were startled. The train of Madame de Gontaut, who with Henri in her arms was trying to step out, was caught up in the moving carriage. A footman quickly disengaged Madame's train, as the governess stumbled and fell forward, to be caught by Louis-Philippe, who happened to be standing by. Thérèse saw the near disaster as her heart flew to her mouth. But a greater danger lay ahead.

Before leaving for church, a mysterious stranger gave Madame de Gontaut a letter addressed to her with the dire words: "Be on your guard at the Pont Neuf, where the carriage will stop, and take care of the prince." Madame de Gontaut was in a panic, but nothing happened, except that a bouquet was presented by the Dames de la Halle. However, after the christening, when the carriage with Henri was rolling into the courtyard of the Tuileries, the guards were forced to fall back so as not to be crushed, and at that instant, Thérèse saw a woman throw a scroll into the vehicle. It hit one of Madame de Gontaut's broad shoulders, from which blood spurted. It had just missed sleeping Henri's head. Madame de Gontaut was happy to take the blow for him.

The entire nation continued to rejoice in the new prince for months and months, as he grew plump, rosy-cheeked and robust, full of smiles and gurgling laughter. The brilliant young poets, Alphonse Lamartine and Victor Hugo, wrote poems dedicated to "the miracle child." Several royalist associations saved enough money to purchase the exquisite Château de Chambord, which they presented to Henri as a gift. As for Thérèse, she could often be found in the nursery, caring for him hours at a time, especially when Caroline was shopping, or visiting her aunt Marie-Amélie. When she sang to him, he did not seem to mind her rasping voice, but smiled contentedly in his sleep.

Chapter Twenty-two:
The Judgment
Summer 1824

> *"We must all be manifested before the judgment seat of Christ." 2 Corinthians 5:10*

It was tea time at Villeneuve l'Etang. Green, sleepy summer had taken possession of the garden at the country villa of the Angoulêmes, and the Duc's spaniels slept contentedly in the shade. Antoine and Thérèse sat in wrought iron chairs by a round table covered with a cloth and laden with a silver tea service, fruit tarts, and cream. The cream in the small silver jug was from the cows that Thérèse had just bought for Villeneuve l'Etang, which she planned to turn into a model farm like her mother's Trianon.

She and Antoine had never had a house of their own before, not in twenty-five years of marriage, and they behaved with almost child-like delight over their small, brick, ivy-covered villa, old enough to be romantic but with a newness that required no extensive repairs. Thérèse had never decorated a personal dwelling before, and in doing so she instinctively sought the uncluttered simplicity and the well-constructed furniture that she had known at Trianon, embroidering chair covers herself, and laying down rugs that she had worked, for like Marie-Antoinette she excelled at tapestry.

Her knitting bag was next to her chair, for any rare moments of leisure she would spend on the endless stockings, caps, shawls, mittens and scarves for the poor and orphaned. She knitted everyday except Sundays and feastdays, when she would instead do fine embroidery on vestments and sacred linens, or else cut out the wax seals from official documents in order to give to impoverished persons, who were able to sell them to collectors.

The daily edition of the *Journal des Débats* and other newspapers were stacked neatly beside her tea cup. She read them every day, making it her business to be informed of the social and political climate. Someone in the family had to do so; the King could not, since he was slowly dying of gangrene. As for Artois and Antoine, they never bothered with the gazettes. Thérèse would relay the headlines to her father-in-law when he visited them in the afternoons, but he looked forward far more to finishing his long-running chess game with Antoine than to hearing the news. An ivory chess set was at Antoine's place, with the red pieces resembling Buonaparte and his court and the white ones resembling the Bourbons, with Thérèse as the White Queen. Antoine was studying his white pieces as he sipped his tea, trying to decide upon a strategy that would push the Red King (a tiny bust of Napoléon) into another Waterloo. With his spectacles perched on the bridge of his Bourbon nose, his striped trousers making his thin legs seem longer, his grey silk coat and striped cravat sprinkled with a few crumbs from the fruit tart, Antoine did not have the semblance of being the warrior prince whom everyone now referred to as "Generalissimo."

A year and a half earlier, the Duc d'Angoulême led an army into Spain to help King Ferdinand VII, who was on the verge of being swept from his throne by the liberals. Antoine won a great victory at Trocadero, the name of which was then given by the King to a park in Paris. When he returned in triumph to the capital after refusing all honors and titles the King of Spain wanted to bestow upon him, and trying to mitigate the fierce reprisals levelled by the Spanish Right against the Spanish Left, the entire the Royal

Family assembled on the balcony of the guard room overlooking the Tuileries gardens. Thérèse, with three-year-old Henri in her arms, stood on the King's right and glowed with joy as her husband knelt before Louis XVIII who, mimicking Buonaparte, said, "My son, I am satisfied with you," to the acclamations of the troops assembled before them. She ignored the scoffing old marshals who had fought in the Napoleonic wars, who said that Antoine's exploit had not been a "real campaign." Thérèse was thrilled whenever anyone addressed her husband as "Generalissimo."

"It all proves that a king in trouble can be saved," she often commented.

"It is a beautiful day, is it not?" said Thérèse to Antoine, as she took up her knitting.

"Ah, yes, Princess," he said, without looking up, "but it will rain tonight." He indicated to his barometer, also on the table beside him. He had become inseparable from barometers, thermometers and weather charts, for studying the weather patterns had become a fascination for him, and he frequently sent one of his aides riding over to the Observatory to inquire the maximum temperature of the day. It was a pleasant distraction, for otherwise he meddled over much in military affairs. In time of war he was a courageous leader and bold strategist; in times of peace he was nothing but a pest, setting his network of spies upon the officers and then interfering in their promotions and appointments.

Thérèse tried to counter his bungling by knowing the names of all the Royal Bodyguards and many officers in the other corps. Whenever she intervened for anyone in the military, she always said, "Do not thank me, thank my husband," or "You can thank Monseigneur d'Angoulême for this." She tirelessly sought to enhance his prestige and popularity.

"Tante Thérèse! Oncle Antoine!" came two little voices, the sound of which to Thérèse surpassed in beauty all the exalted music of earth. Henri and Louise came running into the garden, first to Thérèse, who caught them both up in her arms, kissing their cheeks, and then to Antoine, who did the same. Artois was right behind them, with Madame de Gontaut, the ever watchful

232

governess. Louise was an exquisite fairy of five years, with short blond curls, large sapphire eyes, an expression of gentleness, sympathy and wit which she possessed in overflowing measure. Henri was a robust, masculine version of his sister. The innocent beauty of his plump, rosy cheeks and engaging smile were tempered by a demeanor both serious and wise, so that he reminded Thérèse of certain statutes she had seen of the Divine Child. Thérèse was concerned that Madame de Gontaut's overprotectiveness was causing the little boy to be nervous and shy.

"Henri and Louise begged to come with me," said Artois. "I knew you would not mind, my dears." He kissed Thérèse's hand.

"Of course not, Papa," she replied. "But I know of a little prince and princess who love fruit tarts!"

"May we, Bon-Papa?" asked Louise, looking up at Artois.

"If it is agreeable to Madame la Gouvernante," he said, with the slightly restrained indulgence of a doting grandfather. He was closer to his grandchildren than he had been to his sons, for in the old days he had been too preoccupied being the rakish Prince Charming of Versailles.

"Oh, *amie chérie*, may we please?" Louise asked Madame de Gontaut. The governess was herself the mother of a loving and closely knit family; she conveyed an aura of affectionate security to her charges, who responded with boundless devotion towards her. She assented to the tarts, and in a few moments Henri and Louise were ensconced in chairs with cushions for added height, munching contentedly away, with sweet cream to drink. Artois, meanwhile, sat down next to his son and without another word became preoccupied with the game of chess.

"Where is your Maman today?" asked Thérèse.

"Hunting at Rosny," said Louise. "She will come home tonight." Caroline often held hunting parties at the château bought from Talleyrand's nephew.

"Who would like to go for a pony ride?" asked Thérèse. "And see Oncle Antoine's new puppies?"

"Oh, Tante Thérèse, I do love puppies!" said Henri.

"Then Madame de Gontaut will take you to the stables and to the kennels," said Thérèse, helping the children climb down from their chairs.

"Do not pull the ponies' tails," teased Antoine.

"Oh, *mon oncle*, we would never hurt the little ponies," said Louise.

Thérèse embraced her. "Of course, you would not, *ma petite*." With her brother and governess, Louise skipped off through the gardens in the direction of the stables.

"So Caroline is at Rosny today," said Thérèse, as soon as the children were out of earshot. Caroline had inherited the Bourbon passion for the chase. She went hunting even when Henri was very sick, which horrified Thérèse and Artois, and they both scolded her. "Thank heaven, the summer is almost over, and she will not again be sea-bathing at Dieppe." Thérèse was stunned to hear that Caroline had undertaken the disturbing habit of swimming in the ocean in public and in broad daylight. Others imitated her, and Dieppe quickly became a fashionable resort. Her Tante Babette had told her that the world would never be the same again after the Revolution, but she would never have imagined such doings by a lady and a princess, even if modestly attired in a long bathing dress and thick black stockings. "Well," sighed Thérèse, "I hope Caroline is not keeping company with that Italian gentleman, Monseigneur de Lucchesi-Palli, while over at Rosny. He has been coming so often to see her at the Tuileries."

Artois moved his red king out of danger's way. "Nonsense, daughter," he said. "Monsieur de Lucchesi-Palli is merely a friend from Caroline's childhood. He comes to the Tuileries to converse with Madame de Gontaut, with whom he shares many acquaintances. He calls upon Caroline merely in order to convey messages he has received from her family."

"Oh, Papa, for a man of the world, you are dense!" sighed Thérèse in exasperation. He never saw a calamity until he was in the middle of it. "Would you care to hear any of the news?"

"Yes, my dear, but only news of society. No politics today," said Artois, wincing as Antoine's queen swept the board.

Thérèse took up the *Journal de Débats*. "'Monsieur le Prince de Talleyrand, Chamberlain of the Royal Court, received Their Serene Highnesses, the Duc and Duchesse d'Orléans, at the Hotel de Talleyrand Wednesday last. Monseigneur de Quélen, Archbishop of Paris, was also received. Madame la Duchesse de Dino acted as hostess,'" read Thérèse. "I tell you, Papa, Orléans' friendship with Talleyrand bodes ill for us. They have never ceased to be revolutionaries at heart, and that dreadful Adelaïde scorns us so! As for La Dino, they say her last baby was Talleyrand's. Truly, I do not understand Monseigneur de Quélen."

She was interrupted by Artois, who suppressed an intake of breath as the "Generalissimo" captured one of his knights. "That is all gossip. I am sorry, Thérèse, that you so dislike Louis-Philippe. He is a charming man, who has tried to be amiable to you. Nevertheless, I do not understand if he is so abhorrent to you, why do you constantly shower his children with gifts, but never give presents to Henri and Louise?"

"I do not 'shower' the Orléans children with gifts. I am only…trying to do what is fitting." She found herself at a loss for words and had to unravel some of her flawed work. Glancing up, she noticed Antoine staring at her, a wistful pity flickering in his amber eyes. She quickly looked down again. "As for Henri and Louise, I do not wish to spoil them as others seem to be intent upon doing. I keep plenty of toys for them to use when they are here." Most of the world would never have recognized Thérèse when playing with Henri and the toy soldiers she kept in the small nursery at Villeneuve l'Étang. She started reading and paraphrasing again.

"'Madame la Duchesse de Berry rode the first public omnibus.…In honor of the princess, the vehicle has been renamed a 'Caroline.'"

"That" said Artois, "is almost as bad as when your mother rode in a taxi to a masquerade ball." He referred to an escapade of Marie-Antoinette's which had shocked Paris, although he had thought it very amusing at the time and had written some comic verses about it. Thérèse picked up another gazette.

"'Monsieur le Vicomte de Chateaubriand read from his renowned works *Le Génie du Christianisme* and *Les Martyrs* at the

Abbaye-aux-Bois in the salon of Madame Récamier on Tuesday evening.'"

"That is old news," said Artois. "Madame Récamier has long since gone to Rome."

"It is scandalous how Chateaubriand pursued her," said Thérèse. There were rumors about the relationship between Chateaubriand and Madame Récamier being more than platonic. Even bankruptcy, which had forced her to live in the cell of an abandoned monastery, did not deter her friends from flocking to see Madame Récamier every day, including Chateaubriand, despite his liaisons with other women. "Papa, I do not think he would be a suitable governor for Henri." Madame de Gontaut was urging Chateaubriand for the office of governor, and Artois so often listened to her (she was, after all, the cousin of his late beloved Louise de Polastron), but Thérèse hoped for the appointment of Mathieu de Montmorency to that coveted post.

"Look, Bon-Papa, look!" came Henri's voice. He was sitting on a white pony, with Louise behind him, her arms protectively around his waist. A groom was slowly leading the pony, and Madame de Gontaut was walking along beside the children, her hand on Louise's back.

"Bravo! It is Bayard *sans peur et sans reproche*!" exclaimed Artois. "A brave knight, who has just rescued a fair princess!"

Thérèse froze, for she was reminded of Charles, whose favorite slogan was "Without fear or reproach" when he had played knight. She uttered a silent oft-repeated prayer that Henri would never suffer as Charles had suffered.

"Checkmate!" cried Antoine.

That evening, they all returned to the Tuileries. With the King's condition worsening everyday, no one wanted to be long away from the palace. He was not able to preside at supper, but insisted on being wheeled into the Galerie de Diane where the Court assembled to play cards. The head of Louis XVIII was so sunken upon his chest that one had to kneel close to his chair in order to catch his words. Antoine undertook to amuse him with a game of chess, but the sick man only looked at him dully, and then cried out, "Where is your brother!? Where is Berry!?"

"You are unwell tonight, Sire," said the Comtesse de Cayla, an attractive brunette with whom the old King was infatuated. Thérèse could not abide her presence, and forbade her ladies-in-waiting to have any truck with the "adventuress." Madame d'Agoult disobeyed and showed friendliness to Madame du Cayla, so Thérèse stopped the evening chats before bedtime that she and Madame d'Agoult had enjoyed for years.

"Ah, my dear," said Louis XVIII to Zoé du Cayla, as he returned to his senses. "A king is permitted to die, but not to be sick."

Thérèse rose to depart and after curtsying deeply, she leaned towards her uncle's ear and said gently, "Sire, perhaps it is time to speak to Abbé Rocher?" Abbé Rocher was the King's nominal confessor, whose services he did not seek very often, if ever.

"No, my child, there is plenty of time for that," wheezed the King, his face contorting in pain. The stench of his disease filled the Galerie de Diane.

As she left the Galerie, Thérèse motioned to Comtesse du Cayla to follow her. With her uncle's soul at stake, she must make some concessions.

"Madame du Cayla," she half-whispered in the great doorway, "the King is not long for this world, according to Doctor Portal. He must be persuaded to receive the last sacraments before it is too late. I sense a…a…certain torment in his soul. God willing, he will find peace when he confesses. I beg you to help him to see that it is time."

Madame du Cayla was a good-hearted soul. "Most willingly, Madame," she agreed with a charming smile.

Thérèse retired to her quarters. In the half hour she used to spend gleaning the news from Madame d'Agoult she now occupied herself with reading Sir Walter Scott's novels, highly recommended by Caroline who was an avid reader of all his works. She picked up *Waverley*, but somehow could not concentrate upon it, and decided instead to pay a call on her sister-in-law, who surely had returned from Rosny. Thérèse had noticed Monsieur Lucchesi-Palli lingering outside the Pavillon de Marsan earlier in the evening. His presence did not bode well. Thérèse believed that someone in the family needed to keep an eye on Caroline almost as if she were Henri or Louise.

Not willing to disturb her ladies, she summoned a footman to escort her to the other side of the palace. (It would be very improper for any princess to be wandering through the Tuileries alone.) As she approached Madame de Gontaut's apartments, where Caroline usually spent her evenings, there came the sound of a sweet, soprano voice raised in Italian in an aria of Rossini. Her footman scratched on the door, opened it and announced her.

In the salon, everyone instantly rose. Caroline, who was at the pianoforte singing, came forward with a curtsy. It was an elegant room, the walls hung in sea-green striped silk from when those apartments had belonged to Napoléon's little boy. Caroline looked surprised and rather confused at seeing Thérèse.

"Sister, pray continue," said Thérèse. "I did not mean to interrupt." The Marquis de la Ferronnays, chivalrous as always, brought her a chair, and everyone sat down. Caroline was surrounded by a small group of friends, both ladies and gentlemen, who were sipping almond milk, while playing cards and listening to music. Madame de Gontaut embroidered primly on a sofa, and sitting next to her was Monsieur de Lucchesi-Palli. Thérèse had never before seen him at close range. He was very young, certainly not a day over twenty, yet exhibiting a maturity and poise beyond his years, exuding a certain fierce dignity in his calm, rugged features. Black curling hair and olive complexion, in his simple, dark suit, he was the soul of elegance and nobility in a virile, mettlesome way.

"Sister, you have not met my young friend from Napoli, the Conte Hector Lucchesi-Palli," said Caroline. Her grammar had improved over the years, but the lilt and intonation remained Sicilian. The count stood and bowed low. "He is an attaché at the Neapolitan embassy. He is so sweet, so kind to bring me news of my Papa and all my brothers and sisters." Thérèse nodded to the young man, who quietly resumed his seat.

"What shall I play now?" queried Caroline.

"There was a beautiful aria at the *opéra* last night," said one of her ladies.

"Oh, yes, I shall sing it for you!" exclaimed Caroline. She possessed an uncanny ear for music, which Berry had encouraged her to cultivate before his death. Unable to read a note, she was able to replicate almost to perfection any piece from any opera, after having heard it only once. She launched into Rosini's aria from *Il Barbiere di Siviglia*, "*Una voce poco fa....*"

Thérèse had a narrow capacity for understanding music but she appreciated her sister-in-law's talent, which she saw blossoming in both Henri and Louise in the little songs they loved to sing. She glanced at the young Conte Hector. He was as one transfixed as Caroline sang, his eyes like coals as he steadily regarded her. As she finished, they all applauded. The Conte's lips were parted ever so slightly; his demeanor was radiant.

"Principessa, a boon!" he said when the clapping ceased. "Grant me a boon. Please, most gracious lady, sing '*Voi che sapete*.'"

Caroline blushingly acquiesced, and began to play and sing Cherubino's aria from Mozart's *Le Nozze di Figaro*. Singing of the sweetness and melancholy of love, the words as well as the light, exuberant melody seemed to express Caroline's deepest being. By the last trilling note, Hector's eyes were darker and moister.

"Ah, I have sung alone long enough!" said Caroline. "Will not one of you gentlemen join me for a duet? Monsieur de la Ferronnays, will you join me for '*Là ci darem mano*' from *Don Giovanni*?"

"Madame, I beg to be excused," said Ferronays. "My throat is hoarse today."

"Who else is a baritone?" asked Caroline. She looked around the room at every man but Hector, who rose and hesitantly came over to the pianoforte.

"May I, Principessa?" he asked, softly.

"But of course, Signore," she replied. "I had forgotten that you could sing."

Hector stood behind Caroline, his hand almost brushing her blond ringlets. He possessed a remarkable voice, deep and rich, which blended pleasantly with Caroline's in the frolicsome duet by Mozart. Everyone was impressed. When they finished, there was more applause, as Caroline smiled in almost shy delight, offering her hand to the Conte, who kissed it far too lingeringly, Thérèse thought. She decided she had seen enough and announced her intention of going.

"I shall retire, too," said Caroline, pretending to suppress a yawn. She bade everyone *bon soir*, but when she turned towards Hector, who towered above her petite form, her eyes fluttered downward as if she feared to meet his gaze, while he stared at her with unabashed passion.

"Sister, may I have a word with you?" asked Thérèse.

"Indeed, yes." Caroline led the way to her sitting room.

"Caroline," said Thérèse, when they were alone, "that young man is clearly besotted with you."

"What young man?"

"Monsieur Lucchesi-Palli. You must send him back to Naples at once."

Caroline raised her eyebrows and assumed a defiant air. "I do not know what you mean, Thérèse. He is a very respectable gentleman, from an ancient and distinguished Neapolitan family. I knew him when he was a little boy. He would fight boys much bigger than himself if they did not agree that I was the most beautiful princess in the world!" She laughed in fond remembrance. "He promises to be an accomplished diplomat someday. For me to complain of him without cause, and send him home to Naples, would ruin him! What a cruel thing to do, when he has shown me nothing but esteem! As for his affections, well, perhaps he feels for me a bit of puppy love, that is all. I am almost certain he has a fiancée awaiting him in Capri. Soon he will be married, and forget all about me." She turned abruptly away, and looked out the window at the September moon.

"Dear sister," said Thérèse, firmly. "The privileges of royal birth are few compared to the many sacrifices one must make throughout life. You are the mother of the future King of France, and the widow of one of our princes. Even the very breath of scandal should not touch you. Your behavior must at all times be such so that even the most malicious tongue will be given no excuse to gossip. Thousands follow your example, for good or ill."

Caroline spun around with fire in her eyes. "You are quick to see wickedness in everything I do!" she seethed. "There is nothing wrong between Hector and me. We have only the highest respect and regard for each other. Nothing improper has occurred. Nothing, nothing!"

"I do not see wickedness; only a hint of imprudence," said Thérèse. "In your position, you cannot risk even a hint for the sake of Henri and Louise. It is unwise to keep company with a man who is in love with you, unless he is a man whom you will be able to marry. Hector Lucchesi-Palli is not in that category, I am afraid, because he is not a prince of royal blood. Besides, he is a foreigner. The people would never accept a foreigner as step-father of the future king. If you keep seeing him, I fear it will end badly for both of you." It was apparent to Thérèse that Caroline was almost as infatuated with Hector as he was with her.

"If it were not for Henri and Louise, I would leave this place!" shrieked Caroline. "I would pack my bags tonight, and go home to Naples." She raised her hands grasping at the air. "You…all of you here…you and Antoine and Papa…you are driving me to madness!!" She ran sobbing from the room, slamming the door behind her.

Thérèse hurried to her own apartments, wondering what was going to become of them all. She and Caroline had many altercations, especially over the children, and what Thérèse perceived as being Caroline's injudicious public behavior. She pitied Caroline, and wished there was some available prince for her to marry, one who would not try to manipulate Henri as a political pawn. Her situation was similar to that of the widowed, ill-fated Princesse de Lamballe.

Within a few days, it was evident the King was dying. Madame du Cayla was successful in persuading him to go to confession. Face red and swollen, eyes blind and vacant, he seemed withdrawn into his own universe, unless his dignity was infringed upon. Once the royal physician, Doctor Portal, gave a brusque order to one of the King's valets: "Hurry up and take off his shirt." The old man's eyes flew open, as he spoke in his well-known, authoritative manner: "Monsieur, my name is Louis XVIII. You should say: 'Take off His Majesty's shirt.'"

Antoine and Thérèse remained at his side as the end approached. He would frequently grasp Antoine's hand. "Angoulême, my son, are you there?"

"Yes, Sire, I am here."

"Where is Berry? Where is your brother?"

Tears flowed down Antoine's cheeks. "He... he... has gone away, Your Majesty."

"Has he? Always the rascal...an irresponsible lad." A single tear trickled out of the corner of the King's eye.

In the wee hours of September 16, 1824, the King fell into his last agony.

"Marie-Thérèse!" he called, suddenly. Thérèse knelt by his side. "*Mon oncle?*"

"Your brother– Louis XVII– he lives!" the King gasped. "Do not ask me...how I know of it! Martin of Gallardon, the visionary– told me... years ago that it is God's will...that he... your brother... be restored to the throne of his fathers...." Struggling for breath, he seemed to lapse into unconsciousness.

"Sire?" Thérèse wanted to learn more, but he did not appear to hear her. Then he spoke again so softly, she and Antoine had to lean very close.

"Antoine, under my pillow...a letter...give it to your Papa...." Louis XVIII moaned, and did not utter another word.

Antoine gently reached under the pillow and pulled out a letter affixed with the King's seal. "I will take it to Papa at once." A short time later he returned, looking deeply shaken. "Papa read it, and threw it into the fire, declaring it to be nonsense."

Thérèse began to sob, wailing aloud as she had last January at the Requiem Mass for her father at Saint Denis, when King Louis XVI's will was read. In the meantime, the soul of Louis XVIII passed from this world into the next, and appeared before the Judge of the living and the dead, Whose Kingdom shall have no end.

Chapter Twenty-three:
The Coronation
Autumn, 1824 to Spring, 1825

"He will crown thee with a crown of tribulation...." Isaias 22:18

The Comte d'Artois was King of France. He took the name of Charles X. At the death of Louis XVIII, Antoine disappeared for the entire day. He reappeared the following morning, when he led the Royal Family in showing homage to the new King. Charles X, with his white hair and trim physique, cut a particularly striking figure in his mourning suit of violet silk. Antoine was so accustomed to standing back at doorways in order to let Thérèse pass through first, not only because she was a lady, but because she was the daughter of a king, that the new Madame la Dauphine had to remind him that henceforth, as heir to the throne, he would enter first. "After you, Monsieur le Dauphin," she said.

Thérèse sent for Henri and Louise to speak to them of the momentous occasion that had occurred, the end of one reign and the beginning of another, in which they were to play chief roles. Henri's eyes were round and solemn, but Louise's pale, pointed face was genuinely perturbed.

"Bon-Papa is King, oh, that is the worst thing about it." She kept repeating over and over again "that is the worst thing" and Thérèse demanded to know what she meant, but the little child was unable to explain herself. Finally, Madame de Gontaut intervened.

"Madame la Dauphine, Mademoiselle thinks that now that her grandfather is King, His Majesty will have to be wheeled about in a chair like Louis XVIII." Thérèse had to suppress a smile, and noticed the supreme relief in Louise's face when it was explained to her that Bon-Papa would continue to walk about on his own two feet and that she and Henri would see as much of him as they were accustomed.

One of Charles X's first formal acts as King was to bestow upon Louis-Philippe Duc d'Orléans, the title of "His Royal Highness," which annoyed Thérèse almost as much as the way Caroline was constantly going to see her "Tante Amélie" at the Palais Royal, with Henri and Louise. Thérèse was convinced that Mademoiselle Adelaïde was at the center of a plot against the crown. Talleyrand himself was involved, as he had once broadly hinted to the Baron de Vitrolles: "The Bourbons must take care, for Louis-Philippe is treading on their heels." Her fears were mitigated somewhat by the joyous acclamations of the army and the multitudes for King Charles X whenever he appeared in public.

The Court retired to Saint-Cloud for a time after the funeral of Louis XVIII, in order that the Tuileries could be cleaned (the stairwells and various kitchens stank to such a degree that many persons were made sick by it). When Charles X made his triumphal entry into Paris, the crowds, undeterred by a driving rain, flocked to see the handsome, slender monarch on his white steed, and the *vivats* were deafening. His piety was well-known, and unlike Louis XVIII, who was nicknamed "The Crowned Jacobin" and "King Voltaire," his religious devotion was heartfelt and genuine. Many devout persons believed that a golden age of the Church was about to dawn, ushered in by the reign of a true Son of Saint Louis. The motto of the King was "For Altar and Throne," one of the battle cries of the Vendéan army. Thérèse hoped against hope.

The nation, prosperous and free with a growing population, sparkling with brilliant, new intellectual accomplishment and Catholic scholarship, seemed burgeoning with greatness, ready to lead Europe from the darkness of the so-called Enlightenment and revolutionary epoch into another triumphant age of the Gospel, when all nations would be converted, and the Mohammedans themselves would embrace the Cross they had scorned for so many centuries. What a kingdom to hand over to Henri when his time came! What a new Solomon he would be, a new Henri IV and Louis XIV, except he would be pure and good. Perhaps he would even restore Versailles ... Thérèse prayed and prayed, always ending her petitions with "Thy Will be done."

During his triumphal entry, the King touched many hearts when he rode out of the procession and over to a window of the Tuileries, where two small, blond figures were jumping up and down, calling, "Bon-Papa! Bon-Papa!" Charles X, already famous for his hospitality, began to hold glittering receptions at the Tuileries, replete with pastries and ices and he melted many hearts with the gentle tones of his "*Bon soir.*" Thérèse, the tall, cool Dauphine at his side, in jewelled coronet and a cloud of white plumes, either offended by her frigid manner, or elicited tears by those who saw in her person the chaste austerity of Saint Radegonde and other holy Frankish queens of old.

Her own parties, that she gave for members of her household on feast-days and anniversaries, were simple and homey. She especially excelled at children's parties for Henri and Louise, for then her strong, maternal instincts were allowed to come forth. Unfortunately, her formal soirées, when she would allow the great chandeliers to be illumined, were dreaded by everyone, and by Caroline most of all, for their dullness and stiffness. The guests stood quietly or played cards, waiting for the Dauphine to address them. It was rude to speak to one's neighbors except in a whisper; people were afraid to dance or laugh, and most of the guests escaped early to the salons of the Faubourg. Thérèse, haunted at all times by her mother's reputation for frivolity, did not mind if people criticized her for being too morose and monastic; she was always hoping her ultra-respectable conduct was erasing the last vestiges of gossip and rumors about Marie-Antoinette.

The King's popularity soared at first, as he granted a wide amnesty to political offenders, and lifted all censorship of the press, who lauded him for it. However, in the winter of 1824-25, the King and his government passed some laws not so popular with the liberal elements of society. In order to save money, all officers who had reached the age limit and had not been on active duty since 1823 were asked to retire. So many exceptions were made that the financial benefits of the bill were nullified, without mitigating the outcry on the part of many who saw the move as an attack on the remnants of the imperial army. The indemnification law passed by the Chamber of Deputies, which ordered that all former *émigrés* should receive compensation for confiscated lands, caused an uproar.

The greatest furor of all was created by the new law against sacrilege. In the last four years there had been 538 thefts of sacred vessels. Good Catholics were horrified by the desecrations; many were equally horrified by the proposed remedy. When vessels containing no sacred species were profaned, the crime was punishable by a life of forced labor. If the Sacred Hosts were contained in the vessel, the punishment was the guillotine. If the Host itself was directly profaned, then the malefactor's hand would be severed before the beheading. The penalties were rendered void by the bill itself, which stipulated that the sacrilegious act had to be committed in public, or else the punishments did not apply.

Nevertheless, Chateaubriand led the outcry. "My religion," he wrote in the *Journal des Débats*, "is one which likes to pardon rather than punish, which wins its victories by mercy, and only needs scaffolds for the triumph of its martyrs." The philosopher Bonald disagreed. "Yes, religion commands men to pardon, but requires government to punish....And besides, by punishing sacrilege, what is done if it is not to send the offender before his natural judge?"

The anti-sacrilege law was never carried out in practice. However, the anti-clerical forces used it to conjure up in the minds of the masses lurid tales of the Inquisition and the Saint Batholomew's Day Massacre. Charles X was openly portrayed as an ultramontane bigot in mocking songs and satirical cartoons, in which he was shown to be aided by "Madame Rancune" (Lady Resentment), as Thérèse was labelled. The anti-Catholic hysteria grew with any further measures the King took in order to protect the Church in his country.

Thérèse was not shaken by being the target of the slurs of unbelievers, yet the vehemence of the hatred against religion startled her, since the clergy, the re-established religious orders and newly founded congregations of teaching and nursing sisters had done an immense good throughout the land, caring for the sick, instructing the ignorant, and sheltering the orphaned and aged. The tangible fruits of the good works of Catholic faithful were there for everyone to see; there were few lax clergymen compared to prerevolutionary conditions; she could not understand the sentiments of the anti-clerical forces, and attributed it to diabolical hatred of Christ the King.

In the meantime, she plunged into the preparations for the coronation which was to take place in May of 1825. She poured over antiquated books and ancient parchments to verify all the rubrics of the ceremony, enflaming her already passionate enthrallment with the medieval age, and everything that pertained to Clovis, Charlemagne, or Saint Louis. She longed to share with the French people all that she was learning about their magnificent Christian and royal heritage, about to be reborn on a grand scale. An essential ingredient was missing, however, and that was the Sainte-Ampoule.

The Holy Ampulla of Saint Rémi was the miraculous vial of oil brought down from heaven by a dove to the saintly archbishop at the baptism of Clovis and thousands of the Frankish people on Christmas Day in 498. According to the old manuscripts, the crowd was so immense that the priest with the chrism could not get through to where the half-naked Clovis was about to be plunged into the icy waters of regeneration. So Heaven supplied chrism of a miraculous nature. In the great cathedral built on the site in the town called "Rheims" after Saint Rémi, the Apostle of the Franks, the Kings of France were henceforth crowned, after being anointed with sacred chrism in which were mixed particles of the original contents of the Holy Ampulla. The baptism of their first Christian King made France the most ancient Christian monarchy in Europe, and thus the "Eldest Daughter of the Church." The Holy Ampulla was seen as an essential element at the mystical core of the ceremony. The coronation ritual was inextricably linked to the monarch's own baptism as well as the baptism of the entire nation, so that the words of the Lord to Moses and the Israelites could be applicable; "And you shall be to me a priestly kingdom, and a holy nation." (Exodus 19:6) Through baptism, all Christians share in the priesthood and kingship of Christ, therefore the royal dignity, conferred on the individual sovereign could be gloried in by all the people.

In October of 1793, the Holy Ampulla was publicly demolished by the hammer of Citizen Ruhl, a representative of the new government of liberty and equality. After the Restoration in 1814, several persons came forward, including the former constitutional bishop Seraine, claiming that they had salvaged particles of the dry powdery contents of the Holy Ampulla. The alleged particles were combined and mixed with sacred chrism by Cardinal Archbishop Latil in order to be used at the coronation. Many royalists, however, were perturbed, claiming that there was not enough proof of the authenticity of the particles, except the word of former revolutionaries. If there was no Sainte-Ampoule, then there was no true king, or such was their refrain. Others insisted that both Louis XVIII and Charles X were usurpers, for Louis XVII was alive, but his sister "Duchesse Cain" had not bothered to find him because of her own ambition to someday be the Queen.

Thérèse pondered these matters, praying that at least some of the fragments in the new Ampulla were from the original, and that all the abundant graces of kingship would be conferred upon her father-in-law, since he desperately needed them. His enemies were many, and he still would not read the gazettes.

Duc Mathieu de Montmorency came one day to see her. Over the years, he had been employed in various government posts, including Foreign Minister, so he had left her service, and matters concerning Charles had been taken over by the prefect, Monsieur de Messy. Within the year, he was to be appointed the tutor of Henri, Duc de Bourdeaux, for which his learning, his virtues, his gentleness, and most of all, his strong faith, made him eminently qualified. He was going to prepare for the task by spending more time in prayer and recollection, especially during Lent. As they chatted in her boudoir, Thérèse sensed that he was carrying a weight, for there was a shadow upon his pleasing, amiable countenance.

"Monsieur, you are burdened. What is it you need to say to me?" asked Thérèse, troubled for this most faithful of friends.

"Madame, the times we live in are very dark," said he. "The Restoration has been a ray of light, but I fear it will not last. The Revolution is not over, indeed, it has only been held at bay somewhat. Another Revolution is coming."

"Another Revolution?!"

"Yes, Madame. Perhaps a series of Revolutions, until Christian civilization is annihilated, and only a faithful remnant is left to do battle with the Antichrist."

"Mathieu, you are terrifying me. Are you referring to the Masonic conspiracies?"

"Yes, I refer to freemasonry, and to a terror beyond it. I speak of the Illuminati."

"The Illuminati? Yes, I have heard my husband make allusions to them. The late Abbé Barruel wrote a great deal about that bizarre sect. Many of the Jacobins were Illuminati, or at least, they were exceedingly influenced by their infamous blasphemies, I believe?"

"It is a complicated matter, I fear," said Mathieu. "Permit me, Madame, to retrace a little history. Your Royal Highness is well-acquainted with the machinations of Voltaire and his disciples, whose war cry against the Church was 'crush the wretch?'"

"Yes, of course. Voltaire, Rousseau, Diderot, and the *philosophes* corrupted religion and morals to such an extent that the foundations were laid for the Revolution," said Thérèse.

"Exactly, Madame. By the expulsion of the Jesuits, which they accomplished through La Pompadour, by the influx of anti-Christian books such as Diderot's *Encyclopédie* into every school and library in France, and by the corruption of universities and seminaries by other philosophes, the Masons have sought to convince the masses that the Gospel of Christ and His Church are essentially incompatible with individual liberty, with true equality, and with the fundamental rights and brotherhood of man. It has long been the goal of freemasonry to crush the altar of every priest and overturn the throne of every prince. Princes who could not be corrupted were to be destroyed. The Catholic religion, of course, is to be blasphemed at every instance."

"And they make secret oaths, terrible oaths, which they are not allowed to break?"

"Yes, Madame. If they break them, then the vengeance is terrible, indeed. I am thinking especially of the death of the Princesse de Lamballe."

Thérèse nodded, remembering that the Princesse had been an ex-freemason when she was disemboweled by her murderers.

"Many aristocrats and nobles were taken in, Monsieur le Duc," said Thérèse. "They thought masonry was a pleasant club for civic improvements. Even my mother thought so for a time, and although she never considered joining them, she thought Rousseau's philosophy of natural living to be charming and imitable."

"The essence of the masonic craft," said Mathieu, "is to deceive by hiding depravity with a veil of virtue, and ultimately to pervert public opinion, so that depravity itself is mistaken for virtue. Before the Revolution, the Sophisters gave lip service to the authority of the monarch, while simultaneously undermining it by attributing every misfortune to the King and his ministers, until the King was seen as a tyrant, and the loyal priests as wolves. Philippe d'Orléans bought up grain to engineer a famine, yet was portrayed as a hero in the gazettes. On the other hand, the Emperor Joseph, your mother's brother, was an adept of the Sect, who sought to be seen as a very religious prince, even while he was persecuting the Church, closing down monasteries and expelling religions from his lands."

"I daresay he caused his poor devout mother, the Empress Maria Theresa, to shudder in her grave. But what of the Illuminati you mentioned?"

"In the 1770's, there was at the University of Ingolstadt a Bavarian Professor of Law named Adam Weishaupt, who is alive today, alive and plotting and nefarious as ever. An atheist, devoted to vice and the corruption of youth, he seduced his sister-in-law. In order to prevent the ruin of his reputation among the people, who thought him to be a learned and wise gentleman, Weishaupt procured the murder of his own unborn child. Pardon me, Your Highness, for mentioning such a horror."

Thérèse cast her eyes to the floor, as she mournfully reflected upon the destruction of the innocent that always seemed to be the fruit of depravity.

Mathieu continued. "Weishaupt gathered a following of adherents, originally from among his own students, but spreading soon into the courts of princes. Their mission was to silently and systematically destroy the Altar and the Throne through the teachings of Manes. On May 1, 1776 he formally inaugurated the Order of the Illuminati, a secret society in which members are known by assumed names (Weishaupt is 'Spartacus,' for example), exterior virtue and discipline hiding wicked motives and personal corruption. They desire to impose upon humanity a morality without restraint, a religion without God, and a politics without laws. They discredited by any means possible every man of talent they could not persuade to join them. After destroying the traditional ties of government and religion, the goal of Weishaupt's sect is, and was, to destroy the ties of nature, yes, even the love of one's family and, most of all, paternal authority. In destroying the authority of the father over his children, of the priest over his parishioners, of the King over his people, and of the Pope over the Church, they attack the very authority of the Eternal Father. As we have already seen in the case of Thérèse's royal brother, the goal of the Illuminati is to divide parents from their children, making children loyal to the State alone, and thus children like the Dauphin have been and will be in future revolutions torn from the arms of their parents.

"By the time of the Estates-General in 1789, the regular masonic lodges of the kingdom were united into the Grand Orient, Philippe d'Orléans was Grand Master when the Illuminati arrived in Paris. Orléans joined the Illuminati Sect with all the adepts of his occult lodges, and thus the Illuminati acquired a sway over the whole of French Masonry. From this monstrous association sprang the Jacobins, or Illumined Masons, with all the crimes and horrors of the Revolution. Under their auspices, the child-king was dragged from your mother's arms and hideously corrupted.

"Madame, I believe your brother survived. He did not die in the Temple. But his mind and morals were so warped by the depravity of his captors that he could never reign, as was their intention. Remember, Madame, to destroy or corrupt princes is one of their chief policies. If he lives, hunted or in hiding, the Illuminati have their eye upon him, even if we do not, and if we get too close, I fear it will mean the end of his life."

"Do you think that 'Jean-Marie Hervagault' was my brother?"

"Perhaps, Madame. I have failed to find his mother, Nicole Hervagault. Monsieur de Messy has had no better success. There seem to be no records of the woman's death or burial anywhere. No, Your Highness, I fear Louis XVII is now beyond our grasp. Yet, even after so many years, there are rumors. There is a family in Switzerland named Leschot, the makers of the fabulous automatons that were once brought to Versailles. They claim to this day that they once harbored a beautiful child whom they believed to be the Dauphin. He was drowned in Lake Geneva while escaping from the police."

"I will ask Monsieur de Messy to investigate it further," said the princess. "So you think, Monsieur, that not only have the Illuminati prevented my brother from taking his rightful place in the world, but they will stop at nothing in order to destroy my father-in-law, my husband, and even my nephew?"

"Yes, Madame. There are many artists, writers and journalists among the number of modern adepts, but I fear there are many princes also, and high officials. The wheels of propaganda are turning day and night. The King must be careful. All could be saved or lost in an instant. We must entrust the realm to the Sacred Heart of Jesus and to the Immaculate Heart of Mary."

"I have always done so, *mon bon ami*. We will be united in prayer this Passiontide." Mathieu departed, and Thérèse never saw him again. He died on Good Friday at three o'clock in the afternoon, kneeling before the stripped altar in the Church of Saint Thomas Aquinas. Many poor persons wept for him, for he had been a generous benefactor to those in need.

On Trinity Sunday of 1825, Charles X was crowned and anointed at the Cathedral of Our Lady of Rheims. Jewels sparkled like stars within the gothic heights amid the blaze of candles. In the galleries and nave there was a crush of silk, velvet and plumes. The sword of Charlemagne, *Joyeuse*, was borne in triumphantly, as was the new golden dove containing the Holy Ampulla. Nevertheless, there were those who caustically remarked that the entire event was too operatic and grandiose. Chateaubriand, who was recovering from his disappointment at not being chosen to be governor of the Duc de Bourdeaux (even though his old rival and friend Mathieu de Montmorency had died, the Duc de Damas was preferred to himself), commented that the coronation seemed to him a mere dramatic representation of a coronation, but not a real coronation. Thérèse, weighted by her ermine-lined regalia and the crown jewels, viewed with joy the first such ceremony she had ever witnessed, in the very spot where Jeanne d'Arc had watched the anointing of Charles VII before her fiery immolation.

The former Comte d'Artois, more spry and elegant than ever before, humbly knelt, while his old friend and confessor Cardinal Latil anointed him with sacred chrism, mixed with the particles of the Ampulla, on the top of his head in the form of a cross, between the shoulder blades and at the bending and joints of both arms. He rose, and was clothed in dalmatic, tunic, and royal robe; all were of purple velvet and emblazoned with gold *fleur-de-lys*. His palms were anointed with chrism and the oil of catechumens; he alone among laymen could now handle the chalice and drink of the Precious Blood at Mass. When the Cardinal Archbishop of Rheims took the crown from the altar and set it upon the King's head, the bells of the cathedral began to peel, *vivats* echoed in the streets of Rheims, and the *Te Deum* was intoned. Trumpets blared, doves were released, and cannons reverberated. Three days later, according to ancient custom, King Charles touched thousands of people, for it had long been believed that the anointed monarch had the gift for curing scrofula. "The King touches you, God heals you," he repeated over and over again.

In Paris, the coronation was greatly mocked by the liberals and free-thinkers as coarse, medieval superstition. The King was coldly received when he returned on June 6. The anti-clerical campaign, of which he was the central target, had only just begun.

As for Caroline, she seemed to enjoy the pageantry and festivities surrounding the coronation. Thérèse did not see Hector

Lucchesi-Palli lingering around her sister-in-law, although she thought she saw him at the coronation sitting with the diplomatic corps. She assumed Caroline had taken her advice, and was exercising greater prudence in choosing her companions. But one June night, when the Court was staying at Saint-Cloud, Thérèse, unable to sleep, stood by the open window of her room, soaking in the opalescent moonlight that brightened the firmament, and silvered the glistening and splashing fountains. The mysterious mingling of roses, jasmine, and syringa were a gentle, soothing balm to her mind, too active with worries and memories. As her eyes grew accustomed to the lunar radiance, she was quite easily able to discern the figures of a man and a woman, the latter heavily veiled, emerging from behind one of the fountains. She assumed it was two servants having a tryst, or two courtiers perhaps. She began to back into the shadows of her room. The man suddenly threw himself on his knees before the woman, kissing her hand most passionately. As the lady pulled away, saying, "No! No!" Thérèse heard him utter a few words in the Neapolitan dialect. The lady, who was wearing one of the new hooped petticoats, began to run with light, dancing steps towards the palace, her heavy silk veils billowing behind her like a cloud, shimmering in the moonglow.

"Adieu, adieu forever! We cannot meet again," she called softly back to her suitor, who stood like a statue by the fountain, arms held out in a gesture of despair. Thérèse recognized the whispering voice and graceful bearing. It was Caroline.

Chapter Twenty-four:
Jewels
Summer 1827

"My sorrow is above sorrow, my heart mourneth within me." Jeremias
8:18

"But they laughed at us, *ma chère tante*! After praising and complimenting us, as soon as they thought we could not hear them, they mocked us!" said Louise.

"They said we were small for our ages," piped in Henri. "Are we, Tante Thérèse?"

Thérèse strolled with Henri and Louise beneath the long, tunnel-like pergolas entwined with roses in the gardens of the Bagatelle. The white villa, gleaming in the July sun, could be glimpsed through the lattices. It was the feast of Saint Henry, and Caroline had invited them all to the Bagatelle for Henri's name-day celebration. The invitations were actually issued under the name of Madame de Gontaut, otherwise it would have to be an event for the entire Court, and anyone who had been presented to the King would have to be asked. If the governess hosted the *fête*, then it could be small, delightful and informal, qualities many had come to associate with Caroline's parties.

Thérèse had not seen her niece and nephew all summer, for they had been at Rosny and Dieppe. She rejoiced to be united with them once more in the superlative loveliness of the park of Bagatelle, rich with the hot summer stillness that makes winter an apparent impossibility. The gardens had been planned by King

Charles X when he was a young man, but he had long ago bestowed the property upon Berry, and so officially it belonged to Henri.

Henri and Louise were telling their aunt of a recent disconcerting experience: that of accidentally overhearing what flatterers really thought of them.

"No, Henri," said Thérèse. "You and your sister are not too small for your ages. Your Papa and Maman were and are not persons of great stature, and so you, too, will both be short in height. But that is the will of God and how he made you and so it is a good thing. What else did those silly people say?"

"They said that I was as white as an egg, and that I needed some medicine," said Louise. "But a moment before they had been praising us so, saying over and over again that we were so pretty – oh, I heard them perfectly well. I understand now what flattery means. It means saying the exact opposite of truth, a most wicked thing indeed."

Thérèse nodded. "It is well, *mes petits*, that those people were allowed to visit you and that they spoke ill of you in your hearing. You have benefitted from their rudeness to learn a lesson which many princes never realize in their entire lives: beware of flattering words. Be unmoved by them one way or another. Keep only those persons near you who have courage to speak the truth. Princes and princesses have few friends, and only adversity can teach you who those are. Now, tell me, have you made your feast-day offerings to the poor?"

"Yes, Tante Thérèse," they replied. Every year on the feasts of Saint Henry and Saint Louis, the children made generous donations from their private allowances to the needy.

"That is good. And it is important to do so without ostentation. We do not help the poor so we can be popular, but because it pleases the Good God, Who said: 'Do not let your right hand know what your left hand is doing.'" Thérèse always worried that, as was the case with many of the privileged classes, the children would learn to be generous in order to enhance their reputation and would then forfeit their heavenly rewards. As for herself, her charities were immense in number, and no one, not even Antoine, knew the extent of them, for the majority of her benefactions were made anonymously, and guarded as if they were secrets of the confessional.

She was deeply troubled by the rising prices of bread. Vast numbers of peasants had flocked to Paris and other cities to work in the new factories that were sprouting up every day, and most were shamefully underpaid. Public drunkenness, abject poverty, prostitution and illegitimate births were on the rise. There were many orphaned and abandoned children for the Sisters of Charity and other religious to take care of. Society seemed to be in a state of flux, in constant danger of becoming unglued.

Already there were signs of unrest, due to the anti-clerical forces. The actor Talma died outside the Church, after a life of infamy. When he was refused a Catholic funeral, large demonstrations occurred, and a secular funeral was held, in which Talma was portrayed as a martyr of bigotry and narrow-mindedness. The plays, pamphlets, cartoons, songs and books which ridiculed the Catholic religion were spewed out in vast quantities. When the King undertook to make public reparation for his failings by walking in a penitential street procession with Antoine and Thérèse, the free-thinkers did not realize that his violet cassock was merely royal mourning garb. Rumor spread that Charles X had secretly been ordained a bishop and said Mass in the Tuileries. The phantom ogres of fanaticism and ultramontane extremism were constantly held up before the people by the forces of the Left, who told them they were being oppressed by Rome, when actually they were experiencing the greatest intellectual freedom anyone had known since 1790.

All of this disturbed Thérèse almost as much as the infernal machine found in the road to Bagatelle one day, an iron pot filled with nails, glass, and gunpowder, set to explode when Henri passed by. Mathieu de Montmorency's words never failed to haunt her. She firmly believed that only the angels of God could give Henri the protection he required against such attacks.

They walked along the white gravel paths to the villa, through the rose arbors and past sculptured yews and boxwoods. Thérèse remembered Charles in those very gardens, as naughty as could be, jumping off the paths, and in between the rose bushes, in great danger of being scratched. When his tutor warned him to watch out for the thorns, he saucily replied, "Thorny paths lead to glory!" Well, she hoped he was enjoying eternal glory and beatitude, rather than living a miserable, mad, tortured existence somewhere. If only she knew for certain.

Many of the guests had already arrived. On the green lawn Caroline was presiding over a game of croquet, the leg-of-mutton sleeves of her white organdy dress billowing around her, as she joked gaily with Chateaubriand with whom she loved to exchange witticisms. Thérèse detested Chateaubriand and wished he had not been invited. She thought him the most vain and odious hypocrite to write about religion while neglecting to restrain or renounce his never-ending love affairs.

Then the Orléans family arrived from Neuilly, their summer residence. Caroline ran to embrace her "Oncle Fifi" and "Tante Amélie," while the younger Orléans children began scampering about with Henri, Louise and the other children from the Blacas, Damas and Gontaut families. The older Orleans children, now in their teens, stood by politely. Thérèse thought it disgraceful the way Louis-Philippe insisted on sending them to school in order to appear more democratic, yet they were chaperoned by tutors; only allowed to speak to certain of their classmates, and never permitted to mingle. Thérèse thought they would be better off being educated at home. Whenever she saw Louis-Philippe, Thérèse thanked God that she had not married him. She had once thought him handsome, but the side whiskers that hung from his sagging jowls gave his face a pear-shaped look. He had Louis XVI's self-satisfied expression; determination and ruthlessness flickered there as well. Antoine, with all his defects, seemed to her to be more genuinely noble and kind, for he acted from the heart, not from political expediency. The King insisted that the Orléans clan be invited to every family gathering, a goodnatured gesture which Thérèse did not think was appreciated by the recipients, especially Mademoiselle Adelaïde, who found in every visit more fodder for her barrage of gossip and criticism. She wished her father-in-law was not so naïve and trusting.

Charles X was currently indulging in his favorite form of relaxation, that of playing whist. He sat at a table underneath the trees with Antoine, the Duc de Blacas, and Monsieur de la

Ferronays. Thérèse sat by them with Madame d'Agoult, tapestry in hand. She watched Henri running with his hoop, full of vibrancy, on his short, sturdy legs. She noticed that Monsieur de Lucchesi-Palli was there. He appeared to be fulfilling errands for Madame de Gontaut, for he kept dashing in and out of the house in an animated and high-spirited manner, full of jests and light-hearted banter for everybody he passed. He seemed to be avoiding Caroline, who was laughing with Chateaubriand, and did not bestow upon Hector a single word or look.

"So much the better," thought Thérèse. Then she began to address the ladies sitting near her, beginning with the Duchesse d'Orléans, who being of higher rank than the others must be addressed first as etiquette required.

"*Ma cousine*, what think you of the latest anti-religious attacks? Are they not horrid? Imagine the effrontery of throwing a stink bomb into the middle of the revival at Saint Germain des Prés, and then putting ink into the holy water fonts at Sainte Geneviève."

"Truly lamentable, Madame la Dauphine," replied the Duchesse, "but perhaps it should be attributed only to students' pranks and not to a hatred of religion in general."

"Maybe," sighed Thérèse. "But do you not think, Mademoiselle Adelaïde, that if the youth of today had better religious instruction, they would be more respectful of holy places?"

"I think, Madame," said Mademoiselle Adelaïde in her acidy tones, "that the youth are disgusted with the hypocrisy that prevails in high places, and with the coldness and fanaticism that make religion so unattractive to them. The times cannot be ignored and must be conformed to."

Thérèse was not surprised at such words coming from the daughter of Philippe Egalité, Illuminized Jacobin, and she smiled kindly upon her to show that she was choosing to overlook her impertinence.

"What of you, Monsieur le Duc?" she asked Louis-Philippe as he approached, kissing her hand. "Is there not a great difference between true devotion to God, and the fanaticism which your sister seems to think so rife in France today? Must one practice one's faith in secret, so as not to be considered a fanatic by 'broadminded' intellectuals, who glory in open impiety?"

Louis-Philippe considered her words thoughtfully. Thérèse wondered if he had seen the pamphlet being circulated around the Quartier Latin, addressed to himself: "Let's go, Prince, have a little courage. In our monarchy there remains a good position for the asking … that of first citizen of France. Your Highness has only to stoop to take the jewel that is there on the ground."

"It is my belief," said Louis-Philippe, "that the movement towards democracy obeys the law of gravity, and that the further it goes, the more force it acquires. Perhaps, it is the rôle of the state to accommodate itself to the times, to identify more with the people and less with the Church as an institution, so that politics and religion are not confounded together in the minds of radicals."

"Monseigneur, you surprise me," said Thérèse.

"How have I surprised you, Madame la Dauphine?" asked Louis-Philippe.

"It surprises me that you do not come right out and openly advocate the separation of Church and state. It seems to me that is what you are advocating, in a round about way. But such an idea contradicts the essence of a Christian state, in which the throne is at the service of the altar, and the laws are based upon the Gospels, not upon popular consensus."

Antoine's voice chimed in from the card table. "My dear Princess, these are matters on which we cannot all agree. Let us let it pass, and speak of lighter things."

Thérèse acquiesced to her husband. In the last few years his attentions to her had become more frequent; his devotion, more profound. He delighted in waiting upon her, cheerfully calling himself her "aide-de-camp."

A footman arrived with a letter on an oblong silver tray, which he proffered to Madame d'Agoult, with a soft, verbal message. Madame d'Agoult handed the sealed document to Thérèse. "It is of an urgent nature, Your Highness," she said in an undertone. Thérèse noticed it bore Monsieur de Messy's seal. Opening the letter, it read as follows:

To Her Royal Highness, the most gracious and noble Dauphine of France, greetings!

Dear Madame la Dauphine,

Madame René Hervagault, *née* Nicole Bigot, the mother of the late Jean-Marie Hervagault and widow of the tailor of Saint-Lo, has been found. She is living in Paris not far from the site of the Temple in the Faubourg Marais. She dwells alone in rooms above a cobbler's shop, surviving on a pension from her relatives and perhaps from some unknown benefactor. She has not yet been confronted or interrogated. We hesitate to do so without specific instructions from Your Royal Highness, which we await, at Madame's convenience.

Your obedient servant,

Marquis de Messy, Grand Provost, Île-de-France

Thérèse steadfastly tried to display no emotion as she refolded the letter and stuffed it deep into her embroidery bag, but when she raised her head she noticed that Louis-Philippe was observing her. Not until her eyes locked with his did he look away, and quickly occupy himself with helping his wife attend to one of their younger children.

Thérèse's mind disengaged from her immediate surroundings and began planning how to rearrange her scheduled activities so that she herself could go to see Nicole Hervagault. She had decided that she alone would question the tailor's widow. Had Madame Hervagault allowed her son to be exchanged with Charles? Was the charming young vagrant found near Châlons in 1796 and given the identity of Jean-Marie Hervagault, really Louis XVII, King of France? Why did Hervagault's parents show no interest in him, but rather distanced themselves as his difficulties grew? Thérèse was bursting with the questions that had daunted her unrelentingly for fifteen years.

She was brought back to the present moment by Henri, who ran to her, clutching in his hand a bunch of *immortelles*, the delicate flowers Marie-Antoinette had so loved.

"For you, Madame la Dauphine," he said with a little bow.

"Oh, my precious boy!" exclaimed Thérèse, gathering him into her arms, flowers and all, kissing his cheeks and blond head. May the good God protect you always!" she cried, as she heard Charles' voice ringing in the chambers of her memory, as he handed their mother an *immortelle*: "Oh, Maman, I want you to be like this flower!"

The next afternoon, a coach without armorial bearings lumbered into the Faubourg Marais, having as its only passengers two heavily veiled ladies in summer silks.

"Monsieur de Messy sent us very explicit directions," said Thérèse to Pauline de Béarn. "Yet the coachman seems to be having great difficulty finding the place. An alley off a side street of the Rue du Temple should not be so difficult to find."

"Your Royal Highness forgets that the other vehicles do not know whose coach this is," said Pauline, "and so they are not moving aside for us. Therefore, it is taking longer just to traverse the city."

Thérèse could not help noticing as they passed certain shops that busts of Napoléon Buonaparte and souvenirs of his epoch were being proudly displayed. It was appalling to her that among the younger generation Buonaparte had become a folk hero. "They would not love him so much if they still had to pay the high taxes required by his constant warfare," commented Thérèse, nodding towards one annoyingly conspicuous display.

"Does Madame continue to insist upon going alone to speak to Widow Hervagault?" asked Pauline.

"It is the only way I will learn anything from her," said Thérèse. "She will be terrified enough as it is."

"But is it safe?"

"No, it is not, especially not in this neighborhood. However, I am willing to undertake the venture. Here is a mystery which has long eluded me, and yet the phantoms of the night have not ceased their hauntings."

"Do we know if she will be at home?" asked Pauline.

"Yes," replied the princess. "They have been watching the house and she never goes out at this time. Ah, I think perhaps we are almost there."

They passed the place where the Temple tower had stood, and Thérèse shuddered as if she were cold. Making a sharp turn down a side street, the coach halted at a corner near an alley which was too narrow for the vehicle. Thérèse climbed out of the coach with the aid of an unliveried footman, leaping onto one of the new sidewalks, which under King Charles X had been a welcome addition to Parisian streets.

"I shall return within the hour," said Thérèse to Pauline. With the plainclothes footman following at a discreet distance, Thérèse made her way down the alley, trying not to step in puddles and piles of rubbish, while peering through her veils for something that resembled a cobbler's shop. Vendors, urchins, and other passersby instinctively moved aside for her, making her wonder if she had worn too fine a dress. She spotted a sign carved to look like a large wooden sabot. She entered the shop. There was the immediate smell of leather and wood. Samples of the craftsman's wares were hanging from the ceiling. The cobbler himself was seated on a low bench, carving a child's wooden shoe. He stood up quickly, for no veil could hide the fact that she was a great lady.

"Madame …?" he sputtered, bowing several times.

"Does Madame Hervagault reside in this house?" asked Thérèse.

"Yes, Madame, up those stairs to the attic. I will show you." The stout man started puffing in the direction of a narrow, wooden stair at the back of the shop.

"Thank you, Monsieur, but it is not necessary. I shall find the way." She glanced out the window and her footman was standing solemnly and resolutely in front of the house in the dim alley. She hoped no one picked his pockets. The steps creaked as she ascended them into the increasing dimness of the rafters. She knocked at the low door at the top of the flight. It opened, and Thérèse saw a small but sturdy peasant woman, looking as if she had stepped from the fields of Normandy, especially in her starched cap and white apron. There was no flicker of the type of beauty that one would associate with the former mistress of the Prince of Monaco, except perhaps in her large, blue eyes, fringed with thick lashes in her worn, weathered face, eyes which, at that moment, were dark with fear. The bent little woman united an intake of breath with the sudden clapping of both hands over her mouth.

"Please do not be afraid," said Thérèse, her cavernous voice filling the small, dark stairwell. "You are Madame Nicole Hervagault, the widow of René Hervagault of Saint-Lo?" The woman curtsied tremblingly and nodded. "May I enter? I have some important questions I must ask you."

"Please, Madame. Come in. Pardon my bad manners," said Nicole Hervagault, finding her voice at last. She closed the door and showed Thérèse to a rickety chair. The room was shadowy and stuffy, for the small, square windows were shuttered against the heat of the day.

Thérèse raised her veil, partly in order to breathe. "I am your Dauphine, Marie-Thérèse de France. I do not wish to frighten or startle you," she hastily added, as Nicole Hervagault fell to her knees. "Please get up. I come today not as a princess, but as a Frenchwoman searching for her lost brother. I think perhaps you might be able to help me. Please, Madame, you have no reason to be afraid." The poor widow was visibly quaking, her eyes darting around like a trapped bird's, frequently pausing on the small wooden crucifix that hung over a chest of drawers, not far from a faded engraving of Thérèse's father, King Louis XVI.

"Oh, Madame la Dauphine, it... it... it is not you whom I fear. But...I have long dreaded this day, and yet...long have I expected it."

"You are the mother of one Jean-Marie Hervagault, natural son of the Duc de Valentinois, Prince of Monaco?"

Her face became taut, as her eyes widened, as if in agony. "Yes, Madame. Jean-Marie...was my son...before I married René

Hervagault. His father was the Duc de Valentinois, but René adopted him, and gave him his surname."

"In what year was Jean-Marie born?" asked Thérèse.

"Some eight years before the Revolution, around 1781, I think, Madame," replied the widow.

"During the Revolution, a police commissioner named Rémy Bigot lived in this district. Your maiden name was Bigot. Was he a relative of yours?"

Nicole Hervagault looked at the floor and did not reply.

"In June of 1795 a young boy died in the Temple," continued Thérèse. "Rémy Bigot identified the body as belonging to my brother, King Louis XVII, and signed the death certificate accordingly. I do not think, however, that the boy was my brother. Persons who saw him describe him as looking to be about fourteen or fifteen years old, while my brother would only have been ten. I was in the rooms above, but never allowed to see the corpse, nor even to visit or care for the patient before he died. I wonder, Madame, if you know the identity of the boy?"

From Madame Hervagault's eyes, tears began to trickle, but she said nothing.

"In 1798, your husband went to Châlons, where he identified a young boy of about thirteen to be your son, Jean-Marie, who would have been seventeen at the time. The mysterious boy stayed with you on and off between 1796 and 1799, and it is said that your husband always addressed him in a respectful manner. The boy was finally thrown into prison as a swindler. Afterwards, he joined the navy, but deserted and was imprisoned again in Bicêtre where he allegedly died in 1812. While suffering so many trials, it is said that the young man was abandoned by you and your husband, who would not help him in any way. Can you tell me why this was so?" Thérèse asked as gently as possible, for she pitied the woman, who was shuddering from suppressed sobs.

"Oh, Madame la Dauphine," choked Nicole. "René... René was good to me, but he could be a hard man. My Jean-Marie was the son of a prince...he had a special way about him that my husband did not like. He...he...." She broke off, and covered her face with her hands, convulsively weeping.

"Did René sell Jean-Marie to the revolutionaries through your cousin, Rémy Bigot?" asked Thérèse. "Was it not Jean-Marie who died in the Temple on June 8, 1795, just around the corner from this house?"

"Oh, Madame, forgive me, forgive me, but I fear...I cannot say."

"What do you mean you 'cannot say'? We must never fear to speak the truth. You mean that you have been threatened, and that the day you speak, the truth about Jean-Marie's fate, that day will be your last on earth. Who has threatened you so?"

Nicole said nothing, but only sobbed. Thérèse reached into a small velvet purse, and drew out an emerald brooch, surrounded by diamonds, as well as two garnet bracelets, and a ruby ring. The jewels, luminous in the dark room, flashed with their own sparks of flame. The tailor's widow's eyes widened.

"Madame Hervagault, I would like very much to make you the gift of these jewels," said Thérèse. "I have receipts for each setting, so that you can sell them if you desire, and have a more comfortable life than you have now. But first, I must know everything that you can tell me about Jean-Marie and if he was exchanged for my brother. The boy who was arrested in Châlons in 1798, I do not think was your son. Was he my brother Louis XVII?"

"I do not know," said Nicole. "Oh, Madame. I can say no more. Forgive me, but I swore...never to speak of it. I am too afraid...."

Thérèse put the jewels away. "I am sorry you will not accept my gift, Madame Hervagault. I truly want to help you, and protect you from whomever it is you fear. I cannot and will not force you to speak. But I do have something that I will be able to leave with you."

Thérèse reached into her purse again and took out the lock of chestnut hair that had been taken from the boy who died in the Temple on June 8, 1795 and which did not belong to Charles. She handed it to Nicole.

"This lock of hair was taken from a boy who died not far from here," said Thérèse.

Madame Hervagault examined the lock with trembling fingers, then kissing it several times, she sank to her knees in a storm of weeping. At that moment, Thérèse was almost certain what had become of Charles. Slipping a few gold coins onto the chair, she departed from the cobbler's shop.

Part III: THE DEBACLE

Chapter Twenty-five:

Visions

Spring 1830

> *"My spirit trembled, I Daniel was affrighted at these things, and the visions of my head troubled me." Daniel 7:15*

In 1830, the Third Sunday of Easter, coincided with Saint Mark's Day, and the traditional rogation procession granted to the citizens of Paris surpassed in pageantry and solemnity anything that had been seen in years. In full regalia the King, the Daupin, the Dauphine, the Duchesse de Berry and the royal children led the march, beginning at the Cathedral of Notre Dame, where high pontifical Vespers had been chanted. The focal point, however, was not the King and his family but the silver coffin bearing the incorrupt remains of a simple man, a man who had lived in poverty, who had exhausted himself caring for the poor. The body of Saint Vincent de Paul, founder of the Congregation of the Mission and the Sisters of Charity, was finally coming home to rest in his own Church with his spiritual sons.

During the Revolution, when so many precious relics were destroyed with quicklime, the hallowed body of the priest from Gascony was hidden in the homes of faithful Catholics. The body was at long last to be exposed for public veneration, in spite of the strong, anti-clerical sentiments, for France was taking arms against Algiers, where Saint Vincent had once been a galley slave. The Archbishop of Paris, Monseigneur de Quélen, reluctant at first to risk the rancor of the Left, gave permission for the festivity, hoping to gain the blessing of the great saint upon the royal armies. He himself conducted the magnificent ceremonies, walking behind the precious casket among the other prelates in shimmering vestments, mitres sparking with jewels, croziers flashing in the April sun.

All the clergy and various religious orders were represented in the processions, but pride of place was given to the supernatural progeny of Saint Vincent, to the Vincentian priests in their worn, black soutanes, and the Sisters of Charity in their wide, starched cornets. Among them, quite unnoticed by the crowds, who cheered or hissed with equal alacrity, was a brand new novice, in a black wool dress with large white collar and a black cap with white trim. As she walked among her sisters, behind their beloved founder, eyes downcast as became a humble novice, she truly felt that she was no longer on earth.

Zoé Labouré, or "Sister Labouré," as she was now called, had never before seen the King. She had pictured him looking rather like her father, Pierre Labouré, who was certainly the king of the family farm in the village of Fain-les-Moutiers. No monarch commanded more respect than Pierre Labouré sitting at the head of the table, surrounded by his sons, waited upon by his daughters, as he silenced with a single glance, or the raising of an eyebrow. No sovereign dispensed justice with more authority than Zoé's father, resting by the fire in the evenings, smoking his pipe, silently weighing each side of a question, then settling the matter with one gruff word or quick gesture. In such a moment, he had once conveyed to her his refusal to give his permission for her to enter religion, shattering the dream of her life with one blow of his blunt "No!"

In the plain, determined face of the Burgundian peasant girl shown her father's eyes, quick, blue and still welling from the splendors of Notre Dame Cathedral. Her senses were filled with the incense, the majestic organ and choir, as her spirit soared heavenward. The old, faraway life at Fain-les-Moutiers, the lush meadows and vineyards, the smells and noises of the farm and livestock, receded into the beyond, while remaining part of an intricate woven pattern, a dazzlingly complicated tapestry that was taking on shape and meaning. Suddenly her existence of twenty-four years seemed to harmonize with the past, with Clovis, who donated the land for the ancient monastery of Moutiers; with Saint Bernard, who once prayed and preached not far from Zoé's birthplace, with Burgundian Soeur Marguerite-Marie, who in her Visitation Monastery at Paray-le-Monial had been favored by the Sacred Heart with many apparitions and messages. The glorious possibilities appeared to be endless and unfathomable as the dome of blue sky above, with miracles hovering in the very air she breathed.

The bells pealed in the churches of Paris. Zoé remembered that she had been born as the Angelus bell was ringing in the steeple of the ancient parish church of Fain-les-Moutiers. She especially loved the three mystic hours of the day when the Angelus bell chimed, and the family would stop their chores, kneeling together to recite the Angelic Salutation. "The Angel of the Lord declared unto Mary ..." The Angelus was part of the rhythm of her existence; the church bells continuing their call to prayer even when her mother died and the essence of life at the Labouré farm seemed turned on its head. Zoé instinctively sought the aid of the Most Holy Virgin, climbing on a stool before the statue of Our Lady that graced a shelf in her parents' bedroom, where her mother had expired a few days previously. Taking the statue down, she threw her arms around it, pressing her warm little cheek against the cold one of the image.

"Now, dear Blessed Mother, now you will be my mother!" The statue remained inanimate, as Zoé placed her back on the shelf, but an intensity of love united her nine-year-old heart with the fiery Heart of the Immaculate. A practical, unimaginative child, preferring real life and real work to games and fairy tales, as soon as she was old enough, she took over the running of the house with peaceful efficiency, surrounded all the while by an unseen radiance of a hidden presence. It did not seem to her to be such an extraordinary or impossible thing that someday she might glimpse the Mother of God, even for an instant.

As she daily renewed her consecration to her Mother, a vocation to the religious life seemed to her the most natural, logical, happy conclusion to her girlhood. Instead of allowing her to enter the convent, Père Labouré sent Zoé to work in a Paris bistro owned by her brother. In the noisy, raucous hole-in-the-wall, Zoé rushed from table to table, serving wine, bread, soup, and cheese to rough city workmen, amid loud oaths and foul jokes, her serene hopes almost smashed.

As the majestic procession entered the Church of Saint Vincent, Zoé uttered a prayer of thanksgiving, as she recalled how her dark days at the bistro were brightened by the memory of a dream she had in 1824, a dream of assisting at the Mass of a venerable, bearded priest, who beckoned her to follow him. In her dream, she ran from the church, and went to visit a sick friend, but found the same priest waiting for her in the sickroom.

"You do well to visit the sick, *ma fille*," said the priest. "You run from me now, but one day you will be happy to come. God has plans for you. Do not forget it." She later saw a portrait of the mysterious priest, and was told that he was none other than Saint Vincent de Paul, father of the poor, and confessor of the kings and queens of France. She wondered at this because she had little or no devotion to him, and had never prayed to him.

In the meantime, her sufferings increased, as she was sent away from the bistro to a private academy for wealthy young ladies, conducted by her sister-in-law. Zoé at twenty-three could neither read nor write, and her honest peasant manners were buffoonish in the eyes of the adolescent girls whose company she was forced to keep. The illiterate farm maid, undaunted by hard labor and caring for the sick poor, was unequal to the giggles and snickers of the pampered, middle class demoiselles. But God did not abandon her to such a miserable existence amid excruciating elegance. Her father relented at last, her brothers and sisters provided a dowry, and she joyfully entered the postulancy of the Sisters of Charity at Châtillon, where she finally learned to read. She was sent to the Motherhouse of the order on the Rue de Bac in Paris, in time to bask in the glory of her doggedly, persistent patron, Saint Vincent de Paul.

For nine days, Zoé and the other Sisters of Charity knelt with the multitudes at the coffin of Saint Vincent, pleading for his intercession on behalf of France and her armies. On the fifth day as on the first, the King was present, kneeling at the foot of the altar, the short Dauphin on his right and the tall Dauphine on his left. Yet for Sister Labouré, what had begun as joyous experience became an anguished one.

Every evening of the novena, upon her return to the Motherhouse on the Rue de Bac, she had a vision. In the sisters' chapel, over a reliquary of Saint Vincent's arm on Saint Joseph's altar, Zoé saw a heart, which changed from white to red on successive nights. She glanced around to see if anyone else saw the heart, but the other sisters were absorbed in their own meditations. On the third evening, the heart turned to a deep vermilion, and the novice heard a voice, saying: "The heart of Saint Vincent is deeply afflicted at the sorrows which will befall France."

"Oh, *mon Dieu*, what will happen to my country?" Zoé asked herself. An oppression descended upon her, as she wondered if she were going mad, or if the devil was trying to deceive her, or if she were merely given to vain imaginings, and did not truly have a vocation. When the novena ended, so did the visions, and for a brief time she had peace. The corrections from her Mistress of Novices were a welcome trial compared to the sightings of the heart floating in mid-air.

The tranquility was short-lived. At Mass in the early spring dawns, before a long day of mopping, scrubbing, washing clothes, tending the sick and orphaned, Sister Labouré saw the living Christ within the Host in the hands of the priest. She knew that she was seeing the reality that lay behind the veils of faith, the fact of the Real Presence in the Eucharist, in which she firmly believed, without seeing.

On Trinity Sunday, the vision was manifested to her in a unique way. During the singing of the Gospel, she suppressed a gasp, because standing there on the altar was Our Lord Jesus Christ in all His radiance and glory, looking solemnly at her. He was clad in royal robes, complete with crown and scepter, with a cross on His chest. She could not understand why no one else saw Him, so bright was the magnificence of Christ the King. In the blink of an eye, the Savior was divested of His sovereign regalia, as the crown, cross and scepter fell from him; the kingly mantle melted away.

Zoé felt her heart wrench within her for sorrow, for she was seized with a presentiment of disaster for France, and for France's King. Oh, the poor King! Whatever was about to befall him must be terrible indeed! But who could warn him? Zoé sighed. She was not Jeanne d'Arc. She had to tell someone, though, and who else but her confessor? Father Aladel was a stern man, with no patience for imaginative novices. She trembled at the thought of having to tell him of the visions, but resolved to do so.

Chapter Twenty-six:
The Ball
Spring 1830

"All they enemies have opened their mouth against thee: they have hissed, and gnashed with the teeth, and have said: We will swallow her up: lo, this is the day we have looked for: we have found it, we have seen it." *Lamentations 2:16*

In the heart of Paris, the Palais Royal was illumined like a dwelling of the realm of faery. The Duc and Duchesse d'Orléans were hosting a magnificent ball in honor of the King and Queen of Naples. It was the grandest social event since the Duchesse de Berry's masquerade, more than a year earlier. Caroline had enchanted everyone as a diminutive Marie Stuart, all in white and sparkling with jewels. On the May evening she shone all the more, in snowy organza with pale pink rosebuds wreathing her golden head and creamy shoulders. The stout King of Naples was her Papa and his domineering Queen, her step-mother. Her Tante Amélie, Duchesse d'Orléans, the King of Naples' sister, presided with a quiet dignity, leaving Caroline the unchallenged belle of the festivity. She waltzed with Louis-Philippe's eldest son, the handsome Duc de Chartres, among the other swirling hoops, beneath the great chandeliers, each completely lit. Paganini himself played intermittent solos upon his rapturous violin. On a dais not far from one of the refreshment tables sat King Charles X with the royal guests, chatting amicably.

All Paris had wondered if the King would deign to appear, for the Palais Royal was a liberal hotbed, but Charles X was fond of Louis-Philippe, and would never be so rude as to refuse an invitation from his favorite cousin on an occasion of such brilliance. The Dauphin Louis-Antoine stood close to his father's chair, discussing the war in Algiers with several old generals, but otherwise looking more awkward and out of place than usual. Duty compelled him to accompany the King; he would have happily stayed home to watch the stars with his new telescope, for he detested Louis-Philippe, and hated the Palais Royal.

The Duc d'Orléans, in a uniform covered with gold embroidery, danced rather awkwardly with a slender, dark lady in a shimmering silk of the palest silvery blue. She was none other than Dorothée de Courlande, Duchesse de Dino, Talleyrand's niece by marriage and one of the most infamous courtesans in Paris. Permanently separated from her husband, she resided at Talleyrand's house as his most indispensable hostess and helpmate. Her wit, charm, and amiability had won for her influence and prestige among the luminaries of aristocratic society.

"What an extraordinary *fête* this is, Monseigneur," said La Dino.

"Extraordinary, Madame? But why?" asked Louis-Philippe, brows knit in mock humor."

"So many republicans and revolutionaries all gathered to honor a King and his Queen. Let me see, there is my uncle the Prince, Monsieur de Lafayette, Messieurs Theirs and Mignet, the banker Lafitte, and the Duc de Broglie, to name a few." She laughed. "It does not surprise me that Madame la Dauphine decided not to come."

"Madame la Dauphine does not care for the Palais Royale," said Louis-Philippe. "She cannot forget the *Ça ira* was once played here at one of my father's parties. However, the Duchesse begged her to come, and she may, but it is doubtful."

La Dino lowered her voice. "Perhaps she knows the end is near. As my uncle has said, nothing can now prevent disaster for the senior branch of Bourbons. Ever since last March, when the King's hat fell off during his speech, tumbling down the steps of the throne, and you, Monseigneur, retrieved it, it has been clear to many that it is only a matter of time. After the long, difficult winter, Paris is like a tinder box. The slightest spark will set it ablaze, and then who will step in to take the reins of government?" She raised her eyebrows and stared pointedly at Louis-Philippe, whose face clouded with a distant seriousness.

As they swished past the long refreshment table, Louis-Philippe nodded to Talleyrand, who was plotting behind the huge silver punch bowl with Madame Adelaïde d'Orléans.

"My brother hesitates to throw himself into the fray," sighed Adelaïde, looking more and more like her father Philippe Egalité as she aged, and her aquiline nose became more accentuated. "All we need is one good blunder on the part of the King to bring about the necessary catastrophe which will force Louis-Philippe's hand. He will not openly take a stand against the King, but neither will he allow his family to be exiled again because of the obtuseness of our relatives. You did well, Prince, you and Lafitte, to give money to Thiers and Mignet with which to start the *National*. Its articles are certain to provoke a crisis."

"A crisis! Indeed, Madame, it has already provoked one," retorted Talleyrand. His hair was powdered in the old style; for that matter, his embroidered coat and silk breeches were after the fashion of the *ancien-régime* he had done so much to overthrow. Leaning on his cane, unable, as ever, to dance due to his crippled foot, his complexion was grayish and corpselike, but his deep voice as caressing as ever. "The liberal bourgeoisie have lapped up the ideas set forth in the *National*. They are now convinced that the constitutional *régime* desired by the nation is incompatible with the maintenance of the throne of Charles X and his family. The people think that the King's minister, Prince de Polignac, is a bogey-man, representing all the evils of the *ancien-régime*. In reality, of course, Polignac favors constitutional government, but no one would now believe it."

"As for the Rightest press," said Adelaïde, "you would almost think they were on our side. They are urging the King to follow Article XIV of the Charter, which allows the sovereign to seize, in critical circumstances, dictatorial power! If only he would, what a conflagration it would bring about!"

The very idea of revolution excited Mademoiselle Adelaïde in much the same way it had thrilled her father, the Red Duke. She saw herself as the tool for the fulfillment of Philippe Egalité's dream. Talleyrand did not appear to share her elation.

"It was I who was responsible for the recall of the Bourbons to France," he said, sadly and softly. "I did it to restore peace to France. Now it is necessary to drive them out again in order to maintain the peace." He bowed to Mademoiselle Adelaïde, for the King of France was beckoning to him. Talleyrand hobbled over to the dais, making a low, court bow to his royal master, the friend of his misspent youth.

"Ah, Talleyrand," said the King. "It has been quite some time since we had the pleasure of your company. You must know, of course, of the nefarious plots that are afoot. If any friends of yours are involved, tell them that I am determined to crush such schemes, and will do so, to maintain order. I am not my hapless brother, Louis XVI, and will not give in to their demands as he did."

Talleyrand assumed an impassive, sphinx-like air. "You, Sire, are ever the man of action," he replied. "Your Majesty has never allowed himself to be overtaken by events, as was proved in July of 1789."

Charles X ignored the allusion to his past flight to safety. "They are comparing me to James II of England, and my family to the elder branch of the Stuarts. As I have often said, I would prefer to chop wood than govern like an English king. In France, the King is the source of constitutional authority, not the National Assembly or parliament. They think to cow me with the fate of the Stuarts, but I will not be cowed, or threatened. When a king is threatened, he has no choice but to climb onto his horse and fight; either that or he will find himself in a tumbrel."

"Sire, may I suggest that Your Majesty has forgotten another means of conveyance: the stagecoach," hinted Talleyrand, blandly. Charles X's brown eyes were as wide and uncomprehending as a hurt child's. He nodded a curt dismissal to

Talleyrand, who slithered off to find La Dino, and regale her with a new account of his devastating wit.

Chateaubriand was lingering near the King. He had overheard Talleyrand's impudence, and was seething anew against the apostate bishop. It seemed unfair that such a debased, cynical character possessed the ability to manipulate persons and events like so many marionettes in a children's theater, while he, Chateaubriand, the high-minded defender of religion and the crown, was rendered virtually impotent to prevent a debacle from occurring. It was he, Chateaubriand, who should be in Prince de Polignac's place. Why did the Bourbons always select the most stupid people for the most demanding tasks? Why was his beautiful dream of royal France deteriorating before his eyes? Then his gaze fell upon Caroline, who for a moment was unengaged in an interlude between waltzes. She sparkled like a living star, and he longed to dance with her. Her quick agility and lightsome, impetuous moods had made him dub her "a crazy, Italian tight-rope dancer," but she was his princess and the mother of his future king, embodying to him whatever enchantment was left in the cold, utilitarian, modern world. He took a step towards the Duchesse de Berry, but in that instant a tall Neapolitan gentleman approached her, kissed her hand, and as the music started, swept her away in his arms.

"Monsieur de Lucchesi-Palli, I have not seen you since the Epiphany," said Caroline, lightly, not raising her eyes to his. "I hope all has been well with you?"

"I have stayed away," said Hector in an undertone, ignoring her last question. "Principessa, I... I have striven to avoid you, as you have asked. I came tonight at the request of Their Majesties...and to see Your Royal Highness one more time.

Caroline's lower lip trembled ever so slightly. "You are leaving? You are returning to Naples?" she asked.

"No, Madame. I have asked to be sent to The Hague. I will be leaving tomorrow."

"The Hague!" exclaimed Caroline so loudly that other dancers regarded her with curiosity. "Then, truly, I shall never see you again." She raised her eyes to his, brimming with tears, then quickly looked down again. "It is better this way. I wish you every happiness, Hector."

"If you ever need me," he said, firmly, "I shall come!"

Caroline was prevented from replying by the Duc's chamberlain, banging his staff three times on the floor, and announcing in resounding tones: "Her Royal Highness, the Dauphine!"

The dancing ceased at once, and the orchestra was silenced a moment, until it began to play Gluck's chorus from *Iphigénie*, "Let us praise and celebrate our queen." The assemblage turned and faced the marble staircase, which a woman was slowly and stiffly descending. Every gentleman bowed, as the ladies dropped their curtsies. The white plumes of the Dauphine's headdress made her appear taller than she actually was; the few fine wrinkles on her firm skin and the few silver threads in the braided loops of her chestnut mane, belied the fact that she had passed the half-century mark. The simplicity of her ivory satin gown, dotted with pearls, accented her agelessness, albeit the flared skirt and voluminous, puffed sleeves were according to the current fashion.

"She exudes majesty, and the aura of both the throne and the scaffold," thought Chateaubriand. "If only the Salic law did not prevent her from being the queen regnant, perhaps we would not be facing the present crisis."

Thérèse, in mid-descent, was noticing all the blazing chandeliers, and wondered at the extravagance. She had not wanted to come to the ball, but decided at the last minute to do so, because her father-in-law at the Palais Royal was like a baby in a den of vipers. The political situation was grim, in spite of the victories at Algiers. Her rheumatism made such a flight of stairs difficult, so she took them gradually. Two of her ladies followed with like deliberateness.

Except for her aches and pains, Thérèse at fifty-one was more energetic than ever before. Every morning at half past five, she and Antoine assisted at Mass together, beginning their long, busy days. In the past, difficult winter, she had worn out her fingers making garments for the poor, as well as organizing clothing drives and soup kitchens. Caroline had likewise devoted herself to charitable works, a bit more ostentatiously, however. Thérèse still took great care to be as anonymous as possible, and so received little or no credit in the eyes of the masses.

At the foot of the stairs, Louis-Philippe and Marie-Amélie waited to welcome her. Louis-Philippe wore an expression of sheepish guilt; his wife's face was a mingling of sweetness and worry. Thérèse greeted her cousins, then walked between them through the divided throng to the dais, where Thérèse made her obeisance to the sovereigns. She detested the Queen of Naples, an unendurably bossy woman, one of the Spanish Bourbons. As for the Neapolitan King, he was oblivious to the fact that Paris was on the verge of upheaval, so enthralled was he with the delights of Paris, and Thérèse wondered if he would ever go home. Her father-in-law and Antoine both seemed glad to see her.

"My dear daughter, how pleased we are that you have come," said Charles X. "It would please us even more to see you dancing. If Monsieur d'Orléans would oblige...."

Louis-Philippe bowed in acquiescence and taking Thérèse's hand, led her into the middle of the ballroom. Mercifully, the orchestra played a stately polonaise; Thérèse did not think she could have managed anything faster. Louis-Philippe was a far worse dancer than herself.

"Madame de Genlis thought me to be hopelessly clumsy, and as you can see, she never taught me how to dance," he said, as he trod on her satin slipper. Thérèse's inward flinch did not show upon her face.

"Your Highness's governess preferred to instill in you qualities she thought to be more productive," commented Thérèse, "such as political ambition."

Louis-Philippe raised an eyebrow as if in surprise. "Madame la Dauphine, I am the most content of men, and do not desire to be anything more than what I am."

"Come now, Monseigneur," said Thérèse. "You are your father's son."

"And you, Madame, are your mother's daughter," retorted Louis-Philippe. "I tell you that the bourgeoisie are impatient to partake more broadly in the government. The franchise must be extended to include them."

"Very well, let us then extend the franchise," said Thérèse. "But where will it end? Someday you will have a plebiscite, and plebiscites lead eventually to dictators. Those who are not educated or well-informed; those who are deluded by masonic propaganda, will in the end vote for whoever is clever enough or handsome enough or able to lead an army. You may think, dear cousin, that with your cumbersome relatives out of the way you, with your immense popularity and ability to charm the wealthy factory-owners, will make a superb modern ruler. Alas! You are but a pawn, a tool, a stepping-stone to the next stage. But of that perhaps you are already aware...."

Louis-Philippe clouded with anger, and Thérèse guessed she had been importunate again. "Madame, I have always been loyal to His Majesty. If you accuse me of plots against the King, you are gravely mistaken. It is Your Highness, who for the safety of the dynasty, must urge upon the King the necessity of conforming to the times."

"I shall never waver from upholding the traditions of France," said Thérèse. "I warn you, Louis-Philippe. In the end, the liberal and progressive ideas you espouse will be your ruin, for as I told you many years ago, it is impossible to be a prince and a republican."

To their mutual relief, both the dance and the conversation abruptly ended, for through the windows of the ballroom, piercing shouts of "Long live the Duc d'Orléans!" rose above the strains of music. Thérèse froze, too well did she remember the sounds of a mob, and one had gathered in the courtyard outside. The other dancers halted as well, and many hurried to the windows to see. Huge bonfires had been lit, and flames leaped to the sky.

Caroline found Hector Lucchesi-Palli hovering protectively at her side. She whispered to him; he, in turn, said a few words to the conductor. The orchestra began to play a lively *tarantella*, composed for Caroline by Rossini. Caroline and Hector began to dance with an almost fierce gaiety. The effect was electrifying; other guests left the windows and followed their lead.

The color drained from Thérèse's face at the sight of the leaping flames. As she turned gray, Pauline de Béarn and Madame d'Agoult began to wave a fan over her. The King and Antoine left the dais and rushed over; Antoine put his arm around her.

"Come sit down, my dear," said Charles X. "It is nothing. Have some champagne."

"Oh, Papa, I have heard and seen all of this before! Sire, they insult you! By cheering for Orléans, they deliberately insult their King."

"Nonsense. I shall go onto the balcony and show myself to the people. All will be well, you shall see, my daughter."

"I shall come with you, Sire," she said.

"No, my dear. Once you stood on a balcony and faced an angry mob. You shall never be asked to do so again, at least not by me. Stay with her, Antoine." Antoine took Thérèse's hand, and sat beside her. The dancing resolutely continued, with the music and footsteps almost drowning out the hooting and the shouts. The flames climbed.

"This truly is a Neapolitan ball," said Antoine. "Just as in Naples we feast and dance over a volcano!"

The King walked towards the balcony, his slim form silhouetted against the orange glow of the bonfire. As he stepped outside, the cries grew more hostile. Not a single *Vive le Roi* was heard, rather the shouts of *Vive Orléans* intensified. Thérèse felt cold beads of perspiration break out on her forehead. She was plunged backwards into a churning pool of memories. The King remained on the balcony some minutes, dignified and unruffled. At last he left it, still calm and serene, as the wildness of the mob increased. The troops would have to be called to restore order. The King and his entourage departed soon afterwards from the Palais Royal, thanking the Duc and Duchesse for the ball. Thérèse followed, without a word to anyone. As the royal carriages clattered away Talleyrand watched from a window, with La Dino at his side.

"Charles X is the least capable of the Kings of France," remarked the ex-bishop. "He makes the most mistakes and will continue to do so." He sighed. "Yet I have always esteemed him, because he is the most faithful and one of the best men that I have ever known."

Chapter Twenty-seven:
The Lady
Spring 1830

"And a great sign appeared in heaven: A woman clothed with the sun, and the moon under her feet, and on her head a crown of twelve stars." Apocalypse 12:1

The summer evening was warm but not oppressive as Sister Labouré retired into the small curtained cubicle for a well-earned rest. She had quickly become accustomed to the night sounds of Paris; the voices, carriage wheels, clattering of hooves and various comings and goings of the Rue de Bac did not disturb her repose or meditations. Through the shuttered windows of the dormitory one could glimpse the dusky sky, painted in a color of blue that only God could have invented. Sprinkling the four corners of the cubicle with holy water and then blessing herself, Sister Labouré slipped between the coarse homespun sheets of the narrow, trestle bed. The faint rustling and breathing of the other novices in their own cubicles could barely be heard.

They had all worked very hard that day preparing for the feast of their Holy Father Saint Vincent de Paul on the morrow. No bride had been dressed with as much care as the altar in the chapel of the Motherhouse, with starched and snowy linens; flowers decked among the gleaming candlesticks; the floors scrubbed and waxed. Zoé sighed with happiness, and opening her clutched palm, she kissed a small, square piece of white cloth that she had been holding. It was a piece of Saint Vincent's own surplice, and each of the novices had been given a similar precious fragment.

"Oh, Father Saint Vincent," whispered Zoé. "Please, let me see her. Please obtain that I might see Our Lady."

The only response was silence, and the slight movement of the curtains in the whistling of air that had somehow whisked through the shutters.

"Oh, Father Saint Vincent," Zoé continued to pray. "Be a father to me. Is it too bold of me to beg to be permitted to see Our Lady, my Mother?" A sense of confusion seized her. Zoé's confessor, Father Aladel, had sternly told her that her visions were nonsense; she should ignore them, and give them not the slightest credence. She was resolved to obey him, and struggled to put the memory from her mind, occupying herself with her novice duties and learning the rules of their congregation. Yet the visions had seemed so real, and beyond anything she could have concocted in her mind, being bereft of the necessary imagination to do so.

Zoé trembled from sheer anguish. In a moment of desperation, she tore her relic of Saint Vincent's surplice in half and swallowed one tiny particle of the cloth. She had heard of people being healed by imbibing oil burned before miraculous images and the tombs of the saints, or by drinking water from sacred wells or springs. Surely, if her visions were not of divine origin, it was a malady of sorts, from which she needed to be healed.

"Oh, my Father Saint Vincent, pray for me." She closed her eyes, and as she drifted into a slumber, a sense of peace came to her, then a certain piercing thought: "Tonight, I shall see her. Tonight I shall see the Most Blessed Virgin."

A voice was calling her. "Sister Labouré! Sister Labouré!" Had she overslept? But no, it was still very dark, perhaps only around midnight. Zoé climbed from bed and quietly drew back the curtains of her cubicle. She saw a little boy in a white gown of about four or five years old. A soft radiance shown and shimmered around him, and his feet seemed to barely touch the floor.

Somehow, she knew him to be her guardian angel; he did not seem a stranger to her, but an old friend, although she had never before beheld him.

"Come to the chapel," he said. "Get up and come to the chapel. The Blessed Virgin is awaiting you!"

Sister Labouré quickly retreated behind the curtain and dressed, her nimble fingers managing all the complicated ties and buttons of her habit. She was wide awake, peaceful and elated at the same time. She followed her angel out of the dormitory and down the corridor. All the lamps were lit wherever they went, which particularly astonished her, even more than the fact of the mysterious child, although she did not know why it did. At length they came to the chapel. It was illumined as if for Midnight Mass. Even the candles of the chandeliers were ablaze.

Her angel bade her kneel in the sanctuary near the priest's chair. She obeyed, and remained on her knees for what seemed an eternity, while her little companion stood nearby in rapt attention, like a small soldier waiting for a superior of the utmost importance. Zoé looked around the chapel. There was no one to be seen, not in any of the doorways or windows, no sight of the Blessed Virgin at all. Was this all a trick or a terrible, vainglorious delusion? The child's voice, both wise and sweet, called to her again: "Here is the Blessed Virgin! Here she is!"

Zoé heard a rustling as if from the finest silk in the world. Descending the steps from the Gospel side of the high altar was a Lady. Her beauty was that of the most radiant dawn over Fain-les-Moutiers, of which Zoé had seen many, but the iridescent blueness and whiteness of her mantle and gown put the colors of the morning sky to shame. The Lady's face shone with a surpassing beauty and mercy that was beyond telling. Zoé dared not look into her eyes. The Lady sat in the chair. The child spoke again, but this time his voice was as deep as a man's: "This is the Blessed Virgin!"

Zoé found herself kneeling at the Lady's feet, resting her arms upon the Lady's knees. Blissful awe mingling with filial intimacy swept over her. She slowly looked up into the face and eyes of the Blessed Mother, and almost died of joy. Then the Queen of Heaven spoke to her.

"My child, the good God wishes to give you a mission. You will suffer many trials because of it, but you will overcome them with the thought that it is for the glory of God. You will be tormented. You will be contradicted, but you will receive grace. Fear not. You will see certain things. You will be inspired in your prayers. Give your confessor an account of them. Tell with confidence all that passes within you; tell it with simplicity. Have confidence and fear not."

"But my Mother and my Queen, what of the visions I have seen already? What of the heart, and the appearance of Christ the King?" asked Sister Labouré.

"My child," replied the Holy Virgin, "the times are very bad. Calamities are going to fall upon France. The whole world will be in an upheaval due to all sorts of trouble." The compassionate eyes of the Virgin were filled with sorrow, as if of a thousand worlds. "But come to the foot of the altar. There graces will be shed upon all, great and little, who ask for them. Graces will be shed especially upon those who ask for them, with fervent confidence." The Queen of Heaven began to speak of the Sisters of Charity and the Vincentian fathers, that there were many abuses in the following of the rules, and much relaxation, but when the rigorous observance was restored, there would be peace, blessings, and growth granted to the spiritual family of Saint Vincent de Paul. Then the Lady's face clouded once more, and her words came in a slow and halting manner, as if what she had to say was breaking her Heart. "A moment will come when danger will be great. It will seem as if all were lost, but have confidence. Do not be discouraged. I will be with you."

Tears began to stream from the Lady's eyes. "There will be victims among the clergy of Paris. Monseigneur the Archbishop...." The Queen of Heaven wept so profusely, she was not able to finish her sentence. "My child, the Cross will be scorned. It will be thrown to the ground. Blood will flow. They will again open the side of Our Lord. The streets will stream with blood. Monseigneur the Archbishop will be stripped of his garments...." The Holy Virgin seemed wrenched with anguish, like a Mother watching her child die. "My child, the whole world will be in sorrow." Her face reflected a grief so profound that Zoé's heart almost stopped. The

Queen of Heaven did not speak again, but somehow Zoé was given to know that the catastrophes were not all to befall at once, but within a span of forty years.

"She is gone," said the child, and Zoé realized that in a heartbeat, the Holy Virgin had vanished. The chair was empty. Zoé rose from her knees, and the angel-child quietly led her back to the dormitory, then he, too, faded away like mist on a pond. The bell towers and clocks of Paris were tolling and chiming two o'clock. Sister Labouré crawled into bed, but did not sleep again that night.

Chapter Twenty-eight:
The Hunting Lodge
July 1830

"He has stripped me of my glory, and hath taken the crown from my head." Job 19:9

Thérèse fought a surge of panic and despair, as the post-chaise swayed and bumped through the vineyards of Champagne along the road to Paris. It was viciously hot, even with the windows open, but her mind reeled with the events of the last few days so that she was almost oblivious to her discomfort. She thought only of reaching her family. Every mile seemed to be a thousand. What an unreal catastrophe! Thousands had been wounded or killed in the streets of Paris in the last three days. Almost every town saw riots and the looting of churches. The government had collapsed and the King was said to be on the verge of abdication. She feared what would happen to Henri and Louise, especially Henri. What if the revolutionaries captured him for use as a pawn? What if he suffered Charles' fate? What if he, too, disappeared? Her rosary beads slipped through her fingers as she struggled to steady her nerves by commending the King, the realm and Henri to the hands of the Mother of God.

She had seen it all coming. The coldness with which some members of the family were received in many towns during the goodwill visits of 1828 and 1829 to the Nation had been ominous. The King had sent each of them to different parts of the country. He himself visited all the army camps, and met with hearty greetings. Caroline went to the Vendée, where the welcome was delirious, as the survivors of the Catholic and Royal army brought out their worn, white standards, riddled with musket balls, lining the roads down which she gaily trotted on horseback, acclaiming the brave princess who managed to bring under control a spirited mount, frightened by the salvos. Thérèse journeyed to the south, where she was warmly welcomed, but in other parts of France the enthusiasm for her person was obviously nonexistent. At Nancy, for instance, she was hissed when she appeared on a balcony, and was forced to cut short her speech. "Madame Rancune" and "Duchesse Cain" were the epithets most frequently applied to her. No longer was she seen as the noble, heroic "Orphan of the Temple" but a vengeful, spiteful, ambitious harridan. At Varennes, where she was supposed to make a visit, she had been so overwhelmed with terrible recollections of her family's capture and humiliation, that she ordered her coachman to drive right past the crowds that had come to see her, leaving the town as soon as possible. Such behavior on her part served to heighten the negative impressions of the populace. As for Antoine, he travelled to Normandy, where he found a most frigid reception, which boded ill for him as heir to the throne. The fact that the country was not united behind the Royal Family was not a good sign. A disaffected minority could wreak a great deal of damage.

The first thunderclap heralding the approach of Revolution occurred at the review of the National Guard made by the King and the Dauphin on horseback, with Thérèse and Caroline riding behind in a *caléche*. The soldiers had shouted, "Down with the Jesuits. Down with the ministers!" as the Royal Family passed.

"This is a calamity!" whispered Caroline, while nodding and waving to the men as if she did not hear their rude shouts.

"It is bad, but I expected worse," retorted Thérèse. She was furious when they returned to the Tuileries, and she heard the King telling Madame de Gontaut how the review had passed off quietly.

"Well, you are easily pleased!" she snapped at him, to everyone's consternation. She believed in facing a crisis head-on, and to see the men in her family trying to pretend that nothing was wrong irritated her beyond words.

Industrialization had created slums overnight, where an entire family would be crowded into one tiny room, and such inhuman conditions became breeding grounds for rampant immorality, crime, and anarchy. The last two winters had been long and freezing, with an abundance of ice and snow, and a shortness of bread. Unemployment rose, and at the open air "hiring halls" at the Place de Grève and the Place du Châtelet sometimes as many as 700 workmen came to beg for work, but only about 150 were actually employed on any given day. The price of bread rose, and if it were not for the bread cards provided by the government and soup kitchens opened by charitable institutions, many would have perished from hunger.

In the Faubourg Saint-Antoine the police found a placard which read: "War to the death on Charles X and the priests who want to starve us to death." The King, as well as the Jesuits, were falsely but quite openly blamed for forcing up the price of bread. Riots broke out in factories and working-class neighborhoods. Mercifully, the price of bread had finally fallen again, and order seemed to be outwardly restored. Nevertheless, the King was convinced that the liberals and the press were spreading false propaganda and destroying his people's love for him. He had decided that after the next election, if the liberals triumphed, he himself would launch a *coup d'état* by passing certain "Ordinances." He would dissolve the newly-elected chamber, have another legislature elected according to an electoral system with a more united franchise, and suspend freedom of the press.

Thérèse was against his "Ordinances," knowing that such a measure would be fuel in the fire of their enemies, and political suicide. The King, in the meantime, was urging her to go to Vichy for a short holiday and as a treatment for her rheumatism. She decided to go, against her better judgment.

"But Papa, please do not sign anything while I am away," she pleaded.

"On my word as a king and a gentleman," promised Charles X, who never ceased to be the consummate gambler. Reluctantly, she departed for Vichy with her big, green travelling bag stuffed with newspapers to keep apprised of the swiftly moving events, and the political climate of the realm.

The crowds at Vichy had been happy to see her, and it seemed like the early days of the Restoration again. On July 27, she peacefully began her homeward journey, picking up current newspapers in towns along the way and scanning them in her coach. "Nothing new," she sighed, much relieved. In the villages through which she passed, she was greeted with enthusiastic cheers, banners and flowers. Even politically liberal Châlons welcomed her warmly. The word had obviously been spread abroad that she was opposed to the Ordinances. She planned to break her journey at Mâcon, where an official reception was planned for her, but there the fateful news awaited. The King had signed into law his Ordinances, and Paris was in an uproar.

"Alas, it may turn out a great misfortune that I left Paris," she lamented to her attendants. After a fitful night's rest, she hastened at dawn towards the capital. She wondered if any military precautions had been taken or if even the simplest police arrangements had been made. Probably not, knowing her father-in-law and Prince de Polignac, his kindly but dreamy Prime Minister.

On July 29, Thérèse arrived at Dijon, where she heard grave tidings. Barricades had been set up in the streets of Paris and 1800 people had been killed. The royal troops had been forced back to Saint-Cloud, to where the royal family had retreated, and the tricolor flag was being flown in Paris. Neither the King or the Dauphin had taken their place at the head of the troops, but were said to be preoccupied with card-playing. Thérèse melted from humiliation and disgrace rather than from the soaring temperatures.

She had to do something. She decided to appear in the theater that evening, to appeal to the innate chivalry of the populace. As soon as she became visible in the box she was met with boos and catcalls: "Long live the Charter! Down with the Ministers!" Thérèse sat with serene dignity, watching the performance and ignoring the insults, but then they started to mock her person. "Down with the white feathers!" was aimed to ridicule her plumes. She gave the hecklers her famous look of haughty displeasure, which had in the past great success in intimidating rebellious soldiers and errant princes. The personal jibes ceased but the shouting continued. Eventually, she was forced to retire, and the jeers and hoots of triumph followed her out to her carriage, where she wept bitterly.

That night, a mob tried to burn down her hotel, but she managed to escape before daybreak, dressed in the clothes of her *femme de chambre*. She abandoned her state coach for a plain post-chaise, in order to make better time, for Frenchmen were dying.

"Poor Paris!" she cried. "What have they done! They have lost everything! I knew it would happen!" News reached her that the King and his family had fled to Trianon, and then to the château of Rambouillet, her Papa's favorite hunting-lodge, where he had built a dairy as a gift for her mother, and raised merino sheep. And so she prayed, as the miles dragged by in the heat. By this time, the roads were trimmed with red, white, and blue. If only she knew that the children were safe. If only Caroline had enough wit to keep Henri with her, no matter what anyone said or did.

At last, they rolled through the gates of Rambouillet. The cylindrical towers with cone-like roofs were welcome to her eyes. She climbed out of the post-chaise, dusty beyond recognition, and then she saw the entire household, including the Royal Bodyguards, running out to meet her. In the lead was Henri, running as fast as he could on his short legs. In a moment he was in her arms.

"Oh, my darling child!" she cried, uttering a silent prayer of thanksgiving. If her boy was safe, and his sister, too, then nothing else mattered. But no, there was much else that did matter. Frenchmen were bleeding in the streets. Her father-in-law reached her, his handsome face, worn with anguish. He took her into his arms.

"Oh, Papa, what have you done?" she asked, in something that resembled a moan. "At least, we must never part again."

"My child, can you ever forgive me?" asked the old King.

"Let us bury the past," Thérèse replied, and they went into the château.

Antoine was hiding in the library with a bandaged hand, deeply dejected. The "Generalissimo" had failed to infuse enthusiasm into the troops. He had flown into a rage at Marshal Marmont, and depriving him of his sword, had tried to break it over his knee, but only succeed in slashing his fingers, while grievously offending the Marshal. The Dauphin would never forgive himself for not leading the troops through the barricades. He was sulking especially because Louis-Philippe had shown himself to be very brave by riding alone through a hostile mob to the Hotel de Ville, where on the balcony the Marquis de Lafayette had draped him in the tricolor flag.

There were public proclamations being made in favor of Orléans becoming King, such as: "The Duc d'Orléans is a Prince devoted to the cause of the Revolution." The King had decided to appoint Louis-Philippe Lieutenant-Governor of the realm, since it was almost certain that he and Antoine would both abdicate, and he sent word informing the Duc of this eventuality. Orléans sent back a haughty reply: "I hold my investiture from the representatives of the people."

The following day, Monday, August 2, the King called a family council at noon in the library, and informed them that he was abdicating in favor of his grandson Henri, Duc de Bordeaux. After clasping Henri to his heart, he passed to each of them the letter he was sending to Louis-Philippe:

> My cousin, I am deeply grieved by the ills which afflict or could threaten my people, for not having sought a way to prevent them. I have therefore come to the decision to abdicate my crown in favor of my grandson, the Duc de Bourdeaux. The Dauphin, sharing my sentiments, also renounces his rights. In your capacity as lieutenant-governor of the realm, you will therefore have the accession of Henri V to the crown proclaimed. You will also have all the measures taken to arrange the forms of government during the minority of the new king.

> I renew, my cousin, my assurance of the sentiments with which I remain your affectionate cousin,

> Charles

Thérèse sat down to read it. She could hardly believe any of this was happening. He had formally abdicated. She realized that at that moment, her husband was Louis XIX, and she was Queen of France. It was too sad and too hollow for words. She handed the paper to Antoine. He skimmed it and signed, abdicating in turn. Henri V was King of France. The new little King and his sister were standing solemn and wide-eyed, watching the faces of the adults around them.

Then Louise murmured to Henri, "Some misfortune is going to happen to us, my brother, for they all cry when they look at us. Let us go and pray to the good God." Taking his hand, she led him out onto the balcony, where they both fell to their knees.

Charles X turned to Madame de Gontaut. "Take the children away," he said. "I cannot bear to see them so sad. Go, and amuse them." Madame de Gontaut led the children into an adjoining room, and managed to get them involved in a game. They made a coach of chairs, and Henri pretended to be the driver. When told that he was now Henri V, he only exclaimed, "What! Bon-Papa, who is so good, could not make France happy! And they want me to be King in his place! It is an impossibility! Come, sister, let us go on with our game."

Caroline had been absent during the signing of the abdication. She burst into the library in a smart travelling costume with two small pistols stuck into her belt. "Sire," she said to Charles X. "I beg to be permitted to take my son to Paris this instant, so that he can be proclaimed King."

"No, my daughter, I must refuse my consent for such an enterprise. It is far too dangerous. Henri will be proclaimed here at Rambouillet, before our remaining loyal troops."

"Oh, Papa, that is no good!" cried Caroline, trembling with agitation. "No one will know or care, and they will send us all into exile. Henri will be forgotten! He must be seen by the citizens of Paris!"

Charles X's face was at its most mulish and intransigent. "My dear, you do not know what a Revolution is. People who cheered for you a week ago act with the most unimaginable rudeness. They may throw rocks, and say the most unpardonable things. No, it is better for you and for Henri to stay right here with us. I do not care to hear another word on the matter!"

Caroline was on the verge of tears. "It is better for Henri to be in Paris, at the Tuileries!" she shouted. "The people love Henri! No one will hurt him! My Uncle Fifi would never allow anything to happen to Henri!" She started to flounce in the direction of where Henri was playing.

Thérèse grabbed her arm. "You ridiculous woman!" she said in an icy undertone. "So you think no one would hurt a little boy! You think no one would take him from his mother! You forget that I saw my brother torn from my mother's arms, and to this moment, I do not know where his body lies. As for Louis-Philippe, he has gained the upper hand, but for how long? Revolutions have many masters. The day will come when he may not be able to protect his own family, much less Henri, who is the sole obstacle to his dynastic ambitions!" Caroline's blue eyes widened twice their size. She wrenched her arm away from Thérèse.

"Very well," she said. "I will go to Paris alone!" She started towards the door. Thérèse blocked her way.

"Move aside!" Caroline shrieked. Thérèse slapped her, and Caroline sank to the floor, burying her head upon a chair. "I want my son to be a King!" she sobbed. "I do not want him to live as a homeless exile, without a country! I want him to stay in France, to at least be given an opportunity, and I want to stay with him!" She began to wail.

"Stop acting like a Sicilian peasant!" scolded Thérèse. "You want him to stay alive, which is what we all want, and we want you to stay alive, too."

The next day the revolutionary troops were reported to be marching on Rambouillet. Louis-Philippe begged Charles X and his family to leave the country to prevent more bloodshed. The Duc had made the abdication public, without the least mention of the accession of Henri V to the throne. They made preparations for the journey to the coast.

"What will become of my dogs and my horses?" wondered Antoine aloud. Thérèse wondered when she would have a clean change of clothes. Finally, the trunks she had left behind at Dijon arrived. Dressed in black, she bade farewell to the faithful Swiss guards and Royal Bodyguards. The men kissed her hands and wept.

"Oh, my friends, my friends, this is no fault of mine, believe me," she sobbed to the loyal soldiers. She embraced her dearest friend, Pauline de Béarn, who was not going to accompany them. Henri would need faithful subjects in France. Thérèse's heart told her that she and Pauline would never meet again on earth. The Bourbons climbed into their coaches, and the lily banner on the roof of the château was lowered for the last time.

Chapter Twenty-nine:
Sunset
August 1830

"And of His kingdom there shall be no end." Saint Luke 1:33

Madame la Dauphine walked alongside the huge coach, which had slowed to a crawl. The summer fields bespoke a glory not of this world, and she felt cleansed of painful thoughts by inhaling the sweetness of the sod. She wanted the touch of French soil beneath her feet for every precious possible moment, before she was taken away from it forever. The old King, dressed in civilian clothes like a country gentleman, rode on his horse ahead of the party, hardly speaking to a soul. Thérèse understood that he wanted to forget the nightmare and humiliation he had brought upon himself and his family. She looked at the vast pavilion of sky over the fields; at the clusters of houses dotting the plain, arrayed around an ancient church or monastery; at the rows of trees denoting some age-old boundaries. The meadows of *la belle France*, where knights had ridden to battle, where saints had walked on pilgrimage, which she was leaving behind, the land of her birth, the land of which she was Queen.

For most of the journey, she rode in the same coach with Henri, Louise, Madame de Gontaut, and the faithful young equerry, Monsieur O'Héquerty. They said little, but contemplated the Norman peasants laboring in the wide expanses of grain. In a few of the villages, the citizens assembled to witness their passing and were mostly silent, as if watching a funeral cortège, and some wept.

At last, Monsieur O'Héquerty, leaning out the window, said, "Your Majesty, we will soon be arriving in Charbourg." In spite of her husband's abdication, every member of the entourage referred to Thérèse as "the Queen" and "Her Majesty." She protested that the title was not quite appropriate under the circumstances, but they persisted in doing so.

As they rumbled through the town to the post, Thérèse noticed almost every building was flying the tricolor flag. "Look, Henri, do you see those tricolor flags?"

"Yes, Tante Thérèse."

"That blue, white and red flag is nothing more than Philippe Egalité's racing colors. They were chosen during the Revolution to symbolize the masonic plot to destroy the altar and the throne under the guise of liberty, equality and fraternity. Remember that there is no true freedom or brotherhood except in Christ our Lord, before Whom we shall each stand to be judged. Consider our own beautiful white flag. The golden lilies symbolize the Most Blessed Virgin. Always be faithful to the lilies, my son."

The coaches pulled up along the quay. Immense crowds stood by, bathed in a silence, which veiled the mingling of awe, indifference, and sorrow. The Kings and Thérèse bade farewell to the remaining bodyguards who had accompanied them, and the men brandished their swords, swearing eternal devotion. There was nothing now to do but board the packet called the Great Britain.

Antoine immediately disappeared into the hold of the ship, saying, "There is no mouse-hole small enough to conceal me." The captain was the famous explorer Dumond d'Urville. Thérèse tried to make conversation with the surly seaman by asking him to point out to her the name of the warship bearing the name Duc de Bordeaux.

"It was renamed yesterday," he grunted, pointing to the vessel. "It is now called the *Friedland*."

Thérèse felt an icy chill pass through her. Already, as Caroline had said, all memory of Henri was being wiped from France. She glanced at her boy. His eyes were wide with horror, as he regarded the rude captain, who was speaking familiarly with Charles X. The captain had not removed his hat! He smoked his pipe, and blew smoke into the King's face. Henri had never seen anyone treat his beloved Bon-Papa with anything but profound reverence. The outrage pained him. Thérèse took his hand, and they went to the stern of the ship, and gazed at France as it shone in the setting sun.

"All the kingdoms of this world come to an end, my child," she said, her rasping voice tender with sorrow. "There is only one Kingdom which will last forever, and if we are members of that Kingdom, then there is nothing to fear."

They were joined by Charles X. He silently watched his country sink into the waves. Tears streamed down his face, losing themselves in the salt water that splashed onto his travelling suit. Thérèse thought that he had never looked so noble, so majestic, and in that moment, she loved him as much as she had loved her own Papa. She put her hand in his, and the thick crêpe veils of her bonnet wafted around the three of them like a cloud of shelter, storm and woe.

Part IV: THE BUNDLE OF MYRRH

Chapter Thirty:
The Exiles
Autumn 1832

"For we have not here a lasting city, but we seek one that is to come."
Hebrews 13:14

"Well, my dear, Louis-Philippe's conduct which I have never understood," commented Charles X. He and Thérèse were ambling on horseback through the heather-laden hills behind Holyrood Castle. Their two year Scottish sojourn was coming to an end. The King was relieved to be leaving what he regarded as such a dismal and inclement climate, although he had enjoyed his frequent long rides in the bracing air with Thérèse and their discussions on family matters and politics. The old King never complained of their misfortunes, but sooner or later he would always introduce the topic of Louis-Philippe's betrayal, so greatly was he saddened by it. When first told of Louis-Philippe's usurpation of the crown, Charles X refused to believe his cousin capable of the infamy. It was only after Thérèse showed him the articles in the English gazettes that he began to accept the truth.

"It was a shabby way of repaying your many kindnesses," said Thérèse.

Her father-in-law shrugged off his great generosity to the Orléans family. "It was nothing," he replied. "But what pains me is his treatment of Henri. How could he steal the crown from his own nephew and legal sovereign? And then, he was not even properly anointed at Rheims."

"How could he be anointed, Papa? He is a usurper. Besides, Louis-Philippe does not believe his authority comes from God, but from the French people. That is why he became so-called 'King of the French' in a civil ceremony, without prayers or priest or even so much as a crucifix. No blessing at all was given. His reign has been ratified by violence alone."

"Well, at least we have a little something to live on," said the King. "And it was good of Caroline to lend us her silverware." All of their property and possessions had been confiscated by the Orléans regime, except for Caroline's country estate. She had managed to have her entire silver service smuggled out of Rosny, and it replaced the steel utensils the family had been using in their exile. The royal silver had been rescued, but the King would not send for it because he feared to compromise the faithful follower who was hiding it.

Mercifully, in 1814 Louis XVIII had commissioned Blacas to deposit money in England, a total of about 10 million francs. Thérèse hoped to make it last for the rest of their lives, for they had many pensions for elderly servants to provide, so she insisted that everyone live as frugally as possible, and she herself went about in old, much-mended gowns.

Thérèse watched the clouds sail across the blustery sky, twisting and twirling as they went, like the events of life. The King gazed upward. "It appears as if it is going to rain upon us again. That is all it seems to want to do in this confounded country." He sighed. "Poor Caroline, I wonder where she is? Surely, it was this dreary weather that drove her away from us, away from her own children."

"Caroline had become very melancholy, Papa," said Thérèse. "Her health was affected by it."

During the two winters in Edinburgh, Caroline had fallen into sulky fits, hardly brightened even by her children's First Communions. She brightened only at the mention of Marie Stuart, the tragic Scottish queen with whom she greatly identified. She quarrelled so fiercely with Thérèse that they could not live under the same roof, and Caroline rented a house in the Canongate section of Edinburgh. The previous winter she developed a nasty cough, and had decided to go south to Bath for a cure. She never returned to Scotland, but took ship to Sicily, where she reputedly clashed with her domineering step-mother.

The next thing they heard, or rather, read about in the newspapers, was that Caroline had gone to France in April 1832, intending to lead a popular uprising against the Orléans régime, and retake the throne for Henri. Finding little support, she walked from Marseilles to the Vendée with few companions. Dressed as a man, she rode at the head of a small royalist Vendéan army against the government forces. Her followers were quickly dispersed, and Caroline, disguised as a peasant, was being pursued by the police and the army from village to village all over the Vendée and Brittany. She had apparently gone into hiding, no one knew where. Charles X, who had stormed at Blacas to somehow rid the gazettes of Caroline's name, longed for any news of her at all. Thérèse was proud of her sister-in-law's courage, but was worried about her safety.

As usual, she devoted herself to Caroline's children. They read the novels of Sir Walter Scott together when the children came to visit her on rainy, Sunday afternoons, making Edinburgh more exciting to them when they envisioned scenes from *Rob Roy*, *Waverley*, or *The Bride of Lammermoor*. They loved stories of Marie Stuart, of Prince Charles Edward Stuart, and other heroes who once had walked within the walls of Holyrood, where they themselves now slept. Henri, especially, loved Bonnie Prince Charlie, who had come so close to regaining the crown of England for the Stuarts.

"I hope to be able to reconquer France later," he often said. "But I do not wish to now. I have first to finish my education." His tutor, Monsieur de Damas, took him around Edinburgh, visiting archives, libraries, schools, factories, poor houses, and prisons. At twelve years he was shy but engaging in manner, amiable, kind, with genuine concern for others. He had insisted on himself carrying a leg of mutton to the soldiers during the July days. He loved to draw, especially military subjects and scenes of France that he remembered.

His religious devotion was deep and authentic. With the fervor of a young Saint Louis, he received his first Holy Communion on the preceding February 2, the Feast of the Purification. It was feared by many French people that he would want to be a priest or a monk instead of a king, and they wrote hundred of complaining letters to Thérèse. She saw in him the makings of a great king, a holy king, and it broke her heart a thousand times a day knowing he must grow up so far from his homeland.

"You and Louise will have a pleasant journey together," said the King. "She has reached that delicate, difficult age of transformation, when a young girl so needs her mother to confide in, but, alas, her mother has fled. You will be good for her."

"I hope so, Papa," said Thérèse. She feared that her moody brusqueness and strict, self-imposed regimen would alienate Louise, as it had already estranged Caroline. It had been decided that the King, Antoine, and Henri would go together to the continent and find an available palace somewhere in the Austrian Empire where they could all live. It was important for Henri to begin moving in the world of men. Thérèse and Louise would travel first to London, and then leisurely make their way across Europe, stopping to visit museums, points of interest and the various relatives with whom they were on speaking terms.

"Louise certainly needs some new frocks," said Charles X. "Make certain she gets some in London. It is important that she taste a little more of society. Although I must say, she quite charmed the Duc of Wellington when she and Madame de Gontaut dined with him two years ago. She is becoming a most accomplished princess, I am pleased to say." Louise was a particularly attractive thirteen year old, with rippling blond tresses, Caroline's eyes, and Berry's nose and chin.

"She is a modest and humble one, too, Sire," said Thérèse, "and truly devout." Louise had received her First Communion and Confirmation over a year before. The bishop, Abbé Busson, who had come over from France for the sacred ceremonies, did so at great risk to himself, knowing full well that he would incur the wrath of Louis-Philippe, and forfeit his archbishopric. He did so, and retired to a small village, where he occupied himself by teaching deaf children. Thérèse was sorry for him, but honored that Louise should have had the offices and example of such a saintly cleric. It was more important to her that the children be sincere Christians, than the rulers of kingdoms.

They trotted into the courtyard of Holyrood, and as they did so, they passed Antoine, who was standing in the orchard with his barometer, looking up at the sky. Thérèse handed her mount to a groom, and walked over towards him. She wondered if he was packed for his journey on the morrow.

"Will it rain tonight?" she asked.

"Yes, Princess. But tomorrow will be fair. Papa, Henri and I will have a fine crossing." His fine, thin hair was so windblown that it stood straight up in the air.

"That is good. Everything is in readiness for your journey?"

"My valet is packing this instant," he said, making marks in a small notebook. "How is Papa?"

"He is glad to be leaving this place. What of you? Will you regret leaving Scotland? The rain does not seem to bother you overmuch."

"I will regret nothing," replied Antoine. A pained expression entered his amber eyes. "My only regret is that I was not shot in Paris at the head of the guards."

Thérèse did not know how to help him. The mortification of not having died in glorious battle seemed to consume him. He retreated from society, and when in company, had embarrassing outbursts of temper.

"I, for one, am glad that my husband is alive," said Thérèse, taking his hand.

"Well, I do not care anymore," said Antoine morosely. "My political career is at an end. I would not reign over France, even if she called me back to the throne, especially not after the way Papa was treated. No, I only ask to be able to lead a retired, quiet life."

"And you will find such a place where we can lead one together," said Thérèse. "I will miss you, Antoine."

He kissed her hand. "I am still your aide-de-camp." And he displayed the glimmer of a smile.

Thérèse went to London with Louise and Madame de Gontaut. They stayed for a week, long enough for Louise to be fitted for some autumn and winter clothes, and were visited at their hotel by the Queen of England.

Then they sailed to Holland and disembarked at Rotterdam, where they met with an old friend, General de La Rochejagquebin, a hero of the Vendée, who offered to act as an escort on their short journey to The Hague. No sooner were they rattling along the Dutch highroad, than the General informed Thérèse that her brother, Louis XVII was very much alive. Louise's blue eyes were large with amazement. She had known nothing about Thérèse's search for Charles.

"Are you referring, Monsieur le Général, to the gentleman calling himself 'Naundorff'?" asked Thérèse. "I am well acquainted with the particulars of his claim, and I regret to tell you that he is not my brother. He is a native of Berlin, a watchmaker by trade, who can hardly speak French, and was recently imprisoned for counterfeiting. He possesses none of the physical marks that would show him to be Louis XVII."

"Ah, Madame, you have been terribly misinformed," said the General. "Why, Madame Rambaud, the royal cradle-rocker, recognized him as the lost king. She insists he has the same wrinkled neck and deformed ear."

"Alas, Monsieur," said Thérèse, "Madame Rambaud has also recognized the so-called Baron de Richemont to be my brother. Come now, they cannot both be Louis XVII."

The General drew out a small portrait of a coarse-looking man with a florid countenance, beady eyes, and frizzled hair. "There, Madame, behold your brother."

Each of the ladies examined the miniature. "I think he does not resemble my brother in the least, Monsieur. They say this Naundorff dyes his black hair blond, and has memorized every memoir ever published, including my own, so as to appear knowledgeable of my family. His true name is Karl Werg, and he took the alias of 'Naundorff' after deserting from the Prussian army. A true swindler if there ever was one."

The old General was becoming distressed. "Madame, I beg you not to dismiss him so lightly. The young king escaped, and was smuggled into Switzerland, where he hid with a family named Leschot. Leschot was a watchmaker, and creator of fabulous automatons, which he once exhibited at Versailles, under the name of 'Lebas.' The Leschot family will swear that the same Naundorff apprenticed to the great Monsieur Lebas, that is Leschot *père*, maker of automatons."

Thérèse fell into silence. She had heard of the "Leschot" Dauphin before, but never the link with Naundorff. Something about it caused her great agitation.

"Monsieur le Général, it saddens me to tell you that Louis XVII is dead. I happen to possess information which gives me near certainty of this."

"Are you truly certain, Madame?" asked the General. "Many of your subjects are not."

"How could you believe," she said, with a sudden burst of vehemence, "that if there were the slightest possible doubt, I could hesitate a moment to proclaim it? Is it probable that I should prefer my uncles to my brother?" The General shook his head, giving up his appeal on behalf of Naundorff.

"Tante Thérèse, I do not understand," said Louise. "What is this about Louis XVII?"

Thérèse contemplated the flat Dutch countryside as it crawled by. Then she answered her niece. "Madame de Gontaut will tell you the cruel circumstances, which I cannot speak of to you. I shall start early tomorrow morning, and you will be alone together. You shall know all; and you will then understand, my child, a sadness which you have sometimes mistaken for *brusquerie*."

They supped at a small inn, and stayed the night there. Thérèse lay in an agony of tears until dawn. She rose, dressed, and started walking alone down the road, oblivious to the tidy farms and billowing windmills. Her soul was raw and bleeding as if newly flayed. The mental lacerations of past years were reopened, and the torment that weighed upon her was such that sleep or rest were unimaginable. The traumas of her imprisonment wracked her inner vision. She found relief only in walking, as in the past she had spent sleepless nights pacing in the Tuileries or at Hartwell. All the griefs of her life were upon her that morning, and the bitter chalice of failure, failure as a sister, as a daughter, as a wife and a woman, as a queen and a princess. She had not found Charles, although she suspected where his body lay, but without resolution, there would always be pretenders. She had not succeeded in helping Antoine to be the happy confident man and prince he was born to be; she had not been able to make him love her, not in thirty-three years of marriage. She had not prevented disaster from falling upon France; thousands had died and the Revolution had triumphed once again. (If only they had fought back. The numbers of loyal troopers were greater than they had been led to believe.) Her coldness and lack of charm had alienated many from their cause. But then, her mother had been captivating and charismatic to no avail. Thérèse did not understand. She only suffered. She suffered most of all from the memory of a little brother, who once held out his hand to her.

A pale autumn sun had edged midway towards the dome of the vast Netherlands sky when the coach caught up with her. She was pulled from her dark thoughts by Louise's footsteps, as the young girl jumped from the coach and threw her arms around Thérèse. "Oh, *ma chère tante*, how you have suffered! Madame de Gontaut told me about your life! I never guessed, or imagined! Oh, you are such a great lady and a heroine! Oh, I love you so!

Thérèse clung to her niece. "Silence, dearest child. Yes, I have suffered much. Now that you know it, Louise, we will get into the carriage and go on together." They did so. Madame de Gontaut, observing Thérèse with discreet concern, offered her a pastry and a cup of chocolate, kept hot in a silver flask. General de la Rochejaquelin had begged to be allowed to depart from their company, and go about his business. Louise's adolescent mind was clearly bursting with questions.

"Oh, Tante Thérèse, could you please tell me how you occupied yourself during your long imprisonment? How were you able to survive so many miseries?"

"Only faith sustained me," she replied. "I learned by heart the whole of that excellent book, *The Day of the Christian*. There, I found resignation, comfort even. Also, my beloved and saintly aunt Madame Elisabeth had left me with a bit of wool, which I knitted into a thousand different designs, unravelling each one and starting over again."

"Tante Thérèse, you were very brave to be there all alone," said Louise. "Were you ever afraid?"

"I admit to you, *ma chère*, that I was very much afraid, although I constantly recommended myself to God." She hesitated for a few minutes with downcast eyes before continuing in a halting manner. "One of my greatest trials was never knowing the hours at which my jailors would visit my cell. Madame Elisabeth had obtained a promise from the jailer that he would never come alone. She made me promise her that the guards, when they came, would never find me in bed. I had always to be up and dressed when they came, by day or by night. Unfortunately, one of their cruelties was never having a fixed hour for their visits, so that sometimes I spent entire nights and days listening, fearing, waiting. They never did find me in bed, but always sitting in a chair beside it."

Louise had fallen upon her knees in the coach and listened with her arms hugging Thérèse's legs, her white face, with faint pinkness in the cheeks, resting on Thérèse's lap. No one had ever listened to her with such obvious sincere devotion, at least not for a long time. Louise's eyes were bluer with compassion and love, and reminded Thérèse of Marie-Antoinette's way of looking at someone she felt pitied. She was a little embarrassed and longed to stop speaking of the sad past, but Louise was eager with questions.

"Tante Thérèse, how did you bathe and keep clean?"

"Bathing was impossible under such circumstances, as one can imagine. But I had soap and water, and sponged myself off as modesty permitted. I washed my hair and was even able to wash my underlinen, laying it out to dry between the mattress and the sheets."

"But what of your little brother? Were you never allowed to see him all that time?"

"Never. Not for a single instant. I found out the gruesome details of his sufferings later, and the fact that my poor mother had been aware of them, although she tried to hide her anguish from me, before she was taken away from the Temple to the Conciergerie."

"What did they do to him?" Madame de Gontaut put her hand on Louise's shoulder, and knit her brows, concerned that her charge's curiosity had gone too far. Thérèse continued with unseeing eyes.

"My mother heard the guards try to make my brother say 'The Republic is eternal.' Charles firmly replied: 'Only God is eternal.' The guards beat him savagely for such a brave reply, kicking him in the chest with such violence that my mother could hear the blows." She put her hand to her heart. "I am sorry, Louise, but I must be alone again for a while."

Thérèse signalled for the coach to halt, and she walked along beside it until they reached their destination. She asked Louise never to speak of her sorrows again. Louise obeyed, although it was apparent the memory of her aunt's recollections were engraved forever upon her heart.

Thérèse insisted upon travelling incognito, and registered at the hotel as the "Comtesse de Marnes." They went to the art museum, where Thérèse wanted Louise to see the Rembrandts and other Dutch masterpieces, but it was closed for the day, and the curator shooed them away. In the street, whom should they meet by chance but Louis XVIII's favorite, the lively Comtesse du Cayla, who was quite comfortably living in Holland. She hastened to the museum and informed the curator that "Queen Marie-Thérèse of France" desired to enter, and the doors opened for them immediately.

Madame du Cayla told everyone else in her acquaintance that the French princesses were staying in The Hague, and people flocked to see them. Even the King of the Netherlands hurried to their hotel to pay his respects. One day, as they were crossing the reception hall of the hotel, Louise exclaimed, "Look! There is Monsieur Lucchesi-Palli!"

The tall, gallant Neapolitan was striding across the hall towards them, and in a second he was bowing over their hands. "Comtesse du Cayla was good enough to inform me that Your Majesty was in town."

"It is good to see you, Monsieur le Comte. Please, we are about to dine. Do join us."

"Monsieur le Comte, have you seen my Maman?" asked Louise, as soon as they were seated, much to Thérèse's and Madame de Gontaut's discomfiture.

Hector's solemn countenance glowed at the mention of Caroline, and he appeared to be both delighted and embarrassed in such strong measures that he could not conceal his emotion. "I had the great pleasure of...of seeing Her Royal Highness last April at Massa, immediately before her departure for France. She was in excellent health... and spirits. Her Highness had earlier in the year entrusted me with several manifestos which she bade me to take to the Vendée, to prepare the citizens for her coming."

"Have you seen her since then?" asked Thérèse. "Do you know where she is?"

Hector warily glanced about, and waited for the waiter to leave the room before he replied. "Yes, Madame," he affirmed in subdued tones. "I know where the Duchesse de Berry is hiding. She is in Brittany with a devout family of good royalists, but danger is never far off. I am trying to exert what poor, small influence I possess in diplomatic circles to deliver her safely from her enemies. Let us pray that I am successful."

Louise began to weep. "Oh, poor Maman! She is like Jeanne d'Arc! She is like Marie Stuart!"

"Nonsense!" exclaimed Thérèse. "Your Maman is safe. She should surrender herself to the authorities. Louis-Philippe is her uncle, and will do her no harm. Do not fear for her, Louise." She spoke emphatically, trying to relieve her own worries.

"The Duchesse de Berry is a lady of high courage," said Hector. "I, Mesdames, fear she will not give up her effort to secure the throne for her son until the last hope is extinguished." He continued to extol Caroline in the most ardent manner throughout the rest of the meal, and Thérèse thought it almost indecent, but then he was a Neapolitan.

The news reached them that the Emperor of Austria was going to lend Charles X his own palace in Prague. Thérèse and Louise made their way to Bohemia, while Madame de Gontaut went on holiday, to tour Italy with her daughters. They were reunited with the men of their family at the castle of Hradschin, a huge citadel with eleven vast halls. The Duke and Duchesse of Lucca offered them another castle for their use when the Habsburgs planned to stay at Hradschin. The Duc de Blacas had the entire court well organized, with all the intricacies of etiquette firmly in place, so people backed away from members of the royal family, and scratched on the doors. Faithful Madame d'Agoult's curtsying gave new meaning to the word profound. As for Henri, he longed for France, and hearing a line from a song: "O, my country, be my love always" he asked that the words be inscribed upon his seal.

Shortly after settling at Hradschin, their old friend and Berry's former gentleman-in-waiting, the Comte de la Ferronays, asked for an audience with Thérèse. After the fall of Charles X, he had withdrawn from his diplomatic career, and was planning to spend his retirement in Rome. He presented her with a small silver medal of the Blessed Virgin, sent to him by Archbishop de Quélen. The medal showed the Mother of God with rays of light streaming from her outstretched hands, and all around her were the words: "O Mary, conceived without sin, pray for us who have recourse to you." On the back of the medal was the letter "M" surmounted with a cross, and the Sacred Hearts of Jesus and Mary, surrounded by twelve stars. At the base was the date "1830."

"Your Majesty, this is the 'Medal of the Immaculate Conception,' but it has already come to be called the 'Miraculous Medal,' because of the many prodigies that seem to surround it," Monsieur de la Ferronays explained.

"It is extraordinary," said Thérèse. "Please, Monsieur, what is the story behind it?"

"In Paris, there is a humble Sister of Charity who has been receiving visions from Heaven. No one knows her name, or who she is, except for her confessor, the Vincentian Father Aladel. Our Lady appeared to the sister, predicting the catastrophes of 1830.

The prophecy being subsequently fulfilled, Father Aladel knew her to be an authentic visionary. Our Lady asked that this medal be struck and distributed among the faithful, promising many graces to those who wear it with confidence."

Thérèse kissed the medal, her eyes filling with tears of joy. "Look, she is the Woman of the protoevangelium and of the Apocalypse, for she is clothed in light, and crushes the serpent! And the twelve stars! The Most Holy Virgin has not abandoned France, for this great sign heralds her victory to come, which in many ways has already begun! Oh, this is a wondrous thing! It is a wondrous thing indeed!" And falling to her knees, she offered thanks and praise to God.

Chapter Thirty-one:

The Adventure

Autumn 1832

"For gold and silver are tried in the fire, but acceptable men in the furnace of humiliation." Eccesliasticus 2:5

Caroline shivered beneath her rough, woolen shawl, trying to fend from her limbs the penetrating November chilliness. Comfort was impossible on the narrow, folding chair she used as a bed, and without the down quilt she would have been unable to sleep at all. She had just been napping, which she had started to do frequently of late. She rose from the camp chair and huddled by the dormer window of her garret hiding place to view the sunset. She opened the mullioned pane to better see the cloudless sky, cold and wind-whipped, filled with the breath of the sea and glowing with the colors of elusive, fleeting dusk.

How exhilarated she had been when she had set off from Italy, impelled by happy April breezes and Mediterranean sunshine—she had been convinced that as soon as she set foot on French soil, the people would flock to her, the lily banner would be raised, and she would march in triumph to Paris at the head of an army of citizens in the name of her son, King Henri V. She had several dreams of Berry in which he told her that everything would come out according to God's own decree. Hector had not been so convinced of the wisdom of the plan, but she had not listened to his precautions. Now she was a hunted and proscribed outlaw in Henri's kingdom.

Her bright curls were tucked into the once starched, white cap of a Breton housewife, become quite limp and dingy. She had rubbed her delicate, white hands against the stones of the road to make them rough and calloused. A ragged dress, patched petticoat, and wooden shoes completed her disguise. To throw her pursuers off the track, she had also masqueraded as a stable boy in tattered breeches and a brown wig. Trudging along the roads of the Vendée and Brittany, she would bite her lower lip so that passersby could not notice her distinguishing Habsburg pout. She had not been out of doors since June. It was almost Martinmas, and she was beginning to be sick, especially in the mornings. With a mixture of terror and joy, she wondered about her condition. Was it possible...?

Her thoughts sped back across the months, to her return to Naples in late 1831, when she had sent word to Conte Hector de Lucchesi-Palli that she had need of him. As it turned out, he had important papers from The Hague to deliver to her father, the King of Naples, and so was able to come to her aid. She wanted his advice in plotting the insurrection; she also longed for the sight of him. It was in the gardens of her Papa's huge, orange palazza of Caserta on the Bay of Naples that she laid eyes upon him for the first time since the ball of the Palais Royal, when they had danced the desperate *tarantella* together. Standing by a marble balustrade overlooking the sea, she heard his footsteps on the gravel path behind her. She turned, and meeting his gaze, was overwhelmed with shyness, an emotion entirely foreign to Caroline, Duchesse de Berry. He paused about ten feet away from her, his black hair curling in the sea winds, his face and eyes, stern. They were both speechless for an endless minute. Then Hector spoke.

"I will not chase you all over Europe, *principessa mia!*"

Caroline restrained an impulse to throw her parasol at him. "Hector! What a greeting!" she cried. "What a way to address the daughter of your King! Who is asking you to chase me?! I sent for you merely to seek your counsel as a member of the diplomatic corps, one acquainted with French affairs. If you behave with effrontery, I shall ask someone else!"

"I have waited my life away for you, Madame!" replied Hector, the slightest tremor in his firm, clear tones. "I have striven to forget you, to forget that you live and breathe on this earth, and that the moon and stars are able to touch you with their light, while I hardly dare to raise my eyes to you. My efforts have been vain! Only death, I fear, can release me from this torment, and bring me oblivion!"

Caroline made a gesture as if she longed to clap her hand over his mouth, as she had often done to Berry when he spoke of death, and other unpleasant realities. "Do not make such morbid remarks, Hector!" she exclaimed, taking one step towards him.

"Maria Carolina, when will you cease these cruelties!?" Hector threw himself upon his knees, and held out his quivering hand to her. "When will you consent to become my wife?"

Caroline gasped. "Oh, rise, Hector!" She clasped his hand, kissing it several times. "I see now, yes, I see that it is truly meant to be." She smiled and wept and laughed.

Hector got to his feet, folding both of her hands between his own. "It is meant to be," he said. "We were created one for another." And they were betrothed.

The marriage of Caroline and Hector was solemnized a few weeks later in Rome under the auspices of a Jesuit priest. They spent their honeymoon at Hector's estate near Massa in Modena, where Caroline conspired with the Duke of Modena, who pledged his aid for her cause. The nuptials were to be kept secret from practically everyone, including Caroline's family, until Caroline had reconquered France for Henri, and was installed in Tuileries as Queen-Mother and Regent. Then she could do as she pleased, without interference from either her bossy step-mother or meddlesome sister-in-law, Thérèse; then she would announce her marriage to Hector.

Hector detested the secrecy and her proposed adventure in France, but he did not want to stand in the way of what she believed to be her duty to her son. Nothing discouraged her, not even the collapse of the royalist support at Marseilles, the doors slammed in her face, and the long trek across France, her feet blistered and bleeding from the sabots. She thought of Marie Stuart and her heart was stirred to further boldness. After the dispersion of her small army in the Vendée, she began to experience disappointment, but refused to turn back, hoping for the winds of popular opinion to change.

On a crowded market day in June, she and her loyal companion, Mademoiselle de Kersabiec, were able to slip unnoticed into Nantes, where they found refuge in the house of two spinster sisters of the name of Duguigny, on the Rue Haute-du-Chateau. The long months of weary confinement required every ounce of her courage and faith. She longed for her husband and her children. They probably assumed her to be dead. If only Hector would come, and find a way to deliver her from her predicament.

One stifling, summer night, she awakened in horror at the sound of a man's footsteps coming into the garret. She reflexively huddled into the folds of the down quilt, in spite of the heat. Had the police found her? But no – in a moment she found herself safe in her husband's arms.

"I urged you not to come, *piccina*," said Hector, tenderly. "Thanks be to God and the Holy Virgin, you are safe!" He was travelstained, but radiant with happiness in the light of the single rushlight she kept burning.

"Oh, Hector," sobbed Caroline. "I have realized my great folly and selfishness in these long months in this place. How vainglorious I have been! Can you forgive me?"

Hector pushed her unruly locks of hair out of her face. "Selfishness? It is not selfish for you to want your son to take his rightful place in the world. Vainglory? No, *amore*, you are a princess of spirit and courage. Inaction wearies you, as it does me." He kissed her cheeks. "Now, we must get you home! And that will be no easy task!:

"How did you find me?"

"I met up with your servant, Simon Deutz. He told me where you were hiding. *Bellissima*, I do not like him or trust him. He is said to be in contact with Monsieur Thiers in Paris. The army is stopping and searching every coach in the vicinity. Only diplomatic immunity kept me from being harassed. I dared to come here only under the cover of night."

"It is not possible, then, for me to leave," said Caroline. "We must wait until it all blows over, and they give up the search. Hector, perhaps you should return to your post at The Hague, and keep a close eye on French politics."

Hector sighed. "Perhaps there are some officials who can be bribed into helping me spirit you out of the country. But it kills me to leave you here! My wife, hiding like a bandit, in rags! It is unendurable!" He held her close to him, and his fingers became lost in her hair.

"I promise you, amore, that it will not be for long. Then we shall always be together." She clasped her arms around him as if she would never let him go.

Hector left the garret and the Duquigny house before the first glimmer of dawn. Two and a half months dragged by while Caroline, filled with love and hope, watched from her tiny window. She knew Hector would manage a way for her to escape. On the November evening, as she basked in the embers of the sunset, she heard the tramp of many feet, then saw soldiers below, pounding on the front door of the house. Her gentleman-in-waiting, the elderly Monsieur de Mesnard, came dashing into her chamber, disguised as an unlikely farm hand.

"Madame la Duchesse, soldiers have surrounded the house!" he exclaimed. He was followed by Mademoiselle de Kersabiec, in an ill-fitting peasant costume. "Quickly, Madame, to the hiding place!"

They hastened to one of the other rooms in the attic. In the corner was a scarcely used fireplace. The back of the chimney could be pushed open, leading up into a narrow space between the exterior walls of the house and the chimney, with the rafters above. The crevice was about eighteen inches wide, three and a half feet long and three and a half feet high. Caroline and her companions had no sooner crouched into the hidden area, closing the back of the chimney, than the garret was teeming with soldiers and gendarms. Caroline heard them shouting and ransacking the rooms. Then they stomped downstairs.

"I fear they are still in the house, Madame," whispered Monsieur de Mesnard. "I can hear them talking below."

"Thanks be to God for this secret opening," replied Caroline. It was a vestige from the Terror in 1793 and '94, when many citizens of Nantes, especially priests, were forced to hide in order not to be drowned by the revolutionaries." Caroline was beginning to exult in her safety, when there came sudden blows to the walls.

"O *mon Dieu*, they are sounding the walls with hatchets and hammers!" exclaimed Mademoiselle de Kersabiec in a piercing whisper. They began hacking into the wall of the garret. Chips of plaster and dust covered Caroline's hair and face. The men cursed and swore.

"We are going to be torn to pieces," she whispered. "All is over. Ah, my poor children! And you, my poor friends! It is on my account that you are in this frightful position!"

The search continued until late into the evening. Then they began to hear snores and other noises of sleep. The pursuers must have decided to spend the night in the garret! Caroline and her companions remained tightly cramped together, hardly able or daring to move or breathe. Caroline's arms, legs and back were stiff and excruciatingly sore, but she was resolved to suffer the results of her follies as a good Christian and daughter of Saint Louis, without complaining or thinking overmuch about it.

Morning came, after what seemed an endless darkness. The soldiers and gendarmes could be heard stirring, cursing, spitting, and asking for bread. "It is cold!" one of them exclaimed. "Let us light a fire. There is wood downstairs!"

"Oh, mercy! We shall be roasted alive!" screamed Caroline in her thoughts. To their mutual horror, the fugitives heard a fire being kindled in the hearth of the fireplace behind which they were hiding. In a short time, the stones of the chimney grew too hot to touch, and they scrunched themselves away from it. The wall reddened from the flames, and sparks began to fly into the hiding place. Caroline's dress caught fire. She quickly slapped out the flames with her hands, scorching them in the process. Smoke streamed into the crevice. Monsieur de Mesnard wheezed. Caroline herself gasped for air, as her dress caught fire again. It was more difficult to extinguish the flames the second time, and tears flowed from her eyes at the sheer pain of the burns.

"Who is there?!" called one of the gendarmes, hearing the movements of the writhing prisoners.

"We surrender!" cried Mademoiselle de Kersabiec. "Put out the fire! We are going to open the back of the chimney!" The policemen and soldiers quickly stamped upon the fire, and Caroline led her companions from the hiding-hole, nimbly stepping through the embers in her sabots. Her hair and cap were singed, mixed with ashes and plaster; her face blackened, hands blistered; her gown and petticoat covered with scorch marks.

"I am the Duchesse de Berry," she announced with calm dignity. "I should like to speak with your commanding officer. Please fetch him at once." Some of the soldiers saluted and stumbled over each other to bring General Damoncourt to the garret. He entered with a bow, remembering to remove his hat.

"Monsieur le Général," said Caroline in the same calm tones. "I have done what a mother could to reconquer the inheritance of her son."

"Madame, may I escort you to the château of Nantes?" asked the embarrassed officer, offering her his arm.

"Ah, Monsieur le Général!" exclaimed Caroline, after a final glance back at the fatal chimney. "If you had not made war on me in Saint Lawrence-style, which was rather ungenerous in a soldier, by the way, you would not have me under your arm at this moment." They descended from the garret and left the farmhouse. The street outside was crowded with curious citizens of both high and low degree. There were a few scattered cheers for the courage of the princess, as well as snickers and catcalls. People lined the road to the castle, as Caroline and the General made their way to her prison.

Soon after, Caroline was transferred to the impregnable fortress of Blaye. For awhile, popular opinion swiftly grew in favor of the imprisoned Duchesse. She continued to be sick in the mornings, then asked if she could have larger gowns. A physician was sent for, but by then her condition had become too obvious to hide. To the delight of Louis-Philippe's government, hoping to expose her to public shame, it was announced that the Duchesse de Berry was with child.

Chapter Thirty-two:

The Scandal

Winter, 1832 to Autumn, 1836

"Therefore judge not before the time; until the Lord come, who both will bring to light the hidden things of darkness, and will make manifest the counsels of the hearts...." Corinthians 4:5

Thérèse thought her father-in-law was having a fit of apoplexy as he read the story in the gazette about Caroline. She wished she could have kept it from him, but he would have to know sooner or later. He turned a reddish-purplish shade; opening his mouth, there was no sound, and she hurried to pour him a glass of port. The old King buried his face in his hands.

"She is with child!" he cried. "How can this be? How can she do this to Henri and Louise? It is bad enough to have run off to France without my consent, and get herself thrown into prison! But to allow her reputation to be destroyed and her good name dragged through the mud...! To be the mockery of the Orléanists...!"

"Oh, Papa, perhaps it is not true! Perhaps it is only propaganda!" exclaimed Thérèse, unconvincingly.

"She shall be stripped of her title for this!" raged the King. "She shall no longer be regarded as a Princess of France! Where is Blacas?! He must go to Brittany at once and deal with the situation." He slammed the newspaper onto the table, upsetting his game of chess. At the sound of his name, Blacas entered the room and bowed, his gravity unshaken. "Blacas, you have heard of the unfortunate behavior of my daughter-in-law?"

"Yes, Sire," replied the Duc. "They say Madame's hiding place was betrayed by one of her servants, a Monsieur Simon Deutz. It is a dreadful ordeal for Her Royal Highness."

"Do not refer to the Duchesse de Berry as 'Her Royal Highness'! I have stripped her of her title. She has made our family the laughingstock of Europe! She has destroyed all chance of another restoration by her deplorable misconduct. You, Monsieur le Duc, will travel to Brittany and discover from Madame de Berry who the father of her child is. Perhaps he can be persuaded to marry her, if the dowry is generous enough, and we shall see that it is!"

Thérèse, overwhelmed by the tawdriness of the affair, took to her bed. She was anxious for how Henri and Louise would be affected. Perhaps they would be hindered from making good marriages. The adverse consequences of having a mother who was a fallen woman were innumerable. Because it was in the middle of winter, it took the Duc de Blacas over a month to travel to Brittany, and then it was several weeks before they heard from him. He wrote that he had spoken with Caroline in the fortress of Blaye; she was being treated well and was in reasonably good health, but she refused to reveal the identity of the father of her child. She claimed that she had been secretly married to him since her return to the continent in late 1831. Thérèse had little doubt as to the identity of the husband of Caroline.

"She fears to compromise Hector I suppose, and yet she allows her own reputation to be sullied," thought Thérèse. "We must bring a swift end to this scandal." She wrote to Comtesse du Cayla at The Hague, whose discretion in the handling of prickly situations had been relied upon in the past. Madame du Cayla confronted Hector, who made no secret of his marriage to Caroline and his paternity of her child.

Thérèse ran to tell her father-in-law. "Papa, here is a letter from the Comtesse du Cayla. She has discovered the truth of the matter. Caroline is married to Comte Hector Lucchesi-Palli, Prince of Campofranco. The marriage was contracted in secret, and the gazettes are claiming that no marriage license is to be found."

"Send the Prince of Campofranco 100,000 *écus* as Caroline's dowry. As for the license, surely Madame du Cayla can produce one from somewhere for the sake of the press," said Charles X.

Madame du Cayla pulled a great many strings to secure a copy of the marriage license, while the liberal press took every advantage of the confusion. Hector was depicted as having been paid to marry Caroline, who was depicted as a strumpet. The gazettes crowed over the depths to which the ancient Bourbon dynasty had been reduced. To make matters worse, when Caroline gave birth to a daughter in early May of 1833, her jailers were ordered by the government to witness the event, so that her humiliation would be complete. Thérèse lost whatever shred of respect she had left for Louis-Philippe, who tried to strengthen his throne at the expense of a helpless woman prisoner, his wife's own niece.

Thérèse's health was affected by the unfolding of the events, and she had to repair to the spa at Carlsbad in order to take the waters. Caroline's baby was christened Maria Rosalia. The prisoner at Blaye wrote to the Vicomte de Chateaubriand, begging him to go as her ambassador to Charles X and the rest of the family, explaining the circumstances of her marriage and asking that she be permitted to retain the title of a Princess of France. Chateaubriand was cordially received by the King, in spite of the fact that he had written unkind things about the fallen sovereign, but failed to convince him to reinstate his erstwhile daughter-in-law. So at the end of May 1833, Chateaubriand betook himself to Carlsbad to plead with the former prisoner of the Temple.

Thérèse received him around noon in the small salon of her hotel. As the elegant statesman and author entered, she was conscious of the shabbiness of her gown and the poor simplicity of her quarters. She had been determined to travel as inconspicuously and as inexpensively as possible. She plied her needle on a length of tapestry as Chateaubriand presented his case on Caroline's behalf. She listened in silence to the writer's long-winded pleas.

"Madame la Duchesse de Berry was wise to ask my help," she said when he had finished. "She was quite right, Monsieur de Chateaubriand. I am sorry for my sister-in-law. Pray tell her so."

"Your Majesty, I implore you to read the letter Madame la Duchesse has written to you. It is composed in lemon juice. Permit me to make it readable for you." He endeavored to heat it in the grate.

"Here, Monsieur, you will set it afire," said Thérèse. "Let me do it." She had long practice with letters written in invisible ink.

Madame, my very dear sister (the letter read),

> It is with pleasure that I announce to you my marriage with Monsieur le Conte Hector de Lucchesi-Palli, Prince of Campofranco, solemnized in Rome in December of 1831. It is with great trepidation that my husband permitted me to undertake the thwarted campaign on behalf of my son, Henri V. The sufferings I have endured were only those of any mother attempting to fulfill her duty towards her child. There has been no dishonor in my conduct towards Monsieur Lucchesi-Palli, nor in his towards me. I implore you to exert your influence with our father-in-law so that I, as mother of the King of France, may be allowed to retain the title of Princess of France. The care of my two elder children I sadly but with resignation relinquish to you, my good sister. I thank you for your affection and kindness towards them. I humbly ask for your prayers for myself, my husband and our child. I remain always,

> Your loving and respectful sister,

> Marie-Caroline

"My sister does me justice; she knows I have felt deeply for her in her troubles!" exclaimed Thérèse, as she read the missive. "Tell her I will take every care of the Duc de Bordeaux and Mademoiselle Louise. I am very fond of them. How did you find them looking? Very well? Monseigneur de Bordeaux is strong but of a nervous temperament."

"Madame, as I attempted to express in my 'Ode to the Maternal Virtues of Marie-Caroline' concerning the Duc de Bourdeaux: 'Your son is my king,'" replied the poet. "He is the noble scion of an ancient race, and possesses the complete loyalty of many Frenchmen. As for Mademoiselle Louise, there is in her entire person a blending of the child, the young girl, and the princess. She looks at one, she lowers her eyes, she smiles with native coquetry; one is at a loss whether to tell her a fairy tale or to address her respectfully as one would a queen."

Thérèse invited him to partake of her meager dinner, served within the hour in her salon, and later to join her entourage in the evening recreation. He seemed to be appalled and disillusioned that she enjoyed sitting at the window, watching the comings and goings of the passersby. Chateaubriand began to experience a sort of deflated melancholy in observing Marie-Thérèse, the princess of a throne and a scaffold, remarking upon the mundane doings of her neighbors. As she bent over her embroidery, Chateaubriand was struck how similar her profile was to that of her father, Louis XVI, with the neck drooping as if under the sword of sorrow, waiting for the blade of the guillotine.

He met her at five o'clock the next morning, the hour at which she went to the bath house, for then she was assured of solitude and privacy. She was touched that he should rise so early to pay his respects. Amid the serene birdsong, she strolled around the gardens with Chateaubriand, conversing of a matter that had been weighing upon her.

"What do they think of Monsieur le Dauphin in the army? He is immensely respected, is he not? He is remembered?"

"The Generalissimo is remembered for his impartiality, virtues, and courage," said Chateaubriand, soothingly, with a great deal of mental reservation.

Thérèse smiled with gratitude upon the ambassador of Blaye. Her husband's humiliation was a source of anguish to her. "Call upon me this afternoon, Monsieur le Vicomte, and I shall give you a reply to take to the Duchesse de Berry."

She had the letter ready for him when he returned. "Here is a note for her," she said, handing him an unsealed letter covered with her strong script, even except for the inflated capitals. "I have not mentioned your name, Monsieur, so if anything untoward should happen, you will not be compromised. Pray read it." Chateaubriand read the message.

Carlsbad, this 31st of May, 1833

I am delighted, dear sister, to receive direct news of you at last. I pity you with all my heart. You may always count upon my interest in you and your dear children, who will be even dearer to me now than ever before. My days will be devoted to them as long as I live. I have not been able to deliver your message to the family, as my health has necessitated my coming here to drink the waters. But I shall do so immediately on my return, and believe me, we shall always be of the same mind towards you. Farewell, my dear sister. From the bottom of my heart I grieve for you; I embrace you tenderly.

M-T.

Chateaubriand paled with shock at the cold, unfeeling tone of the letter. He assumed, as did many, that the princess' English sojourn had left an irretrievable mark upon her character, soaking all her modes of expression in a detached stiffness. He gazed in despair at the uncrowned queen in her patched, worn silks, with the frayed, straw bonnet, as decrepit as her dignity. Where was the exalted splendor of the princess who in 1814 entered Notre Dame Cathedral like the morning rising, amid the lilies and palms of white martyrdom? She was gone, lost in the demeaning trivialities of the nobly born, all the while dying the death of the thousand pin pricks of ordinary existence. He could not comprehend the mundane suffering of years, the poverty of humiliation in the loss of worldly grandeur. Is this where it ended for Marie-Thérèse de France– in dismal pettiness and illusions, in squabbling over empty titles? His mind churning with such questions, Chateaubriand departed from

Carlsbad, convinced that his days as a Royalist were coming to an end.

"Thank you, Monsieur for your services to our family," said Thérèse before he left. "Please tell my friends that I love France, and deeply miss my country. I am at heart a loyal Frenchwoman, and will always be. I am French, yes, I am."

In June, Caroline and Baby Rosalia were deported to Sicily, where Hector met them at the port of Palermo, dashing onto the ship to embrace his wife and child. Unfortunately, little Rosalia was taken from them by death less than a month later. Caroline sank into the deepest grief, and longed more fervently than ever for the sight of her other children.

One summer's day, in a splendid coach and four, Caroline and Hector drove uninvited through the gates of Hradschin Castle in Prague. The King would not turn them away, but he refused to restore her royal title. She was happy to see Henri and Louise, and they to see her, after eighteen months or more, although she remained touched with sadness.

Thérèse sat in the seclusion of her boudoir writing letters one morning, as all the clocks began to chime eleven o'clock. Antoine had during their exile developed a particular craze for punctuality, so he insisted that every chamber of their apartments have some noise-making, time-telling device installed therein. He had managed to rescue some of his pet birds, which were moved to sing at the telling and chiming of the clocks, many of which were cuckoo clocks. The clamor of the cuckoo clocks and canaries at every hour was such that Thérèse thought her head would echo with bells and birds forever.

When the ringing, chiming, and chirping ended, she realized that someone had entered the room, and turning from her sécrétaire, she saw that it was Caroline. Caroline was pale and pensive, yet quivering with agitation. She left the door slightly ajar, and from the rustling and whispering noises, Thérèse assumed that her sister-in-law's Italian entourage attentively waited outside. Caroline took a few steps forward; Thérèse realized that she was white with wrath.

"My dear sister, what is the trouble?" asked Thérèse. "How can I help you?"

"You can help me by not turning my son into a monk!" cried Caroline. "Abbé Moligny is too severe with Henri! Furthermore, you have stolen the affection of both my children from me!"

"Madame, I have stolen nothing," replied Thérèse. "You deserted your children, and they naturally turned to me, who love them as my own. As for the Abbé, yes, he is at times excessive in his descriptions of hellfire, but we try to balance it with instilling in Henri confidence in the love and mercy of the Sacred Heart."

"I did not desert my children," seethed Caroline. "You bitter old woman! Your cold and critical attitude would kill any true devotion in a child's heart! A critical spirit sours Christian charity! You always think the worst of people! Why, you have always thought ill of me! You assumed that I had sinned when you heard I was with child. Well, I was married!! Yet I am deprived of my royal title! It is a disgrace for my children, for my husband, and for Rosalia, which neither they nor I deserve! Now my poor baby, whose birth caused such a scandal, is dead! I hope you are satisfied!!"

"Caroline, your alliance with the Prince of Campofranco was brought about in a hasty and imprudent manner. You did not inform your family of your marriage, so what was anyone to think?" queried Thérèse.

"You do not know what it is to be in love!" cried Caroline. "You do not know what love is!"

"You are mistaken, Madame," said Thérèse, hoarse, as tears welled into her eyes. "I know far more than you will ever comprehend!"

"You and Antoine are imbued with each other's fussiness!" exclaimed Caroline. "You both agonize over trifles of etiquette, making the least infraction into a vice. You disgusted everyone in France, and we all pay the price for it with a life of exile. Oh, we know how much you pray, but it seems that the more you pray, the gloomier you make yourself and those around you, the brusquer and more irascible you become! You are not the only person in the world who has lost loved ones! I have lost my mother, a husband, and three babies. Stop nourishing your griefs!"

"Believe me, if I had not prayed, I would be far worse," wept Thérèse, wiping her face with her handkerchief.

"And I say, depart from your incessant moroseness at once, especially in dealing with my children. I will not have the sunshine blocked from their lives, when our religion is one of joy, and life is abundant with goodness, with beauty! I do not want them surrounded with bleakness, mourning and tears!" Caroline paused, looking suddenly ashamed. She flounced from the room to join her attendants, who were chattering in rapid Italian, with not a few titters, leaving Thérèse in a state of misery, tears causing the ink of her letter to blur.

Caroline soon afterwards departed with Hector, who bought her a palazzo in Venice. Before the middle of the following year, she had a new baby in her arms. She grew in happiness with Hector, whose diplomatic career flourished, and he was granted the title of Duke Della Grazia.

Thérèse and the rest of the family moved from palace to palace. Their tiny court suffered from many defections due to the bickerings of the courtiers and the tyrannies of Blacas. Fleeing from a cholera epidemic late in 1836, they came to a town in the eastern marches of the Habsburg empire called Gorizia.

One windblown, November day, Charles X was doubled over by piercing stomach cramps and convulsions, and had to leave his game of whist. Horror seized Thérèse; she had never known him to be so sick as to not finish a card game, especially when he appeared to be winning. The court physician examined him, and came to Antoine and Thérèse with a blanched countenance.

"It is cholera," he said. "His Majesty could be dead within hours."

They rushed to the old King's bedside. Antoine always behaved towards his father as if he himself were the humblest valet at the Tuileries, and all the more so in the hour of crisis. He fell to his knees beside his father. Thérèse stood beside him, leaning over her father-in-law.

"My dears," gasped Charles X. "I am done for. The very scourge I sought to avoid has pursued me. It is highly contagious. Do not allow Henri and Louise to come near this room. I beg both of you to depart from me this instant."

"I shall never leave you, Papa," said Antoine.

"Neither shall I," said Thérèse.

"Then, before my tongue fails me, I ask you once again, to forgive me. Forgive me for bringing calamity upon you, for depriving you of your crowns."

"It is the will of God, Papa," said Antoine. "And we accept it."

"Indeed, we do accept it," echoed Thérèse.

"And that," said the King, "is the greatest scandal of all.... The one most misunderstood and most repellant....It is the scandal of the Cross, the acceptance of the crosses sent by God."

They were with him for every moment of his gruesome agony. In spite of their efforts he became completely dehydrated, and went into shock. Before lapsing into unconsciousness, he received the sacraments of the church with childlike devotion. Early in the morning of November 6, he surrendered his soul into the Hands of God. Antoine and Thérèse covered his cold face and hands with their tears. The children and the faithful retinue were broken with sorrow, especially Henri and Louise, who had been unable to bid their adored Bon-Papa a final farewell.

Charles X was buried in the crypt of a Franciscan monastery in nearby Castegnavizza, high in the foothills of the Austrian alps, an ending unforeseen when he was the most gallant, handsome prince of Versailles, in a world that was gone. It was autumn, and there were few flowers. Louise adorned the altar of the church with paper flowers she had made. While praying before the tabernacle for her Bon-Papa's soul, Louise and Madame de Gontaut were startled to see the paper flowers catch fire. Behind the tabernacle was a picture representing the souls in purgatory, lifting their hands in supplication to Heaven. In the midst of the flames, before they were extinguished, it appeared that one of the souls seemed to have raised itself higher than the rest. It occurred to Louise that it was her Bon-Papa, and they redoubled their prayers for the soul of Charles X, King of France.

Chapter Thirty-three:
The Village of Joy
Spring 1844

"While the king was at his repose, my spikenard sent forth the odor thereof. A bundle of myrrh is my beloved to me....Till the day break, and the shadows retire." Canticle of Canticles 1:11, 12; 2:17

The palace in Gorizia shone rose-gold in the sunrise as Antoine and Thérèse left for their morning walk. Each of them had a cane, yet they clung to one another, uncertain as to who was upholding whom. Thérèse was far stronger and still full of energy, yet some mornings her rheumatic pains and stiffness flared up, but she would never forego the daily constitutional after Mass, for those moments with her husband were precious to her. Antoine's health had deteriorated over the last five years, and he had become so frail that they postponed their departure from Gorizia, where they had spent the winter. Thérèse hoped that lingering in the foothills of the Alps would help him; she firmly believed that there was nothing that plenty of fresh mountain air could not cure. He could still manage a walk in the morning, as long as they stopped to rest along the way.

In his thinness Antoine was lost in his already oversized, shabby blue coat, a scarf around his skinny neck, a battered stove-pipe hat pulled down to his thick, gray eyebrows. Thérèse was clad in a charcoal gray linsey-woolsey gown with a parsley shawl and felt bonnet, all threadbare but adequate against the vernal chill, rushing upon them from the mountains. The birds chanted in the shrubs of the park and amid the shadows of the forest, surrounding Antoine and Thérèse in an unseen tide of living praise. It was marvellous to Thérèse, as was every moment of life, along with the realization that the person who had once been her greatest annoyance had become her beloved.

Seven years earlier, before Antoine began to fail, Thérèse had occasion to encounter her first love, the Archduke Karl von Habsburg. During the Octave of the Epiphany they had travelled to Vienna, for the wedding of Karl's daughter, the Archduchess Maria Thérèsa, to Caroline's half-brother, King Ferdinand II of the Two Sicilies. The city was draped in snow and ice; the austere Augustinian church adorned in silks and tapestries. Thérèse witnessed the marriage with great emotion, for in that very church Marie-Antoinette, as a girl of fourteen, had been married by proxy to the Dauphin of France, whom she had never seen.

The ceremony was followed by a sumptuous ball in the stately palace of the Hofburg. The Bohemian crystal chandeliers were so heavy with tiers of blazing candles they seemed to be floating just over the heads of the dancers. The galleries were festooned in greenery; several tall fir trees glowed with tapers. Thérèse recalled how she had thrown her champagne glass to the floor and run from the ballroom upon hearing that Karl had accepted the rank of Field Marshal, knowing that he had sacrificed her in order to obtain it. In order to save face, her French entourage had let the rumor circulate that she had rejected his suit, but Thérèse would never forget standing over the River Wien, longing to plunge herself into it.

She had not been certain how she would feel being there and seeing him after so many years, but now it seemed that it had all happened to someone else. The blond princess with the bittersweet gaze, who had left Vienna to marry the Duc d'Angoulême, would never return, for she had died somewhere amid the snows of Courland and Lithuania.

In a gown of ivory silk *moiré*, she sat with her friend, the brilliant Archduchess Sophie, along with Karl's wife Archduchess Henrietta, the bossy Queen Mother of Naples, and other dowagers. Caroline and Hector were there, waltzing and looking more rapturously in love than did the bride and groom. Sixteen year old Louise danced with one of Caroline's half-brothers; she reminded Thérèse of herself, when she had danced with Karl in that same ballroom. Henri was trying not to sulk in his elegant black suit, for he longed to wear a uniform, but it was impossible, for he could not even hold an honorary rank in the French army as he did as a small boy. He was being consoled by the smiles of the fair Ferdinanda, Caroline's younger half-sister.

Then Thérèse saw Karl coming towards her in his white and red Field Marshal's uniform. The military hero who had so enthralled her as a girl of seventeen had given way to a balding, middle-aged courtier. He bowed to all the ladies, making a few courteous quips, and then asked Thérèse to dance. In a few moments, they were swirling around the room.

"The years have altered you very little, my dear, if at all," said Karl.

"You dance as well as always, Highness," said Thérèse. "But come now, as far as appearance goes, we have both changed. It has been almost forty years."

"Ah, still the enchanting frankness of speech!" exclaimed Karl. "No, I shall never forget when I first saw you in the park of Schonnbrun, running after your little dog, to keep him from being trampled by my horse. You shall always be to me as you were then, the orphaned princess, so brave yet so exceedingly vulnerable. I was devastated when you jilted me!"

"What nonsense, Karl von Habsburg," scolded Thérèse. "It was you who jilted me – and our betrothal on the point of being announced...! But then, it was for the best, for I was already betrothed to Angoulême since childhood, and here, you have been happy these past years why, what handsome children you have!"

"Yes, I have been much blessed in life," replied Karl. "The paths ordained for each of us have been rocky, and have not run together by Divine decree. And yet we meet once again. No, I will never forget my Madame Royale, who had to drink deeply of a bitter cup, whose sweet example inspired me…and broke my heart. But know one thing: I did not jilt you."

Thérèse did not ask him what he meant. She allowed the conversation to trail off, while burying in her heart the remnant of regret that had once burdened her. She felt that she had found the young girl she had been, the maiden who had been loved by a gallant prince, who had not jilted after all. She experienced a peaceful acceptance of her life with Antoine and saw clearly in her soul that it had all happened for a reason. As the music ended, she felt Antoine's touch on her shoulder, and nodding to Karl, she allowed her husband to escort her over to the buffet table. She gazed at his homely face, which had so often looked straight into the eyes of tragedy with her own, and she loved him.

A sigh from her husband transported Thérèse back to the spring morning in Gorizia.

"Let us sit and rest for awhile," she suggested, and they ambled over towards one of their favorite benches, near an urn full of blooming narcissus.

"We received a letter from Henri yesterday," she said. "He is doing quite well in England, and has received Monsieur de Chateaubriand. His trip to Ireland was extremely interesting. He made the acquaintance of the hero Daniel O'Connell, who offered to help him raise an army to reconquer France! Imagine!"

"Henri is a son to be proud of," said Antoine. They had both come to consider Henri as their son. "I will never forget the stir that occurred when the Pope received him. The Holy Father was very impressed. How humiliated Louis-Philippe must have been! Yet I pity him, for his eldest son's death was a cruel blow."

Thérèse nodded. "I pity Louis-Philippe and Marie-Amélie in their loss, and I am glad we had a Mass said for the poor young Duc d'Orléans. We would have worn mourning, but as you said, my dear, they would have taken it as a reproach since they refused to wear mourning for Papa."

"In such situations it is better to pray in silence," said Antoine.

342

"Caroline said Henri did so well during his naval training in Venice," continued Thérèse. "I cannot help thinking, Antoine, what a truly great ruler of France he could be!" The news that travelled to them from France showed that the country had not improved under Louis-Philippe, the "Citizen-King," rather unemployment and crime had increased. Visitors from home and faithful friends in letters complained that there was a slow, steady breakdown in morality. Adultery was rampant again; people worked on Sunday and blasphemed God.

"They say there will be another Revolution in France," said Antoine.

"I have no doubt that there will be another. Revolutions will keep happening until the world is in flames," said Thérèse.

"But there is great good in our country. What of that village *curé*, the great miracle-worker that we hear so much about?" asked Antoine.

"Ah, yes, the Curé of Ars," said Thérèse. "There is also Mère Barat of the Mesdames of the Sacred Heart, and good Mademoiselle Jaricot. I am glad that we sent Pauline Jaricot some money. Do you remember, Antoine, how she helped to start the Society for the Propagation of the Faith?"

Antoine smiled serenely into the blue beyond. "Many seeds were sown while we were there. They needed only a Christian climate and God's own time in which to flourish. Your prayers and sacrifices, *ma princesse*, have not been in vain. They have helped to bring about the harvest of saints – French saints."

"I have had nothing to do with it," said Thérèse. "Rather, I weep for my sins. It is Our Blessed Mother, who has not forsaken our poor country. Look at all the conversions from the Miraculous Medal, not the least of which is that of Monsieur Ratisbonne."

They often spoke of the extraordinary event that had occurred in Rome two years earlier. Their good friend, Comte Auguste de la Ferronays, Berry's former gentleman-in-waiting, and father of Henri's secretary, had retired to Rome. One evening, dining at the Palazzo Borghese he spoke with a friend, the Baron Bussières, who told him that he had given a Miraculous Medal to the wealthy, Catholic-hating Jew, Alphonse Ratisbonne of

Strasbourg, persuading him to wear it and recite a *Memorare*. Monsieur de la Ferronays promised to pray for Ratisbonne and went to the Basilica of Saint Mary Major, where he recited more than twenty Memorares. Upon his return home, he died of a massive heart attack. His funeral was to take place at the Church of San Andrea della Fratte, whither Monsieur Ratisbonne went with Barron Bussières, to make the arrangements. Inside the church, Ratisbonne experienced an apparition of the Holy Virgin Mary in which he was converted to the Catholic Faith. "Oh, how that gentleman has prayed for me!" he exclaimed, and that night kept vigil by the body of Monsieur de la Ferronays in the Church of San Andrea della Fratte. He publicly renounced his errors and was baptized.

"Perhaps Henri will be called upon to return someday," said Antoine. "But I prefer that first of all, he be a good Christian. As Monseigneur Frayssinous said to him, it matters little that he may be King; God alone will decide that; but what is more important is that if he is not on the throne, each road and each footpath that he takes should make him more worthy to ascend it."

"There is peace only in total abandonment to Divine Providence," said Thérèse. "People may accuse us of fatalism, but I think that surrender to the Will of God is a far cry from that extreme."

Antoine did not respond for a few moments. Then he slowly said, "Oh, Thérèse, Marie-Thérèse, my wife, I am truly the weakest of men and among princes the greatest of misfits. My – my ineptitude has brought harm to many. What balm for my tortured soul is the practice of true devotion to the Most Holy Virgin. She will bring good to our country in spite of my mistakes."

Thérèse put her gloved hand through his. "She has and she will. Does not Grignion de Montfort say that the greatest saints will be those of the latter days, and they will be singularly devout to Our Lady? We do not know what is prepared for our country. What is left for you and I to do is to offer the sacrifice of our lives, all they have been, and all they might have been, for France and the world through the hands of the Immaculate."

Antoine leaned over, picked a narcissus, and handed it to Thérèse. "You have been my only earthly joy," he said. "You are my bride, and I failed you so greatly. Have you forgiven me?"

Thérèse nodded and rested her head upon his shoulder, until it was time to go in for breakfast.

Antoine's physical strength continued to fail. Thérèse suggested that he help her in the garden, for she thought the air and light exercise would be invigorating. He cut himself on a gardening tool and contracted blood poisoning, in addition to the stomach cancer. His arms and legs swelled up, and by early June, the end had come.

On June 3, after piously receiving the last rites, Louis-Antoine died, with Thérèse, Henri and Louise at his side, overcome with long-expected yet unimagined sorrow. His body reposed in state in the chapel of the Celestine Franciscans on the craggy slopes of Castegnavizza, where his father was entombed. Surrounded by yellow wax candles, Louis XIX rested in an ermine-lined, blue velvet mantle, covered with gold *fleur-de-lys*, a large Maltese cross emblazoned on his uniform, for he was a knight of the Order of Saint John; spurs on his feet; a sword in his hands, clasped upon his breast. A solemn grandeur was in his emaciated face, dominated by his Bourbon nose; not a hint of the ridiculous was left, only majesty and peace. They laid him at the side of Charles X, in a stone sepulchre borrowed from the family of Thurn-and-Taxis.

Thérèse departed from Gorizia, resolving to settle permanently somewhere. She chose a small *schloss* thirty-five miles south of Vienna, purchased for them by Stanislas de Blacas, the son of the late Pierre de Blacas. It was a creamy, yellow villa called "Frohsdorf," meaning "village of joy."

"Come, my children," she said to Henri and Louise. "We are going home at last. We are going to the village of joy."

Chapter Thirty-four:

The Pretender

Autumn, 1845 to Autumn, 1846

"Is there no balm in Galaad? Or is there no physician there? Why then is not the wound of the daughter of my people closed?" Jeremias 8:22

Queen Marie-Thérèse of France leaned over her rose bushes, pruning the branches with great precision, her face hidden by an old-fashioned, floppy straw hat. There were few things which delighted her more than a well-appointed garden in late summer. The park of Frohsdorf, with its ancient oaks, yews, and firs was a place of repose where one could easily and happily become lost; a solitude within a solitude; beyond time, yet unflinchingly in the present. The fragrance of her roses exuded memories of Trianon, while foreshadowing happy times to come. Reigning over the garden, the queenly, white statue of the Virgin stood between the rosemary shrubs and an apricot tree. When busy among the herbs and flowers, wading, cultivating, or harvesting on any given morning or afternoon, Thérèse would sometimes catch her serene glance, and for a moment, among the glistening glory of sunshine that danced upon the foliage and petals, as among a multitude of colored prisms, the day would merge with eternity. "Forever and ever and ever..." the September locusts seemed to cry.

Thérèse had settled into her new house with eagerness and alacrity. The creamy-yellow villa was large enough to hold all their frequent guests and many dependents, but small enough to possess all the comforts of a private home. It was decorated in a gentle blending of the past and the present, with a predominance of the past. In the parlor, the white velvet curtains had been embroidered with gold *fleur-de-lys* by Marie-Antoinette. In the front hall hung a Vigée-Lebrun original of the Martyr-Queen. Proudly displayed in the library were the *panache* of Henri IV and the *gilet blanc* of Louis XIV, along with Henri's thousands of books, for he read almost incessantly. Her chamber, on the north side of the schloss looked out onto the gardens. She relished the country life, the raising of horses, managing the estate, the hunting parties, and visiting the peasants, who reverentially kissed her hands. Feast days were marked with the simple celebrations that Thérèse loved, with dinner served in the gardens when the weather permitted. Sometimes, a band of gypsies would come and play for them, and everyone would dance. It was the perfect setting in which to receive the delegations of young and old, which came often from France to honor him whom they acknowledged to be their true King.

Aft Antoine's death, Henri issued a circular letter to all the courts of Europe, declaring his legal claim to the throne. "I shall never renounce the rights which in accordance with the ancient laws I hold by my birth. These rights are bound by great duties, which by the grace of God I will fulfill." Thérèse had never referred to Henri as "the King" until both Charles X and Louis XIX had died. To the rest of the world he was known by the name he used when travelling: the "Comte de Chambord." As for Thérèse herself, as widow of a King who had reigned, even for a mere ten minutes at Rambouillet, she ranked higher than her nephew and any bride he might take to himself. She spent hours a day writing letters to political allies in France, building up support for Henri's cause. Over the back of her chair hung a bag of diamonds "for emergencies," she said.

347

Thérèse had always been partial to mystical and prophetic works. She was intrigued by prophecies pertaining to the "Great Monarch," the descendant of Saint Louis and the Holy Roman Emperors, who would rule France and most of Europe after a time of chaos and travail. She wondered to herself if Henri was destined to be the Great Monarch. He was certainly qualified for the role, being the most devout and accomplished prince. He seemed to fit so many of the prophecies in an almost uncanny fashion. Saint Caesarius of Arles had predicted in the fifth century that when the entire world, especially France, had suffered the greatest upheavals and miseries, then there shall arise a prince who had been exiled in his youth, and who shall recover the "crown of the lilies." In the ninth century, Blessed Rabanas Maurus foresaw that in the latter days one of the descendants of the Kings of France would reign over all the "Roman Empire." He would be the greatest of the French monarchs, and the last of his race. The rule of the Great Monarch was to coincide with that of the "Angelic Pastor," a pope of unique sanctity, who would reform the Church, bringing an end to heresy and schism. After the reign of the Great Monarch would come the Antichrist. Was it already so late in time? Thérèse wondered. One of the prophecies said that the Great Monarch would have a limp, which Henri had from a serious riding accident.

As she gardened, Thérèse wondered how Henri was faring in Naples, where he had gone to woo and win a bride. He had become quite smitten with Caroline's half-sister Princess Ferdinanda of Naples, whom he had met frequently the previous summer at his mother's palazzo on the Grand Canal in Venice. Caroline and Hector lived happily together with their five children in both Venice and near Graz, Austria. At the Palazzo Vendramini they became renowned for their bountiful hospitality and delightful entertainments. In their home there could generally be found the scions of the most ancient families in Europe, as well as many artists, writers, poets, and musicians whom Caroline patronized almost indiscriminately. Henri frequently and discreetly paid the debts his mother incurred through her many benefactions, he and Louis visited her and Hector often, although they considered Frohsdorf to be their home. Caroline had become exceedingly plump, but her voice as sweet as ever and movements graceful. Her increasing girth had not diminished Hector's fondness and admiration for his princess-bride, whom he treated with the deferential, adoring esteem of a prince-consort.

Ferdinanda was yet another fair-haired, vivacious Neapolitan princess, who had captivated shy, reserved Henri. Thérèse had decided that Henri could press forward with his suit, as Ferdinanda was to be preferred to the schismatic, Russian Grand Duchess whom some wanted Henri to marry. How proud she had been of him the day he left Frohsdorf. She, Louise, and the entire household stood on the front steps beneath the lily escutcheon to watch their young King drive away.

From the steeple of the village church came the jubilant Angelus bell. Thérèse remembered that she had enough time before dinner to look in on one of their mares who was about to foal. Walking down the slope to the stables, she passed the maples, whose highest branches plunged upward into the vaulted immensity of blue, as the garden called to her, in barely audible whisperings of endless bliss and celestial peace.

She returned from the stables to find Henri standing in the front hall of the villa. "Henri!" she exclaimed. "We did not expect you for another fortnight! What has happened?" She threw her arms around him and kissed his cheeks. He was built very much like Berry, with broad shoulders, a barrel-chest, and short legs. His wavy blond hair was definitely his mother's, as were his sparkling blue eyes, although they were tinged with disappointment at that particular moment. Surely Ferdinanda had not refused him!!

"Tante Thérèse, Ferdinanda will not marry me. Her mother is against it. She...she...." His usually cheerful, musical voice trailed off discordantly.

"Tell me, Henri, tell me everything."

"When I arrived at the Palazza Caserta, the Queen Mother Isabella received me coldly and asked who I was. 'Henri de Chambord,' I informed her. 'Ah, so you are the French pretender,' said she, and I was told there was no room in that vast palace for me to stay. I was sent across town to less exalted quarters."

"I never liked her," said Thérèse. "What is this 'Pretender' nonsense? A 'pretender' is someone who is trying to become a king. You, Henri, are the King of France. You were proclaimed King before the troops at Rambouillet, after your grandfather and uncle abdicated in your favor. Well, the Queen Mother of Naples is a ridiculous, pompous woman who is afraid of offending Louis-Philippe. Pay her no heed. But did you not speak with Ferdinanda?"

"I was allowed one dance with her at the ball, Madame. I merely glimpsed her at the opera, for I was not permitted to sit in the royal box."

"Well, that was foolish of them, as distinguished as you are in evening clothes. You would have made the rest of them look better!"

She could see that Henri was tired and did not wish to speak further of his humiliations. He withdrew to his chamber to change for dinner. Thérèse felt rising tears of anger on behalf of her beloved nephew. The grandson of Charles X treated like a poor relation in the land of his mother's birth! The King of France forbidden to sit in the royal box or stay in the royal palace! The heir of Saint Louis not thought worthy enough for the princess of his dreams! Thérèse's hopes of the Great Monarch seemed absurd and pretentious as she forced herself to stare at the unpleasant reality of a young man in exile, without a country, without rank in the army, with no authority whatsoever beyond the boundaries of Frohsdorf…truly a pretender if there ever was one!

"This must be a chastisement for my sins, for my negligence in seeking Charles," she thought to herself as she climbed the stairs to her own room. Perhaps she had not sought hard enough, especially in the last twenty years or so, because her main preoccupation had been insuring Henri's eventual succession to the throne of France.

"Deep in my heart, maybe I did not really want him to be found. I did not want Charles to interfere with Henri's inheritance. But now we have lost everything…is it a punishment? O *mon Dieu*, have mercy!" she prayed as she changed out of her garden clothes.

That afternoon Thérèse and Louise strolled through the gardens, discussing Louise's upcoming wedding. She was to be married in the chapel of Frohsdorf in a little over a month to Duke Carlo of Lucca, son of the Duke and Duchess of Parma. Everyone was relieved, for Louise was twenty-six; people had begun to refer to her as an "old maid." Thérèse was delighted at the thought of a wedding in their new home, but her heart was heavy as she walked with Louise.

"Tante Thérèse, what is the matter?" asked Louise. Sturdy but graceful, she was calm and decisive in her movements; tube-like, honey-blond ringlets framed her face while the rest of her hair was bundled into a net at the base of her neck.

"Henri's journey was unsuccessful, *ma chérie*," said Thérèse.

"He told me of it," said Louise, bending over to pet the spaniel who scampered beside them. "I am sorry for him. I will pray to Saint Philomena that Henri finds a bride. She works many miracles."

"Her intercession is recommended by the Holy Curé of Ars, and by Mademoiselle Pauline Jaricot, who was healed at Saint Philomena's shrine in Mugnano," said Thérèse. "She seems to be the thaumaturge of our time. I hope that God will someday send us a French, wonder-working saint, a saint for this revolutionary age of growing atheism. A great heroine and virgin-martyr like Jeanne d'Arc is what France needs."

Louise's fair, gentle face darkened somewhat, as she hesitantly asked, "Tante Thérèse, I know you requested that I never again broach a particular subject with you, that of your unfortunate brother. Please grant me a boon; allow me to speak of him, now, before I leave this house as a bride."

Thérèse nodded in silent assent. Louise continued. "Tell me, *ma tante*, did your brother die in the Temple?"

Thérèse calmly responded, "Let me tell you that the boy who died in the Temple on June 8, 1795, and buried in the Sainte-Marguerite Cemetery, was not my brother. Of that I am almost completely certain. There is a probability that Charles was murdered in January 1794 by his so-called 'tutor,' the cobbler Simon. However, from what we have discovered over the years, it is highly likely that my brother escaped from the Temple prison, but what he suffered in his body and mind rendered him vulnerable to vice and disease. I do not think he lived to be thirty years."

"How is it, you are certain he is dead?" asked Louise, pulling her shawl closer around her shoulders, for a sudden breeze bore with it the nip of impending autumn.

"Several incidents have led me to infer his demise with near certainty. However, I will never be entirely sure. Hervagault may have been my brother. There are some who said Hervagault did not die in prison in 1812, but escaped, and someone else was buried in his place."

"Do you know beyond a shadow of a doubt that the late Naundorff was not Louis XVII? Remember, *ma chère tante*, when he approached us at Carlsbad saying, 'Sister! Sister!'? But then he could not answer the questions you sent him."

"Naundorff was a mystic degenerate," said Thérèse. "I do not say that because he brought a lawsuit against me. He was anathematized by the Pope." Naundorff had invented a new "Catholic" Evangelical religion, which he expressed in his book *The Celestial Doctrine*, published in 1838. He tried to make Catholics in England and Ireland renounce their faith and join with the Protestants. He moved to Holland where he found a successful market for his clocks, bombs, and explosives. He had died the previous August, and by orders of the King of Holland, had the name "Charles-Louis de Bourbon" inscribed on his tombstone. (Louis XVII had been christened "Louis-Charles," one of Naundorff's many inaccuracies.) His family were calling themselves "Bourbons", and had stolen the Bourbon coat-of-arms, placing the Sacred Heart upon it, hoping to appeal to devout Catholics in France. They continued to sue Thérèse for recognition and for a share in her estate.

"What of the pretender known as the 'Baron de Richemont'?" asked Louise.

"Monsieur and Madame de Béarn have kept me informed of the Richemont affair," said Thérèse. "As early as 1831, when he published his bogus *Memoirs of the Duc de Normandie*, the police discovered him to be one Claude Perrin, son of the butcher of Lagnieu, also a forger, member of at least one secret society, including the *Carbonari*, a Bonapartist movement. He and his brother Jean Perrin take turns impersonating each other, as well as pretending to be my brother. My friends in France have learned that

Jean Perrin was probably in the pay of the secret police of Louis-Philippe's government in order to be a foil for Naundorff."

"But, it is extraordinary that anyone should believe or support such rascals in their trickery!" exclaimed Louise.

"Alas, many good people have supported them."

"What of the 'Leschot Dauphin'? Is he the same as Naundorff?" asked Louise.

"Definitely not, child. Monsieur de Béarn and other contacts of mine have investigated this matter for me. It seems that in 1797, a twelve year old boy was brought to Geneva by an old man dressed as a beggar. Père Leschot hid the lad in the home of his father-in-law, Doctor Himly, whose nephew had been a Swiss Guard at the Tuileries. The police came to the house to seize the boy; he set off across the lake and was drowned. One of the daughters of the family, still living, Marie Leschot, has claimed that the French boy, the 'Dauphin', did not drown in Lake Geneva. Rather, her father, old Leschot, had sent his own son, Henri Frédéric Leschot, as a decoy in the Dauphin's place. It was, she alleges, Henri Frédéric who was drowned, to the father's great despair, for later as he lay dying, he called out, 'My son, my son Frédéric! The Dauphin!'"

"What became, then, of the mysterious French boy?" asked Louise.

"He stayed with the Leschot family until 1804, learning the clock-making trade. Naundorff may have been there, too. At any rate, he assumed the name of 'Henri Frédéric Leschot' and set off for Russia, in hopes, perhaps, of being recognized by me. On his way he fell in with the adventurer Naundorff, to whom he confided his story. Naundorff gained possession of the young man's 'special papers' which supposedly proved him to be Louis XVII and which were later seized by the Prussian police. I think, perhaps, that Naundorff borrowed much of his own tale from what that young Frenchman told to him. The Leschots, you see, were makers of automatons, and Naundorff, in his turn, became the most clever 'living' automaton of all. As for the mysterious 'Dauphin', he wandered Europe in misery. He died in Geneva several years ago, or so I am told. Once in the park of Versailles, I met a young stranger. I chased him away. I wonder if it was he?"

Louise was silent, as if stunned by the tragic complexities of the affair. Thérèse haltingly continued. "Louise, it seems that my every attempt to find my brother has been blocked in some way. I do not know what else I should have done...." She thought of Louis-Philippe's son, the Prince de Joinville, going to visit the missionary Lazare Williams during his tour of America, and promising him money if he renounced his claim to the French throne. The pretender refused.

Louise was married to Duke Carlo-Ferdinando of Bourbon-Parma in the chapel of Frohsdorf on November 10, 1845. Crowned with a wreath of lilies, the *fleur-de-lys* embroidered upon her gown, she shone with wisdom gained through prayer and adversity, and with the determined innocence of one who has resolved to live in the world, but not be of it. Duc Carlo, aged twenty-two, gazed upon his bride as upon a comet or stellar phenomenon that one is privileged to glimpse once or twice in life. The couple departed for the duchy of Parma, which they were destined someday to rule.

Henri left for Venice, to bathe his injured leg in the Adriatic. Caroline had made sea bathing as fashionable in Venice as she had once made it in Dieppe. At one of his mother's many parties, Henri encountered the two daughters of the Duke of Modena. The younger and prettier daughter being already betrothed, Henri found himself conversing at length with the serious, elder daughter, the Princess Maria Theresa. Thérèse was pleased when she heard of Henri's friendship with the young lady, who was two years Henri's senior, for she was said to be very devout and so extraordinarily plain that her family had given up trying to marry her to anyone, and she seemed destined for monastic seclusion.

"It is good that she is not very beautiful," thought Thérèse. "There will never be any gossip about her, or scandal attached to her name. When a Queen is surrounded by rumors of impropriety, it can unsettle an entire nation." She had met the princess from Modena once or twice, and remembered her as being a very proper young lady, scrupulously attentive to her elders, but otherwise quiet and unobtrusive. A perfect Queen of France!

When Henri returned to Frohsdorf in the spring, Thérèse encouraged him to propose to Maria Theresa. He did so in a letter, and she consented with the words: "With joy!" They were married in Austria at her family's castle at Bruck in November of 1846. As the bride came down the aisle, Thérèse wondered if she had been right to advocate the match, as she peered at Maria Theresa through the latter's misty veils. She truly was one of the plainest women Thérèse had ever seen. Her face was actually deformed, one side being smaller than the other, with coarse, black hair and dull, sallow skin which no pomades or cosmetics could give sheen or luster. Yet Henri smiled upon his bride as if he had won the hand of Guinevere or Helen of Troy. Thérèse, because she knew him so well, detected a hint of noble resignation in his face. Otherwise, he was so merry at the wedding breakfast that no one would have guessed that his heart had ever been broken.

During the wedding day festivities, Thérèse noticed an undercurrent of muffled conversation. Caroline pulled her aside, her plump countenance bursting with news. She generally had cognizance of everything that was going on.

"Have you heard?" asked Caroline in an undertone.

"No," said Thérèse. "Tell me, sister, what has happened?"

"The Most Holy Virgin has appeared in France, in the Alps of Dauphiné, near a remote village called La Salette," related Caroline. "Last September two peasant children, a boy and a girl, both working as shepherds, saw her high on a mountain, surrounded by a globe of fiery light. She sat upon a rock, weeping."

"Weeping?" queried Thérèse. "Weeping for France?"

"Yes, indeed. She was weeping for France and the world. The Mother of God lamented to the children over the fact that so many people today work on Sundays instead of going to Mass, and take the Lord's Name in vain. She said that there will be a chastisement from Heaven by means of a terrible famine. The parish priest believes the children, and the Bishop of Genoble is investigating the phenomenon. Several miracles have already occurred on the spot, for a miraculous spring bubbled up close to where Our Lady sat weeping, and many sick have been healed in its waters. Pilgrims are flocking to La Salette, although it is quite out of the way, and travel through the mountains is difficult. But there is more...." She lowered her voice. "The Most Holy Virgin confided to each of the children secrets of great import, which they are not to make public until a later date. It is whispered, however, that the secret given to the little boy, whose name is Maximin, concerns the truth of what happened to your brother, Louis XVII. Our Lady is alleged to have declared that he is still alive!"

Thérèse paled. "But if it is a secret, then how can they know for certain what it is about?" she asked.

"They do not," said Caroline. "The children are going to write both of the secrets down (as soon as they are taught to write, for both are illiterate), and send them to the Pope. No one will know for certain until the secrets are made public, whenever that will be. But is this not extraordinary, especially with the exhumation having just taken place?"

She was referring to the exhumation of the body of the young prisoner who had died in the Temple on June 8, 1795. The lost grave in the Sainte Marguerite cemetery had been found at last, and in it were contained the remnants of chestnut gold hair. The bones, however, in the opinion of several surgeons, belonged to a boy of fifteen or sixteen, not to a boy of ten, the age of Charles. It corroborated the testimony of the guards in the Temple during the last days of the captivity, who were astonished at the great stature of the prisoner in his bed. It confirmed to Thérèse what she had already believed for many years, that her brother had been replaced with another boy, probably the woeful son of Nicole Bigot Hervagault, but did not prove to her that Charles was among the living. Nevertheless, she wondered.

Upon returning home to Frohsdorf from the wedding, she closeted herself in her chamber. She went to the cupboard at the back of the *prie-dieu*, the *prie-dieu* made from the stool her Papa had used in prison. She unlocked the cupboard and opened it, moving aside the folding screen to reveal a bloodied linen shirt, yellowed with age, enclosed in a gold frame. She lit the two candles on either side of the souvenir, and kneeling, prayed to God for the soul of her father, begging also his intercession, whose shirt was before her.

Inside the drawer of the prie-Dieu were other precious souvenirs: the fichu which had blown from Tante Babette's shoulders on the scaffold, and a lace cap her mother had crocheted in the Conciergerie.

"Oh, Papa! Oh, Maman! Oh, Tante Babette! I have had to go on for so many years without you. I have not found Charles. Where is he? Oh, help me, pray for me, who have failed so miserably in so grave a matter. How is it that Charles has eluded me? Did I frighten him away from me that day in the gardens of Versailles? Oh, pray for me! For I have had a long way to go, and may have to travel on further still."

Chapter Thirty-five:
The Weight of Glory
Autumn 1851

"For that which is at present momentary and light of our tribulation, worketh for us above measure exceedingly an eternal weight of glory." 2 Corinthians 4:17

"Madame, the Archduchess Sophie has arrived," announced Monsieur Stanislas de Blacas. "Shall I tell Her Imperial Highness that Your Majesty's illness prevents you from receiving guests?"

"Oh, no, Monsieur. She is the Emperor's mother!" said Thérèse, struggling to sit up. "Please bring her to me in five minutes."

"But Madame, is this prudent?" asked Henri's wife, whom everyone called 'the young Queen,' in her thin, unpleasant voice. "Doctor Rougé said that Your Majesty must stay in bed." The young Queen Maria Theresa had been reading to Thérèse from Venerable Grignion de Montfort's *True Devotion*. She had been caring for her husband's aunt as lovingly as if Thérèse were her own mother.

"I am feeling better today," said Thérèse, as she started to get up. "It was foolish of me to go for such a long walk without my shawl. Furthermore, this is my feast-day! It is Saint Teresa's day! I cannot lie ill on such an occasion. Look how the sun shines on the colored leaves! Come, I will put on my wrapper."

Two days ago, Thérèse had walked for an hour or more around the district. The countryside was a panoply of colors and she wanted to drink it in. She stopped to chat with some of the villagers, but then the sun had disappeared. It grew cold, and began to rain. She already had a light cough, but by the time she got home she was feverish. The doctor's diagnosis was pneumonia.

She insisted upon rising at dawn the next morning for Mass, but had to leave the chapel immediately after the Consecration, so ill had she become, and had remained bedridden ever since. She missed the time she usually spent in her beloved chapel everyday, the glow of the sanctuary lamp, the serene colors of the stained glass, as she knelt by the carved altar rail, communing with the Eucharistic Savior. She hoped she was better by tomorrow, so she could spend the anniversary of her mother's execution there, as was her custom.

At seventy-two, Thérèse was slender, erect, and more energetic than at thirty-two, but the pulmonary infection had so rapidly taken its toll she could hardly stand up to don her white dimity wrapper and paisley shawl. The young Queen helped her over to a favorite chair by the window, from where she could look down upon the asters and chrysanthemums in her garden. In the last few years her face had softened; the lines graven upon her face were somewhat altered, for she smiled more than in the past, in spite of her bad teeth. Wrinkles only heightened the impression of innocence and nobility on her countenance. Beneath her ruffled nightcap hung a single, thick chestnut braid down to her waist, threaded with silver, like frost on the leaves of the oak outside her window.

There was a scratching at the door, and Monsieur de Blacas entered. "Her Imperial Highness, the Archduchess Sophie," he announced, and bowing low, he withdrew. A tall lady with auburn ringlets, wide, sparkling blue eyes, and a forceful manner, whisked into the chamber. During the Revolution of 1848, which shook the Habsburg monarchy to its foundations, Sophie had managed to keep her hands on the reins of government in order to salvage the throne for her young son Franz Josef, who thus became Emperor at the age of eighteen. Thérèse and Sophie had grown to be fast friends over the years, having had husbands of similar temperaments.

"Do not embrace me, Sophie dear," said Thérèse, as the Archduchess curtsied and came forward. "I have a bit of a cough. Please, sit there...in the chair by the fire. You have driven far to see a sick old woman."

"Not far at all Madame. It is never too far to Frohsdorf. I wanted to congratulate Your Majesty on your feast day."

"Thank you, Sophie," said Thérèse, while the young Queen Maria Theresa curtsied silently and departed.

"My nephew's wife is the soul of discretion," said Thérèse.

"She always appeared to me to be full of sense," said the Archduchess.

"And how are your sons?" asked Thérèse. "How is the young Emperor?"

"My children are in good health, Your Majesty. As for my eldest son, Franzi, well, I tremble for him, for he is fascinated by his cousin Sisi, a fey, temperamental creature. Her older sister, a prudent, dignified girl, would make him an admirable Empress, but Franzi will have no one but Sisi. Be grateful, Madame, that Henri listened to your advice in the choice of a bride."

Thérèse sighed. "Yes, the King is very attentive to my opinions. The young Queen makes him an excellent wife. But I must tell you, Sophie, that I worry about her. For one thing, they have no children, which is a deep disappointment. Maria Theresa is prone to melancholy, and has the greatest dread of revolutions, although she has never seen one. Her dread is so great that she really has no desire to ever go to France, if the monarchy were to be restored, for she is both timid and terrified."

"So many dreadful revolutions all over Europe!" exclaimed the Archduchess. "And famines, too. What is God saying to us?"

"That we are sinners and that we should repent, beginning with the great and mighty, or else the innocent will continue to suffer with the guilty. The finger of God is in everything." She thought with sad irony of the overthrow of Louis-Philippe during the bloody February Revolution of 1848, in which the Archbishop of Paris was shot down in the street. The Orléans family fled into exile. Louis-Philippe died in England in 1850, and Thérèse had a Mass said for the repose of his soul.

"Austria is at peace for now," said Archduchess Sophie. "We can be grateful for that mercy. But what a task my son has before him. The Empire must be held together. The stability of Europe depends upon it."

"Well, we hope he chooses an Empress who can be a source of strength to him," said Thérèse. Sophie looked doubtful.

"Will Your Majesty be wintering in Venice again this year?" she asked.

"I hope so," said Thérèse. "I must say, I enjoyed the last two winters there. The family, you know, were all in Venice after Christmas. Louise and Carlo, and now Henri and Maria Theresa, have residences along the Grand Canal. But as usual, we spent most of our time at my sister-in-law's *palazzo*, with children scampering everywhere, and one never knowing what is going to happen next." She shivered, and began to cough convulsively into her handkerchief. Sophie hurried to Thérèse's chair, taking her hand.

"You are burning with fever, Madame!" gasped Sophie. "You are very ill! I did not realize! Your Majesty should be in bed!" The Archduchess insisted, and Thérèse allowed Sophie to tuck her back into bed.

"Oh, Sophie, it is Saint Teresa's Day," murmured Thérèse drowsily. "What *fêtes* we would have at little Trianon on such days." She coughed again. "How the world has changed. As my mother said, it does not require courage to die, it requires courage to live." She closed her eyes and seemed to sleep. The Archduchess kissed her forehead, and left the room.

The following day was the anniversary of Marie-Antoinette's execution. Thérèse struggled to rise and go to the chapel. "Nothing shall prevent me from going to the chapel to pray for Maman. I have never failed to do so in fifty-six years." But she had not the strength. Henri consoled her, drawing the down quilt up to her chin.

"Be comforted, Tante Thérèse," he said. "Your heart is in the chapel with the Saviour. You have been faithful. As Monsieur de Chateaubriand said, you have been as faithful to suffering, as suffering has been faithful to you."

"I have not tried to be faithful to suffering," Thérèse replied. "I have only tried to be faithful to My Lord."

She did not attempt to leave her bed again. She coughed and slept while her fever intensified. She lost track of the days and the hours. Henri did not leave her side.

"My son," she called to him, as if from far away.

"My Mother?" he responded.

"I do not wish to be embalmed," she said.

Night passed, and another day. It was dark when she opened her eyes. Henri was snoring in a chair beside her. She turned her head towards the door. A little child was there. It was Charles, the way he was before being given over to Simon. He grinned at her mischievously in the candlelight. He stood upon a chair, then jumped to the floor, and began peeking at her from behind it. She tried to tell him that he was naughty, and should not jump around so in the house. Suddenly, he was no longer a little boy, but the young man whom she had seen in the park of Versailles. He stared at her with tormented eyes, and holding out his hand, he pleaded, "Sister!"

"Go away!" she exclaimed. "Why did you tell those lies about our Maman and Tante Babette?!" He turned and faded into nothingness. She felt the splash of holy water sprinkled upon her by Maria Theresa, who had just come into the room. "No, do not go!" Thérèse called to the young stranger. "Forgive me! Forgive me!" The young man did not return. Then she realized she could barely breathe.

"I must go to confession," Thérèse said between gasps. "Please send for Abbé Trébuquet. It is time...." As she struggled for every intake of breath, she faded in and out of consciousness; therefore it was daylight again when she was able to confess to her chaplain. Afterwards, he administered the Sacrament of Extremunction and the Apostolic Blessing. She received Holy Viaticum, for the last leg of her pilgrimage had come. The clocks ticked on, and the sun sank behind the mountains. It was the evening of October 19. The shadows deepened in her chamber. Thérèse was vaguely aware of Henri at her side, his arm cushioning her head. His wife sat on a stool nearby, holding a lighted taper.

"Papa's watch…" she gasped. Henri handed her the watch of Louis XVI, which she kept on a table by her bed. She remembered seeing her father look at it in the hour of his last farewell. She kissed the watch and then replaced it in Henri's palm. The clocks chimed, as midnight drew near, and the Bridegroom's coming was imminent.

Thérèse opened her eyes; she fixedly stared at the foot of her bed. Scintillating in mid-air was a Child of surpassing beauty, surrounded by a soft radiance, wearing a glittering crown, a glimmering mantle of gold, and in His left hand He carried a shining orb. He solemnly and silently regarded her; His words were clear in her mind.

"Do you accept these trials for My Name's sake?" In a single moment she saw the loss of her family, the searing disappointment of her marriage, and Henri's years in exile. With her last ounce of strength, she raised her left hand to her lips and kissed the wedding band that Antoine had once slipped onto her finger, the same that her father had reluctantly removed on his way to the guillotine, and which inside bore the inscription. "M.A.A.A." for "Marie-Antoinette, Archduchess of Austria." She gave her assent. The Child smiled. He held out His pierced Hand to her, and Marie-Thérèse of France rendered Him her soul.

Abbé Trébuquet began to recite the *In Paradisium*. "May the angels lead thee into Paradise…."

After a quiet requiem Mass in the chapel of Frohsdorf, Henri and his Queen took Thérèse's body to Gorizia to be laid to rest beside her husband in the Franciscan Monastery. They walked up the mountain, ahead of the hearse, which was drawn by six white horses. As the coffin passed, draped with the white lily banner, the peasants blessed themselves, and whispered one to another: "She was the daughter of a king."

The End

BIBLIOGRAPHY

(Author's Note: *Trianon* and *Madame Royale* are works of historical fiction, not scholarly dissertations. However, for those who are interested, here is a list of some of the sources consulted for both novels.)

Anthony, Katherine. *Marie Antoinette*. New York: Alfred A. Knopf, 1933.

Barruel, A. *Memoirs Illustrating the History of Jacobinism*. Fraser, Michigan: Real-View-Books, 1995.

Belloc, Hilaire. *Marie Antoinette*. New York: Doubleday. Page, and Company, 1909.

Bernard, J. F. *Talleyrand*. New York: G. P. Putnam's Sons, 1973.

Bernier, Olivier. *Secrets of Marie Antoinette: A Collection of Letters*. New York: Fromm International, 1986.

Bertier de Sauvigny, Guillaume de. *The Bourbon Restoration*, trans. by Lynn M. Case. Philadelphia: The University of Philadelphia Press, 1966.

Bluche, Françoise. *La Vie quotidienne au temps de Louis XVI*. Paris: Hachette, 1980.

Boigne, Adéle de. *Memoirs of the Comtesse de Boigne, 1781-1814, Vol I*, edited by M. Charles Nicoullaud. New York: Charles Scribner's Sons, 1908

Boyer, Marie-France. *The Private Realm of Marie-Antoinette*. New York: Thames and Hudson, 1995.

Brown, Jr., Marvin L. *The Comte de Chambord: The Third Republic's Uncompromising King*. Durham, NC: Duke University Press, 1967.

Brown, Raphael. *Saints Who Saw Mary*. Rockford, Illinois: TAN, 1994.

Campan, Madame de. *Memoirs (2 vol.)* Philadelphia: George Barrie and Sons, 1898.

Castelot, André. *Queen of France*, trans. by Denise Folliot. New York: Harper and Brothers, 1957.

Charles-Roux, J.M. "Marie-Antoinette: The Martyred Qeen of Christian Europe." *Royal Stuart Review*, Vol. 6, Number 3, 1987 and Number 4, 1988, pp. 55-62, 72-85

Chateaubriand, Vicomte de. *Memoirs d'Outre-Tombe. 2 vol.* Paris: Flammarion, 1949.

Clouard, Henri and Leggewie, Robert *Anthologie de la litteréature française, Tome 1*. New York: Oxford University Press, 1975.
Connor, Edward. *Prophecy for Today*. Fresno, CA.: Apostolate of Christian Action, 1956.

Crankshaw, Edward. *Maria Theresa*. New York: Viking Press, 1969.

Cronin, Vincent *Louis and Antoinette*. New York: Wm. Morrow and Co., 1975.

Dennis, Mary Alice. *Melanie and the Story of Our Lady of La Salette*. Rockford: TAN,1995.

Desmond, Alice Curtis. *Marie Antoinette's Daughter*. New York: Dodd, Mead, and Company, 1967.

Dirvin, Joseph I. *Saint Catherine Labouré of the Miraculous Medal*. Rockford: TAN, 1984.

Ederer, Rupert J. "The false goddess: Liberty." *Fidelity*. Vol. 8, Number 8, July, 1989.

Elizondo, D.C., Sr. Juana. *A Light Shining on the Earth: the message of the Miraculous Medal*. Strasbourg: Editions du Signe, 1997.

Faÿ, Bernard. *Louis XVI ou la fin d'un monde*. Paris: La Table Ronde, 1981.

Gaulot, Paul. *A Friend of the Queen*, trans. by Mrs. Cashel Hoey. New York: D. Appleton and Co., 1893.

Gontaut, Duchesse de. *Memoirs of the Duchesse de Gontaut*, trans. by Mrs. J. W. Davis. 2 Volumes. New York: Dodd, Mead, and Company, 1894.

Greenlaw, Robert W., editor. *The Social Origins of the French Revolution*. Lexington, MA.: D.C. Heath and Company, 1975.

Grignion de Montfort, Saint Louis. *True Devotion to Mary*. Rockford: TAN, 1985.

Henrey, Robert. *Letters from Paris: 1870-1875*. London: J. M. Dent and Sons, 1942.

Herold, J. Christopher. *Mistress to an Age: A life of Madame de Staël*. New York: Charter Books, 1962.

Hibbert, Christopher. *Versailles*. New York: Newsweek, 1972.

———*George IV: Regent and King*. New York: Harper and Row, 1973.

Hunt, Lynn. *Politics, Culture, and Class in the French Revolution*. Berkeley: University of California Press, 1984.

Hyde, Catherine, editor (Marquise Gouvion Broglie-Scolari). *Secret Memoirs of Princess de Lamballe*. London: Walter Dunne, 1901.

Jardin, Andre and Tudesq, André-Jean. *Restoration and Reaction, 1815-1848*, translated by Elbog Forster. Cambridge, Cambridge University Press, 1983.

Jordan, David. *The King's Trial*. Los Angeles: University of California Press, 1979.

Knapton, Ernest John. *The Empress Josephine*. Cambridge, MA.: Howard University Press, 1982.

Kuehnelt, Leddihn, Erik von. "Operation Parricide: Sade, Robespierre, and the French Revolution." *Fidelity*, Vol. 8, Number 8, July 1989.

Latour, Thérèse Louise. *Princesses, Ladies and Republicaines of the Terror*. New York: Alfred A. Knopf, 1930.

La Vergne, Yvonne de. *Madame Elisabeth of France*. St Louis: D. Herder Book Company, 1947.

Lenotre, George. *The Dauphin or the Riddle of the Temple.* New York: Doubleday, Page, 1921.

Louis-Philippe. *Memoirs 1773-1793*, translated by John Hardman. New York: Harcourt, Brace, Jovanovich, 1977.

Macfall, Haldane. *Vigée Le Brun.* New York: Frederick A. Stokes, 1922.

Manceron, Claude. *Their Gracious Pleasure, 1782-1785*, trans. by Nancy Amphoux. New York: Alfred A. Knopf, 1980.

Maurois, André. *Chateaubriand: Poet, Statesman, Lover*, trans. by Vera Fraser. New York: Harper and Brothers, 1930.

Milligan, Harold Vincent. *Stories of Famous Operas.* New York: Permabooks, 1950.

Minnergerode, Meade. *The Son of Marie Antoinette.* New York: Farrar and Rinehart, 1934

Mitford, Nancy. *Madame de Pompadour.* London: Hamish Hamilton, 1954.

Nagel, Susan. *Marie-Thérèse: Child of Terror.* New York: Bloomsbury USA, 2008

Nolhac, Pierre de. *Marie Antoinette.* London: Arthur L. Humphreys, 1905.

Orczy, Baroness. *The Turbulent Duchess (H.R.H. Madame la Duchesse de Berri).* New York: G. P. Putnam's Sons, 1936.

Peppiatt, Michael. "The Hamlet of Marie Antoinette." *Architectural Digest*, October, 1998.

Pick, Robert *Empress Maria Theresa: The Earlier Years, 1717-1757.* New York: Harper and Row, 1966.

Pinkney, David H. *The French Revolution of 1830.* Princeton: Princeton University Press, 1972.

Raspail, Jean. *Sire.* Paris: Editions Fallois, 1991.

Reynolds-Ball, E. A. *Paris, Volume II.* Boston: Dana Estes and Company, 1900.

Saint-Amand, Baron Imbert de. *The Youth of the Duchess of Angoulême.* New York: Scribner's, 1901.

—*The Duchess of Angoulême and the Two Restorations*. New York: Scribner's, 1901.

Schama, Simon. *Citizens: A Chronicle of the French Revolution*. New York: Vintage Books, 1989.

Seward, Desmond. *Marie Antoinette*. New York: St Martin's Press, 1981.

Stevens, A. de Grasse. *The Lost Dauphin*. London: George Allen, 1887.

Toqueville, Alexis de. *The Old Regime and the French Revolution*. New York: Doubleday, 1955.

Turquan, Joseph. *The King Who Never Reigned*. London: E. Nash, 1980.

—*Madame Royale: The Last Dauphine*. New York: Brentano's, 1910.

Van der Kemp, Gerald and Meyer, Daniel. *Versailles*. Paris: Editions d'Art lys, 1981.

Webster, Nesta H. *Louis XVI and Marie Antoinette before the Revolution*. London: Constable, 1937.

Wight, William W. *Louis XVII: A Bibliography*. Boston: T. R. Marvin and Sons Printers, 1915.

Wharton, Grace and Philip. *The Queens of Society*. New York: Harper and Brothers, 1861.

Woodgate, M.V. *The Abbé Edgeworth*. New York: Longmans, 1946.

Made in the USA
San Bernardino, CA
04 September 2014